S0-BIQ-722

"Instantly compelling."
—*The Detroit Free Press*

"Surprise upon satisfying surprise."
—*Baltimore Sun*

"Transports readers to a place they might really go."
—*Portland Oregonian*

EXTRAORDINARY ACCLAIM FOR PETER GADOL'S *THE LONG RAIN*

"Delivers plenty of action . . . Gadol is a gifted writer."
—San Francisco Chronicle

"Spellbinding . . . you will find yourself eagerly turning pages."
—The Santa Rosa Press Democrat

"THE LONG RAIN is a mature book: carefully written, painstakingly plotted and a joy to read. One wishes that more contemporary writers would take the care that Gadol has taken in writing THE LONG RAIN, presenting the reader with a coherent philosophy with which to agree or disagree and a memorable story which makes one think."
—The Grand Rapids Press

"A beautifully written, richly atmospheric novel."
—Jennifer Egan, author of *The Invisible Circus*

"THE LONG RAIN is at once dark and radiant, moving and chilling. It tells a harsh story in seductive, irresistible prose; it explores the most universal human weaknesses by giving us all the particulars of a unique and mysterious world."
—Michael Chabon

more . . .

THE LONG RAIN

Peter Gadol

St. Martin's Paperbacks
Picador USA ⋈ New York

THE LONG RAIN

Copyright © 1997 by Peter Gadol.

All rights reserved. No part of this book may be used or reproduced in any manner whatsoever without written permission except in the case of brief quotations embodied in critical articles or reviews. For information address Picador USA, St. Martin's Press, 175 Fifth Avenue, New York, N.Y. 10010.

Library of Congress Catalog Card Number: 97-15662

ISBN: 0-312-96638-5

Printed in the United States of America

Picador USA hardcover edition / September.1997
St. Martin's Paperbacks Picador USA edition / October 1998

10 9 8 7 6 5 4 3 2 1

For Stephen
and for my father

Some afternoons that first autumn in the valley, I would sleep until four and then take a long drive. If I drove fast, I didn't have to think about anything except the road ahead of me, and so I would race past all of the fallow vineyards with their neat stripes of dead vines and past the chalky slopes of the vineyards that had been turned into quarries. I would rush across a shallow gulch of white stones where a river once flowed and then I would tear down the straight, somnolent highway that divided the basin, until at some random turn I would peel off onto one of the anonymous dirt roads that branched from the highway like the veins of a dead leaf. I would head up into the foothills, where the air was bluer and cooler and the tall trees were not oak, but all pine, where I could lose myself in the wend of the mountain road as it traced the sheer granite cliffs and slouched back into the verdant run of the forest, a road that would, if I was lucky, carry me into the singed dusk settling over a new valley. I suppose that if I had an ultimate destination in mind during these drives, it was the distant snow, the north-listing peaks of the range, but I never made it that far—I never even made it beyond the foothills that banked my own valley—because somewhere along my climb, I would pass the stone shell of an old winery, and then I would get out and explore.

I don't remember why they intrigued me or what I
expected to find when I prowled these ruins. Usually the roof
of the building would be gone, and the windows, too, and
sometimes a swarm of bats would flap out of a deep round
vat. Even though the cellars with their high walls of empty
shelves had remained dormant for over a decade, the air was
still thick with the stench of mold, of fruit fermenting, and it
seemed to me like night poured first out of these cold chambers, seeping into the valley like a sinister fog. All of the
wineries looked as though they had been evacuated in haste,
as if enemy troops had launched a fast and sudden approach,
and I often found tools or supplies that had been left behind,
granted, nothing of value, but objects that would be of use to
someone, I thought. A hoe, a pair of pruning shears, a cache
of corks, heavy oak barrels with warped and chinked staves.
And the stone rooms were littered with empty bottles, the last
of the vineyard reserve spent on the eve of bankruptcy or
maybe finished off by looters. I expected to run into squatters
or to find their trash, but in the same way that you never saw
anyone camping out beneath the fractured pediments of
ancient temples, there was no evidence that anyone had taken
shelter in the wineries, not even the ones with roofs intact, as
if using these rooms for anything other than the making and
aging of wine would be sacrilege.

I toured all of the old wineries that fall. There was the one
with the turrets and the iron gate that made it look like a
model château. There was the one with the palladian array
of pilasters and arched windows. I walked around a winery
designed to look like a country cottage with a thatched roof.
I found a winery constructed from logs, a sturdy cabin on
the edge of a meadow. In a way, I preferred the wineries like
the one my grandfather had built, a simple stone house nes-
tled into the slope of a hill, and I should note that all of these
ersatz villas that I am describing were the exceptions; most
of the wineries appeared to be little more than utilitarian
sheds with plain pine siding and corrugated metal roofing;
their cellars were concrete bunkers.

I was hardly methodical about my archaeology—I only explored the wineries that were visible from the road—but there was one place that I came back to many times. It was a yellow stucco house capped with a red tile roof, and most of the tiles had fallen away, leaving piles of terra-cotta shards everywhere. One side of the house had collapsed down a hill, but the other walls remained standing. The floor of this winery was carpeted with grass and tufts of clover and a bramble of sumac. Some wisteria and other vines had begun to climb the stucco. The winery had been abandoned, left for the slow scavenge of the Pacific wind, and yet it looked to me as though the surrounding landscape had embraced the ruins. A stand of cypress now grew in the center of the main room, six or seven adolescent trees in a semicircular huddle around a fermentation tank, green and skinny and fragrant, bowing in the breeze of the impending evening.

When I was in a loftier mood, I believed that the trees growing amid the ruins had to be a good omen: My fortunes would soon improve and I might recover the charm of my youth, which had eluded me in recent years. When I was feeling sorry for myself and lonely, I decided that the surviving walls would eventually fall down and that sagebrush would enshroud the tumble of stucco in time and obliterate the foundation, that this was the way of the world: Once a civilization collapsed, it was soon forgotten. I admit that my mood back then was gloomier more often than not, but I kept coming back to the winery, and with each return, I would stay longer and sit beneath the cypress trees until it was dark, and then I would pocket a piece of a broken tile as a souvenir.

After I had walked around the winery, I climbed back in my truck and continued driving farther up into the foothills, and some nights I did make it as far as the mountain road. I wanted to cross the Diablo Range. I wanted to keep driving clear across the state and into the desert, deep into the American vastness, where I knew no one and no one knew me. I wanted to drive for days and, wherever I finally stopped, take a new name and start my life over. And so I

way up a switchback. I skimmed a cliff. I sped
close of pine. I looked for any road that might lead
a natural pass through the range, but I never found
on and I suppose that if I had really wanted to escape, I
would have consulted a map.

Some nights I drove up to the mountain road only to turn
around, and some nights I inadvertently made a circle. I
would recognize a road that I had already driven earlier that
evening, and I would follow it back down into the foothills,
back to the highway cutting through the valley, back to my
own dirt road branching off of the main drag, across the
arroyo, then up to my own vineyard and the winery and the
stone house that my grandfather had built on the crest of
the property, where I poured myself a glass of wine from the
bottle that I had uncorked the day before, where I would add
the latest fragment of a broken roof tile to my collection,
arranging and rearranging all of the scraps on a table as if I
were trying to piece together the skeleton of an extinct bird or
maybe the elaborate design of an ancient mosaic. With each
shape that I added, I came closer to seeing an image in the
tiles, the bird, the face of a hero, but I could never seem to
make any real progress with this puzzle, and that frustrated
me. Inevitably I would end up making a fire and spend my
evening staring at it, brooding.

These were the facts of my life: I had met a woman in college and fallen so profoundly in love with her that I never
would have imagined that a decade and some years later that
same woman would barely be able to look me in the eye.
Our marriage was over, and now I would rarely see our
young son. He would not kiss me on the cheek before he
went off to school in the mornings, and in the evenings, I
would not help him with his algebra and social studies. In
the past year, I had lost my mother and I had lost my job. My
home was no longer my home, and I had drifted into a vol-
untary exile from the city where I had grown up and had
thought I would grow old. If only I could spin out of the mud
that trapped me and move on. If only I could take the first

step toward remaking a life for myself—but where, with whom, doing what?

Looking back, I know that my fog that autumn was too thick for me to realize that I had already come to the place where I could begin a new life. Everything that I needed was within my reach, but I didn't see it right away. But looking back, I also wish I could return to the strange safety of that fog and linger there, because back then, I had so little, if anything, to lose. I had nothing to protect. I had proffered no lies. I had committed no crimes.

My original plan when I came to Oak Valley was to sell the land that I had inherited, what was left of my father's estate. I thought that my family had wasted enough hope on one place, and I had no intention of leaving the deed to my own son. Part of the reason that I stayed and didn't get around to listing the property—so I told myself—was because I believed that I should paint the house inside and maybe clean up the grounds in order to get a better price. I could refinish the floors, maybe reshingle the roof of the garage. I accomplished nothing during those first months, however, and if I did start to paint an upstairs bedroom, I never got beyond priming one wall before I found myself staring out the window at the slope to the south of the house where the last remaining plot of vines had grown wild.

At one time, my father had owned twenty vineyards throughout the valley—he had bottled five different kinds of wine—but a fifteen-year drought in California as well as a prolonged recession had wasted his empire along with the farms of all of the other vintners in the region. Without rain, my father's vines had yielded less and less fruit, and what grapes he did manage to harvest had made thin and bitter wine. He had to shut down the winery to avoid bankruptcy, and then he began to sell off his various vineyards to survive, all of them except the original one below the house,

...er, my grandfather, had planted earlier in the
...father was left with a large stone house that he
...fford to heat and the winery, which he pillaged
...rels and whatever other oak was lying around, for
any w od that he could burn during the winter to keep
warm. He either burned or bartered away almost all of the
furniture in the house, all of the old chests and writing desks
and ladder-backed chairs. He finished off whatever bottles
of cabernet he found in his cellar and spent his last days in
a daze, sitting vigil by a window, watching his valley pale
from green to gold to brown. He saw his world turn to dust,
and in a way, my father died of thirst. He didn't live to see
the end of the drought.

Most of the vines in the valley had dried and withered, if
not during the long drought, then from subsequent neglect,
and so it was something of a miracle that my grandfather's
first plot had survived. The vines had apparently thrived
recently with renewed rainfall, coiling like barbed wire into
an untrellised tangle of sticky leaves and shoots. I had arrived
in November, and the fruit of that autumn's crop lay rotting
on the ground, flooding the air with a citrus rankness and
moistening the soil with a bloodred juice, the red wine mixing with the red clay. I stared at the vines for weeks before I
actually went down to the plot, and when I did walk down the
hill, I couldn't get very far without a machete or some sort of
tool to cut a path into the vineyard. I couldn't find anything
sharp enough in the garage, so I purchased a pair of pruning
shears at the hardware store, one of the few shops that had
not been boarded up in the town center at the southern end of
the valley. One day that January, with the shears in hand, I
began pruning the vines, ostensibly to clear a path.

Once I started to prune the vines, I couldn't stop. Pruning
turned out to be like driving fast—velocity deterred regret. I
lost myself in the rhythmic clip-clip of the shears, the elbow
flap, the tedious groom. Pruning was a safer distraction, too,
and I was accomplishing something. I was tidying the property, getting ready to sell the family stead—that was how I

justified a seemingly sisyphean labor that left me with sore shoulders and an aching lower back—and slowly I could measure my daily progress by looking behind me at the barbered plants and the piles of wiry trimmings in my wake.

I began to spend the better part of each day hunched over the plants, hours and hours out in the cold field, chopping at the vines that had begun to weave into one another and fold in on themselves, scissoring my way down the long rows of the square sloped plot. I had to saw off the thicker branches in order to cut the vines back to their cordons, saving only a young shoot here and there on each branch. Eventually I uncovered the old trellises, and I rewired and restaked them. I pruned all day, and I still liked a glass of wine at dusk, and then I would sink up to my ears in a warm bath before I went to bed, strangely eager to get up early the next morning and get back to the vines.

Before long I had fashioned a monkish routine for myself, pruning and sleeping, pruning and sleeping. I would pull on a poncho and prune when it rained. I pruned even though it became quite cold that February. I hacked away in the early evening when I couldn't really see what I was doing. I hewed each vine down to its muddied trunk and lowest bifurcation—there were one thousand separate vines in all—and carried away the clippings in my father's old pickup. I had spared a few shoots, as I say, because I remembered that the men who worked for my father would always leave the sturdiest new growth on the cordons when they pruned the vines in the months after the harvest, but I worried that in my zeal I might have mortally wounded the plants. I worried that I would wake up one morning and my vines would be dead beyond resuscitation, just like all of the other vines in the valley.

I expected to sell the house and the vineyard in the spring, and when I drove up to San Francisco at the end of March to visit my son, I promised my soon-to-be-ex-wife Julia that I would promptly send her the money I had promised her in our settlement. I had some cash in the bank, as well, enough

to last me through the summer, but I needed to sell the vineyard and knew that it would take time, and so I had decided
to contact a real estate broker when I returned to the valley.
But when I did get back to the vineyard, I discovered that the
shoots that I had left on the cordons had begun to sprout
bright green, almost incandescent buds, and frankly, I was
astonished. You have to understand that I had never grown
anything in my life—I had maimed every kind of plant, from
ferns to cacti, at one time or another—and so I found myself
wanting to stay on in the valley just to see what these brave
new buds would do.

I checked on them every day, I inspected every sprig.
When the rainy season ended, I dragged a hose down from
the house—the irrigation pipes had all rusted and cracked—
and I watered my vines one by one. The buds sprouted new
tendrils and then leaves. Flowers blossomed. With the flowers came clusters of berries, inverted prisms of hard nascent
fruit. The berries became grapes, each one a plump green
globe that began to redden and purple and swell with juice
by the end of the summer. In September, I began to test the
ripeness each day by crunching a bunch in my hand. One fall
morning I opened my fist and saw that my palm was sticky;
it was time to pick the grapes.

I had been quite lucky, given what I would later learn
about tending vines. I had neither sprayed the plants with
fungicides nor taken measures to safeguard against frost and
mildew; I hadn't properly thinned the canopy of leaves to let
the sun get to the fruit or performed any of the most basic
gardening, the weeding of the beds, the training of the vines,
the cluster thinning, which most people who had spent any
time around grapes knew to do. I ended up with a harvest that
left me wearing a stupid grin for weeks, and the fact that this
crop was what most growers would consider a low yield
didn't bother me at all. The yield was low, I knew, because
my vines were the same vines that my grandfather had
planted when he came home from France after the Great War,
and that meant that they were seventy-five years old—in their

seventy-fifth leaf, as winemakers say—whereas most growers replanted their vines after forty leaves, sacrificing the rich
loaminess of wine made from the grapes of elderly vines for
a crop that provided a more abundant and profitable vintage.
My harvest may have been modest, but I made some calls
and found that there was definite interest in my venerable
cabernet sauvignon grapes. A respected vintner from a northern valley bought my entire harvest to blend with his own
cabernet franc, fruit from considerably younger vines.

I spent most of my second autumn in the valley
fixing up the old stone house. At the time of his death, my
father had occupied only two rooms, the kitchen and the
adjacent living room with its generous hearth. He had placed
a cot in front of the fireplace, and it was my impression that
he never went upstairs, but when I had come to the house a
year earlier, I found drop cloths spread out over the warped
oak floors in several of the bedrooms and in the hallway. I
found brushes and rollers and mostly unopened cans of
white paint in the corner bedroom where I used to stay when
I came to visit my father in the summer when I was young.
All of the rooms had grayed with dust and cobwebbing, but
the walls of my old bedroom looked somewhat less dingy
than the rest. I rubbed away the grime on a paint can to read
the date marked on its lid. The year fell somewhere in the
middle of the drought.

I bought new paint and spent several months sanding the
floors and waxing them, fixing doors and replacing broken
windowpanes. I bought tables and a bed and a desk at a flea
market. I found a dark blue leather couch and two matching
armchairs. A wicker settee, a chest of drawers. I chose one
bedroom upstairs for myself and left the others unfurnished.

Both the house and the winery on the hill below it had been
built from a smoky stone, and the house, buttressed by two
tapered chimneys, had a green roof and green shutters. The

window frames were green, too. The shutters on one side of the house had been removed, and I found them in the garage. Another unfinished project. My father—I had to assume that my father was responsible for this renovation—had been in the process of replacing broken slats and giving the shutters a fresh coat of primer. Looking at the paint cans, I could see that he had intended to paint the shutters black. I kept them green.

And I found incomplete projects everywhere I turned. Outside the winery, my father had begun but not finished the job of repairing the stairs that descended the slope and connected the tiered rooms housing the gravity-fed fermentation tanks with the cellar at the base of the hill. Out in the vineyard, my father—or whomever he might have hired—had begun to build a tall wooden fence around the plot of vines to keep out the deer. Only one corner of the new barrier had been erected. It seemed strange to me that my father had commissioned this work when he was broke or that he might have been undertaking this kind of repair work himself when he had given up on the vineyard. I tried to put up some more of the new fence, but I was not a man who had worked much with my hands, and I ended up hiring some local men to help me with the carpentry.

It wasn't until I was cleaning out the shelf of a closet in the study and I found a folded page of Dark Oak Wines stationery tucked into a leather-bound ledger that I began to understand the last chapter of my father's life. It was a list written in my father's looping, left-slanting hand, and it was dated around the same time as the cans of paint that I had found; it was a list of projects, which included repainting the house inside and the shutters outside, repointing the gray stone, and repairing the splintered rafters in the winery along with the stairs down to the cellar. The list mentioned the new fence. Plant rosebushes outside the dining room, my father had written. Sage and rosemary by the kitchen porch, plus lavender, plus larkspur. New shelves for the pantry. Rewire the trellises. See about trading in the pickup. The list reminded my father to trim a pear tree, which by the time I had come to the vineyard had been axed to a stump. Tractor needs a new fuel pump. Sod the back lawn. Hang a hammock. And then along with a neat diagram at the bottom of the page, my father had sketched plans for a broad slate terrace and a lap-length swimming pool on the side of the house that overlooked his vines and the rolling vale beyond.

The citizens of Oak Valley tended to congregate in the late morning at the hardware store—this was where they had always gathered, even before the wineries went out of business—and I went there with my father's list and asked some of the people who knew him what he may have been up to. I don't remember who it was, but someone said, We all made lists that year. Which year? I asked. The one year during the drought when it rained, someone else explained. We all made lists, and then we tore them up the next winter.

What I had not realized was that the fifteen years of drought in California had not all been dry years. There were seven in a row with no rain, but then there had been a single rainy season that had lasted from November through April, a wet spell that was followed by seven more years of brutal dryness. If I didn't know about the one season of rain, it was probably because I was out of the state at the time; I had gone to college and law school in the East. Ultimately that isolated span of six months hadn't mattered; not enough rain fell to restore the water table or fill up the reservoirs. One season of rain had not saved the valley, and yet one season of rain had apparently been enough to inspire my father and all of his friends to scribble lists of chores and errands and dreams. Life would return to normal, they thought, and there was so much work to do, so much renovation that my father had not known where to begin. He must have darted from task to task without making much progress anywhere, from the shutters to the fence and then the winery stairs.

That evening, I paged through my father's ledgers. My rapport with him had always been formal at best. I was aware that he had been proud of me when I did well in school, but we had never found a way of talking to each other. I hadn't seen much of him during his decline. And now for the first time, I was able to fathom his sorrow, his long fall, as I pored over his records, his journals of rapid expansion and then slow, malignant defeat, as I studied the accumulating accounts payable and the trickle of income and the sad ink recording the acre-by-acre sales of the family land. From the dates of certain transactions, I determined that my father had not shut down his winery until the first dry winter after the one winter when it had stormed. He had not sold off any land, I realized, until the second wave of the drought. I suspect that he had somehow remained optimistic throughout the first seven years, hopeful, holding out, refusing to give in to a despotic sun. He had prayed for rain, and I could picture him dancing in the cold rain when it finally did pour. That spring he made his list, he was going to hang a hammock—a hammock—my father, who was a farmer at heart and not a man who ever napped—but then he must have died inside when that one wet winter proved to be nothing more than a fluke turn of weather. The long drought itself was not really what killed him; it was that single season of rain and the false hope that it engendered that had made his life unlivable.

I wished that I could have told my father now that I understood the trials that he had endured. I may have understood when it was too late to tell him, but I also believed, as all sons do, that I would not repeat his mistakes. I would never allow my own life to take the turns that his had taken. I had gone through a drought of my own, but as I pruned back my vines a second time, I vowed never to let it resume. I pruned my vines again, and that was when I plotted out my new life.

I discovered that the valley needed a lawyer, and so I rented a storefront one block down from the hardware store and set up an office in what was once a cheese shop that had catered to the weekend tourists who used to visit the wineries. A year earlier, I never would have guessed that I would end up back in practice. The same week that Julia and I had decided to split up—and this came a month and a half after my mother died—I had learned not only that I was not going to make partner that year at the big firm where I was working but also that I never would make partner in any future year. The managing partner suggested that I consider moving on to a new firm, but as far as I was concerned, I was through being an attorney. I had ended up hating the law. The law had been a mistake for me. The law bored me, but then I found myself staying on in Oak Valley and needing money—even though she wasn't pressing me for it, I felt obliged to send Julia what cash I had in the bank—and I didn't know what else to do. Much to my surprise, however, I began to enjoy my work, and before long I had built a modest but sustainable practice.

I was glad to help clients whom I knew and had befriended, as opposed to the corporations or investors whom I had represented in the big city. In the city, I had become a tax and bankruptcy attorney, but in the valley, I ran more of a legal general store. I drew up wills and real-estate contracts and handled some claims against the quarries taking over the vineyards. I picked up a case that had to do with disputed water rights. When I needed to bring in a little more cash, I would take an overflow assignment from the San Benito County public defender's office, and for that freelance, usually the weeklong defense of a first-time larcenist or minor drug offender, I would receive a flat fee. I looked forward to the hour's drive up to Hollister, where I would make the occasional courtroom appearance, although it was the practice of the Legal Aid department to dispatch most of its caseload through rapid poker hands of plea bargaining. And my background in California bankruptcy law came in quite handy because much of my work in Oak Valley, the most rewarding work, as it turned out, involved the renegotiation of various vintners' foreclosures, the filing and refiling for certain protections against creditors and so forth. Here were people who had been destroyed by drought, and I was able to help them hold on to their homes and their dwindling retirement savings; that work seemed worthy to me.

All the while, I was fixing up my house and tending my vines, and so my life became busy. I made friends in the valley; I was invited to dinner. I dated a woman for a while, my contact in the public defender's office, and we had fun while it lasted, but a season of reasonable passion was followed by a single half hour of pleading our felonious affair back down to a misdemeanor friendship. I knew—and my friend knew, too—that the woman with whom I really wanted to spend my life was Julia—Julia, my one great friend across the years—and I have to be honest and say that even while I was seeing my friend in Legal Aid, I was contemplating the various ways that I could lure Julia down to the vineyard.

We had not spoken much during our first year apart. When we talked, we talked mostly about our son.

"So how were Tim's grades this term?" I would ask.

"He gets good grades," Julia would answer.

"Good grades. What, like *A*'s and *B*'s?"

"Those would be good grades," Julia replied.

But gradually, perhaps with a certain distance on our long union and our fast drift, we chatted with greater ease, more like the old friends that we truly were. Although that is not to say that I actually looked forward to our conversations, quite the opposite. Julia had a way of unnerving me, of catching me off guard, she always did.

"Am I calling at a bad time?" she asked one midwinter evening.

I had just come in from the field and I was trying not to track too much mud into my kitchen. I told her it was a great time to talk, and I tripped as I kicked my boots off and reached for a juice glass and bottle of wine.

"So tell me a good book I should read," she said.

"A good book," I said.

"You're always reading a good book," Julia said, "and I'm really craving a good book right now."

"That's why you called," I said.

"That's why I called," she said.

I made my way upstairs to one of the unfurnished bedrooms, where I stretched out on the floor with my wine and the cordless phone. I sat in the dark.

"How are you?" I asked.

"Bored," she said. "Tim's at a sleep-over. I need company. I need a good book."

"I haven't had much time to read lately," I said. "What free time I have, like today, I spend out in the field."

Julia was silent.

"Looking after my vines," I said. "I told you how I brought back the vines—"

"But isn't that, you know, a summer thing? Gardening?"

I didn't think that she meant to belittle my farming. "It's more of a year-round obsession," I said.

Julia was silent again. Then she said, "You see, I still have all of your books—"

"Right," I said. "I should come and pack them up." Once upon a time, I had been a voracious reader, and I had amassed quite a collection of novels and travelogues—what I liked to read—and when I left Julia, I had left these books behind, along with most of my possessions.

"No, no, they're fine here," she said. "What I meant was . . . Well, you used to want me to read the books you were reading, do you remember?"

I remembered.

"And I never had time," Julia said.

For much of our marriage, she had been working toward a doctorate in art history at Berkeley and didn't have time to read my books, let alone her academic journals, all the while breast-feeding or keeping our toddler occupied. She had abandoned her dissertation.

"I have time now," Julia said. "I have a lot of time these days, it seems. Like right now. So. Tell me, what should I read?"

I listened to her breathe awhile.

"I'm supposed to come up and see Tim in two weeks," I said. "And I was thinking maybe it's time for him to come down to the vineyard and stay with me here."

When I saw my son, I usually went up to San Francisco, rather than having Julia make the one-hundred-plus-mile drive south to the valley. I didn't think Tim would much like hanging out in the valley, and I wasn't keen on disrupting his city life.

"Maybe," Julia said.

I took a deep breath. "And I was thinking maybe you'd bring him down and stay over one night before heading back, and then I'd drive him home at the end of the weekend."

"Oh," Julia said. "Interesting. Except, see, the problem is that I'm kind of busy these days. I don't have a lot of time. I'm thinking of getting back to work on the big D."

My chest sank. "Really? That's great, Julia," I said.

"Yeah, so I'm not sure I could swing it. But I'll ask Tim. Maybe he wants to go down to the vineyard—"

"Or maybe I should just come up to the city like usual," I said.

"Yeah, maybe," Julia said.

"We'll see," I said. And that was the end of our dance that evening. I lay on my back in the dark bedroom and stayed there for a long time before facing the bright rest of my house.

Something had happened during that conversation. I couldn't say what exactly, but I convinced myself that Julia wanted what I wanted. We just needed to proceed slowly, at a glacial pace. She called again a few days later, and I took my glass of merlot up to a bedroom and talked to her for an hour. I don't recall precisely what we talked about, but I do remember that Julia wanted to draw me out about my legal work.

"This whole public defender–good works deal you've got going," she said.

"What about it?"

"I'm proud of you, Jason," she said. "I mean, you always

talked about doing that sort of thing but never got around to it. I never thought you would."

"I only take a case now and then," I said. "More often during the winter, because for some reason that seems to be when I need the cash, and don't make me out to be a saint, Julia, because, listen, it's not very much money, and it's just income."

"Good deeds are good deeds," she said. "Take the compliment."

"Okay," I said. "Thank you."

Days later, I called her.

"Tell me more about the dissertation. Would you choose a new topic?" I asked.

"I would have to," she said. "Somebody published a book about my guy." Her guy had been a little-known quattrocento miniaturist. "Besides, I think I want to hang out in this century now."

"That's probably a good idea," I said. "Seeing as this century is almost over."

"Tim is really looking forward to coming down to see you," she said.

My heart raced.

"If that's still something you're ready for—"

"Definitely," I said.

"And I'll stay over one night, if that's okay. If you have a couch," Julia said.

"I have a couch," I said, and as soon as I hung up, I bolted downstairs to plump up its cushions, as if Julia would walk through the door any minute and expect to lie down.

This was what I wanted to happen—what I had been angling for—for Julia to bring Tim down here to the vineyard and to see me here, on my new turf, because I knew that Julia's memory of the place was mostly of my father during his saddest years. What I wanted to happen was happening, and that amazed me because I had never been much of a conductor; I was more likely to be found playing second violin. I had never been a great planner—this is what I'm trying to say—I lived my life from day to day, and so I began to wonder if during my year and several months away from Julia, I had perhaps changed the way I had wanted to change. Maybe I was a new man, for once in charge of my destiny.

It was either the last week in February or the first of March that year, a Friday at dusk, when Julia showed up. She parked her sports car by the twin eucalyptus that stood sentry at the end of a long path leading up to the house from the vineyard road. The sun lit her from behind as she walked up to the front door, giving her long limbs, her narrow taper, a sharp, luminous edge. She looked as if she were on fire, and I was quick to hug her, to smother the flames with my embrace. Her lips brushed against my neck. Her breath warmed my left collarbone, my ear. At that moment, I wanted nothing more than for her to unbutton my ironed white shirt and peel it off of me and run her palms up my forearms and biceps and across my chest in the way that she once used to touch me, in a way that had always made me feel strong.

When she pulled away, I asked her where Tim was.

"At a friend's," she said. "I forgot all about how he had this big birthday party to go to, another sleep-over, and I'd promised him he could go. I figured you could come up next weekend to see him. . . ."

I must have been frowning.

"I know, I'm sorry, I'm sorry. I should have called," Julia said.

She had come alone, which for the most part thrilled me, and my frown wasn't a grimace of anger, but one of sudden fear.

"No, hey, I'm delighted," I said.

Julia stepped back. "Show me around," she said.

I gave her a tour of the house first, what there was of it to tour, the living room with the cracked leather sofa and chairs, the wicker settee, the writing table. The dining room with its beat-up long mead-hall table. The study, my bedroom with my flea-market four-poster, sans canopy.

That was it, but Julia said, "I like your decorating."

"My decorating?"

"Your style."

"My style? I think it's called bargain-basement," I said.

"You have a definite style," she said. "Spare, lean, handsome."

"I think it's called neo-flea market," I said.

"You never used to have a style."

"I didn't?"

"You definitely did not know how to furnish a room," she said.

I wanted to point out that I could have easily furnished our six-room floor-through plus deck in San Francisco, but I had always deferred to Julia, with her penchant for anorectic furniture, for spindly chairs and polished maple; I had always let her choose the mattress ticking for the upholstery and the muslin for the curtains; she had decided which wine-country landscapes we would hang on which walls. I was in no mood for stale bickering now, however, and so I ushered her out to my vines.

I had finished cutting them back in time for the new growing season, and I didn't think that Julia would be as impressed as she might have been if she had visited during the full leafiness of the high summer or in the early autumn, when there was color on the vines.

"I have to tell you something," she said as we headed down the hill and the groomed plot came into view.

The last sunlight of the day caught her steel-rimmed glasses, which she almost never used, except to drive and read, and which she propped up on her wheat-colored head like a hair band most of the time. The glasses gleamed like a tiara.

"I never believed you about your vines," she said. She left me standing at the edge of the plot and, even though she was wearing a pair of unscuffed leather shoes, headed down an aisle between the muddy rows of the serpentine trunks.

"You thought I made it all up?" I asked.

When she came back toward me, I could not tell whether she was blushing or merely rouged by the March air.

"You want me to be impressed?" she said.

Now I was the one who was blushing.

"It worked," she said. "I am."

I took her hand. I led her back up hill. "Let's eat dinner," I said.

"Can you get decent takeout in Oak Valley?" she asked, and then, when we were back in my kitchen and I removed a chicken from the oven: "Who cooked that?"

I saluted her with an oven mitt.

"No way," she said. "You can't cook. You cooked that?"

This was the only meal that I knew how to prepare that turned out well every time. A roasted and stuffed chicken and then some no-nonsense vegetable on the side. Glazed carrots that night. I had left the chicken in a little too long, but that had only made for a crispier roast. Similarly I had overcooked the vegetables, and yet there was something soothing about the sweet soft chunks of carrot. And the fresh sage that I had chopped up and mixed into the stuffing—too much sage, I thought—filled my dining room with the pungent grassiness that any Californian will identify as the smell of the vernal equinox. The scent of sage and of candle wax, too, surrounded us in my dining room as we supped together for the first time in over a year, and although I knew that I had accomplished what I had set out to accomplish— for there I was, a model of self-sufficiency, an independent man who could make a life by himself, for himself—this wasn't enough. I wanted more. I wanted to know that Julia would go upstairs with me later and sleep with me and wake up with me. I wanted Tim magically to appear at the breakfast table. I wanted our life back, transplanted here, and even if this evening was a first step, that ultimate goal seemed so far off that I worried it might be unattainable.

Julia didn't stay the night—she needed to pick Tim up in the morning—and her second hug when she left a few hours later, that second embrace just about paralyzed me. When I shut my front door, I suffered such a profound welling-up inside, a sudden mourning nearly equal to the mourning that I had known when my mother, sick for years, had finally died, the shock, the spine chill, the shudder, the buzz in my ears, such grief that I slumped against the wall and wept for a good hour in the oak-wainscoted foyer of an old stone house in which I could not fathom living one more day now that I knew so clearly, so precisely what it was missing. What made my life so obviously and, I feared that night, permanently incomplete.

And yet we plodded forward, Julia and I, cautiously and inevitably forward. There was no other way. We spoke often, and with each conversation, I became more patient. We ate meals together when I went up to see Tim. He did start coming down to the vineyard, and he and I made pizzas together and took long hikes, and although he had become hard for me to read—he was eleven going on twenty—I believed that Tim enjoyed my company and liked the break from the urban bustle that a few days in the country gave him. Julia never stayed over, however, and at some point that spring, I found out that she had been seeing a man back in San Francisco, a painter, and so she used the time when I took Tim for the weekend to be alone with this new man. An artist. I wished that he had been a stockbroker. Julia had always had a thing for artists, and I think that when she and I got together our senior year in college, all of her friends thought I would last for about thirty seconds, given that I could barely draw a tree. She told me that she was seeing a man, and I remember that I felt ambushed. I knew that she had dated other men, just as I had dated other women, but I often made the mistake of assuming that Julia's life followed a parallel course to my own. If I was mateless now, then so was she. But that was not the case, and as we became closer that spring and then that summer, Julia wanted to tell me about her man, and I let her, although I was never happy about it. Or I should say that I was only happy to hear about a fight or disagreement that she and the painter had endured.

I hated hearing that they had made up. I made sure that I never met him when I went into the city.

One night late in the summer, Julia brought Tim down to see me, and after dinner—I'd learned how to make salmon fillets in a lemon-dill sauce and I'd concocted a couscous dish to go with it; I had practiced this meal a dozen times before making it for Julia and Tim—Julia and I were doing the dishes while Tim was in the living room playing with his computer. We were standing close to each other, and I don't remember what we were talking about; in truth, I wasn't really listening to what Julia was saying; I was admiring the way her neck sloped so gently into her shoulder. And it was a warm evening, so Julia was wearing a loose-fitting white blouse—she wore only white in the summer and then was exclusive about browns and blacks in the winter—and I could see her dark nipples beneath the shirt, and suddenly I was buzzed by the mere shape of her. I wanted to drink her in a single gulp. And she looked over at me. And she grinned. And she combed back her loose bang with the dry back of her hand but couldn't get her hair out of her face. So I put down the plate I was drying and I swept her hair behind her ear for her. Then I touched her neck and shoulder with my finger. She turned toward me and she was red, she was hot, and I stepped closer to her to kiss her. She let me kiss her. That kiss lasted for all of a second, yet I felt as though we were driving through a long tunnel beneath a mountain, spilling out on a canyon road that ran down to the ocean, winding down the road at an amazing speed but never quite reaching the coast. I thought, I have her back.

But then Julia pulled away from me. She reached for a towel and dried her hands, and before I knew it, she was kissing Tim good-bye, and she was out the door, and even though I called after her, she didn't turn around. She marched down the path to her car and was off in a cloud of dust. There I was, slumping against the foyer wall again, but I couldn't afford to be sad, because Tim was calling me. He wanted to show me something on his computer, and I stood behind him and watched him zap through the game that he had mastered, but all I could think about was how I'd blown it. Julia would tell me that I was just as self-absorbed as I always had been. I didn't know what she wanted at all. I'd blown it.

When I took Tim back to San Francisco at the end of the weekend, I met the painter. He was sitting in the kitchen, the bastard, right where I used to drink my morning cappuccino. Julia was polite with me. She apologized for running off, and I said I was sorry that I had misread her, and she told me not to be sorry, and that was that.

The painter had a big chest, big arms. Shoulder-length hair and earrings in both ears. I sat down with him while Julia got Tim in bed, and I had absolutely nothing to say to the man.

"So what kind of trouble have you two kids been getting into this summer?" I finally asked.

"What?" the painter asked back. He was wearing a thin leather choker. He looked a little cross-eyed to me.

"Has it been as brutally hot up here in the city as it has down in Oak Valley?" I asked.

The painter sipped his beer. He said, "I don't mind the heat. I kind of like it."

"Do you?"

"Yeah, I really dig it when the streets, you know, get all wobbly and wiggly. I mean, I think the heat can be pretty cool," he said.

I laughed. The painter cocked his head. He frowned; he didn't know what I was laughing at. He couldn't hear his own joke.

"The heat can be pretty cool," I echoed.

The painter shook his head again. He still didn't get it, and so I laughed even harder, and when Julia returned to the kitchen, she asked what was so funny.

I didn't tell her. I wanted to say, Your painter is so stupid. I wanted to give her a hug because I felt such relief. I knew that this man couldn't last. His arms were huge, sure, and maybe he was a good lover—maybe his paintings were terrific—but without any wit, there was no way he would last.

I could take him, I was sure of it. And it occurred to me that if Julia wasn't ready for me, and if she had to date someone, I would rather have her date a dumb lug like this guy than someone who might actually steal her heart, a man whom I might not be able to outrun when it came time to sprint for the golden apple.

And so I returned to my vineyard, and in an odd way, I became less anxious. I could be patient. The new me could take my time. I began to enjoy this period in our lives when we counted on each other as friends yet maintained our physical distance. As long as Julia and I spoke, I was happy, and we did talk on the phone, some nights for hours. Rare was the evening when we didn't check in with each other, if nothing else merely to say good night, sleep well. I could be patient.

I don't want to pretend, however, that I wasn't lonesome that fall, because I did suffer spells of exacting melancholy, although at the age of thirty-five, I had finally learned how to live alone. I looked forward to the chores that I assigned myself to fill the day, stripping an old breakfront or hoeing the hard soil around the vines or burrowing into a classic novel that I had always told myself I would read. I looked forward to the shifting seasons in the valley and the different skies that each promised—the gray of the winter weighing against me like a heavy coat, the cathedral ceiling of the spring, the colorlessness of the summer air, that ocean without water. I looked forward to the autumn most of all, and not because its mood swings matched my own breeze and gust, nor because the fall landscape appealed to me—the entire valley turned gold, the hills, the trees, the sunsets—but because I had become a man who spent his entire year growing grapes and his autumn reaping a harvest and then walking around with the buzz, the deep satisfaction that a harvest behind you brings.

My second crop was larger than the first, again not because of anything I did or didn't do. I had pruned the vines in the winter and watered them in the summer, that was all. I had measured the stickiness of the fruit each day when they colored up, and then I went at the vines with a small curved knife, a miniature scythe, and I picked my grapes bunch by bunch. Once again I sold my harvest, and while I didn't earn much from my grapes, I did make some money. I had become a small-time farmer.

A few days after the fruit had been trucked away, I went into town and stopped off at the hardware store before going to my office. The crowd there, my friends in the valley, applauded me when I came in. I wasn't sure why. People patted me on the back. Everyone wanted to say hello and chat with me, and it quickly became apparent that I was being congratulated and embraced because, quite simply, I had grown some grapes and sold them. No matter how insignificant my commerce was, it meant a great deal to the people of Oak Valley. If some city boy could come along and grow some fruit and sell it for a fair price for two consecutive harvests—that I had proven myself two years in a row was key, because consistency meant everything to vintners—then there was hope for everyone else.

I never intended for my farming to become symbolic in any way, to take on public meaning, but that was what happened. I had not set out to inspire anyone, but more than one vineyard owner informed me that morning that he was going to see about getting ahold of some new rootstock, some new vines. In the days and weeks that followed, several vintners stopped by my office to talk seriously about how they might restart their wineries as new enterprises free from the debt of the failed ones. Veteran farmers began to ask me for my agricultural secrets, and I wished that I had secrets that I could dispense. Someone baked me a plate of brownies and left it by my office door one morning along with an unsigned note that said, Thank you for coming to the Valley. A few people asked me if they could work for me, as if I were my father back in his heyday, with a score of vineyards to manage, and I was sorry that I didn't have jobs to offer anyone. Suddenly there was talk of the prosperity that lay ahead. I would go into town and notice the giddier pitch of the conversation in the hardware store, a gleeful chatter that holiday season, as if the rumor was that a distant war would soon end. The fighting had already subsided and lasting peace was inevitable.

I had never played the role of the hero before. I had never scored a winning touchdown or rescued a child from a well or given a stirring speech from the steps of a city hall or put forth a theory of gravity or written a story that captured the mood of an era or done anything remotely like that. I had merely lived my life and made a mess of it, and all I was doing now was attempting to make a new life for myself, nothing more. I was not entirely comfortable with this new role and the burden to succeed that came with it, yet at the same time I have to admit that I liked the way people looked at me, as if there was some sort of glamour in my relative youth and my innocent faith that I could make something grow from tired soil. The way people looked at me, as if I was a man with a golden touch, made me believe that perhaps I had become lucky again, charmed, as if nothing that I would now do could go wrong.

And so one evening when I was driving home during my third year in the valley, I decided that I would save some grapes from my next harvest rather than sell off the entire crop, that I would keep part or maybe even all of my harvest so that I could fulfill a mission that I had only intuited before but now understood as my destiny—so that I could make my own wine.

One Saturday morning that winter, Julia arrived unannounced. She had Tim with her, and for a moment I thought that I had misread my calendar; I wasn't due for my monthly weekend with my son for another two weeks. Tim ran in the house, carrying a package of glow-in-the-dark constellations that he wanted me to help him paste to the ceiling of his bedroom, the corner bedroom where I used to stay when I visited my father. Julia collapsed into a club chair in the living room. She looked tired.

"Are you okay?" I asked.

"I haven't been sleeping," she said.

Tim called down to me.

"Go," she said. "Put up the stars."

Julia was quiet all day, and I didn't push her. She said nothing during dinner, and it wasn't until Tim went to bed that she told me that she had broken up with her painter beau. I did my best not to smile, but I couldn't help but grin a bit.

"I know you never liked him," Julia said.

"No," I said. "I liked him." My lie sounded as thin as the evening air.

Julia became teary. "I'm the one who broke up with him," she said, "so I don't know why I'm so upset. He didn't seem all that bothered, but I'm a mess."

"Hey," I said, "it's okay," and I drew her to me, into my arms, and moored her with a firm hug. I let her cry softly in my arms. I knew that I had to play this very carefully. She seemed fragile to me now, and if I wasn't careful, I would crush her weakened frame. I took her hand and led her to the couch.

"I'm sorry," she said.

"Don't be sorry. Cry away," I said. "It's better to cry now than to . . ."

I didn't really know what to say, and then I realized that I didn't need to say anything. She had chosen me to be the one to whom she turned when she was sad, and all I had to do was hold her. She buried her head in my chest, and so now I could afford to let go of the wide smile I had been keeping in check, wide, but not wide enough to match my intense glee at that moment.

I insisted that Julia sleep on the couch rather than drive home when she was upset, and she finally allowed me to turn the couch into a comfortable cot. I kissed her on the cheek and went up to my bed, but I could hardly sleep.

Here they both were, Julia and Tim, asleep in my house. I touched the plaster behind my bed with my palm, and the walls seemed warm, as if they were vibrating with all of the life they unexpectedly contained.

The next morning Julia was in a better mood. She made banana pancakes. I had a big stack in front of me, but I didn't want to eat any of it. I just wanted to watch Tim and Julia pour syrup over their plates and hack away at the formidable stacks.

I had not told Julia—indeed, I had not told anyone yet—that I intended to restore my winery and hold on to my harvest for my own crush. I told her now.

"Hey, Jason. That would be amazing," she said.

"I'll have a lot to do this summer," I said. "In terms of getting the vats and tanks ready and so forth."

"But do you think you really know how to make wine?" Julia asked.

"I'm sort of hoping that the grapes will just do their thing," I said.

"I think it's more involved."

"I know. I need to hire a gang of chubby women to hold up their skirts and dance on the fruit," I said.

"For starters," Julia said. "Preferably while the menfolk hoot and play their accordions."

"It's kind of a secret," I said. "My making wine, I mean. So I'd appreciate it . . ." And then I felt foolish, because who was Julia going to tell? She didn't know the folks in the hardware store. She didn't have anyone to tell, and I wasn't even sure why my plans needed to be secret in the first place.

But Julia said, *"Tu secreto es mi secreto,"* and she winked.

She began coming down to the vineyard with greater frequency. We abandoned whatever visitation schedule had been worked out in our custody agreement. She had won a grant to work on a new dissertation, and she claimed that she enjoyed these weekends in the serene country when I could watch Tim and she could get some serious reading done. She arrived with a stack of library texts and took over my desk in the study. Meanwhile, Tim would run a phone line from my bedroom down to his room and spend hours upstairs modeming his various friends; I went out into the fields to do some work. Then we came together for a great feast, and we made a fire at night. Julia slept on the couch.

I have to confess that while I was eager to move much faster toward that final station where we all knew we were headed, the last stop on a long line, I also appreciated the rhythm of Julia's coming and going. This was something that she and I had missed out on when we were younger, and now I could see that it was a significant part of any romance, that early phase of living apart that no lovers should rush, the to-and-fro, the commute between your home and the home of your paramour. When Julia and I first met, we were seniors in college and I was living in a dorm and she shared a house off campus. We moved in together right after graduation; three months after that, we eloped, and it was too soon, way too soon.

Now, all these years later, in the days before she came down to the vineyard, I would prepare my house, filling vases with whatever I could gather from my land, rosemary and lavender and poppies and lacy fennel, stocking my pantry with snacks, with grains and soups, my refrigerator with cheese, juice, cramming bowls with more fruit than our small family could eat. And I liked being alone after she and Tim left. I would go for a jog down the vineyard road, and then I would take a long shower. I would take a good novel to bed with me. If we had carried on like this for a year or so more, I think I would have been content. Maybe I am exaggerating. Anyway, I had become a farmer now, and a farmer had to plan his seasons; he had to take the longest view. Then again, a California farmer also had to cope with the neuroses of a fragile climate. I could be patient, but Julia and I had a history, and history, we are told, repeats itself, or so we hope that at least peace will follow war, but not necessarily war after peace.

Late in April, I heard a troubling weather report on the radio. When Julia and Tim arrived that same day, I was pacing amid my vines. Julia sent Tim into the house and asked me what was wrong.

"I've been lucky so far," I told her, "but everyone gets hit by a frost at one time or another."

"What will happen?" she asked. "Could you lose the whole crop?"

"I could," I said. "But hey, that's the worst-case scenario."

"What will you do?"

I listed my options, which were few.

Julia was wearing a dark brown shirt, which the wind pulled back against her chest. Her hair blew back, too, and she looked as if she might be carried away. When she took my hand, I thought it was to anchor herself.

She said, "Don't worry, Jason. We'll survive the frost," and she smiled, and I believed we would.

That afternoon Julia and I dug shallow pits at five-yard intervals all around the plot. Tim helped for a while, too, but he had a science project to which he had promised his mother he would devote some of the day. So it was mostly Julia and I alone clearing away the brush and twigs and tossing them into the pits along with some logs from the woodpile in my garage. We also filled the dozen metal buckets that I had bought at the hardware store with sticks and wood chips and some coal, and we positioned these buckets around the grapevines. It was dark by seven-thirty. Then we waited out the evening and watched a movie with Tim, put him to bed when it was over, and around midnight, as the temperature dropped according to the forecast, Julia and I put on sweaters and our warmest coats and trudged out to the field, armed with matches and cans of fuel, and we lit the brush and twigs and logs and coal in the pits and the buckets.

We monitored each fire to make sure that they all burned steadily, and some of the small pyres went out in the night breeze, but most burned well, and the buckets, our smudge pots around the vines, kept the plants warm as the morning broke and the chill in the air numbed our faces, as the insipid white glaze of the predicted frost blanketed the valley. If my irrigation pipes had been working, we could have watered the vines and let them ice up; they could recover from ice but not frost. That was what everyone in the hardware store had told me to do, but with my pipes still rusted, I had no choice but to resort to the older, time-proven practice of smudging.

Picture a vineyard in the eerie green light of a cold morning before dawn. Eventually the fires burned out and the embers smoldered in the pits and the buckets, and a veil of warm smoke—a savory smoke because of the oak twigs and the sagebrush and the pine logs that we were burning—curled around the vines with their buds and new leaves and first white flowers. It was a sweet-scented smoke but not an entirely benevolent fog, because there was something menacing about this floating gauze that made me nauseous after a while. Julia said that she didn't mind the fumes, but she looked a little queasy to me when I shined my flashlight at her, slower in step as the morning moved along.

"Go inside and take a rest," I said, but she wouldn't go in.

We paced the aisles between the vines together, arm in arm. We could watch the ground around us, the lawn, the trees, all the less fortunate flowers of the slope, fall prey to the heartless dew, and it was only around five in the morning, when the sun began to rise across the valley, and rise fast, in a hurry to relieve us from our watch, that we could compare the frozen lawn to our smoke-pampered vines, still bright green, dripping with the warmed moisture, and know that our smudge had worked.

"I told you not to worry," Julia said.

When the sun was higher, we stamped out the last of the smoldering cinders with our hiking boots and headed inside, peeling off our layers of coats and sweaters, and then, in the mudroom off the kitchen, despite our fatigue, our sweatiness, we embraced. We were not just congratulating each other for a job well done, and we knew it. I held her against me tightly for a while, and then we kissed briefly, and we kissed again, or I kissed Julia's neck and pulled back her shirt so that I could kiss her shoulder, and this time she didn't tell me to stop. She whispered something in my ear, but I couldn't quite make out what she said. Don't let go, I think. And I obeyed. I didn't let go of her even as we stumbled together into the living room—was I afraid that if I let go of her, she might have doubts and run away?—to the couch, me with my pants undone and falling around my knees, my ankles, and Julia with her shirt off, her T-shirt off, no bra. We would worry about tenderness later, we would take our time later.

During our first hasty romp at dawn, however, I didn't pause and remember that Julia liked to be kissed along the side of her breast and ribs, nor did I wait for her to stand behind me and massage me until I was ready to explode. We were clumsy, we were reckless—drunk without sleep—and the only way I can describe our first sex after so many years apart would be to say that I had the distinct sensation that I was sobbing the entire time—even afterward when Julia sat on the floor, her back against the couch, and I lay on my side with my head in her lap and she stroked my cheek, both of us staring at the pile of cold ash in the fireplace—or to say that our making love again felt like falling from a considerable height, tumbling, plunging fast, faster, but never quite crashing into the riverless bed of white stones that ran through the valley.

julia came down to the vineyard every weekend that spring; we shared the same bed. We talked about moving slower, as if we had not already moved slowly enough, but the unspoken plan was that Julia and Tim would move down to the vineyard at the end of Tim's school year.

For his part, Tim became increasingly taciturn as the weeks went on and that move approached. I thought that maybe he was anxious about leaving the city and his friends there, but something else was going on. At the vineyard, he spent more and more time alone up in his room, doing what, I didn't know. He went on-line for hours at a stretch; this much I know because I paid the bills. When I made the very grave mistake of knocking on his door and entering before he gave me permission to come in, he shrieked at me and covered his computer screen with his arms. He had a friend in the valley whom he played with sometimes, but only one friend, and I worried that he had become the kind of boy who tended to know one boy well for a few months and play with him exclusively until he made a new friend and sought only that new boy's company. This was a pattern that had made me a lonely child, and I didn't want that for my son, but Julia said that this sort of habit was beyond our control. My son seemed wary of me. If I was, say, reading the newspaper in the dining room, Tim would stand in the door frame between the dining room and the kitchen, hovering at the threshold, balanced on one foot, his arms folded tightly across his chest, and he would make small talk with me for several minutes about the weather or what we would eat for dinner before he would sit down with me at the table. And I couldn't blame him for not trusting me.

Why should he? I had left once. Nothing I could promise him would make him believe that I wouldn't leave again. During those first seasons away from Julia, I hadn't seen a lot of Tim, which I greatly regret. I was not very good at talking things out with him, and so I didn't know what he had really gone through, and I didn't think Julia did either. But during this last year when I was around and when Julia and I clearly became closer, my son had appeared overjoyed. I had caught him grinning at the dinner table when we passed around the salad bowl. We had taken some long hikes together, just him and me, and we'd had fun, or so I thought, identifying trees from field guides and picking out the constellations on cold nights. I had thought that he wanted his mother and me to be together, so when we were together at long last, I didn't understand his sullenness.

"I expected it to be the other way around," I told Julia.

"Maybe he knows something we don't," she said.

"Like what?"

"Maybe he thinks we've gone too far too fast," she said. "Maybe he thinks we'll just fall into our old habits."

"He's eleven. Who are we talking about here?" I asked.

"Maybe he thinks we'll fuck up again," she said.

"We won't fuck up again," I said. "He doesn't seem angry with you. He trusts you." I had noticed how Tim behaved much more like his old buoyant self when he was, say, alone with his mother in the kitchen while she made dinner, and when I walked in the room, he switched mood channels: he didn't smile; he refused to laugh. "Why won't he trust me?"

Somehow I had to win back his affection. But how?

Summer arrived and Julia and Tim moved down to the vineyard. I had taken on more cases than I could manage and went in to my office every day, even on weekends, but Julia helped me out by taking over the weeding and the watering of the vines. Whenever I wasn't at my office, I was busy restoring the winery.

The winery was more of a compound of small buildings than a single structure, each shed or stone room riding its own steppe down the hillside, snug beneath the level above it. Building the winery down a hill meant that my grandfather and then my father could rely on gravity to draw the grapes or the must or the pressed wine down from one tank to the next during the wine-making process. And every structure on every level now needed some kind of repair. The top level, which was also my garage, was where I would dump the grapes after I picked them, into a wide funnel—it needed to be replaced—that emptied into a series of chutes—so did they—that carried the fruit down to the second level, the shed that housed the fermentation tanks. I had three tanks, each an eight-foot steel square, ten feet deep— my father had replaced my grandfather's original wooden tanks—and I needed to ready only one of these for our first vintage. But that meant climbing down inside the tank and making sure that there were no leaks; that meant scraping away patches of rust with a nasty ammoniac solvent, which was smelly and tedious work.

All of the plastic hoses and mesh screens, all of the alimentary connections between the levels of the winery, needed to be replaced or refitted. I had to get ahold of some presses for level three midway down the hill—my father had pawned his presses—and then I also had to clean out the holding tank the next level beneath the presses. The next structure below that one—a windowless cottage rather than a shed—housed the fining tanks; this was also where the wine went into the aging barrels and then later would be racked, and while these tanks were cleaner than the ones above them, my father had burned all of his barrels. I didn't worry about the cellar on the lowest level, a vault encased in stone, a catacomb for the finished bottles, because I wouldn't bottle any wine for almost two years.

I purchased some of the necessary equipment, the hoses and mesh and whatnot, but all of the hardware turned out to be rather expensive. The barrels were particularly costly because the grain of American oak was either too tight or too loose for aging wine—I could never remember which—and if I was serious about the quality of the wine I was trying to make, I should have been importing my barrels from France, where the oak trees had a grain deemed perfect for wine making. Usually vintners ordered their barrels a year ahead of time, and you had to pay a surcharge when you tried to get them without ample notice. My law practice could sustain my family for the time being, but I didn't have any cash left over for an amateur exploit that might prove entirely frivolous in the end should my wine turn to vinegar. I did buy some of the air locks and siphons that I needed, and then one night in the middle of the summer, I asked Tim and Julia if they wanted to take a drive.

Julia said yes, and Tim said no, and then Julia convinced Tim to come along. Then when we were all out in the garage, Julia changed her mind—she flashed me a wink—

and headed back inside. Tim said that he didn't want to go out either.

I said, "Tim, please. I could use your help." And for reasons as baffling to me as any of his swings in mood, he did not follow his mother into the house.

We headed out of the vineyard in my truck, an elderly but reliable four-by-four—my pickup had more room in its bay, but it needed new headlights—and I steered us across the gulch and followed the main highway awhile until I found the unmarked road that I had in mind on the opposite side of the valley. We headed up a hill, snaking our way around unfamiliar knolls—several times Tim had to get out and clear away the brush or tumbleweed obstructing our path—until we arrived at a barnlike structure with a squat windmill next to it, the vanes of the windmill broken and torn and altogether too battered to turn in the wind. Tim hopped out of the truck first, and I followed him inside the winery.

"Mostly we're looking for barrels," I explained.

"To steal," Tim said.

"Think of it more as recycling," I said.

We looked around and found a long oar, a paddle for stirring the must in the fermentation tank. We found a hand-corking machine and a wad of foil to capsule the corks. We found some unused bottles, but no barrels. I didn't consider the search to be all that successful, but Tim, having never explored these ruins the way I had when I first came to the valley, walked around with his flashlight aimed from his hip like a gun, his mouth agape. When I was ready to leave, I found him in the darkest corner of the room, by a vat, and when I stepped over to him, he kicked the tank. A few gray bats swarmed out of it and up to the rafters, banging into what was left of its ceiling as if they were drunk on whatever dried lees they had licked from the tank.

"Cool," he said. And he smiled.

In my company, Tim smiled. It was a genuine high-wattage grin that was contagious and made me beam, too.

"We should get out of here before someone hears us," I said.

Tim kicked the vat again and one more bat flew out. "Cool," he said, and he laughed. Another kick did not produce any more bats.

"C'mon," I said, and tugged at his elbow.

We went out again the next night. We drove to one of the vineyards that had been transformed into a quarry. In the darkness, the naked limestone looked like snow; the hacked-at hillside could have been a slalom course. The air smelled like soap. Now our trespass seemed more dangerous because we ran the risk of running into a night guard or of leaving some trace of our break-in for a quarry worker to find the next morning. We made it to the old winery, however, without getting caught, and Tim jumped out of the truck before I did again and galloped over to the chain-link fence that had gone up since the last time I had come here. It looked like the winery was being used as a mechanic's garage; tractors and flatbed trucks were parked beyond the fence, and floodlights illuminated the compound. I turned around to think about where else we might drive instead, but when I turned back toward Tim, he was standing on the other side of the fence, having discovered that the padlock on the gate was broken or never locked.

The winery itself, as it turned out, had been converted into an office. We tiptoed around the desks and file cabinets, and just as I was about to head back to our truck because there was clearly nothing there for us to take, Tim pointed at a table in the corner of the main room, a low round table with a coffeemaker and a mug tree on it. The table was a barrel turned on its end, a fine and perfectly usable one that we did not think twice about stealing.

Tim hummed all the way home. He was back, my happy-go-lucky son. He said, "We have to hit every winery, Dad."

"If you say so," I said.

"We've got to loot the whole damned valley," he said.

Naturally I worried that I was setting a bad example for

my son, and I reminded him that theft, no matter how petty, was still criminal. But most of the wineries we rummaged through had been abandoned—I decided to stay away from the other quarries—and so our thieving seemed harmless enough. The fact was that Tim still did not seem to want to talk to me much during the day, but at night, during the forays that became a regular part of our week that July and August, I knew that he would giggle and play. Julia never came with us. It was a guy thing, she said, all of this cat burgling.

We found a wonderful basket press with a broken crank and we found plenty of funnels and a cracked hydrometer that I couldn't really use, and occasionally, if we were lucky, we came across an oak barrel. Tim was always steps ahead of me when we explored the wineries, the one with the turrets or the one built from logs. He wanted to be the one who actually stumbled across the treasure first, and that was fine by me. For my part, I felt as if I was showing him the various haunts of my youth, especially when we came to the winery with the stand of cypress.

In three years, the trees had grown taller than the stucco walls, and the walls themselves had cracked and faded and eroded. A broad-leafed ivy had consumed one side of the winery, and while I found no evidence of other intruders, no litter, no clothes or blankets left by squatters, I had the sense that we were not the only visitors. The grass around the trees was worn, and so was the path we had followed up from the road. I sat down beneath the trees and watched my son pick through the piles of broken tiles.

"There's nothing here," he said.

I was staring at the stars. I don't remember what I was thinking about.

"Dad, let's jam," Tim said. "Dad?"

"Go on back to the truck," I said. "I'll be there in a second." And when Tim was gone, I dug my fingers into the cool soil and I may have cried, just a wince. Then I cleared my throat and returned to the truck, too.

We collected about a dozen barrels—I would end up having to buy some—and we would have continued our treasure hunt, but the grapes began to swell and redden, and each day they became darker and sweeter. Tim started school—the school was in New Idria, the next town to the east of Oak Valley—and he seemed to like his new teachers. Each day before he rode his bike down the vineyard road to catch his bus, Tim helped me squeeze a bunch into the beaker of the hydrometer that I had purchased—the sticky-palm approach was no longer scientific enough if I was going to make my own wine—and then we dunked a calibrated glass tube into the beaker; it reported the specific gravity of the juice. We could determine the level of acid in the grapes, and we could measure the steady rise in the percentage of sugar, until one morning late that September, Julia set aside her books and Tim didn't ride his bike down to the highway to catch his bus, and all three of us grabbed our buckets and our recently sharpened miniature scythes and began slicing off the grape bunches from the vines.

The harvest took two days. We let Tim stay home from school. Seeing him hunched over behind a row of vines, his blond head occasionally popping up, observing his steady diligence through the leaves, made me think fondly about my time with my own father long before the drought, although I had never actually helped my father around the vineyard and I always returned to school in San Francisco before the crush. What I remembered now was a certain olive tree that I used to climb—it stood on a parcel of land that my father had sold off—and I remembered learning how to whittle from a cellar worker whose name escaped me. Mostly I thought about the summer when I was Tim's age and my father poured me my first splash of cabernet, barely a shot, and I came to the conclusion that with every sip of wine, one became a little wiser. Wine made you see the world with greater clarity; every leaf on every oak and eucalyptus took on a sharper edge, each leaf catching the breeze that I could barely feel against my arms or face. Of course, the wine, the few sips I had, also made me want to lie down on the lawn and nap, but I could not understand why my mother had moved us away from the source of this amazing elixir or why she condemned my father for devoting his life to bottling it. Wine was mysterious to me, and I thought that the people like my father and grandfather who knew how to make it were privy to some deep secret of nature, an alchemy that the rest of us would never know. Years later, I think that I still believed this. Anyone could grow grapes, but only a few sage souls could transform that fruit into something more profound.

We collected all of the grapes in our buckets, and we dumped the buckets into the pickup, and then we emptied the harvest into the chutes at the top of the winery. It was a satisfying sight, the cascade, the million tiny orbs, fat garnets rolling into the deep vat. With the grapes piled up in the fermentation tank, the steel walls took on a violet cast. Like both my grandfather and my father, I did not destem the grapes—I should say that I was constantly consulting the ledgers that I had saved from past Dark Oak vintages, which meant that I was in effect following my grandfather's recipe—nor did I crush the grapes the way, so I had been told, the vintners did at the large industrial wineries in the north. The grapes at the bottom of the vat broke beneath the weight of the grapes above them, and grapes on top split during the initial fermentation. I added sulfates right away—again an amount prescribed in my grandfather's and father's meticulous annals—and the sulfur killed off all of the native yeast, the natural airborne yeast, along with the bacteria that could have turned the wine to vinegar. Then, with the long paddle that looked like a gondolier's pole, the oar that we had salvaged from the first winery that we pillaged, I mixed in a dose of the cultured yeast that would give me the slow and controlled fermentation that I was after.

Nothing happened for two long days. If I had read the ledgers more carefully, I would have discovered that this was ordinary, and on the third day, bubbles began to rise to the surface of the vat. A thick pinkish foam fizzed to the surface of the must. Twice during the next ten days, Julia helped me punch down the cap with the paddle; I wanted the skins and stems and other debris that had floated or been pushed up to the surface by the fermenting to stay mixed amid the juice for as long as possible; and the cap, exposed to the air, could also fall prey to the vinegar bacteria.

After the must had finished fermenting, I let it sit in the vat for a couple more days before I opened a valve in the bottom of the tank and let the wine pour freely down to the next level—here was the test of all of the food-grade plumbing that I had installed, and so far so good, no leaks, no spills—and then I scraped the skins and lees from the bottom of the fermentation tank and shoveled them into the barrel press, and bit by bit Julia pressed this pomace to squeeze out the last juice into the holding tank with the free-run wine. I went through a process of stirring a prescribed amount of another culture into the must to kill off the remaining bacteria, and after that secondary fermentation, on a cloudy Saturday afternoon, Julia and Tim, too, helped me carefully siphon off our first young ruby-red vintage from the holding tank into the purloined barrels.

The wine would age and absorb some flavor from the oak. In the months to come, we would insert a thief, a long pipette, into the bunghole of each barrel and perform some simple chemistry to make sure the wine matured with the right balance of acid and sugar and to be certain that no bacteria ruined the batch, and occasionally we would rack the wine, siphoning it into fresh barrels. In fifteen months, we would bottle it. Two years beyond that, we would drink it. Tim would be fifteen then, and Julia and I would be turning forty. A good life ahead had never before seemed so simple or so clear.

During the summer, I had revealed to the folks in the hardware store that I was trying to bring back the winery— I had no choice but to tell the truth, what with all the equipment I was buying, with all of the questions that I was asking the veteran vintners about how to use a hydrometer or how long to let the wine sit on its lees after fermenting—and in the fall, everyone waited for me to emerge with some final word about my crush. After the wine was in the barrels, the town threw a small party for my family. Champagne was poured on a makeshift patio behind the store, and all three of us were toasted, saluted, and praised, and when it began to drizzle, we moved inside and mingled among the garden supplies and video rentals and toaster ovens. For the first time that I could remember, with a plate of cake in one hand, a plastic flute in the other, I felt as though I lived in a place where I belonged.

Over the next year, Oak Valley appeared to blossom again, literally flower when other vintners replanted their fields—it would be several years before they could make wine from the grapes harvested from their infant vines—and with some of them starting to restore their wineries as well. While the quarriers did not exactly close down their operations in the face of such a determined renaissance, the prevailing sentiment was that one day they would all shut down and their butchered slopes would be covered with fresh loam and converted back into arable vineyards.

I pruned back my vines again. I practiced law, Julia worked on her dissertation—she made occasional research trips up to the city and Tim entered the junior high school in New Idria. He found some boys to pal around with. He had a small part in a play. My son and I grew closer; we took long weekend walks in the woods. Julia and I made love often and with deep passion. The next summer my vines looked even greener than they had the previous year. I thought that the swells and meadows of the entire valley looked more virid and alive, but this was what happened when your life went well: The place that you inhabited appeared preternaturally lush. When the jasmine bloomed, it bloomed with a sweeter perfume. When a hill turned gold at the end of the summer, it glistened like a pile of antique coins.

I had done exactly what I had longed to do. I had turned my life around. I was a father and a lover and a lawyer and a farmer and a vintner, a hero to some. My life in the valley seemed complete.

And so I had no way to explain, none at all, why it was that I still went out on long drives alone at the end of the day or why it was, when I worked my way toward the mountain road each dusk, I still dreamed of disappearing.

No matter where I have lived or wandered, there has always been something about the slow dim of late afternoon that has made me restless. Something about the fade of the day that has filled me with doubt and made me prone to panic, as if my self-confidence diminishes with the sunlight. Even when I lived in the city, I would take long walks instead of long drives; from my office, I could never go directly home. To my own ear, I sound hyperpoetic, and I don't mean to exaggerate these vespertine moods; I think that this restlessness that I am describing was really quite ordinary. I was hardly the only one who went wandering at dusk; witness all of the men and women like me whom I would find lingering over a glass of red wine or a latte in the bars and the cafés at the edge of the evening, people everywhere who had difficulty surrendering the order and the routine of the workday for the unscripted formlessness of the approaching night. As long as you could busy yourself with the errands and chores of your various callings, you could be by yourself all day and somehow never get lonely. But at night, you could dine with your family or see a friend or lie down with your lover, and still you might feel utterly and hopelessly alone. And it was that possibility of feeling isolated even while being in the company of the people whom I loved most that I think I dreaded.

So I would be working at my desk, a lamp-lit island in the darkening room, and I would finish up a task, and then I would head home in my truck, speeding north along the main drag, and I would have every intention of veering off at my regular turnoff and crossing the arroyo and heading up the vineyard road. But I would pass my turnoff and keep driving. And I would cross the riverbed farther north. And I would follow another road up into the foothills and beyond.

When I first came to the valley, the mountain highway had been an unknowable maze, but now it was a familiar track, without riddle. The cliff turns and the bends through the forest, the slow coils, the sudden drops. It was not a heavily trafficked road, and I rarely, if ever, passed anyone when I drove at dusk. I could drive fast down the center of the two lanes. The longer I drove, the calmer I became, the less restless. Maybe the curve and meander of the road hypnotized me; maybe I lapsed into a trance. I drove way too fast, dangerously fast, and yet I felt completely safe in my truck, navigating the river of a road, confident and in control when I shifted gears and stepped on the gas, when I leaned into the wide turns, when I raced through the black of the woods.

I would drive for a half hour or so, but I never clocked myself and I never knew how long or far I had traveled. At some point, I would snap out of my trance, as it were, and I would follow a hill back down the valley and begin to make my way home. Back home, I would kiss Julia hello and breathe in her familiar scent of lemons and pekoe, Julia stirring some splendid sauce at the stove, listening to the news on the television, and I would tousle my son's hair, Tim working through a math problem at the kitchen table. I would open a bottle of wine and help get dinner on the table. But I never told Julia that I just had gone for a drive by myself— these jaunts were my one deep secret—and I don't think she had reason to suspect that I didn't come straight home from my office. If she did, I doubt that she would have cared.

And why would she care? What was the big deal? I needed to go for a drive, I needed to lose myself for a half hour or an hour, so what?

It was what I thought about while I followed the curves of the mountain road that was the big deal. It was the fact that I kept these drives secret that stained me with the telltale bruises of adultery. And what I thought about was what I used to think about way back when my life was a mess, during my first autumn in the valley. What I thought about was how easy it would be to find a pass that would lead me to a new valley. And from the new valley to the central valley of the state, and from that valley across another range. Then deep into the desert. Then anywhere. And to tell Julia about these drives would have meant confessing more than the mere fact of them; it would have meant telling her about my loose and vague fantasies of escape, too, and my naked honesty would hurt her, or so I believed.

I left my office and I went for a drive, and when my life was getting better, when I became busy with my farming and my practice, I went out once a week. When Julia came back into my life, I drove alone at dusk maybe twice a week. Then every other dusk when she moved down to the vineyard, then every night that summer. I always thought, even as the drives became more frequent, that each one would be my last. I wanted each drive to be my last. What I was doing was reckless and I knew it. And there is this to say, as well: I craved some kind of danger; I drove way too fast. Imagine if I had driven off a cliff. Imagine if I had stranded Julia and imagine if I had abandoned Tim, who seemed to be finally secure about me and secure about his home. What I was doing was selfish and I knew it. So I told myself to cut it out, and once or twice, I came straight home and took a walk in the woods instead of driving, but the walk didn't do the trick. I had a horrible sleepless night; I tossed and turned; I was cranky the next day.

I needed motion, I needed to drive fast. The drive cleared my mind. The drive allowed me to dream in a way that I didn't dream at night. The drive became a substitute for dreams and the release that dreams provide. The turns, the bends, the coils, the drops. The cliffs, the tall trees. The

more familiar the mountain road became, the more I craved
its twist and stray.

What was I doing driving so fast? Did I need to test
myself? Did I need to push the limit of my contentment?
Why did I dream of running away? Maybe I wanted to cross
some border and journey far away to see just how badly I
needed to come home. And when I did go home at night,
why did I feel so alone? My life in the valley was complete,
wasn't it? So why did I suspect that something was missing?
I heard an echo in a hollow canyon deep in my gut.
Something was missing—I didn't want to admit it—but
what, what?

I don't know. I can't answer these questions. All I do
know for certain is that I went out on these drives when the
sun went down, and that was how my troubles began.

early one evening my fifth autumn in the valley,
I left my office and climbed in my truck and headed fast into
the foothills. It was October. Julia and Tim and I had harvested the best crop yet. We were midway through the crush
of our second vintage, which had gone well so far. The rainy
season was just beginning, and that afternoon, it had been
drizzling. I had to wear a warm coat, a long scarf. It was still
drizzling, and when I reached the mountain road, the pavement looked as though it had been swabbed with ink. I drove
north for about five minutes before it started raining much
harder. It really began to pour. It was only six or so, six-
thirty maybe, but it was completely black along this unlit
road.

And the road became slick, almost icy, and water rolled
down my windshield in sheets, more rain than my wipers
could push aside. The storm had quickly turned the night
from black to gray and, whenever I caught a glimpse of the
valley, an unsettling ocean green. I couldn't drive at my
usual speed, but I still drove fast. I followed the road to a

cliff and swung into a slow turn, and then I hurried back
through the trees. Down a hill, up another rise. I stepped on
the gas only when I needed the push; I braked only as much
as I needed to brake to avoid wiping out.

I drove for only about fifteen or twenty minutes before I
decided to head home. I was somewhere in the middle of the
vast forest, but I knew that in a quarter of a mile I would
reach a turnoff, a road that would plunge toward the valley
basin. I drove faster. I leaned back in my seat with both of
my hands on the steering wheel, and I sped down the narrow
black channel with slim dark trees on either side of me, the
countless pine and the occasional birch.

And then I saw a figure in the shallow cast of my headlights—

I saw a man walking down the center of the road ten yards
ahead of me.

I slammed my foot on the brake, but the road was glassy
and the truck swerved all over the pavement. There was virtually no shoulder, no way that I could turn off without
crashing into a tree, and I stepped hard on the brake and
tried to turn to the left and I banged my fist against the horn,
but I needed both hands to steer.

"Stop, stop"—I was actually shouting stop, as if that
would work, but the wet road became like a rope, like a
weighted pulley drawing me toward the man, faster and
faster, faster, and he had to have heard my tires skidding—
he had to have heard me coming at him, because he glanced
over his shoulder. I saw him look at me, I saw his eyes, I saw
them widen. But he froze, he didn't jump out of the way.

And I was still trying to stop my skidding truck and leaning my shoulders, my entire body into the turn, but I was driving too fast and the road was against me, reeling me in, and
the rain was against me, too, flooding my windshield, blind-
ing me so that I could see nothing, and I could hear nothing
except for the guttural screech of my tires, a sharp thrown
wail in the night, and then the dull thud at the right-front
bumper of my truck—a thud like a branch had fallen on my

hood—a thud and a crunch of wood, my tires running over the branch, crushing it, pulping it, and then something like a bird fluttering up my windshield. A bird fluttering off in the rain.

My truck began to tip over and so I pulled the wheel quickly to the right, and I probably would have capsized if I hadn't run into a birch by the side of the road. It was a slender ghost of a tree, which, when the truck bounced back, teetered and snapped and fell halfway across the highway. I rocked back in my seat and fell forward against the steering wheel, and I banged my head hard against the windshield. I had ended up facing the opposite direction, with my headlights illuminating nothing but the road that I'd just driven down and the broken tree and a black umbrella being carried away by the wind—the fluttering bird—an umbrella somersaulting and drifting, trying to fly but not quite taking off. It disappeared into the woods.

My ribs were sore. My forehead throbbed. I became dizzy and the back of my neck and face were cool. My heart beat so fast that I couldn't catch my breath. I reached for a flashlight that had rolled under the passenger seat, and I hopped out of the truck and into the rain, pelting now. I wound my scarf high around my chin, and I aimed my flashlight everywhere, sweeping the road with it, panning the trees, but I couldn't find the man anywhere.

For one fleet moment, I believed that I had dreamed the entire episode. Something had spooked me and made me think that I'd caught a man in my headlights, when I hadn't really, and I had spun out and taken out a birch tree and nothing more. I would never go out driving alone at night again, lesson learned. For a moment I believed this, but then I tripped over something on the road. A backpack.

I was still standing near my truck, so I opened the passenger side and flung the backpack onto the seat as if—as if what?—as if I was going to find the man and give him a ride somewhere? The backpack was proof that I had not imagined him, but I still couldn't find him, and I stepped forward and called out to him. My throat was dry, I could barely speak. I jogged down the road a few yards and still didn't see anyone. I jogged farther, and I thought that I might have misunderstood the physics of the crash, that maybe I was looking in the wrong place, which actually was the case, because I finally did spot a body farther, much farther, alarmingly farther down the road than I would have thought possible—twenty, thirty feet away—a body in the same lane that I had ended up in.

He was lying on his stomach with one arm under him and the other reaching toward a tree. One of his legs was bent at the knee, twisted at a queer angle.

I ran to him. I knelt down next to him.

He was not moving, but his left arm, the extended arm, twitched, and I saw that he had grabbed hold of a large pinecone. He was holding a pinecone, and I thought that he was alive, unconscious but breathing, and maybe all I had to do was get him up on his feet and brush him off and he could continue collecting pinecones or whatever else he had been doing out here in the middle of nowhere during a storm.

I spoke to him—I don't remember what I said—and he didn't open his eyes. A dark liquid seeped out from underneath him, and at first I thought that it was the rain forming a puddle around his body, or mud, but then I realized it was blood. My heart galloped again, and I screamed at him.

I yelled, "Hey." I yelled, "You hang in there." I yelled, "Just hang in there."

He was choking, gagging on something, gurgling, and I knew that I might kill him if I moved him, but I didn't want him to suffocate, and so I pushed at his shoulders until I had eased him over onto his back, and when I saw his face, I recognized him. His eyes were swollen and his jaw was puffing up, and there was blood all over one side of his face, like paint. A trickle of blood dribbled from the corner of his mouth. He was not a man at all, he was just a boy. That thud, that crunch my truck had made—I heard it again like a delayed echo bouncing back at me, swallowing me. What had I done? What had I done?

"Hey," I yelled, "you hang in there. Hang on."

He was a local kid. I had spoken to him only in passing. He was only sixteen or seventeen—three years older than my son at most—tall and lanky, an athlete, beloved, and I couldn't stop him from dying.

"Hang on," I whispered.

I wanted to shout for help, but who would have heard me? I didn't have a phone in my car. I was a half hour away from the nearest house with a phone. What I needed was for someone to drive by and help me, but I couldn't make that happen. We were all alone, and I thought that the only thing I could do would be to drag him to my truck and lay him out on the backseat and take him to the hospital in Hollister. Which would take an hour. Plus I would risk killing him if I tried to pick him up. He wouldn't make it, no way.

"Help," I screamed. "Help, help," even though I knew it was useless.

The boy was going fast, there was no stopping him. And here I was, a virtual stranger, a reckless driver, his killer, and I was the only person he had to hold him and tell him that the next world was a better place and all that other nonsense I didn't believe. I shifted his head and shoulders up onto my lap.

"Help," I screamed. "You hang on," I whispered.

He seemed to be choking again—or not so much choking as sighing, letting go of whatever air he had left in him—and he was still holding on to the pinecone, but blood was pouring out of him everywhere now in a rush, onto my lap, mixing with the mud and the rain, flooding the road like an oil slick. I pulled off my coat to blanket him because he was shivering. I wadded my scarf into a pillow. I held the back of his head with one hand and his chin and cheek with my other. I wanted to steady him. I wanted to stop his body from trembling, but I was shaking, too, shaking with him.

"You're safe," I said. "Hang on." I couldn't stop him from shaking. "You're safe," I said.

I have no idea how long I sat there by the side of the road in the cold rain, how long I sat there with his head in my lap before his eyes opened, round brown eyes, and he looked at me—no, through me first, as if I weren't there at all, and up at the tall trees instead, and then back at me finally, focusing on my face, searching my face, reading my face. It wasn't like he was asking me for help, and he wasn't absolving me, and he didn't even look angry with me, just confused, just baffled, just lost— Who are you? That was what he seemed to be asking me with his eyes. His brown eyes dilating, going black. Who are you?

Then his lips parted as if he might speak. Then his mouth opened wide as if he might scream, but no sound came out, not even a gasp. Then his body stopped shuddering and the fingers of his left hand uncurled and the pinecone rolled away. I was still shaking, but he had stilled, and in a matter of seconds, that was it, he was gone—he became as cold as the road beneath me.

The evening was so violent. The rain breaking against the highway. The boughs of the trees banging against one another, keening, their branches falling. I set the boy down on the ground and got up on my knees first before I stood all the way, and I staggered a few yards into the woods, where the canopy of the trees reduced the storm to a drizzle. I threw up. I vomited until my throat burned. I sat down on the damp carpet of needles.

The rain pounded the boy's body, and I couldn't leave him there, so I crawled over to him and reached under his shoulders and dragged him off the road and under the trees. I took my coat back but didn't put it on, even though I was cold. It was soaked with mud and blood. I half-expected a car to drive by, a ranger, someone who could have radioed for help now that help would be too late, but no one came along. I needed to report the accident, and I could hear myself describing how it had happened: I was driving too fast to brake— How fast? the ranger would ask me. Well, sixty or seventy— In this weather? Okay, fifty, but no one else is ever out driving at this time of night, let alone walking this road— How fast did you say?

I buried my head between my knees and rocked back and forth. I had killed a boy, I had taken a life. Even if I didn't look at him now, I could picture his last glance, his melting eyes searching my face. With his last breath, his confusion had become my confusion. With his last sigh, his worries became my worries. He would rest now, but I would have to try to figure out why this had happened and what would happen now—

What would happen now? I sat in the woods and tried to remember the penal code with all of its definitions and degrees, but I couldn't think straight. Could I be prosecuted? Could I go to jail? I tried to picture the boy's sad parents. Would they sue me? Would they go after my vineyard? I could lose everything, the new life that I had made for myself, everything. All I wanted to do was go home and kiss my wife and hug my son. All I wanted was to hold him until he made me let go.

I looked at the boy, and I knew that it didn't matter, that it changed nothing, but I told him that I was sorry. There was nothing I could do for him now except be sorry for the rest of my days. There was no saving him, he was gone. He was gone. So I sprinted back to my truck and I climbed behind the wheel and I noticed the backpack on the passenger seat. I got out of the truck and hurled it as far as I could into the woods, and then I got back behind the wheel and I turned the key and I shifted into reverse and pulled back from the broken birch tree. I lurched forward with a skid. And I drove away.

i

If you live with a lie long enough, the truth becomes a kind of fiction. The truth begins to seem fabricated, the facts mutable. The truth can be told any number of ways, and where you start and what you leave out gives your confession its slant, its spin. I want at long last to report what went down as it actually went down, although I know that through the repeated vending of my various lies, I have lost some of the truth forever. I want to glue together an urn that I regrettably and foolishly smashed during a reckless spree of panic, and while I hope that the urn will look as good as new, I know that is impossible; no matter how expert my restoration, I will still end up with cracks and chinks and even missing pieces by the time I am done.

What I am trying to say is that I am not sure that all of this will make sense. What I am trying to say is that it doesn't make sense to me.

I want to speak the truth before it's too late, before I lose any more of it, and yet so much has already slipped away. Now, for instance, I can't remember how I got home that night. Did I drive off the road when I crossed the arroyo and did I change my tire? Or was that just what I told Julia? Was that how I explained the bruise on my forehead and the blood and the mud on my clothes? Now I can't remember how I made it upstairs without Julia or Tim noticing me—I must have slipped in the front door rather than the door to the mudroom and kitchen—and all I can remember next is sitting on the edge of the tub in the bathroom off my bedroom—stripped and shivering—when Julia walked in.

"Jason? Where have you— Jason," she said, gasping. "Honey, what happened?"

She knelt down beside me, but I couldn't look her in the eye, and instead I stared at the flaking eagle claws of our old tub.

"What happened?" she asked again. "Look at you— you're white, you're freezing."

"I didn't want Tim to see me like this," I said.

Julia touched my forehead with her fingertips. It stung. I looked across the room into a mirror and could see the deep red bruise taking shape. She grabbed a towel and threw it over my shoulders.

Finally I looked at her. "I had an accident," I said. "I . . . I was driving . . ."

And then, here, this was the moment. Looking back, I can see that this was the moment—not when I drove out of the forest, not when I headed up the vineyard road or when I snuck in the house and upstairs, but here, after some of my panic had subsided, this was when I made my first real choice. But I don't remember why I decided that I couldn't confide in the woman who was rubbing my hands with her hands, trying to warm me up. I don't recall what exactly I was thinking, but I can remember the heaviness that suddenly weighed me down, like my arms were stone, like my legs were stone, and I do remember that I had to slide down to the floor of the bathroom. This was the moment when I began to lie.

"I was driving in the rain, not even that fast," I said. "I crossed the riverbed. The wheels slipped. I skidded. The truck nearly turned over."

Julia gripped my hand.

"And then I managed to turn off the road," I said. "I ended up in a ditch. I had to change a tire," I said, and I proceeded to improvise elaborate and probably unnecessary detail. I lied, and I think that even then I realized that this was no small fib; it was a high-mountain lie from which a widening, ever-rushing river of greater lies would inevitably flow.

Julia slumped down next to me on the bathroom floor, and her eyes brimmed with tears. "You really could have been hurt," she whispered.

"I'm fine," I said. "Just a little shaken up."

She hugged me. "I'll tell Tim. He'll be cool about it. But you, you're okay?"

"I just need a hot shower," I said. "Then I'll come down for dinner."

Julia began to gather the pile of muddy clothes.

"No, I'll take care of those," I said. "You go and tell Tim I'm okay, and I'll be down soon."

I turned on the shower, and soon I was scrubbing at my skin, furiously rubbing every inch of myself with a rough loofah. I had lied to the one person who might have offered me the counsel that I needed. I had lied, and I was honestly amazed at how easily the truth washed free from me along with the forest mud down through the drain.

"Wicked," Tim said when he noticed the bruise on my forehead.

"Timothy," Julia said. "Your father could have been seriously injured."

I gave him a wink. "What do you have there?" I asked him, and pulled his math book across the table.

"Gee, I'm a tree," Tim said. He was in a silly good mood.

"You're not supposed to be doing these proofs for another—what?—five years," I said. This was my way of complimenting my genius son.

He beamed. "Test tomorrow. The proof will be one of these," Tim said, taking back his book. "So I figure if I do all ten problems tonight, I'll ace the quiz."

"Need help?" I asked.

Tim blinked. "Sure," he said, although he didn't really. I reached into the dark recesses of my brain for dusty axioms. I found a certain solace in the straightforward demands of my son's homework.

Dinner, the dishes, the most usual of routines. An evening like any evening. Tim worked at the dining room table, and Julia and I took to opposite ends of the couch, she with a text about a group of once-avant-garde sculptors, and I with a novel that I only pretended to read. A fire glowed in the hearth. Outside the rain pounded the lawn.

Fourteen years earlier when I had become a father, I had started driving with a greater wariness of other drivers on the road. I stayed to the right on the freeways and I drove much more cautiously than I had before or than I later would, and I don't mean just when Tim was riding in the baby seat; I mean whenever I drove, with my family or alone. I had heard about new parents who became afraid to fly and I always thought that they were silly, but then I, too, avoided travel of any kind. And I remember something else, that before I became a father, I had a habit of buying myself expensive ties, but after Tim was born, I stopped buying ties or anything for myself. I owned many more ties than I could wear, some hundred silk cravats; it was a fetish. But I didn't need them all and it somehow seemed selfish to go in a store and buy myself these or any other material things. I can't explain it except to say that my whole notion of myself shifted when I became a father, and shifted seismically at that. I wasn't living my life for myself alone, I suppose; I had a son. And then my son grew up. And I may have allowed myself certain indulgences again. Driving fast, for one, and look what happened.

Tim was absorbed in his work, and I didn't think that he noticed that I was watching him. He had his laptop, and his fingers bounced gracefully across the keyboard as if he were playing a piano. Julia scribbled a note in a blank book and then looked back at the text in her lap. She glanced at me, saw me watching Tim, and smiled. And this was all I wanted in the world, an evening like this one. Here was everything that I had to lose—everything that I had already lost once in my life and reclaimed—and although it may seem melodramatic to make such an assertion in hindsight, that night of the accident my emotions were large and I thought that I was on the brink of losing everything again. And I could not, I simply could not let that happen.

I set my novel down on the arm of the couch. "So, Tim boy?"

"So, Dad man?"

"Can you turn off the lights and make sure the fire screen is in place?" I asked.

Julia took off her glasses.

"Can do," Tim said, not looking away from his screen.

"Your mother and I are retiring early," I said.

I took Julia's hand, and I led her upstairs, shutting our bedroom door softly behind us. We stood by the bed and faced each other, and I heard myself sigh. Then, without the normal tease and without the regular play, I was hard and lifting Julia's nightshirt over her head and then I was quickly inside her, and I think that she held me with a tighter grasp than usual, an almost frightened clutch. We fell into an instant frenzy at first, but then we slowed down, and we made love with a certain caution, as if we were fragile creatures who might break. Julia needed to tell me that she was relieved I hadn't been hurt, and I think that I was trying to pretend that nothing bad had happened on the mountain road, that I had possibly dreamed it all. Nothing bad had happened, and I was safe. We nested beneath our commodious down quilt, and Julia's breathing shallowed, and I drifted off for a while, too.

At midnight, I woke up.

Julia pulled a pillow over her head and turned away from me and kept sleeping.

I lay there on my back, and I tried to shut my eyes, but as soon as I did, I pictured the mountain highway, wet and black, and then with a blink, I saw the boy in front of me on the road, turning, looking at me over his shoulder. My braking foot jerked forward in the bed, and even when I opened my eyes, I couldn't escape the sight of him lying broken on the road, with his knee askew and the puddle of blood and mud widening beneath him, enveloping him.

I got up and sat in a rocking chair across the room from the bed, and I was cold again. I could feel the boy shivering in my arms, losing all heat, losing all air, and then he looked at me.

I went to my dresser and traded my boxers for a pair of flannel pajamas that Julia had given me and that I never wore. I put them on, and a bathrobe, too, but I was still shaking.

I could see the boy looking at me and his brown eyes read my face as if my face were a stele inscribed with an ancient language that he couldn't decode. And then he went limp: He became stone, he became the mud, he became the rain—

Stop, I heard myself say, although I didn't actually speak the word aloud. Stop.

I made my way down the hall to Tim's room and eased his door open. I crept over to his bed. He was smiling in his sleep.

I should not have run away, it was wrong and I knew it. I should not have left the boy in the woods, as if his life had been worth nothing. His poor parents were probably wondering where he was now, making calls, worrying themselves sick. And soon they would get a knock on the door. Their worst fears would come true. A deputy would tell them that the great hope of their lives had been left for dead on the mountain road; and I had done that to them. I hadn't just killed a boy, I'd killed his parents, too. If it were me, if something had happened to Tim— He twitched with a dream. It was unfathomable.

I thought about my life before the accident, and I think that I could say that while I had made countless mistakes, I had lived according to some sort of moral code, even if I could not articulate what that code was exactly, even if I had never really thought about it. Now I had to consider what would be moral, what would be right, and what would be moral and right would be to turn myself in and deal with the consequences of this accident, whatever they might be. And I needed to do this before the situation got out of hand, before the boy was found in the woods. I thought that I was being pragmatic, too, because if I turned myself in and if I had a lawyer with me, I stood a better chance of navigating the system than if I didn't take charge.

It was clear. I knew what I had to do. The next morning, I would see about finding a lawyer. I would have to go to the police. The next morning, I would tell Julia what had happened.

When I woke up the next morning, however, I seemed to be slightly out of phase with everyone moving around me—this would be the case all day—and I couldn't seem to catch up. I woke up in my son's bedroom, curled up on the floor by his desk, covered by one of his wool blankets. I was stiff. My chest ached, my eyes burned. I felt as though someone had drilled a hole in the back of my skull.

Both Tim and Julia were already down in the kitchen, dressed and ready for the day. Julia was at the stove, making eggs in a skillet, and Tim was at the table, reviewing his math. Here they both were, just as I had found them when I had come home the night before.

I croaked good morning and sat at the table—Tim did not say good morning back—and before I knew it, Julia slid a plate of food in front of me, the eggs sunny-side up, along with some bacon and a stack of toast. She gave me a glass of orange juice and a mug of coffee. She set the entire pot of coffee in front of me. She had made breakfast for herself, too, but when she joined me, she didn't lift her fork.

Julia watched me eat. Tim glanced up at me once and then returned to his proofs.

I knew that I needed to explain how I had ended up sleeping on the floor of his room, but all I managed was, "Couldn't sleep."

Julia refilled my coffee mug. When I reached for a carton of milk, she said, "You should drink it black."

"Black, why?" I asked.

She didn't answer me.

I ate the eggs quickly, and the bacon and toast, too—my hunger surprised me—and I downed three mugs of coffee.

Julia took a bite of some toast, but that was it.

"You're not eating," I said.

She turned to the newspaper.

"Hey, Tim boy," I said.

Tim looked up.

"You all set for your big test?"

He had inherited both his mother's blondness and my dusky coloring, but his eyes were all his own. They looked greener to me that morning, less polished; maybe it was the dim light in the kitchen that darkened them. The storm had continued into the morning, and it was gray out, pouring now.

"All set," he said. He looked at Julia, and she nodded, and he closed his book and retreated from the table. I heard him pound upstairs.

I glanced at the clock on the coffeemaker. I had woken up an hour and a half later than usual. Normally I was the one who prepared breakfast; in our household division of labor, it was my chore. Normally I assembled Tim's lunch, too, but a plump paper bag on the counter looked already packed.

"I checked on the wine," Julia said.

Normally I checked on the wine first thing at six-thirty. "Thank you," I said. "And is it foaming?"

"Like the ocean," she said. "Although I think we need to punch down again."

"That sounds right," I said.

"I have a doctor's appointment in Hollister," she said.

"You do?"

"I told you I did," Julia said, although I didn't think that she had. "And then I thought I'd do some shopping, see a movie. Kind of have the day to myself," she said.

"I couldn't sleep," I said. "That's why—"

"Right," she said. Suddenly she was clearing the dishes from the table and dumping her uneaten breakfast in the trash. "So can you handle the punch-down?"

"Julia?"

"Because I kind of need a day to myself," she said.

"The first time wasn't that difficult. I can take care of it," I said.

It was at this point in the morning that Julia usually retreated to the study and burrowed into her research. We were alike in that we each thrived on routine. Instead she pulled on a pair of boots in the mudroom and grabbed a long raincoat and was gone without a kiss good-bye.

"Julia?" I called out to her. "Julia, wait."

She didn't answer me.

"There's something I need to tell you," I said.

Moments later I heard her sports car zip down the vineyard road.

Tim came back through the kitchen. He put on an old peacoat of mine that he had made his winter coat; it was way too big on him. He slung his knapsack over both shoulders. He stood in the door frame, his weight on one foot.

"Listen. I couldn't sleep," I said, "and I wandered into your room to see if you were okay—which may seem strange, but it's something fathers do—and I just fell asleep there. That's all."

Tim looked past me at the clock on the coffeemaker.

"Thanks for throwing your blanket on me," I said, although I didn't know if it was he or Julia who had covered me.

The gutters couldn't catch all of the rain, and water streamed down the windows in a steady curtain.

"I'll drive you down to the bus," I said.

"I'm getting picked up," Tim said. He grabbed his lunch from the counter.

I looked away. When I turned back toward him, he was gone.

•

I threw on some clothes and went down to the winery. The dank shed smelled less like wine in progress than wet bark or a wet lawn. I climbed up the ladder next to the fermentation tank and studied the layer of crimson foam

fizzing to the surface. I checked the clipboard hanging over
the vat like a hospital patient's chart. I made a notation with
a red felt-tip. Day eleven, so far so good, but Julia was
right: The skins and stems that had floated to the top needed
to be pounded back into the juice. With the long pole that
we used, I was able to puncture the cap, but standing at the
top of the ladder, I was able to make only a small hole. A
gurgle of juice and foam bubbled up, but then the hole
closed. The first punch-down of the crush had been much
easier; the cap had caved in after a few gentle prods. I
pounded the pole at the cap again, and I made only a dent
in the strata of skins.

I was wearing the knee-high black rubber boots that I
sometimes put on for the winery work, and I swung one leg
over the side of the fermentation tank. I tapped the cap with
my foot; it was as hard as ice. I held on to the edge of the
tank and swung my other leg over the side, and then, still
holding on to the edge of the vat, I jumped up and down. I
jumped higher each time, as high as I could without hitting
the rafters—there was not too much room between the top
of the tanks and the roof—and slowly I worked my way
around the rim of the vat, jumping all the while, until the red
mica beneath me began to crack, until it showed a few fissures and dents. I pulled myself back over to the ladder and
punched down hard with the pole where I had weakened the
cap. The layer of skins broke and large pieces began to fold
and fall into the depth of the vat. I punched the cap into the
must and stirred the mixture as briskly as I could, stepping
around a ledge at the top of the tank, until I could be certain
that I had thoroughly churned the juice.

It took a lot out of me, stirring the fermenting fruit soup
in a vat ten feet deep. My lower back ached. But I quickly
wished that I could have launched myself into another consuming chore, because as soon as I climbed down the ladder
and plopped down on the cement floor and caught my
breath, my mind began to turn with what I would need to do
now. The steps I needed to take. First I had to find a lawyer.

Then I would have to meet with the lawyer right away. Then head up to the sheriff's station. I knew there was a right way to go about this to minimize my liabilities, but I just wanted to blurt out my confession to the sheriff now. I wanted to phone it in. I just wanted to get it over with. To say it once: I did it. To let go of the truth like a helium balloon.

I picked myself up and I went inside and hurried through a shower. I dressed. I came back out to the garage, and when I pulled open the barn doors, I had to hold my gut. I didn't want to be so weak, so fragile about this, but my pulse raced when I faced my truck. I didn't want to drive it, I didn't want to drive at all. And then it occurred to me that unless I wanted to get caught before I issued my confession, I probably shouldn't take the truck out on the road. It was a forest green and fairly dilapidated jalopy with ten-plus years of dents and scrapes, but I knew that some of those dents and scrapes had to be fresh. I inspected it now, but my problem was that I couldn't remember what dents had been there before the accident. There was a shallow crater over the right wheel that could have been new. Eventually, of course, what had happened would become known around the valley, and I had no way of knowing what the reaction would be, but right now, I didn't want to go into town and have someone examine my fender and say, Hey, Jason, it looks like you were in a crash. Looks like you drove into a tree. Or a kid.

I had never gotten around to repairing the pickup, my father's truck—there was something wrong with the wiring—and now the windshield wipers, in addition to the headlights, didn't work; I only used it out in the field. Someone might ask me why I was driving it, and so as I headed down the vineyard road, I tried to come up with a simple and reasonable excuse. If I didn't get the truth out soon, I could see how I would end up spinning a web of fibs to cloak my meaner secret, and I knew that all the deceit, no matter how minor in the scheme of things, would only make matters worse for me. I pushed the pickup as fast as it would run.

*   *   *

the limping yet steady recovery under way in
Oak Valley would not have been evident to a stranger passing
through town, because most of the stores along the main drag
remained boarded up. Among the shops that had survived
were a food market and a liquor store and a small nursery; I
never could figure out how the latter had stayed in business.
We had a two-pump gas station with a garage. The schools
and banks were in New Idria. I ran my law practice out of the
old cheese shop, but all of the doctors and real-estate brokers
were up in Hollister. Most of the signs had been taken down
from the clapboard false fronts of the shuttered stores, and the
signs that had not been removed had paled with each passing
season, so that now you could barely read the names of the
erstwhile framer or butcher. Even the signs of the open stores
were illegible, except for the hardware store, because it was
red neon, although no one ever turned it on.

I always popped into the hardware store before settling in
at my office, and I wasn't going to bother that morning, but
I noticed so many cars and trucks parked outside and wondered what was going on. The usual minyan around the
counter at the back of the store next to the key-copying
machine had swelled to a considerable gathering, and I
spotted familiar faces everywhere, down the aisle of lamps
and light fixtures, down the aisle with the birdfeeders and
picture frames and candles. No one nodded or said hello;
everyone was too absorbed in noticeably muted conversation.

As I pardoned my way past the paint supplies, I heard
someone say, "He was the only one on the team who could
kick the ball."

And someone else replied, "A dean from Stanford per-
sonally delivered an application to his house and told him to
mail it in early. I heard they were talking full scholarship."

It was not possible that the boy had been found already.

Without my coming forward, I would have expected it to take a day or two at least. It was not possible.

I greeted Will Clark. He owned the store.

"Good morning, Jason," he said. "Except it's not a very good morning, is it?"

He was sitting on a stool next to a rack of blank keys. He always kept a pot of coffee going for anyone who stopped by, but the pot was empty. He was a big-bellied man with long arms that he had a habit of flapping while he spoke, as if he were trying to take flight but was too heavy to lift off from his stool.

"You've heard?" he asked, and flapped once.

It just wasn't possible that the boy had been found so soon. I thought about playing dumb, but I nodded instead.

"It's a gee-damned tragedy," Emma Hodges said. She used to run the bakery three doors down, which she had recently talked to me about reopening.

A vintner named Alex Marquez pushed his way up to the back counter. He owned one of the larger defunct wineries in the valley, and he, too, was someone I was trying to help rise from the ashes of bankruptcy. He was very tall and had long black hair pulled back into a silky ponytail. "Is it true?" he asked.

All of us answered him with solemn nods.

"Of all the kids," he said. He shook his head in dismay, and his ponytail swung from side to side. "Who found him?" he asked.

"Some ranger," Will Clark said. "He was driving the Oak Leaf this morning. Checking the road after the storm. He saw a tree that had fallen across the road. He got out to move the tree, and he noticed the skid marks."

"The skid marks," I said.

Emma Hodges looked at me.

"Then he saw the blood," Will Clark said. "A puddle of blood. He spotted a body just off the road in the woods. It was Craig Montoya lying in the mud."

I wished that there were some way that I could have lived

my life and never heard his name. The boy I killed, that was how I would have preferred to remember him if I had to remember him, in the abstract, pretending that he was a nameless stranger who would never be identified. But he was not a stranger, he had a name. Craig Montoya lying in the mud. The stone heaviness returned to my limbs and I wanted to sit down on the floor.

"Did you ever see him play soccer?" Alex Marquez asked me. "No one ever got the ball away from him. The ball was a part of him."

"He would have done something someday," Emma Hodges said.

"He could have been governor," Alex Marquez said.

"No, I mean he could have really done something," Emma Hodges said.

Everyone stared at me.

"Yes, something for the valley. It's very sad," I said.

"His parents are a nightmare," Emma Hodges said.

"Emma," Will Clark said.

"I mean that I saw them about an hour ago. They were with Harry Padillo."

Harry Padillo was the San Benito County sheriff.

"They looked like ghosts," Emma Hodges said. "Like part of them died, too."

"Craig's father used to work for your father," Will Clark said.

"Right," I said. I had forgotten the connection.

"Harry said right now he's calling it a hit-and-run," Emma Hodges said.

I had to take a deep breath. To hear my crime defined made it finally real and irrevocable.

"What kind of maniac would do that to a good kid like Craig Montoya?" Alex Marquez asked.

"What kind of coward is the question," Will Clark said. "To hit a boy and then just—"

"Drive away," I whispered.

"But," Emma Hodges said, "Harry says he's got a lot of questions."

I swallowed hard.

"Like how did Craig get there?" she asked.

For a moment I thought that she wanted me to answer her.

"Because his car is missing," she said. "His parents say that he never came home last night, but they didn't notice until the morning. And you know, he was an honor student. It was a school night. What was he doing out walking the Oak Leaf?"

"No one ever walks that road," I said.

"Exactly. It doesn't make sense," she said.

"They're hard to catch," Will Clark said. "According to Harry, that is."

I blinked.

"Hit-and-run drivers," he said. "They're hard to catch. They have to slip up. They have to do something like bring a banged-up car into a garage or— Your head," he said. He nodded at the bruise above my brow.

I had pulled on a baseball cap, but I had not completely covered my bruise. "Oh, that. Yeah, I was punching down," I said. I didn't know why I thought I needed to come up with a new lie, a nonvehicular lie. "Right, and I was jumping on the skins and I hit my head on a rafter in my winery. If you can believe that." I forced a chuckle.

Again Emma Hodges stared at me.

"Anyway, Harry Padillo's already got a manhunt going," Will Clark said.

"A manhunt," I said. "That's, that's good. Good that he's moving so fast." I gripped the counter because I was afraid that I might fall back into the display of paintbrushes and rollers. I was running out of time.

Alex Marquez pointed at my bruise. "I never punched down. I always pumped over," he said, referring to a method that involved running a pump from the bottom of the vat to keep the surface of the juice moist.

"And your merlot was always a little shy," Emma Hodges quipped.

"My merlot was hardly shy," Alex Marquez said.

"You two stop it," Will Clark said. "Show some respect for the dead."

More people were making their way into the store. Before long the entire valley would be assembled.

"I don't think we've ever had a carjacking in the valley," Emma Hodges said.

"Wait a minute—a carjacking? I thought Harry was calling it a hit-and-run," I said.

"Harry says he's calling it a hit-and-run now, but maybe it was carjacking," Will Clark said. "Somebody took the kid's car."

"I can't remember the last time," Alex Marquez said.

"The last time what?" I asked.

"Ten years ago," Emma Hodges said.

"That woman killed her husband over in the flats," Will Clark said.

"No, I mean the last time someone murdered a child," Alex Marquez said.

"Hold on," I said. "Aren't we jumping to conclusions? A hit-and-run is one thing, but murder—"

"Someone must have meant to hurt that boy," Alex Marquez said.

"You're saying that the hit-and-run was deliberate," I said.

"You don't think so?" he asked back.

"I just don't think we should be jumping to conclusions," I said.

No one said anything.

I cleared my throat. "But if Harry thinks that it's more than a hit-and-run," I said, "then maybe we should be talking"—I swallowed—"murder."

"Think the worst, Jason," Alex Marquez said. "Always think the worst."

"Harry left in a hurry," Emma Hodges said.

"He got beeped," Will Clark said. "Drove off with his lights flashing. Of course, he likes to show off."

I had to get to a phone.

"Let the games begin," Emma Hodges said.

•

I practically ran down the street to my office, but when I sat down behind my desk, all I could do was stare at the storefront window with my name stenciled in gold. I didn't really know what I was facing. I pulled my copy of the California penal code down from a shelf next to my desk.

I could be charged with vehicular manslaughter. I had not been committing a felony, but if a prosecutor established that I had been driving with gross negligence, if that could be somehow proven by the skid marks or how far the boy had been thrown or who knew what other evidence that would inevitably be gathered from the forest, then I was looking at a fine and a possible jail term. Fleeing the scene and not trying to call an ambulance could be considered negligence, despite the fact that I had watched the boy die and knew that he was beyond rescue. With every hour that went by, the fact that I had still not reported the accident didn't help me. Even without gross negligence, I could be prosecuted and punished. Sentencing had become more severe in recent years—I could still get a year. Even a term reduced to probation could hurt me. If the truth be told, a dismissal of all charges could hurt me.

I hadn't thought about it before now, but sitting in my office and staring at the code, I suddenly remembered a man who had been represented by a firm where I'd been an intern one summer during law school. The man was a computer executive who was backing out of his driveway one sunny fall morning on the way to work when he ran into a kid riding a tricycle on the sidewalk. The child had slipped into the man's blind spot. The man was driving three miles an hour. It was a complete accident, but he was arraigned on criminal manslaughter charges, and there was eventually a two-day trial, and even though the man had issued a confession, his lawyer argued that it was an admission of remorse, not guilt, that the accident was an unfortunate but inevitable accident, and the man was acquitted. However—and this was what troubled me—even with that exoneration, the man's life still fell apart. He couldn't concentrate at work and he was let go. His wife left him and took their three children with her; she filed for divorce. She left him the house, but the man couldn't stay in the neighborhood because no one on the street would look him in the eye, no one would talk to him. He was ostracized. He was ruined.

I was in trouble.

Although. This man, the computer executive, had turned himself in. He'd had no choice because all of the children in the neighborhood on their way to school had seen him back up over the kid on the tricycle. There were witnesses. He had to come forward, whereas I did not. No one had seen my accident on the mountain road. No one knew about my drives at dusk. No one had seen me cradling the boy in my arms, and no one but me had seen him die. I didn't have to come forward.

No. This was not what I had decided to do. I had to turn myself in, there was no way around it. I picked up the phone to call my contact in the public defender's office, the woman whom I had dated briefly. We had remained friendly and she always called me first when she was doling out freelance gigs. In confidence, I could ask her what to do. Or I could pretend that I was phoning for advice about someone I was representing.

I dialed my friend's direct line. I hung up when she answered.

Even if I somehow wiggled my way free from criminal prosecution, there was still the prospect of a civil suit if I confessed. The Montoyas would go after my home and my land. The question was not whether they would sue me; the question was when. That was the way of the world: When you lost something, you sought revenge. A jury would sob when the mother took the stand, and I would have to pay. I could pay for the rest of my life, and I might never recover. Telling the truth came with a price, a potentially steep price, and I had to wonder, Was it worth it? It seemed like a mean question, but I had to ask: Was telling the truth worth it, given what I might put my family through?

I paced the length of my office. My stride quickened. I felt like a big dog in an undersized run.

But why shouldn't I pay? Why should I recover? I had killed a boy. Not a boy—he had a name—Craig Montoya. I had run over Craig Montoya. It was an accident—I hadn't meant to hit him—but I was to blame. What if I had been driving at a safer speed? What if I hadn't been out driving at all? And the boy had died alone. Craig Montoya had died alone. I was there, holding him, but he looked at me and he didn't know who I was, so he died alone, far from home and the people who loved him. No one should die alone. So why shouldn't I pay a price for what I had done?

I stopped pacing and picked up the photo of Tim that I kept on my desk. I didn't have any recent photos of him. This was a shot that Julia had taken during our time apart and sent me because she said that it reminded her of me. She and Tim had gone on a vacation to the Mojave when the poppies were in bloom, and so the shot was of Tim sitting amid an orange carpet of flowers, the poppies running all the way to the horizon, and it was a cloudy day, so the sky was gray, giving the flowers even more flame. Tim wasn't looking at the camera. He was staring off in the distance, as if he had gotten tired of waiting for his mother to snap the shot, and he had turned his chin. That was what Julia meant when she said the shot reminded her of me; this used to be a sore point between us, although one we grew up enough to joke about—the way I complained that she took forever to set up and frame and actually take a photograph, the way she took her time and tarried just to annoy me. There were no existing photos of me actually looking at the camera, none that Julia took anyway. So here was our son amid the desert

bloom, impatient, daydreaming. He was happy now, doing
well in school, but he was still a child, easily upset.

I started thinking about Julia and what it would mean when
I told her about the accident. In a sense, I had already wounded
her with my first lie. When I told her the truth, I could try to
explain why I had lied initially, but there would be a scar. Some
of the renewed trust between us would decay. She would see
me through whatever trials I endured, literal and figurative, yet
I worried that these trials would not bring us closer, but would
distance us instead. I know it will sound strange, but even after
Julia came back to me, I suffered from the residual soreness of
her long absence, even as we shared the same bed night after
night. Those years apart had left me with a familiar bone ache
that I always noticed when I got up from a chair. A familiar rush
in my heart, as if I'd had too much coffee. A dull pain like the
way my ears ached when the wind was raw. Maybe this
absence would eventually vanish—I desperately hoped it
would—but I thought that coming forward, confessing, admit-
ting my lie to her, whatever happened next, I thought that all of
this would make the ache last much longer. I loved Julia deeply,
but I lived for that day when I would love her without any ache
whatsoever. Somehow—and here is an example of something
that I am not sure I can make sense of—somehow I started to
convince myself that Julia knowing the truth about the accident
and my flight and my lie would make this ache that troubled me
forever chronic. It would never go away.

I flipped through the penal code again. I looked up the
penalty for carjacking. Carjacking could get you three, five, or
nine years. Murder, I did not need to look up. Murder got you
twenty-five years. Murder while committing a felony like carjacking could be qualified as a crime with special circumstances, which meant life without parole or even death— Wait,
this was crazy. Carjacking, murder—this was absurd. I was letting the rumors get to me. I knew what had transpired, and
obviously I had murdered no one. Not by legal standards anyway, not with malice aforethought. I had definitely not carjacked that kid. Hey, I myself wanted to know where his car

was and what he was doing walking down a road that no one ever walked. What was aforethought in his mind during those seconds when he looked over his shoulder at my headlights?

I flipped back to the vehicular crimes and reread the definition of gross negligence. With gross negligence, you could get two, four, or six years. Okay, there it was. That was what I was facing. And the civil action. And hurting my son in some unforeseeable way. And wounding Julia, wounding us. And putting my home and my winery in jeopardy. Anything else? At the very least, I needed to speak to a lawyer. I could afford that confidence.

My friend in the public defender's office answered her phone. "Are you ready to file on that drug case?" she asked.

I had picked up a case defending a repeat-offender charged with cocaine possession, which I was in the process of diverting with pledges of rehabilitation. "Almost," I said.

"It's a zoo here," my friend said. "You've heard about the kid who was killed?"

Did the entire county know already? "It's very sad," I said. "In fact, that's—"

"Harry Padillo's launched a manhunt, so we're expecting lineups all night. You know what Harry's like. He'll haul in his sister's kids, if he's in the mood."

"Right," I said.

"And Dreyfus has gone completely insane," my friend said.

Eric Dreyfus was the district attorney. He faced an election in less than a month.

"I'm sure he's pressuring Harry to solve this one quickly," I said.

"Mostly because he's behind in the polls. What will the voters think about a man who can't catch a child-killer? Well, lucky for him, Harry's got a lead."

I held my breath. "A lead, you say?"

"He has someone to chase," my friend said.

I had to know, I had to ask: "And do you know whom he's chasing?"

"Some lowlife who tried to shoplift a bottle of soda and a bag of chips at a gas station–convenience store outside Salinas last night. The manager ran after the guy with a bat. The guy got away, but the manager got a partial on the shoplifter's plate. It matches the dead boy's car."

Someone was being chased.

"Jason? Are you there?"

"How do you know all this?" I asked. "Are you sure?"

"What do you mean, how do I know this, am I sure? It's all anyone is talking about," my friend said.

"How did the guy get the Montoya boy's car?" I asked.

"Who knows? Presumably it was not a gift."

"Do they have a description of the man?" I asked.

"They have his handsome in black and white on the security video. So I'm told."

Someone was being chased, but not me.

"We're talking what, grand theft auto?" I asked, and began looking it up in the penal code.

"Dreyfus will go for carjacking," my friend said. "Much more glamorous."

"Then he'll try for felony murder," I said.

"Maybe he'll snag a plea before election day."

"The guy will wise up and dump the car," I said.

"Or Harry will have the feds pick him up crossing the border," my friend said.

Someone else was being chased, and that bought me more time.

"So what's on your mind?" my friend asked. "Why are you calling anyway? How's Julia? How's Tim? Are you making wine again this year? Jason?"

I should have answered her, I should have, I'm in trouble and need your help. I should have said, I want to do the right thing, but I don't want to hurt my family. But someone else was being chased, and I think it was at this point that I began to play a game, the rules to which I improvised with each move. I would wait and see what happened next.

I should have said, It was me. I did it and I want to come

forward. But what I said to my friend was, "I'll file on that drug case soon," and I hung up.

I managed to work most of the day. No more news came in. When I went home, I wanted to deal with the muddy clothes that I had been wearing in the forest. I had collected them in a garbage bag—I'm talking about everything I had on, including my boots and jacket—and I had temporarily hidden the bag in a closet in one of the unused bedrooms upstairs. I didn't want to wash anything, because that might be construed as destroying evidence. And besides, I had no intention of wearing any of those things ever again.

When I pulled into the garage, I noticed that Tim's bike was there. He was home early, but Julia's car was not back.

There was nothing that I needed to do in the winery, but I decided to check on the wine just the same, and it was a good thing that I did. The pointer on a gauge attached to the vat— a thermometer that I should have but hadn't read that morning—had dipped into the danger zone. The heat generated by all of the anaerobic fervor in the vat threatened to wipe out the yeast before its work was complete. A loud school bell–like alarm should have sounded, and I was not sure which device had malfunctioned, the temperature gauge or the alarm. I climbed the ladder next to the vat and saw that the gurgle of pink fizz had indeed slowed, that the foam around the rim of the tank had settled, and when I plunged my hand in the must, I could feel for myself that the juice had become too warm.

The wall of the vat was actually a thin shell that could be filled with chilled water; this was the one higher-tech innovation that my father had sprung for in his flusher days. I scrambled down the ladder and turned the knobs to open the pipes, and I held my breath until I heard the cold water rush into the shell of the tank. We hadn't had to chill the must during the previous crush; I hadn't even bothered to have a plumber in to check out the pipes until this last summer.

I could feel the sides of the steel tank become noticeably cooler. Back up the ladder, I stared at the must, but the fizzing and bubbling remained subdued. I should have known that punching down, that poking and stirring the wine as vigorously as I had that morning might accelerate the chemistry; I should have waited around and measured the temperature. I stared at the strawberry foam for a half hour, longer, and just as I was about to go in the house and tell Tim that the wine might be ruined, a ruby geyser spurted in the center of the vat. In a matter of seconds, the bubbling became effusive, and I found myself standing and bouncing on my toes, bouncing faster as the fermentation itself regained momentum.

Tim didn't answer when I called out his name. I checked his room, but he wasn't there, and when I went back downstairs, I found him stretched out on the couch in the study. He was staring at the ceiling, and the television was on with the sound turned down. All of the lamps were off. I switched one on. Tim covered his eyes with his arm.

"Hi, guy," I said.

"Hey," he said, looking at me eventually.

I sat down on the arm of the couch. "How did your test go?" I asked.

"No test," Tim said. He swung his legs around and sat up. "We got out early."

I knew to take this conversation slowly.

"I didn't know him," Tim said.

"Craig Montoya," I said.

"I mean, I knew who he was, of course. Everybody did."

"He was the captain of the soccer team," I said.

"He hung with the cool crowd," Tim said.

"You're upset," I said.

"I'm not upset," he countered.

I nodded. "Why don't you get a fire going. I'll make dinner, and we'll eat it in front of—"

"I'm not upset, Dad," Tim said.

"I hear you," I said. "We can talk about it later—"

"I'm not upset, okay?"

"Okay," I said. "So your mother isn't home yet?"

Tim's eyes had teared up.

"I just checked on the wine," I said, "and it was a good thing I did. . . ."

He looked away from me.

"I'm going to go in the kitchen," I said. "That's where I'll be, if you need me."

I wanted to cook a wonderful dinner for my family. I decided to make what Julia had planned to make that night. I stuffed some game hens with wild rice. I peeled away the thin bark of a butternut squash, seeded it, and began hacking it with a cleaver. I poured myself a glass of pinot because I needed to relax. Tim came into the kitchen, and without really thinking about what I was doing, I removed a second goblet from the breakfront and poured him half a glass, too. He switched on the kitchen television.

We caught the top story of the local news in medias res. The anchor was speaking in a somber voice, an obituary pitch. A yearbook snapshot filled the screen: a handsome boy, his shoulders at an awkward angle, his hair combed, Craig Montoya saying cheese. Cut to a reporter standing beneath an umbrella on a wet road that could have been any road, not necessarily the Oak Leaf Highway. A strand of yellow police tape whipped in and out of view. The reporter spun out the latest allegations, everything that my friend in the public defender's office had already given me, including the theory that the boy had been carjacked. And the reporter, when questioned by the anchor back at the studio, referred to the possibility of murder. He sputtered legalese. Lying in wait, exceptional depravity. Leaks had become rumors, and rumors news.

Tim sighed loudly. I could see that the news bothered him, but I had to see it. I had to know how my accident, the manhunt, how all current events were portrayed. When I flipped to another station, Tim left the kitchen.

The second report was image for image like the first, except it included a blurry rendering of a man whom I had never seen before, a still photo taken from the security video in the convenience store. The man went unnamed, but if you saw him, say, speeding on a freeway or lifting a bag of cookies from your neighborhood grocery, you were supposed to dial the hot-line number superimposed on the screen. I knew that everyone at Legal Aid must have been groaning, because the photograph was so fuzzy, so ill-defined, that a dozen innocent men would be confused for the suspect and stopped and harassed and maybe even brought in for questioning.

Given the fluorescence in the store and the angle at which the security camera was aimed, anyone would appear as washed-out and culpable as this man did. And yet the longer I stared at him, the more average he looked. He had dark hair, neither long nor short, and the tracings of a goatee. He wore glasses, black oval-framed glasses, which I thought were oddly chic for an alleged killer. The collar of his jacket was pulled up high around his neck. Although it was impossible to tell from the photo, he didn't seem like a large man. To the contrary, he looked wiry, as if he didn't occupy too much space in the world. He looked like a grown-up version of the boy whom you did not want but could not stop your teenage daughter from falling in love with. Cool, intelligent, but trouble.

The video still was replaced by a shot of a station wagon parked on the side of a rural highway in Marin County. According to a reporter, it was Craig Montoya's car, abandoned. Maybe this man, whoever he was, had in fact harmed Craig Montoya in some way. Maybe he had committed a crime against the boy before I came along, a crime for which he could be prosecuted and punished. And then maybe my own crime might not need to be pursued, not if a certain amount of justice had been delivered. The Montoyas would have somebody else to sue. Maybe my crime could go unsolved. I am ashamed to admit it, but you see, this was my thinking, that I might not need to come forward. I could pursue a course of private penance, and that might be enough without a damaging public reckoning.

"Hey, Tim? Should I make the squash the way you like it with the honey and the ginger?"

No answer.

"Tim?"

He was not in the study. He had not gone up to his room. From the window in my bedroom, I could see a flickering light out in the vineyard. Which was where I found him, in the middle of the plot, a flashlight in hand. He was crying. I stepped over to him so that he was sheltered by my umbrella.

"Sorry," Tim said.

"Don't be sorry," I said.

"It's not like I knew him," he said.

"But it's okay to be sad about it," I said.

I felt like someone had punched me in the gut. Whatever pain my son now suffered had been triggered by the death of his peer. The boy was dead, and I was to blame. My son despaired, and I was to blame. I would never find any transport from the cold fact of my crime, no acquittal from what I had done, never, so why was I even looking for a way out? There it was, immutable, accident or no accident, and I was and always would be to blame.

"I'm sad about it, too," I said. "I'm sadder than you know."

I steered Tim back toward the house. Inside, he toweled off and I told him a story, a true story, about a girl in my high school, no one I had known well, no one anyone had known well. Her boyfriend—no one had even known that she had a boyfriend—was driving her home from a church youth group meeting when he plowed into a parked car. The boyfriend wasn't hurt, but the girl lay in a coma for about a week before she died. I didn't know her, I told Tim, but her death affected me deeply; it affected all of my friends. We walked around in a daze and some of us wept as if we had just been waiting for someone to grieve for—it didn't matter who. It felt odd at the time to lapse so easily into a state of mourning for someone I barely knew, somewhat hypocritical, but in retrospect, I told my son, I saw nothing wrong with it. We think about the people we know and love, I said, and we think about what it would mean to lose them suddenly. We want to find them and squeeze them to know they're alive.

"And that's why I ended up in your room last night," I said, "because I was thinking about the boy dead on the road, and I was thinking about how crazy I would be if you were the one who—"

I stopped. I realized my mistake. I was presenting a chronology that was implausible. Last night would have been too soon for me to know about a hit-and-run; the ranger hadn't found Craig until early the next morning.

But then Tim gave me a hug, a long and tight embrace, a squeeze to know that I was alive—or maybe he was letting me know that he was alive—and he was sniffling again, and I didn't think that he had caught me in my lie. Not yet anyway. I wanted to tell him that no matter what happened in the days ahead, I would protect him and Julia and our life and our vineyard. Maybe the news had emboldened me, the remote possibility that a false chase might give me cover. I wanted to make that promise, although it wasn't really one that I could make.

When he pulled away from me, he rubbed his nose with his sleeve. "Can I have more wine?" he asked.

"Will there be school tomorrow?"

He shrugged.

"With dinner," I said.

Both of us turned toward the door when we heard a car come up the vineyard road. Soon Julia came in; in each hand, she carried about five shopping bags, which she dropped all at once in the mudroom.

"Here you are," I said. "I was getting worried."

"Looks like you did some shopping, Mom," Tim said.

She had apparently gone to the hairdresser, too, and had her already-short coif shorn to a shag that made her look about fifteen.

"Nice do," I said.

"You think so?" Julia asked.

"I think so," I said, and offered her a glass of wine, which she declined. "Did you buy anything for me?" I asked.

"No," she said.

"What about me?" Tim asked.

Julia rummaged through the bags until she found one in particular, which she tossed across the kitchen to Tim. He held on to the contents and let the bag fall to the floor.

"Oh, that's mean," Tim said. He was holding a shining and bovine-smelling black leather jacket with epaulets. He hopped across the room and gave his mother a kiss.

"Is that going to be warm enough?" I asked. My real question was, How much did that cost?

Tim tried on the jacket. He looked sharp. "Who cares?" he said.

I eyed the other bags. "It looks like we're in for a fashion show," I said.

"You're in a good mood," Julia said.

"Am I?"

"Or a better one than I left you in this morning," Julia said.

"Two glasses of pinot, I guess," I said, and offered her wine again.

"I shouldn't," she said.

Julia tried on her new clothes for Tim and me. She disappeared into the bathroom and came out wearing a chocolate sweater, baggy in the sleeves, and a pair of tight black trousers. Her new togs looked exactly like her old ones—she had left that morning wearing a brown sweater and black trousers—but I didn't say anything. I did call into question the purchase of a pair of fine suede bucks.

"I hear it rains a lot in these parts during the winter," I said.

"Maybe I'm not planning on ever leaving the house," Julia said.

"You're not going to become agoraphobic on me, are you?"

"What, and miss the Oak Valley ballet season? I don't think so," she said.

Tim poured himself another splash of wine.

"Hey," Julia said.

"Dad said I could," Tim said.

Julia looked at me.

"Tim was upset," I said.

"Upset?" she asked. She looked at Tim. "Bad test or something?"

And then I realized that she hadn't heard the news. I didn't know how it was possible, but somehow drifting from shop to shop in Hollister, somehow while turning from one music channel to another on the car radio, Julia must not have heard the news.

"A kid at school got killed," Tim said before I had a chance to wind my way through a more delicate explanation.

"What? At school?" Julia looked at me.

"He doesn't mean at school," I said.

"A kid was in a car accident. He got run over last night," Tim said.

"Who? Where? How?" Julia asked softly.

I told her. I gave her the facts as everyone except me knew them. I passed along the latest news from the television reports. I fed her every rumor.

"This is so sad. He was such a sweet kid," Julia said. "I mean, I only knew him to say hello to, but still, he was so sweet."

Tim looked grim again.

"You're upset," she said to him. "That's understandable—"

"I'm cool about it now, Mom," Tim said. "Dad and I talked."

Julia looked at me. She squinted as if she knew she wasn't getting the whole story. She glanced back at Tim. "Well, it's very sad."

"It's very sad," I agreed.

Tim wore his leather jacket all through dinner. Julia had on her new shoes. We ate quickly and without much conversation. After dinner, Tim said good night—I think the wine made him sleepy—and he headed upstairs. Julia followed, and so I was left alone in the cold and empty downstairs. When I went up a short while later, I could hear that Tim was not asleep—I could hear the occasional chime and beep coming from his computer—and I found Julia sitting on the edge of our bed, still dressed in her new clothes, holding one of her new shoes in her hand, absentmindedly brushing the suede back and forth with the other.

I sat down next to her. "Hey," I said.

"Hey," she answered. Her salon-styled hair smelled like pineapple.

It was now or never. I had to stop lying. I had to tell her.

"There was something I wanted to say this morning," I said.

"I know," she said.

I let my shoulders drop. I closed my eyes. So she knew. Of course she knew. There was no hiding anything from my oldest friend. Had she pretended not to know about the accident for Tim's sake?

"But look," Julia said. "I don't know if you should be apologizing. I think I may have overreacted, running off the way I did."

"No," I said. "I understand. You wanted to get away to think."

"But nothing really happened. You couldn't sleep. You got up, you checked in on Tim, and you fell asleep," she said. "That's not so horrible."

I had to smile. She didn't have a clue.

"I guess it reminded me of that really bad stretch after your mother died," she said. "You know, back in San Francisco, when you started sleeping in the study."

In a ridiculous effort to save our marriage—I don't know what we were thinking—we had agreed to live as roommates rather than as husband and wife. It was supposed to be a trial separation conducted within our own home, but it was really the last rip that we could sustain. Occasionally we would share the same bed to go through the motions of cold and robotic sex. Then that stopped, too, and not too long after, I fled to the vineyard.

"You went to another bed for one night," Julia said, "or not a bed, but the floor—and I think Tim understood, I don't think it freaked him out really—but in my mind, I made a big deal out of it. Which was foolish. I apologize. What were you going to say about it?"

"That it will never happen again," I said.

"Well, look, if you can't sleep—"

"It's not worth it if it makes you sad," I said. "I'd rather lie awake in bed than remind you of . . ." I put my arms around her rather than finish the thought.

And then Julia said, "Jason," and she whispered, "I'm pregnant."

My heart skipped. I slipped down to the floor and knelt in front of her and put down the shoe that she was holding. I took both of her hands. "Tell me again," I said.

"I'm pregnant," she said. "A month and a half, we think. Two months tops. The doctor—"

"Your doctor's appointment, right. You didn't tell me that you suspected anything," I said.

"Because I didn't want you to get excited for nothing," she said.

Now and then we had talked about having another child, sooner than later, but we had made no plans. We weren't trying.

"If you are excited," she said.

I stared at her hard. I placed her hand against my speeding heart.

"That could just mean you're nervous," she said.

"Well, I am. Nervous and thrilled," I said.

"I don't know," Julia said. "I mean, I know I'll still be able to work on the big D and all. But. Well, I wasn't ready for this. Not yet. I'm not even sure . . ."

"We should have this child," I said. "We should. We want it." I wanted it. I thought about the pure exhausting joy that I had felt when Tim was born. I had loved Julia then more than ever. I had loved her without any heartache. In those days, I told her everything. I harbored no secrets.

"I had to go Hollister," Julia said. "I did have to get away and think. I should have called you from the doctor's office and told you. I'm sorry."

She should have told me when she missed her period weeks ago, but who was I to talk about withholding information?

"But I was all upset, waking up and finding you in Tim's bedroom, crumpled in the corner," she said.

I pulled myself up to the bed and held her again. I stroked her hair, what hair was left. "We want it," I said.

Now I had more to protect. Now I had even more to lose.

Julia undressed and got into bed and I followed her even though the hour was early, and she fell asleep and I lay in bed and stared at the dark stripes of the exposed ceiling beams. My pale truth was becoming increasingly expensive, and I didn't know how much longer I could afford to hold on to it.

I don't remember much about the next day, except I know that Julia and I checked on the wine together early the next morning. The must was fizzing with less brio but without a rise in temperature. And then Tim went to school and Julia hit her books and I went into town—I drove the truck because I couldn't keep it locked up forever—where I listened to the rumors at the hardware store—no one had anything new to say—and I ended up at my office and lost myself in my work for a while. Every couple of hours, I would call the public defender's office. I would come up with minor questions relating to the case I was handling to mask my more pressing query, but there was no word about the hunted man being found. I figured that if he had wised up and dumped Craig Montoya's car, then he probably also knew that he should make his way to another continent. That evening the fermentation of our second vintage did stop. I wanted to let it settle in the vat before pressing it. Tim hid out in his room and spent the better part of the evening on-line, and Julia and I went to bed early again. I ended up sitting in a chair by the window and looking out at my vines.

I do remember every moment of the day after that. The rain stopped and a raw freezing wind swept through the valley, laminating the roads with a thin layer of ice. I put on black clothing, as did Julia, and Tim wore his new leather jacket because it was the darkest coat he owned. We took Julia's sports car because I thought it would be perverse to take the truck; no one questioned me when I said I wanted to take the less comfortable car. We joined the rest of the town at the cemetery. Our district attorney had reportedly pulled some strings and finagled a speedy autopsy so that Craig Montoya's body could be returned to his family. That gesture won Eric Dreyfus a place next to Craig's parents during the funeral.

We arrived at the cemetery early to visit the graves of my grandparents and my parents, the two couples—including my divorced mother and father—buried side by side, and because we were there before anyone else, because we watched everyone arrive, I think I became numb to the sight of the furrowed faces, to the stoic front that Will Clark put up, to Alex Marquez and Emma Hodges, who looked bleached and older to me in the harsh light of a cloudless noon. I watched the teachers and the coaches and all the weeping students, and the more histrionic the ensemble, the more aloof I became. Tim left Julia and me to stand with his friends, but he came back to my side before the Montoyas showed up. Even the appearance of Craig's mother, a rotund woman draped in a black shawl, and Craig's younger sister, a smaller, Russian-doll version of her mother, along with Craig's father, staggering and swaying and clearly plastered—I could smell the whiskey from a distance of some yards—even the sad family portrait with its gaping hole, its obvious wound, did not move me the way I thought then or think now I should have been moved.

I should have made a scene. I should have run up to the velvet-swathed table with the bronze urn of ashes and at the very least ripped the lapel of my blazer. I should have thrown myself at the fat black-stockinged ankles of the grieving mother and prayed for her forgiveness. If I believed in a supreme being of some kind, which I did not, I could have dropped to my knees and looked up toward the blanched heavens and ripped out my hair. Instead I observed the scene like a deranged arsonist who stands in the crowd watching the firemen put out his blaze. To be honest, what concerned me was what our sheriff was up to, because, except during the funeral ceremony, he carried on an inaudible conversation on his cellular phone. Occasionally he blinked in the direction of Eric Dreyfus, and I desperately wanted to know what new facts he had acquired.

We did not have a church in Oak Valley, and the Montoyas had not arranged for a Mass or any kind of service in one of the chapels in a nearby town. They had requested that the priest be quick in his ministrations. I didn't pay attention to what liturgy he served up or what he offered by way of an explanation for how an athlete could die young. Why we had even come to the cemetery puzzled me, since it was the practice of the Montoya clan, like many of the families who had spent the better part of the century in constant migration up and down the state, to cremate and spread the ashes of their deceased. And the cemetery in Oak Valley, a minor mesa of wind-effaced markers and modest tombstones on the eastern flank of the basin, was a depressing place to come these days because one of the larger quarries loomed in the near distance. From where we stood, we could hear the low hum of the heavy machinery gnawing at the hillside, and we had a clear view of the balding slope and the corrugated chutes carrying chunks of stone down to the heaps of rubble, over which a fine mist of talc hovered.

Soon the priest opened the bronze urn and tossed the first fistful of ashes over the side of the hill as if he were sowing the frozen brush with new seed. Mr. Montoya followed suit and then he managed to help his daughter do the same, and it was Mrs. Montoya, her shawl blowing back off her shoulders and into the mourners behind her, who grabbed the entire container and all at once flung what was left of her son into the wind. The ashes hung in the air, buoyed for a second, caught the sunlight and sparkled a bit, and then settled slowly, lazily over the chaparral.

I looked at Tim, who was crying, but without sound, swallowing his sobs, and I gripped his arm. Julia was crying, too. I looked over at the Montoyas again, and then I noticed that Harry Padillo had slipped away. I had not seen him leave.

Tim bolted away from the crowd and ran back through the graves to the car. Julia jogged after him. When I caught up with them, they were holding each other, and I put my hand on Tim's shoulder, but he wiggled free from my grasp. He didn't seem to want me to console him. We drove home in silence.

The wind died down and the air remained quite cold that evening, and I thought that I heard a distant siren, its plaint and wane. The still of the night troubled me. I slipped off to the study and I called my friend from Legal Aid at her home.

"You heard?" she asked.

"No," I said. "What?"

There were voices in the background, a clink of glasses.

"What?" I asked again.

"They caught him up in Del Norte County. He hadn't crossed into Oregon."

"He didn't get very far," I said.

"I don't get the sense that he's too bright. He stole another car, which was traced, and since he didn't cross the state line, he'll probably be back in Hollister by tomorrow."

I asked where exactly he had been picked up.

"At another convenience store," my friend said. "He was stealing food. And you know, I heard something kind of funny. Well, not so funny for this guy. Apparently the dead boy's car ran out of gas. That was probably why he ditched

it, not because he thought he was being chased. Listen, I
have guests," she said, "but are you okay? Is something
wrong with Julia or—"

"No, no," I said. "Everything's fine."

I fell asleep later with unusual ease, but that sleep didn't
last, because at around two in the morning, I awoke with a
jolt. I hadn't really thought out the latest turn of events, and
it occurred to me that while there was a suspect in custody,
someone who would be questioned about my crime, a suspect who might be charged for it, arraigned, and tried, I had
no idea what this man would say.

Was there any real evidence against him, save the fact that
he happened to be driving Craig Montoya's car, or so it was
alleged? What if he had an alibi? What if he could prove he
wasn't in the woods at the time of Craig's death? Or what if
he had been in the woods and what if he had seen the accident? What if—and this was what got me up out of bed and
wandering downstairs, where I could pace without waking
up Julia—what if he was a witness to what actually happened? I had no reason to believe that the arrested man, the
shoplifter, the car thief, would be unable to maintain his
innocence, at least in the crime of the hit-and-run, or however it was trumped up. And maybe he would end up helping the police. Maybe he would become a star witness for
the prosecution.

It was a horrible thought, but I decided that I would have
been better off if the man had been found dead, a suicide, or
if he had been killed in a shoot-out when he was apprehended. Then the case would probably be closed and the
man would never get to say anything at all. I had not thought
far enough ahead, not nearly far enough, because once this
suspect was cleared, the true criminal would be hunted down
by an impatient posse with a lust for justice at any cost. I had
been a fool to wait as long as I had before coming forward.
By delaying my confession, I'd only made it harder on
myself, and now I had to worry about what this man in jail
would say. What would he say?

* * *

Julia and I headed down to the winery at dawn. Tim got up earlier than usual to help us. We opened the valve at the base of the fermentation tank, and with a weak sigh and then a gush, the wine poured through a filter screen into the hose that ran down to the holding tank on the level below. I stood on a ladder propped up against the holding tank and made sure that the free run remained steady and even and that the wine did not splash too much, especially as the lower tank filled up.

I gripped the hose and felt the blood of the grapes coursing through the tube, and maybe because the roar of the liquid filling the tank was so loud or because the mere sight of the immense red flood was so mesmerizing, I didn't hear Tim shouting at me and I didn't notice that I had inadvertently tugged down on the hose and created a gap between the filter of the fermentation vat and the plastic tube, a sliver through which a spill of wine began to run down the cement step between the levels of the winery. It was only when my hand became sticky and Tim rushed down the outer staircase and into the room with the holding tank that I realized what I had done, and I shoved the hose back into its proper position. I had to hold the hose in place for the rest of the free run, another half hour, longer, which made my lower back ache, and which meant that the next chore, the scraping of the skins and stems and other fruit debris from the bottom of the fermentation vat into our barrel press, left me stiff and sore-limbed and cranky.

"You couldn't sleep again," Julia said.

"I slept just fine, thanks," I snapped.

She raised her eyebrows, as if to say, Sorry I asked.

"My mind just keeps wandering," I said, and apologized for being curt.

Tim and Julia took turns cranking the barrel press, squeezing the juice out of the pomace—because we had only one press, this task had to be broken down into a dozen batches—and the pressed wine spilled into a tray with a spout that I angled into the holding tank.

"Where?" Julia asked.

"Where what?" I asked back.

"Where does your mind keep wandering?"

She was giving me another chance, an opening.

"It's a case I'm working on," I said. "I was just thinking about it."

"It's bothering you," Julia said.

I nodded.

"Are you working for someone you know is guilty?" Tim asked.

I stared at my son. I had somehow not really noticed it before that Saturday morning, but he was not as scrawny as he used to be, still lanky, but not so thin. He had begun to fill out in the shoulders, yet at the same time, his face, his jaw had taken on the delicate angle that was unmistakably his mother's.

"Something like that," I said.

"And the guy will walk," Tim said.

"It's more involved," I said. "It's a complicated situation. This man, he did do something wrong, but . . . Well, what he did—or what he should have done . . ."

Tim was shoveling the pressed pomace into a garbage can. He leaned on the shovel and looked at me.

Tell him, I thought, just tell them both.

"Yeah, he might walk," I said. "If he's lucky."

We left the wine to settle in the holding tank for a few hours and had a long lunch. I slipped into the study to make some calls, to gather what gossip I could, but no one at the public defender's office could tell me anything new. I called Will Clark, of all people, and he, too, had nothing new to say, although he did mention hearing that the suspect had definitely been transferred to the sheriff's station in Hollister.

That afternoon we mixed a cultured bacteria into the wine in the holding tank. I should say that Julia handled the malolactic fermentation. She knew that I was distracted, and so she was the one who measured the culture and gave the tank its first stir before handing me the pole. She bossed me around, which was fine by me. She told me to hold the barrels while she operated the siphon from the holding tank, a skill she had mastered during the first crush. She made sure that there was no air in the barrel. She sealed the bunghole.

Tim helped me carry each barrel down the stairs to the next building down the slope, where we stored them on their sides. We kept these newly filled barrels, our second vintage, separate from the barrels we had filled and racked the previous year. This room smelled less like sour fruit than the upper floors did; here the aroma was a blend of freshly turned soil, of mushrooms with a trace of vanilla. And when we were done racking the barrels, Tim and Julia and I stood and faced the wall of oak casks, and then we shook hands and hugged one another, and I knew that I should have felt nothing but pride at that moment, with a second vintage barreled, having made wine with my family, but I was dragged down instead by an undertow of dread.

Outside the late-afternoon wind had picked up again, and the air was heavy and green with a new storm blowing in from the ocean. We dined on leftovers. I collapsed on the couch in front of the hearth after dinner, but I was too spent to build a fire. Tim watched some television and then he went up to his room. Julia said that she was feeling achy and wanted to take a bath. She asked if I would join her eventually, and I promised her I would.

As soon as I was alone downstairs, I retreated to the study to make a round of calls again—I wanted to know what was going down at the sheriff's station, and I thought my friend might have some word if the suspect had requested a public defender—but when I picked up the phone, I heard a series of blips and beeps, and then my son hollered at me from upstairs because he had gone on-line—we only had one phone line for him to use—and I had interrupted whatever electronic message he was sending or receiving.

I paced the entire length of my house, from the hearth back to the study. Back and forth. I began to imagine all of the townfolk, having heard a new rumor about who really ran over the soccer star, gathering at the base of my vineyard road, torches in hand, beginning the long march up to my door to demand instant justice.

A half hour went by. An hour. Finally I couldn't stand it anymore. I couldn't wait any longer.

First I checked on Tim. I thought that he might have gone to bed, because there wasn't any light spilling into the hall from the crack beneath his door, but then I heard him typing at his computer. The blue-gray computer screen appeared to float in the darkness, and except for that rectangle of illumination, the only other light came from a series of tea candles on the windowsill next to Tim's desk.

"What, are you E-mailing the devil?" I asked.

"Can I help you with something?" Tim said. The computer chimed, and he glanced at the screen and typed a few words on his keyboard.

"No, no, it's just that . . ." I scratched my brow.

Tim didn't look at me. The computer chimed again, and he smiled at whatever appeared on the screen. It was my turn to hover in a door frame.

"Dad?" Tim asked.

"I love you," I said, and I shut his door.

Then I wandered into my bedroom and the bathroom, which was filled with steam. Julia lay in the tub beneath a blanket of bubbles.

"It's about time," she said. "I was about to give up on you." She, too, had lit candles all around the tub.

"You're not going to believe this," I said. "That was Legal Aid who called just now."

"I didn't hear the phone ring," Julia said.

"I picked it up on one ring," I said.

"Oh. And?"

"I have to drive up to Hollister."

"Now?" Julia whined. She splashed some bubbles at me.

"It's that guy I've been representing. My drug case—"

"What happened?"

"He got busted again," I said. "This time he was dealing."

Julia didn't say anything. She sank deeper in the tub and a mountain of one knee broke through the surface of bubbles.

"He's all strung out in the lockup at the sheriff's station, and I've just got to go make sure he doesn't say anything stupid or do anything that's going to get him in deeper trouble." My lie sounded so thin to me that I doubted Julia would buy it.

The wind rattled the single window behind the tub. The glass was wet with rain.

"It's not like I can get the guy arraigned tonight," I said. "It's too late, but I should—"

"Okay," Julia said. "Go."

"I'm sorry," I said. "All I really want to do is get in that bath with you. Honest."

"Go, if you're going to go," she said, and splashed me again. Her splash extinguished two candles.

"I love you," I said, and then I headed out into the rain.

the mountain road was called the Oak Leaf Highway because as it traced the perimeter of the valley with its fan of glens and passes, its notches and points, it defined the shape of a giant leaf, although you could only really see that shape if you looked at the entire route outlined on a màp. Under certain conditions—during the dramatically shadowed dusk after an uncommonly clear autumn day, for example—you could also see the oak leaf if you stood at the edge of an unnamed high rock due north in the valley, a moss-dusted, arrow-shaped ledge that jutted out from the forest. Only natives knew where to park in the woods and which path between the pine trees to follow to reach the rock, and because of the sheer drop beneath the cliff, because the granite was treacherously slippery when it was wet, no one ever talked about this natural monument, as if the adults in the valley worried that their children would bike up to the precipice and eventually one of them would have an accident, or, similarly, that teenage lovers might meet some untimely fate if they rendezvoused on the secluded cliff to make out.

I had gone to the rock from time to time during my first lonely autumn in the valley, and I will admit while I hiked up from the road and through the tall trees, I pondered my mortality. I didn't know of any reported suicides from the cliff. By the time I would reach the vista and squint and fool myself into believing that I could indeed limn the shape of a leaf, I didn't want to jump. Regret gave way to wonder, I suppose. Forget about the alleged topography of the valley. The way the setting sun made the hills look vaguely like hibernating bears, the way that you could see the blue horizon of the Pacific to your right and the silvered jag of the Diablo Range to your left and believe that you had climbed to the ultimate summit of the known world—the champagne air at this elevation, the lave of mint and fir—all of that was enough to keep me going for another day. I would hurry back through the trees to my truck and head home.

I had gone up to the rock often during my first year in the valley, but then I had stopped making the hike and more or less forgotten about the cliff completely. And what I hadn't realized until my late-night drive to Hollister was that my accident in the woods had happened not too far from the turnout where I used to park my car before heading into the tall trees, maybe a quarter of a mile away.

First I had to drive past the site of the accident itself, and even though I had prepared myself for my trip back, my heart pounded when I came up to the straightaway and I found myself taking my foot off the gas in order to brake this time. To steer around the boy and not wipe out. It was a mistake to drive the truck, for that memory alone was enough to make me sick. Then I saw what was left of the birch tree, a sharp spike of a trunk, and I noticed some untethered strands of glowing police tape curling and uncurling around the pine trees—the trees themselves on either side of the road looked to me as though they were bowing slightly, leaning toward me, slowly falling down on me, if not to crush me, then to trap me here—and I closed my eyes and accelerated. It was a miracle that with my eyes shut, I didn't have another accident, especially since the rain was coming down harder and my tires slipped as I picked up speed. When I opened my eyes, I realized where I was, following a bend and then a steep ascent up toward the high rock. On either side of the rock, the road that hugged the cliff was supported by a bridge of sorts, a trestle of steel stilts, a crosshatch of iron exes and girders that reached far down into the steep ravine beneath. The trees here thinned out somewhat, and so the storm became fiercer, the rain slapping my truck and the road, pounding hard.

I pulled into the turnout. I killed the engine. I wanted to hike up to the rock, although I knew that I wouldn't see much of anything in the rain. I remembered the one hot summer day that my father had taken me out to the cliff when I was six—it was shortly after my parents had split up—and I recalled the way he had knelt behind me at the edge of the crag, his right arm belted around my waist to keep me from slipping on the moss, his other hand holding mine and making a gun with my fingers. My father used my pointing finger to delineate the foliate basin, and even though I couldn't picture the leaf, I told my father that I could because I liked the way he had taken my hand in his. I asked him to outline it for me again, which he did, around and around the valley.

I sat in my truck for a long while, listening to myself breathe. And then, for the first time since the accident, I cried. I mean that I really let go, I wept. I don't know whether I was feeling sorrow for myself or for my family because of what I had and would put them through or whether I was trying to figure out how I would explain myself one day to my unborn son—I was convinced that it was a boy sleeping inside Julia now—or whether I was finally overcome with regret for the family of the dead boy and regret for the dead boy himself and the prosperous life that I had stolen from him. In any case, I wept and I wept until, charged with a surge of courage that I knew wouldn't last, I started up the truck. I knew what I had to do—I had always known what I had to do—and finally I would do it. I tried not to predict what consequences my belated honesty would bring, and I concentrated instead on the wet road north.

a deputy at the sheriff's station in Hollister was standing behind a round reception counter when I arrived. There was a dark window behind him, smoked glass, through which I could make out only the occasional flicker of the dispatch's control panel. He greeted me by name, which I had to assume was because he was waiting for me.

"This is some night," he said, "isn't it?"

I thought I should make matters easy and so I removed my watch and placed it on the counter.

"With all this rain . . ." The deputy looked at the watch and then at my face.

I reached in my pocket for my wallet and placed it on the counter next to the watch.

The deputy rubbed his nose. He was wearing a gargantuan college ring.

"Go ahead," I said. "Tell them I'm here."

The deputy smiled politely and then spoke into an intercom.

I was about to take off my belt and remove the laces from my shoes when, seconds later, Eric Dreyfus himself emerged from a door behind the desk.

"Jason?" Eric Dreyfus shook my hand. "I'm surprised to see you."

"Well, I'm . . ." My throat was dry.

"But I think there's been a mistake," he said.

"Well, yes, a mistake," I said.

"We didn't put a call in for counsel," he said.

"You didn't what?"

"We asked him every five minutes. I ran the interrogation myself. I didn't want to take any chances. He insisted—no lawyers."

"Now, when you say 'he,' " I said, "you're referring to—"

"Did Legal Aid wake you up?"

The deputy behind the desk looked at me and then at the district attorney.

"Because the fact of the matter is," Eric Dreyfus said, "we just finished taping the guy's statement." He smiled a grin so broad that I could see the coffee stains on his molars.

"When you say his statement," I said, "do you mean—"

"He sang."

"He sang?" I smiled, too.

"He confessed."

"Confessed to what exactly?" I asked.

"To killing the Montoya boy, among other things. It took all day, but he went for the deal. I'm sorry they woke you up, but we don't need anyone from Legal Aid tonight."

I pocketed my wallet. "It's no problem."

"But wait. As long as you're here," Eric Dreyfus said, "maybe you can make sure everything is kosher. Know what I mean?" He winked at me.

I put on my watch and winked back.

From the windows in Harry Padillo's office, you could see the entire empty squad room, a city grid of desks and filing cabinets. The sheriff had greeted me with a friendly slap on the back and directed me to a chair. He sat at his desk, and behind him, flanking a skinny sentry window, were maps of San Benito County, each map a bulletin board pierced with variously colored pushpins. I immediately noticed a pin stuck in on the right, the southern half of the county, one red pin at the edge of Oak Valley.

"Hope you weren't sleeping," Harry Padillo said. A bushy mustache made him look a little puppetlike when he spoke, his mouth opening without really forming the shapes of words. "Okay," he said, lowering his voice, "I think you should know we didn't lean on the guy. We just talked reason. The man listened."

Eric Dreyfus handed me a folder.

I learned the name of the accused man. It was Troy Frantz. The folder contained the waivers that he had signed, abdicating his right to a trial by his peers in order to enter a plea of guilty. I looked at a photocopy of his expired driver's license—he was in his thirties, about my age—and a copy of the warrant for his arrest. I read the charges against him. There was the carjacking and death of Craig Montoya—no surprise there—but then there was a second carjacking upstate. Also a DUI from when the arrest was made.

"What's this upstate jacking?" I asked.

Eric Dreyfus and Harry Padillo glanced at each other.

"The guy confessed," Harry Padillo said. "You can watch the tape."

Eric Dreyfus cut him off. "He knows. Jason, all we really want is for you to tell us this stuff looks clean, and then we can go home. It's always better if we can say to a judge that even though the defendant refused counsel—"

"I'm not the man's lawyer," I said.

"You're just a watchdog representative from Legal Aid making sure that we're doing our jobs right," Eric Dreyfus said. "You want to know about the second jacking? Troy Frantz stole a minivan out of a supermarket parking lot a few miles north of Mendocino. He drove off with a kid in the baby seat, the mother running after him, and he's just lucky he stopped long enough to give the woman the kid back before he headed north."

So he had committed a crime, all on his own, a crime that had nothing to do with me. "No weapons?" I asked.

"No weapons. But he did kill the Montoya boy," Eric Dreyfus said. "He stole the kid's car and then ran him over."

"And he confessed to that?" I asked. "To running Craig over? Did he say it was an accident?"

"You know that it doesn't matter if it was," the district attorney said. "With the carjacking, we've got special circumstances. Plus, we think Troy exhibited exceptional depravity. We think—"

"What about evidence? Do you have any evidence?" I asked.

Harry Padillo leaned forward in his swivel chair. "You can watch the tape—"

"It's okay, Harry," Eric Dreyfus said. To me: "I'll lay it out for you. Briefly."

It was at that point that I knew I had crossed a line. Maybe I was not Troy Frantz's lawyer in point of fact, but I was behaving as if I was, and as his de facto advocate, with my conflict of interest, to put it mildly, I was violating a code of ethics, for which I could be disbarred. I didn't care. I needed to know the facts. I needed to know if this man's confession would float when a judge reviewed the plea.

"Craig Montoya's car had major dents consistent with the accident on the Oak Leaf Highway. Clearly Troy was driving Craig's car. We have prints, we have fibers. We'll have the formal forensics soon," Eric Dreyfus said.

"Just because you have Troy's prints doesn't mean that you can prove he hit Craig," I said.

"We found blood on the right-front bumper of Craig's wagon," Harry Padillo said.

Blood on my car certainly, but on Craig's car?

"Forensics soon," Eric Dreyfus said. "Then we have mud from his shoes—we can put him in the forest—pine needles from his clothes—"

"But do you really have the corpus for the Montoya carjacking?" I said. "Grand theft auto maybe. I give you that, but carjacking—"

"Don't forget the woman in the parking lot upstate," Eric

Dreyfus said. "Pattern of behavior. But back to the forest, Jason. There's more. Troy Frantz dragged the kid off the road in a truly amateurish attempt to hide the body. He tried to get rid of the kid's backpack, too, but we found that. And what else? We found some hair on the corpse that I'm sure will match up with Troy's."

No, but it would match my hair.

Harry Padillo to the district attorney: "Tell him about the vomit."

Eric Dreyfus wrinkled his nose. "Somebody puked in the woods. Nasty stuff, but rich in DNA. If it's Troy's, bingo. If it's Craig's, sounds like torture or something ugly was going on there."

A single drop of cool sweat ran down my spine.

"Don't forget about the footprints in the mud," the sheriff said.

My footprints.

"And the skid marks."

From my truck.

"Better than that. Troy dropped an article of clothing," Eric Dreyfus said. "Not too swift. The Montoyas say it didn't belong to Craig."

I tried to remain cool. "What did he drop?"

"A scarf," Harry Padillo said.

My gray cashmere scarf with the black tassels. I could picture it right where I had left it, the makeshift pillow I had wadded under that poor boy's head. I tried to speak, but no words came out. They had me. All the evidence they would need to turn their video camera on me. If only they knew— they had me. Whatever moral conviction I had summoned back in the woods was evaporating fast.

"If I went to trial," Eric Dreyfus said, "I would have asked for the needle. Troy Frantz is smart. He saw the deal was good for him."

When the evidence was fully analyzed, only some of it would point to this man Troy Frantz, if Troy Frantz indeed had been driving Craig's car. Some of the results would indicate the presence of another man at the scene of the crime, and I had to wonder how long it would take the sheriff and his men to connect me to the scarf and the other scatological detritus. Unless, of course, no one really studied the evidence too carefully. Unless, of course, with Troy Frantz's confession on tape, no one wanted to know what other story the forensics told. I had to hope that the district attorney was more interested in being able to say to his constituents that he had solved a heinous crime than he was in true justice. Here was my gamble, my risk: Let Troy Frantz go down and pray that nobody asked questions later. And frankly, in my brief experience, that was the way the system worked when you cobbled together a plea. Nobody went back to check the math, the continuity, the dueness of the process; if a man was willing to take the blame, nobody cared.

"We forgave him for the DUI," the district attorney said.

I looked over the plea deal. Five years for the upstate carjacking and a plea down to murder in the second degree for killing Craig in the woods.

"Fifteen years," Eric Dreyfus said. "That's way too fair. But hey, I'm a fair man."

That the terms for the two crimes would be served simultaneously and not consecutively surprised me, and I said so.

Eric Dreyfus played with his tie again. "He held out for that. That was what made him deal."

Fifteen years in prison, that was the punishment, with a possibility for parole after seven and two-thirds served. And I thought that if this man Troy Frantz did commit that carjacking, a car with a baby in it, then maybe he did deserve to do some time. And what if he had in fact stolen Craig's car from him? That made more sense than anything else I had heard that evening. That would explain what Craig Montoya was doing walking the mountain road.

"Counselor?" Eric Dreyfus said. "I think a judge would accept this plea, don't you agree?"

Something troubled me. If the district attorney had gathered so much physical evidence against the accused, then why not wait for the forensics and why not go all the way to trial? Wouldn't that make him more popular with his voting public? I could understand why Troy Frantz might take a plea, but why would Eric Dreyfus settle for one? It seemed clear to me that the district attorney probably did not have as solid a case as he pretended, that he knew he could prove only grand theft auto but not necessarily carjacking, and without the carjacking, he couldn't go for felony murder. Talk of the death penalty was pure bluster. Maybe he would have been able to squeeze out manslaughter. But he had gotten lucky. Troy Frantz was willing to confess, and his confession secured the district attorney a greater victory than he might have been able to claim without it.

I should have stopped the wrong man from going to jail. I was the one who should have confessed, but there I was, being offered a way out. If Troy Frantz was already going to pay for one or two crimes, then why not let him pay for mine?

Eric Dreyfus inserted a videotape into a machine on a cart in the corner of the sheriff's office. Troy Frantz's face appeared on the small television. Another unflattering pose, head-on, Troy looking much the way he had for the security camera, except now he wasn't wearing glasses and he was sitting at a table, his hands folded in front of him.

"First I would like to say I'm sorry for what I've done," he said.

He sounded genuinely weary with regret. His voice had more bass to it than I had expected. He spoke slowly but without pause. He said that he had been drinking. He had been drinking for a month straight, for longer than that. He said his life was a mess, although he didn't say why. He said that he was out of his mind. He stole Craig's car. Craig got in the way, and Troy said that he ran into him. He admitted that fiction. He tried to hide the body and then he sped away, and he only ditched the car when it ran out of gas. He hitched a few rides. He stole the second car. He didn't see the baby at first, and strangely, the baby didn't cry until Troy handed him back to his mother. He made it to a forest, but then he got hungry, he needed food, he was arrested.

Why? he was asked. Why did he do what he did?

Troy Frantz shook his head, bewildered himself, it seemed, and then he broke down, he cried. I didn't get the impression that he was acting.

"I'm so tired," he said. He rubbed his shadow goatee. "I thought I hit a deer."

A deer? he was asked. Where, in the woods?

"I was so fucked up," Troy Frantz said. "I was so trashed. I had no idea." Tears streamed down his face into the stubble of his beard. "I thought I hit a deer," he said. "And it ran off, I didn't even think I killed it. Did anyone . . . Did anyone find a dead deer?" he asked the camera. Then he said, "I thought I hit a deer, but I hit a kid. A kid." He buried his head in his arms on the table, and his shoulders rose and fell with his sobs.

The screen went blank. The sheriff and the district attorney looked at me.

I was thinking, A boy is dead. It didn't really matter whether it was Troy Frantz who ran him over or me behind the wheel. The boy was gone—that was the bottom line.

I turned to Eric Dreyfus and I said, "He actually thinks he did it." I realized how odd that sounded, so I was quick to add, "And he states unequivocally that he did it. I don't think a judge will give you any grief."

"That's your opinion?" Eric Dreyfus asked. "We can say we ran it by someone from the public defender's office and he said it was clean?"

I nodded. "But I have to tell you something," I said as he ushered me out through the squad room. "Nobody called me and told me to drive up here."

"No?"

One more lie was in order. "I was here in Hollister and got delayed—car trouble—and I wanted to call home and say where I was," I said.

I was about to step through the door when I saw two

deputies on the other side of the room walking toward us. One deputy gripped Troy Frantz's arm, Troy with his hands cuffed behind him. He was as pale in living color as he had been in black and white. I had been right: He didn't occupy much space in the world; he was short, skinny, fine-boned. He came toward me, within a yard, and he glanced my way. His eyes had no white to them; they were black dots with red edges.

He looked at me. I opened my mouth to speak. But then when he looked away, I said nothing.

After my grandfather returned wounded from fighting in the trenches of France, he retreated to Oak Valley in an act of personal isolationism and planted his vines. But he planted them right as Prohibition began, and so he could neither legally make wine nor sell it for over a decade. Which is not to say that he obeyed the law; during the dry years, he built his winery and made his first wine, experimenting with small batches in order to perfect his oenology. What wine he did covertly bottle, he stored in a grave-sized vault in the floor of the winery cellar. To reach the vault, you had to remove whatever bottles had been stored on floor-to-ceiling racks and then swing aside the racks themselves. Since I had not yet bottled a vintage, all I had to do was pull out the wooden rack. The lock was gone, but, like a window that had not been opened for years, the door to the vault was stuck, and I had to use a crowbar to pry it open. The cement tomb was musty and cold and completely empty. I had never shown it to Julia or Tim.

I had crept upstairs to the empty bedroom and the closet where I had stashed my bag of clothes, and I tiptoed my way back downstairs with it, out to the winery, here to the vault, and I dropped the evidence into the ground. I decided that in a few weeks, I would take these things someplace far away and burn them. I closed the vault and pushed the rack back against the wall and into the corner.

Back up in the garage, I wiped down my truck. I wiped away all of the mud I had accumulated that night and any previous grime that I might still be carrying around from the accident. I spent over an hour polishing the truck, paying the most attention to the front fender and the hood. I threw away all of the rags that I used; I thought about burning them. I kept an old vacuum in the garage and I used it now to clean the upholstery and the car rugs. I vacuumed the truck three times. I threw away the vacuum bag. I tried to think about what else I could do to cover my tracks, but all I really wanted to do was go to bed.

Julia startled me when I went in the house. It was five in the morning. She was sitting in the kitchen, eating her way through what was left of a chocolate cake.

"I guess nobody can sleep anymore," I said.

"The house was loud," she said.

"Loud?" I asked. "You mean creaking?" I removed two glasses from the breakfront and the milk from the fridge.

She handed me a fork. "More like crying," she said, and carved off a sizable wedge of cake. "It wouldn't shut up."

"How rude," I said.

I ate some cake and then I said, "You're not going to believe what happened." I made up some garbled tale about how I had gone to the wrong station to meet up with my drugged-up client, how he had been arrested in a different county but nobody had bothered to tell me. Then I told her about Troy Frantz and his confession.

Julia didn't look me in the eye and kept eating the cake. She was wearing one of my denim shirts, unbuttoned, and as she reached across the table for the milk carton, I could see a crescent of her breast.

"He took a deal," I said. "He figured—"

"So it's over?" Julia asked.

"A judge has to accept the plea," I said, "and make sure the man understands that he is giving up his right to a fair trial and so forth. Then it's over."

"When does that happen?" she asked.

"Tomorrow or the next day, I think."

"Good."

"Yes, I suppose it is good," I said. "Why drag on with a trial when—"

"We should go away somewhere," Julia said.

"Okay," I said.

"Somewhere warm. We need a vacation," she said.

I nodded. "I've never been so tired," I said.

"Go up to bed. I'll join you later," she said.

I followed her orders, although she never joined me. I slept out the rest of the morning and I slept away the afternoon. I would drift and wake and note the passing hour on my alarm clock and decide to get up, but then I would drift off again. I slept until four.

When finally I woke up, I was thinking about the near and distant future. Julia and I would run through the paces of our daily rounds, and meanwhile, our wonder son would grow up in front of us here on the vineyard, as would his younger brother. We would continue to wait out seasons of rain and each spring our vines would flower. Each fall we would pick the fruit and crush it and treat the juice and barrel it. Maybe we would plant other acres of new vines and eventually blend the pickings from our various plots to make an ever-richer and more layered wine. We would age that wine and bottle it and perhaps sell it, a robust ruby cabernet, which would become a prestige vintage. It would taste like the shade of an oak tree. People everywhere would crave it, ask for more, never get enough. The harvests would pass, the leaves fly by, and I could imagine that down the road I might give up my law practice and make wine full-time. Maybe Julia would teach somewhere. Maybe we would divide our lives between the city and the country to accommodate her schedule. Sooner than later Tim would leave the old stone house and venture out into the world, but I expected that we would always know a close friendship and that he would call and visit us often. Eventually the younger boy would travel away from us, as well. And Julia and I would have each other. And we would grow old together. That was the simple future that I imagined for myself, and that afternoon, it seemed possible, even inevitable.

I would let another man be punished for what I had done. So be it. I didn't expect to forget about Craig easily, what it felt like to feel his life slip away from him—how could I? But I would have to forget about him eventually. If I wanted to get on with my life, hard as that sounded, I would have to forget about this boy. I would have to forget, and so by the first anniversary of the accident, I would have already begun to rewrite that cold October night in my mind so that I might believe that Troy Frantz was in truth serving out a punishment for a spree of crimes, every one of which he had indeed committed. If I hadn't convinced myself of this in a year's time, I would persuade myself by the following harvest. As the years went by, everything that had truly happened in the woods would be forgotten.

And I look back and I have to ask, What if my story ended here?

The wrong man goes to jail. Fin, fade to black, the end.

Why not? Other men let the wrong men pay for their misdeeds; it happened all the time. One man went to prison while another man, the real villain, the true criminal, remained free. It happened all the time, and so why should my life have been any different? Why didn't my story end here?

Tim knocked on the door. "You said we would go for a drive today," he said.

I yawned. "Where's your mother?" I asked him.

"Out. Doing something in the winery," he said. "I don't know."

I wondered if Julia had told Tim about the child on the way. No, he would have mentioned it.

"You said if it stopped raining, you would let me drive," Tim said. He would not get his learner's permit for more than a year, but we had already taken the occasional spin together, with him behind the wheel and me gripping the dash with both hands.

It was a blustery dusk, and even though Tim followed the curves of the mountain road with extreme caution, the wind pushed us from behind, so that I kept telling him to slow down. I had started us off at a point that I thought was far enough away from the site of the accident so that we wouldn't pass it, but we ended up driving farther north than I intended, and when I told Tim to pull over, he groaned.

"One more mile," I said. "Then we go home."

We rounded a cliff and headed into the forest, and I braced myself—I decided not to point out the scene to Tim, and I hoped that he wouldn't notice the police tape—but before we reached the jagged birch trunk, I happened to glance away from the road and into the woods, and when I did, I saw a brown creature moving amid the black pine. An animal of some kind. An animal in distress. I needed a closer look.

"Pull over," I said.

"Dad, you said—"

"Tim, stop," I said.

He veered off to the side of the road. He killed the engine.

"Stay here," I said. I hopped out of the truck and jogged back toward the animal.

"Dad?" Tim chased after me. "Dad?"

I reached the animal. Tim came up behind me and I pulled him close to me so that he wouldn't frighten it. It was a young deer. One of its hind legs was badly wounded, twisted and maimed. It didn't even seem to notice us as it staggered a yard and then collapsed with a muted bray. It managed to stand up and hobble another yard.

"Oh shit," Tim said.

I gripped his arm. I could see that the deer's coat was matted with blood and pine needles, and its belly was thin, its haunches protruding, bony. It would die soon, a slow and wicked death.

"You should shoot it," Tim said. "Put it out of its misery."

But I didn't have a gun with me—I didn't own a gun.

"You have to do something, Dad."

Here it was, Troy Frantz's true victim. His exculpatory deer. It stumbled a few yards deeper into the woods, holding itself up against a pine and finally looking back at us, its eyes wide with fear. It couldn't run away.

"You have to do something," Tim said. He became frantic. "Do something, Dad. You have to."

"Do what? What can I do?" I asked.

Tim started combing the ground, searching for something—what?

"What can I do?" I asked again.

He shuffled around until he picked something up by the side of the highway. He ran back to me and handed me a large flat stone.

"You can't be serious," I said, although I took the stone from him.

Tim was white. He looked scared. "You can't leave it like that," he said.

"I'll screw it up and won't really kill it. I'll just make it worse," I said.

Tim pushed me toward the deer. "You have to," he said.

"Okay," I said, "okay. But you go back to the truck."

He walked away. I waited until I heard him slam the truck door.

I followed the deer. It shuffled another yard and fell down. I stood behind it, the heavy gray stone in my right hand. The deer did not glance back at me. It picked itself up and brayed its weak lament. I raised the stone above my head. I aimed my pitch at the head of the wounded animal. Then the deer looked at me. Brown eyes going black.

And I hurled the stone beyond the deer, at the trunk of a pine tree, and I ran back to the road.

The trees lost their leaves. The ground hardened. The sky paled, but the wind that winter remained mild, without the usual bone chill, even humid on certain days. It did rain, but with less frequency and with less confidence. We saw mist and spit but few gusting storms. No one was talking about another drought just yet or about how a low rainfall might adversely affect the clay, but a definite uneasiness settled over the valley. Witness the terseness with which people greeted one another outside the hardware store or when they drove past one another on the main drag or the way everyone would stare at the sky when it drizzled, the way everyone would squint with obvious suspicion at the white dull-edged sun peeking between the clouds, a sun that seemed to be up to something, planning some mean trick, an indifferent tax that it would levy sooner or later—but when exactly, when?

The warm weather made me anxious, too, and when I pruned back my vines, I often wore only a rugby shirt and a sweatshirt, and I would end up taking off my sweatshirt. At night I would carry logs inside for a fire, but it seemed like a waste to burn wood when I didn't even have the heat turned up, and so I tried not to light a fire until I absolutely craved one, and then I would have to open windows in order to justify it. The weather was strange, but all in all, my life on the vineyard appeared to run according to a routine schedule and a calendar that had become familiar.

That January there was a minor problem with our wine.

Early into the new year, Julia and I inserted a thief into the bungholes of all of the barrels in my winery and withdrew samples from both my first and second vintages. We set up a makeshift lab in my kitchen with the kits that we had purchased at the hardware store. We needed to make sure that there would be no further yeast fermentation or bacterial activity once the wine was in the bottles, and the first vintage, as it had in the past, tested well. According to a text we consulted, the acid content was perfect for cabernet. But when we tested the samples from our more recent vintage, the wine that we had barreled only months ago, we discovered a high amount of malic acid in several, but not all, of the batches. The malic acid should have turned into lactic acid during the secondary fermentation; that was the desired chemistry. The acidity of the newer wine was too high, and we needed to add some cultured bacteria to convert the malic into lactic acid, to lower the overall acidity, in effect. And that was no simple task. Practically speaking, this meant dropping in a specified amount of bacteria through the bunghole, fine, but the issue was how much to mix in.

I wanted to check the Dark Oak Wines logs and rely on that record as a guide. Julia insisted we ask the folks in the hardware store and do what they said. Emma Hodges, not a winemaker herself but a certified know-it-all, told us that we needed two cups of one type of bacteria per barrel, which she promised would make the cabernet nice and buttery, but Alex Marquez—this was when he was still speaking to me—said that acidity itself was not a bad thing and that our only goal should be to stabilize the microbiology of the wine by adding only one cup of another kind of bacteria per barrel; he said that we did not want our wine to get too milky. Then he said we would need to mix in some sulfates to kill the bacteria that we added, and Emma Hodges argued that sulfates made red wine too bitter. We ended up more confused than ever and Julia decided to contact the oenologists at the agriculture school up at UC Davis, but whatever information they gave us proved even more befuddling.

All the while, the wine was sitting in the barrels unattended, and so one afternoon I finally decided to mix in some of the bacteria that we had used before, a small amount, the amount prescribed by my forebears. I went down to the winery while Julia was out, and when she came home and found me, she was furious.

She said, "So it's your wine now. You just do what you want to it."

"No," I said, "I just didn't want to let—"

"It used to be our wine," she said, and, of course, she was right. I shouldn't have gone ahead and decided on a recipe without her. "I thought that we were making the wine together," she said. She folded her arms across her chest, which accentuated the swell of her abdomen, otherwise barely detectable, given the loose sweaters she always wore. She said, "Well, do what you want," and retreated toward the house.

"It's still our wine," I called after her.

I had only treated two of the problematic barrels, and I was all set to finish the chore, but then I suffered a head rush of doubt. Like great chefs, winemakers require a certain flash of arrogance to do what they do well, but my spat with Julia made me not trust myself. With the next barrel, I decided to follow the wisdom of the Davis oenologists, which was what Julia had wanted to do in the end. I told her when I went in the house.

"And we'll wait a week and then test the wine again and see who has more malic acid, you or me," I said.

"Oh, I get it," Julia said. "This is a competition."

"No," I said, "it's not a competition—"

"It doesn't matter," Julia said, and left the kitchen.

"What do you want me to do with the last barrel?" I asked.

"It doesn't matter," Julia said, her voice fading as she went upstairs.

So I went back to the winery and finished the chore.

Later, that night, Julia made a point of leaving whatever room I entered, but we eventually had to end up in the same bedroom, in the same bed.

I tried to apologize. I said, "I shouldn't have gone ahead and—"

Julia cut me off with a snort. "Got that right," she said. Even in her nightshirt, it was difficult to see her stomach.

"I'm trying to say I'm sorry," I said.

Julia shrugged. "It's your wine now," she said.

"Great," I said. "I'll take the blame when it wins all the prizes."

"See you in three years," Julia said.

Moments later, in the darkness, with my head under my pillow, I sighed so deeply that Julia couldn't ignore me. She reached her arms around my waist and let one hand roam up my chest. She kissed my back, and I heard her say that she was sorry. At that point, I should have turned around and taken her in my arms, but I suppose that I felt I had been wounded twice, and I didn't respond to Julia's belated gesture. We fell asleep and didn't talk about the wine the next day.

We never did go on the vacation that Julia had said she wanted to take back in October—I don't recall why; I think we were simply too busy leading our day-to-day lives to plan one—but I doubt that any pleasant respite somewhere warm would have made a difference. I don't know when it started, but Julia and I lapsed into an all-too-familiar weather pattern that winter, flashes of heat followed by fronts of cold air, and I think that this constant back-and-forth cracked our new masonry. I don't want to go into all of the other fights except to say that they became increasingly trivial, and that rather than grind through a difficult discussion about, say, whether we needed new curtains in the bedroom, one of us, Julia more often than not, escaped the argument and the room by pretending to give in and not care. At some point, we began to spend our evenings on different floors of the house, usually with me downstairs, back in the study, trying to ignore the noise that Julia made up in our bedroom. I believed that this was a phase and that it would pass.

I should have realized that our visible discord would have had an effect on Tim, but I didn't stop to think about it. During this time—in fact, I would say that this behavior started soon after Craig Montoya's funeral—Tim began to withdraw from both Julia and me, and he spent even more time up in his room. He didn't try out for the play that fall. He didn't seem to have any friends beyond his on-line acquaintances, and despite my complaints about the phone bill, he was spending still more time on-line, so much so that Julia and I got him his own line to free up our phone at night.

I just thought that Tim was being a typical teenager, now affectionate, now sullen; his meteorology was cryptic and unpredictable. He started cloaking himself in all black—a black T-shirt and black jeans and black boots—but so what? I had worn the same uniform at his age. Often when I asked him a question—for instance, I remember trying to engage him in a discussion about the troubling malolactic chemistry—he would answer me with blank stares and shrugs. His pose in the door frame: Do I really need to sit down with you and talk about this? I guess that I thought that as long as Tim didn't feel compelled to rebel against his mother and me with excessive drink or serious drugs, we would all survive his middle adolescence. This, too, was a phase that would pass.

And so it was not the best winter for us, and yet it was hardly the worst. When I was down, I dreamed about the spring. I pictured the buds on the vines, the flowers, the berries. Then it would be summer and we would have a new child, another wondrous child, and then autumn before we knew it, and we would harvest the next crop and make our next vintage; by then, the trouble of the winter would be forgotten. We were going to have a great year.

Late one night early in February when Julia and I were making our way to bed, she became dizzy and sat down on the closed toilet in the bathroom. She squinted at me and

issued the softest moan. She turned as white as the tiled
walls. She stood up, and as she rose, a cascade of water
poured down between her legs. Her nightshirt clung to her
thighs. The suddenness, the force of her water breaking,
threw her back, except she didn't land on the toilet; she
ended up on the floor, sitting in the spill from her womb. She
whispered my name and rested her head back against the
tiles beneath the sink, and she passed out.

I bolted over to her, my mind reeling with the math of her
pregnancy. How many months were left, how many had
gone by? Six months had gone by, only six months.

I panicked. I didn't know what to do.

"Tim," I yelled. "Tim, wake up."

I lifted Julia up and carried her to the bed and covered her
with a blanket—she was so pale that I could see every vein
in her body—and I grabbed a pair of trousers, but then I realized I needed to call an ambulance—no, I needed to get Julia
into a robe because she was shivering. I noticed blood on the
blanket between her legs. An ambulance, I should have
called for an ambulance right away.

"Tim," I screamed.

"What?" Tim said—he was still dressed, he hadn't gone
to bed—and then he screamed, "Mom." He immediately
began to cry.

"Ambulance," I blurted.

Julia blinked herself awake, and in a weak voice she said,
"Drive me."

Tim was holding the phone by the bed.

Julia glanced at him and then at me and said, "Isn't time.
Drive me."

"We'll wait for the—"

"Can't," she said.

"Dad," Tim screamed. He was as pale as Julia. He ran
down to the bathroom at the end of the hall. I heard him
retching.

"Can't," Julia said.

In the end, I don't know whether it mattered. It would

have taken an ambulance at least a half hour to reach us, probably more like an hour. And it was raining, of course. All winter so far, we had seen little rain, but that night, it had to pour. It had to squall. The rain pelted the bedroom windows at a sharp angle.

I threw on a shirt and found shoes and wrapped Julia in the blankets from the bed, and Tim came back into the room and helped me carry his mother downstairs. She seemed weightless. We didn't stop for coats and we charged outside through the cold downpour to the garage. Tim slipped into the backseat of my truck and I lay Julia down across the seat, with her head in his lap. Blood seeped through the blankets. Tim was sobbing.

As I headed down the vineyard road, I noticed that I had left the front door to our house wide open. I raced past our plot of vines and across the gulch and then north on the main drag, up another road, up to the mountain highway.

"Talk to me, sweetie," I said, reaching back to hold Julia's hand. I couldn't hold her hand long because I needed both hands to drive.

She was unconscious.

"Dad," Tim said, and winced.

"Keep her warm," I said. "Okay? That's your job. You keep her warm. Make her talk to you."

"Mom?" Tim asked. "Hey, Mom? Mommy?"

The patch of blood around her legs had darkened and widened, and I drove as fast as I could through the rain. But the road was slippery. I hit a slick streak as I pushed through the woods, and the truck swerved, and I lost control and steered off the road, nearly into a tree and into a rut of mud. The skidding threw Julia forward, against the front seats. Tim grabbed hold of her and eased her back onto his lap.

"Mom," he said. "Talk to me, Mom."

I tried to drive us out of the ditch, but the tires were spinning. We were trapped. I had to shift into neutral and get out and try to push the heavy truck forward and then get back behind the wheel and try to drive forward, and still the tires spun and whirred, and the right rear of the truck seemed to sink deeper into the mud.

"She's bleeding bad, Dad," Tim said.

I didn't know whether he should help me with the mud or hold his mother. "Keep her warm," I said. .

I hopped out of the truck again, and I was soaked and soon covered with mud and I threw all of my weight against the hood and pushed the truck backward instead of forward; behind the wheel again, I slammed into reverse. No luck. I got out and pushed the hood again. I tried reversing out of the ditch. The tires spun, but with more noise, with more friction. On the fifth try, it worked.

Back on the road, I headed north for Hollister, but I had to drive slower than I wanted to because I was afraid of wiping out again and Julia was cold and bleeding, and I thought, This is it, this is it, this is it, I'm going to lose her. Please, no, I can't lose her.

I noticed that Tim was shivering, too. "Tim? Timmy?"

He didn't answer me and his lips were so blue that I realized he was going into shock. This fucking road would kill us all.

I made it the hospital, where emergency room attendants ran out to my honking car and took over. Nurses took Julia away on a stretcher. Another attendant wrapped Tim in a blanket and ushered him away, too.

I was alone in the waiting room. A nurse brought me a blanket and a mug of hot chocolate. She gave me updates. The child, a boy, was born dead. Julia's hemorrhaging was under control, but she had lost a great deal of blood. Tim would be fine, but he had lapsed into shock, as I had thought he had—from fear, from the cold—and he had been given a mild sedative and a bed to rest in.

When I finally saw Julia, she was lost amid the tubes and machinery of the recovery room, and she was too drugged up to do anything more than blink my way. Tim was lying on a cot in a dark room next to her room, but his eyes were open. I told him what had happened and that he had been brave, but I didn't think that he heard me.

Julia stayed in the hospital for a week. I spent much of each day with her, reading aloud to her from the paper or from a novel she had requested, but she didn't appear to be listening. She brightened up a bit when I brought Tim, but after two visits, he asked me if he could stay home; the sight of his mother, even as her complexion pinked up a bit, made him nauseous. So I saw Julia alone, and during most of my visit, she would gaze absently out the window at the hills beyond the hospital.

A few days after I had brought her home, I had to ask her, "Are you mad at me?"

I asked because I thought that there was a dullness to her glance when she looked at me as if I were—what?—ugly to her now. A monster who had done this to her, ripped our new child from her. As if I were to blame because I had trapped her here in the middle of nowhere.

"Not everything is about you," she said.

"I know, I just—"

"Try not to be so self-absorbed," she said.

"Is that it? Am I being self-absorbed?" I asked, I begged. How should I be?

Julia glared at me. "We should wait a while before we talk about any of this," she said.

"Okay. Right," I said. "What you need now is rest and relaxation."

"Did you know that you have this tendency to talk in clichés when you really have no idea what to say?" she asked.

Now I was afraid to speak at all.

"I'm sorry, Jason," she said. "We'll get through this," and that sounded to me like the great lie of our life together. We can get through anything. But I tried to believe her. I needed to believe that what she said was true.

In a few weeks, it was time to bottle our first vintage. Julia was not supposed to move around too much, which I knew disappointed her, because she had looked forward to the first bottling. She did what she could, and Tim surprised me by offering to come down from his cell and help out.

On the first morning of his winter vacation, we separated several dozen eggs, discarding the yolks. Down at the bottom of the winery, we emptied all of the barrels from the vintage into the fining tank, blending the various batches. I climbed a ladder and dropped the egg whites into the vat—three whites per barrel was what my grandfather's recipe called for—and then I had to stir the wine with the long paddle and stir it fast, because the egg whites did not carry their positive charge for too long; that charge was what attracted all of the stray unwanted particles of sediment to the bottom of the tank.

We let the wine sit on the finings for a day, and then I ran a hose down to the next level of the winery to begin the slow process of siphoning the wine into the bottles. I worked the hose carefully so as not to spill any wine, and Tim carried the finished bottles, four at a time, over to a table where Julia, seated on a stool, inserted the bottle first beneath a corking machine and then a press that applied the capsule; this much she could do without too much strain, although the process seemed to take a lot out of her. Tim carried the finished bottles over to the racks built into the wall, then scrambled back to me to retrieve the bottles that I had filled.

We fell into a simple rhythm, Julia and Tim and I, and we worked silently all day and for most of the day after that. We became increasingly efficient and faster, filling the slender green bottles with cabernet and corking them and racking them, one after another, achieving a kind of fevered harmony. I thought that this was perhaps just the distraction that we needed, that this straightforward task would do wonders to mend our wounds, and when we were done with the bottling, I held Julia on one side of me, and Tim stood on the other side of me, and we stared at the wall of bottled wine, our wine. I knew that my smile was goofy and broad because some sort of order seemed restored. We had been tested, the three of us, but we had survived. Now we would return to the good life we had been living. It would take time, but we were strong and we would get past this loss.

This was what I kept telling myself. We were strong. We would move forward.

but I found that I wasn't strong; I couldn't move forward. I couldn't move forward because I couldn't seem to put the accident on the mountain road behind me. I didn't expect to forget about it right away, no, but the opposite proved true: The more time passed, the more frequently I had to wake up in the middle of the night to stop myself from skidding into that boy one more time.

And I didn't need to be asleep to drift back to that October night. In the middle of dinner, I would look at Tim and inevitably think about Craig Montoya letting go of his last breath. I would be drafting a contract, staring at my computer screen in my office, absorbed in my work, and somehow my mind would drift, and I would ask myself, What would a kid like Craig Montoya be doing this February, this March? He would have been accepted early at Stanford, and I pictured him taking it easy and cutting classes to drive his girlfriend to the beach. I pictured him wandering the coast in search of a deserted cove where he could make love with her on the sand. Or I saw him at school, in class, the kid the teacher called on. The kid with something to prove. I saw him eating his lunch off a tray at a long table in the cafeteria, the center of a group, everyone wanting to hang out with him, be near him, know him because he was the guy to know. I tried not to think about him, and days went by when I didn't, but then I would be lying in bed or cooking dinner or watching the news on television, and I would picture Craig Montoya alone on a playing field, a great green field with the mountains in the background. I'd see Craig in knee-high black socks and black shorts and an oversized striped shirt. The boy I killed kicking a ball across the grass. The ball soaring. The ball crossing under the white frame of the goalpost. And then these visions always ended in the same way. With rain. With me on the mountain road. Spotting the body on the road. Seeing his knee bent at an impossible angle.

"Earth to Dad," Tim once said. We were eating breakfast. "Earth to Dad," he said.

"Oh. Sorry," I said.

"You look like a vampire," he said.

I swallowed some coffee, and I grinned or I winked or gave him some sign of life. But I looked at my son, at the blush in his cheeks, and it didn't seem fair to me that while he sat across from me and read the comics, there was an empty chair at the Montoya table. There were times when I thought perhaps my punishment for taking Craig's life was Julia's miscarriage—tit for tat, a life for a life—but that was foolish reasoning, I know, and I am frankly embarrassed to admit that I even entertained that kind of notion, a bartering of fates. No, the fact was that my life rolled on, but the Montoyas' lives, I imagined, had stopped that morning when the police knocked on the door. Their lives fell apart. I knew that to be the case; I wasn't just speculating. Sometime that winter, Mr. Montoya left his wife and daughter, and meanwhile, Mrs. Montoya was perpetually ill with a flu or arthritis; her daughter was taking care of her and missing a lot of school.

I wanted to do something for Mrs. Montoya and her daughter, although I didn't know what, and the only good deed that came to mind was to send money anonymously. Which would have helped, sure, but what I really wanted was to express my deep regret, and my regret had no tangible value. I went so far as to drive to the Montoya home at the southern end of the valley, in the flats, where many of the people who used to work on the vineyards and who now worked at the quarries lived on a hill-less grid of barren streets. The houses were small and made smaller by how far apart they were spaced. They didn't have lawns, just plots of dirt and brush. There were no trees. A few had satellite dishes out front. I drove up to the Montoya home at the end of one of these streets one day at dusk, a white house that had yellowed with neglect, a house with missing shingles and a raw wooden beam supporting one side of the front porch. Chains for a swing dangled in the wet breeze. But what could I possibly say to make a difference? Even the truth seemed too absurd now, however sad and simple it was, and the truth would not bring back Craig. The truth would probably not bring back Mr. Montoya either. I drove off without coming to a stop.

That was in March, and I think that it was around this time that my role in the town began to change. Or I should say that it was around this time that I noticed a change that had probably begun earlier in the year without my realizing it.

First of all, my involvement in the Troy Frantz plea bargaining, however tangential and technically anonymous it was, had become known. The sentiment at the hardware store was that Troy Frantz should have received a sentence of life in prison without the possibility of parole—or even better, death—and that I had somehow intervened on his behalf, me with my big-city-liberal heart, and that I had saved him by arranging for his lesser punishment. Which of course was not the case, since the deal had been brokered before I stumbled along, and I couldn't be sure, but I suspected that our narrowly reelected district attorney had said something to someone about my being at the sheriff's station the night of the confession; or it could have been Harry Padillo who exaggerated my role. It didn't really matter.

"He should have fried," Will Clark said.

"They don't fry them, they gas them," Emma Hodges said.

"They don't gas them, they shoot them up," Alex Marquez said.

"You should have let him fry," Will Clark said to me.

"Actually I didn't have anything to do with it," I said, and tried to explain the extent of my nonrepresentation. No one seemed to hear me.

Meanwhile, rumors would surface about Troy Frantz and just how evil he was.

Emma Hodges: "He left a wife and child starving back in Eureka, while he went off to Hollywood to make sleazy horror films."

Will Clark: "You know he was running dope into the New Idria high school."

Alex Marquez: "He once kidnapped a boy in L.A.—no, listen, it's true. Took him into the woods, kept him there, but something got screwed up with the prosecution, so he never went to jail. And he was trying to do the same with the Montoya boy. Maybe the kid was luckier to have just gotten run over."

The truth of the matter was that none of us knew anything about Troy Frantz, who, without the forum of a public trial, had denied himself his only chance at recrimination. Troy Frantz remained an enigma. I tried not to think about him, and I had more success at removing him from my mind than I did with Craig Montoya.

Regardless of my connection to Troy Frantz, such that it was, I also fell into disfavor in the town for another reason. It had to do with my legal work.

On the same day at the end of March, an hour apart, two clients showed up at my office unannounced. In the last two or three months, while many of the vintners back in the game had pruned back the first year's growth of their new vines, while some even made wine with grapes purchased from coastal growers, the Oak Valley quarriers had begun buying up parcels of land with a new fury, paying whatever they needed to pay to get the slopes they wanted, which was not much. And they were starting to move in on my clients' resuscitated vineyards, the ones that I had rescued from bankruptcy.

What I had done for these two clients who came in to see me—and I am simplifying matters—was help them form new businesses that in effect became partial creditors awaiting debt repayment from their old, failed enterprises; the way that was done was by paying off some of the old creditors, not with cash but with shares in the newly incorporated concerns. Which I know sounds completely illegal, buying your own debt without repaying it exactly, but it was legal, and bankruptcy trustees approved of the maneuver. There were loopholes; there were ways of circumventing the legal order of things; I did not invent this practice, nor did I apparently grasp it. Quite frankly I just did not understand the arcane laws of the state with real fluency, I never had, and what I had not anticipated was what began to happen: First of all, the creditors who had not received offers in the new vineyards sued; and second, the creditors who had taken the bait started to sell off their shares in the new businesses to the quarries. Which I had thought that I had safeguarded against with certain contractual language, but which I had somehow not done at all. More loopholes. So the quarries were grabbing control of the vineyards when they wouldn't have had access to the land if I hadn't intervened in the first place and played with the firmer protections already in place. I had made my clients vulnerable.

They were not happy, and the only reason that the two stopped by that day was to collect their files to take to another attorney. Then there was general panic among my other clients in similar situations, and in two cases, the vintners caved in before the summer and sold all of their land directly to the quarriers.

My clients started leaving me. I began to have trouble finding new clients. I wasn't earning as much money from my practice as I needed to bring in. Another phase—this had to be a phase, I kept telling myself. Eventually I would recover my good standing. I had to be patient and I had to work hard. I would recover.

One client who felt betrayed was Alex Marquez. I overheard him talking to Will Clark in the hardware store. I didn't think that they had seen me come in and wander down the aisle of lamps and electrical supplies, but maybe they were just pretending not to have noticed me.

Alex Marquez said, "He's no better than his father, if you ask me. His father told us all to expand. His father told us to buy land, to plant more vines, to bottle more wine, and we did. He told us to go the bank and take out loans if we had to, and we did. Show the folks up in Napa-Sonoma, he said, show them we can make better wine and more of it. And then look who was still standing after the drought, them or us? Not us. I'll tell you that. Not us."

Will Clark said something I didn't hear.

"Tell me how he's any different," Alex Marquez said. "Leading us all down the dirt road to doom."

I heard him say this—it stung—and I left the store without buying anything.

•

In April we racked the second vintage, transferring the wine to fresh barrels, including the ones that we had treated with the different cultures back in January. We had checked these barrels along with all of the others in subsequent weeks and found nothing to worry about. The acid content was average, the sugar spent, the wine, we thought, stabilized. But when we began to rack one of the problem barrels, we had to pinch our noses. Instead of the woody and caramel scent with a trace of cider that we expected, we smelled a rank and acrid fume, and when I inserted a pipette into this barrel and released just a single drop of the wine on my tongue, I had to grab at my thermos of sweetened tea and then the muffin that I had been eating—at anything—to get rid of the bitter taste. The wine had fallen prey to the vinegar bacteria.

"How?" I asked Julia. "A month ago, everything checked out fine. How did it turn?"

We checked the other problem barrels, and another one had gone bad, but two of them were okay. We had lost two barrels to the acetic fermentation, one hundred and twenty gallons. We were fairly certain that the majority of barrels were fine, although now their ongoing chemistry became suspect and we realized that we would have to worry about the entire vintage until we bottled it the following winter. I should have just spilled the bad wine out, but I couldn't bring myself to do it, so I racked the ruined barrels anyway, and set them aside from the others in the vintage.

As I say, two of the problem barrels had not spoiled, and when Julia wondered why that night, I had to tell her.

"The barrels that I treated according to my recipe," I explained, "were the ones with the vinegar."

"And the ones that didn't turn?" Julia asked, knowing, I was sure, what my answer would be.

"I added the amount you were leaning toward. Your recipe," I said.

Julia said nothing.

"So you win," I said.

"I win," she said. "Swell. What's the prize?"

We were lying in bed, and when I crept closer to her, Julia turned away from me. I caressed her shoulder, her hip, and she shrugged me away. When I woke up in the morning, I didn't find her next to me. Her pillows were missing. I found her in one of the unfurnished bedrooms on the spare futon on the floor, a quilt pulled over her head.

Soon this became a habit: Julia went to sleep next to me but ended up in a bedroom down the hall before dawn.

"You're having trouble sleeping," I said one morning.

"I never sleep well in the spring," Julia said, which was news to me. "And you know, you're like a ship in a storm," she added.

"I'm like a what?"

"Tossing, turning. It's a wonder you don't capsize," she said.

Soon Julia began napping in the afternoon, and when I went to bed, she remained awake, mostly watching television in the study. Actually I had no idea what she was doing all day or while I was in bed; I never saw her. Eventually she gave up on our bed entirely. We were making love about once every ten days, and then not at all.

I knew where we were headed. I couldn't deny it. We'd

been down this hill before, and I didn't know how to slow us down. I rehearsed conversations in my head. I said, Julia, please, I don't want this—we don't want this. But whenever I was around her, my heartbeat quickened and I couldn't remember my lines, my scripted truce, so I said nothing at all. I said nothing, and we fell faster.

One night, one morning around three, I got up to use the bathroom and heard some noises downstairs, what I thought was crying. But echoes have a way of changing shape in a stone house. A creak in a joist becomes a very human moan. A brush of a branch against the eaves becomes a plate breaking in the kitchen. I went downstairs and discovered that the crying I heard was actually Julia making a fire. It had been a cold spring, so a fire in late April was not all that extraordinary, but at three in the morning, I found it a little odd. She must have gone out to the woodpile behind the garage for logs, because we had used up whatever supply we had carried into the house. The wood was wet, it was hissing.

"We have to talk," I said.

And I immediately regretted saying anything at all, because what Julia said in response was, "I should tell you that I'm not interested in trying again now."

"Just like that, you decide," I said.

"Not just like that," she said. "Obviously not just like that."·

"Okay," I said. "So you don't want to try again, when, anytime soon?"

Julia didn't answer me.

"Ever?" I asked.

"The thing is, Jason, I never really wanted another child. You knew that."

"I did? We talked about it," I said.

"You talked about it," Julia said. "I said that I could go through life without another child, and you said you wanted another. Tim is great. He's enough for me."

"He is a great kid, I agree, but that's not the point," I said.

"We never figured it out," Julia said.

"We should talk about this later," I said. "Obviously, I'm tired, and you're—"

"I'm what?" Julia asked.

The wet logs were turning black but not really burning.

"I'm what?" she asked.

I couldn't remember what I was going to say. I kissed her on the cheek and went back to bed.

A few days later, there was a frost, which I hadn't seen coming. I had enjoyed a rare night of decent sleep, of tossing and turning, but sleep just the same, and when I woke up around six, I looked out at the glazed lawn and hillside, the crystalline slope. I pulled on a pair of jeans and bolted downstairs and ran out shirtless into the cold field.

For some reason, the frost had not spread up to the higher level of the property, and my grapevines had survived the night unharmed. The vines were in full flower, but I didn't lose a single one. I could have lost the entire crop, but I had been lucky. And yet, somehow I did not see myself as lucky.

When I had woken up, Julia was nowhere to be found, and I assumed that she was sleeping down the hall. She startled me, then, when she sat up on the window seat in the living room as I came inside.

"There was a frost," I said.

"I know," she said. She was wrapped in a blanket. "I was up last night. I saw the temperature drop."

"You did?" Both of my fists clenched, almost a reflex. "You should have woken me up," I said. "I would have set up the smudge pots."

"How are the vines?"

"They're fine," I said. "It's a miracle, but they're all fine."

"So?" Julia asked. She let her blanket fall away from her. She was dressed, wearing a sweater and dark jeans.

"So," I echoed.

"Why are you so angry?"

"That's not the point," I said. "The point is that you knew how cold it was and you should have woken me up."

"Great," Julia said. "But the vines are okay, right?"

· "You don't understand at all," I shouted. I heard a door upstairs creak open.

"I understand perfectly. You're upset because the vines weren't ruined," she said.

I looked at her, and at that moment, I believed that she did not know me very well. Or maybe she knew me too well.

"I'm going away," Julia said.

Wait. This wasn't fair. She was raising the stakes.

"Look, I'm sorry," I said. "I shouldn't have yelled."

"For a month or so," Julia said.

"Don't," I said. "Please, don't."

"Back to the city."

"Please," I said.

"I need to get back to work," she said. "I need to be closer to the library—"

"And Tim?"

"Tim should stay here," she said, "and finish out his school year."

At that, I heard a door slam upstairs.

"Julia," I said, I pleaded. Slow down, let's talk. We can talk this out, can't we?

She had lost weight. Her sweater fell off her shoulder and revealed a thin bone.

"And you're right," she said.

"About what?" I asked.

"I should have checked the thermometer and woken you up, and I did think that we would have a frost. In fact, I knew we would. But you see . . ."

"What?" I couldn't look at her. I stared at the parallel grooves of the floorboards.

"I wanted the whole damned valley to freeze," she said.

I didn't know what to say. Nothing I could say would keep her here with me.

Later in the morning, she had a talk with Tim, and Tim didn't leave his room for the rest of the day. Julia packed some luggage and was gone by dusk. She promised to call me from San Francisco with a number where she could be reached, and when she did call the next day, I thought that she was lying. She sounded so far away, as if she had traveled to another continent, that I thought she had given me a bogus number.

After I hung up, I called her right back to test it, and when she answered and I didn't speak for a minute, Julia finally said, "I'm sorry, Jason. I am sorrier than you know."

Tim spent all of his time at home up his room. I could hear him tapping at his computer. I knew that he spoke to his mother every day, but he took the calls upstairs and I didn't eavesdrop. Julia and I spoke once every three days— we only chatted about Tim—and then once a week. Meanwhile, I tried to draw Tim out about whatever I could whenever we did spend time together.

Over breakfast, for instance, he was spreading jam across a piece of toast, and I asked him, "Did you hit any cool Web sites last night?" I felt like I was speaking textbook French to a native Frenchman and was a little embarrassed.

Tim didn't answer me at first, but then he said, "No."

"No? So, what? Did you talk to your friends on-line?" I asked.

"I played Homer all night," he said.

"Homer," I said.

And then Tim actually looked at me and talked to me, and I didn't really know what he was talking about, not specifically—he was describing the interactive computer game that was all the rage among his set at school—but I was thrilled to see him this animated.

"And did you win?" I asked.

"It's not something you win," Tim said. "You find clues."

"Clues," I said.

"Basically you're trying to get home," he explained.

"And did you get home?"

He issued a single ha. "Only, like, one person has ever made it," he said.

"Well, that's troubling," I said.

"The game is really new," he explained.

And then that was it. I didn't know what else to ask, and Tim turned toward his toast again, and in a blink, he was gone, off to school.

His math teacher called me one day to warn me that he was failing the semester.

"But you're so good in math," I said to him that night at dinner.

Tim shrugged.

"I know it's been hard with your mother gone," I said, "but she—"

"You know she's not coming back," he said. "You know that, right?"

I took a deep breath. "She told you that," I said.

"Can I move to Los Angeles?"

"Can you what?"

"I didn't think so," Tim said. He left the table.

"Wait, I'm not finished with you," I said, but he pounded up the stairs and that was it; he was gone for the evening, gone but for a glimpse at breakfast the next day.

Had Julia really told him that she wasn't coming back? I decided not to believe this. I decided that it couldn't be true. She would be back in a month, two at the most. She needed time alone, that was all, and meanwhile I would stay aloft in a holding pattern. Meanwhile I had other things to worry about, like money.

I could still pay my bills, but barely. Most of my clients had deserted me and I wasn't picking up cases from the public defender. Something else that I hadn't realized was that I had lost the esteem of my friend and contact at Legal Aid. She, too, had frowned upon my conversation with the district attorney on that evening back in October; she had sent me a terse memo, a reprimand for acting beyond my authority. She had continued to send me freelance work during the winter, but the assignments had petered out by the spring, and I had to wonder if there was any connection to my bankruptcy blunders. I was not getting any work when I needed it most. I needed to cut costs, and although the rent was cheap, I gave up my office in town. No one came by to try to stop me; no one even seemed to notice me loading boxes of files and books and furniture into my truck. I turned my study at home into an office.

Actually it worked out well, being able to look over a contract and then go out to the vines and then come back in to make calls and so forth, although I think that Tim wasn't keen on having me around so much. Against my protests, he began eating his dinner up in his room, and I ate mine at my desk and pretended to work, but I often ended up solving crosswords. At night I lay in bed and made calculations about how much I might earn from the bottled wine, if I could actually sell it, and I figured out just what I needed to bring in from my legal work to stay afloat. But Tim would need a car next year, and I didn't want him driving any old jalopy. And then before I knew it, there would be his college tuition to pay. Money was tight, and thinking about it gave me insomnia, and one morning in early June, I saw a doctor in New Idria who prescribed some sleeping pills. They worked, but I felt drowsy or not quite with it for much of the next day. Nevertheless, I took a pill each night to get some rest.

One night when one of these pills was beginning to kick in, Julia called.

"I'd like it if Tim could spend the summer with you," she said.

I heard a low voice in the background.

"Where are you?" I asked. "Wait, what do you mean, spend the summer with me? Won't you be spending the summer with me?"

"I have a new address," Julia said.

"Your son is failing math," I said.

"And a new number," she said.

"Math," I said. "His best subject."

"Here's my number," she said.

I managed to scribble it down. "Julia, please. Let's see

each other." I wanted to say more, but the tranquilizer made me swallow my thoughts before I could get them out.

"We'll talk soon," she said, and hung up.

No, I thought. I couldn't let this happen again. How could we drift apart so fast? I couldn't let it happen. I called her back at the new number.

A man answered. It was the painter. "Hold on," he said.

She had gone back to the idiot painter. I hung up before she came to the phone, and she didn't call me back. She didn't chase me. I slammed my fist against the plaster behind my bed and promised myself that I wouldn't chase her either. Good riddance, I thought. Forget my holding pattern. Then I crashed; then I wept. I wanted to come up with some sort of resolve, but all resolve escaped me. I cried myself to sleep.

I threw myself into my farming. My vines needed my affection. I thought that this was one thing that I did well, growing grapes. I nurtured the plants. I sprayed for mildew; I sprayed herbicides. I trained the vines, curling the tendrils around the upper wires of the trellises. I watered them. I devoted myself to my gardening because this had worked for me before. Taking care of my vines had brought me great contentment when nothing else had.

Then one morning—it was still June—I noticed a dime-sized bright green gall on the bottom of one leaf on a vine. I checked the other leaves on the same vine and found more of the bristled sores, and then I noticed the growths on some of the younger shoots.

I quickly examined the other vines in the row and found the lumps everywhere I looked. I found more on the vines in the next row down the slope. And the row after that. When I cracked one with my thumbnail, I wanted to throw up. The galls were orange inside, sticky with gluey larvae.

I ran into the house and found a book about grapevines and paged through the appendix titled "Pests." I had to read through pages and pages of descriptions of mites and moths and all manner of hoppers before I found the description of my symptom, and the way the list was arranged, the worst plights were saved for last.

It was the phylloxera louse. I was in trouble.

In 1869, according to this text, the phylloxera louse had wiped out much of the rootstock in Europe; an epidemic had broken out in California at various times late in the last century, as well. I had read about it in the newspaper recently because agriculturalists at Davis were warning that a new strain had come into being and threatened the West Coast crops, but I thought that there was no way that I could be affected. For one thing, my vines were ancient; I had not introduced any new plants to my vineyard. Second, cabernet sauvignon grapes were supposed to be at low risk for phylloxera.

This may have been the coup de grâce for me at the hardware store. It was a mistake to go into town with news of my infested vines, but I panicked. I needed advice. Will Clark took two steps back from me, as if I breathed an airborne disease. Alex Marquez left the store, but then again, he wasn't speaking to me anyway.

"Shit, Jason," Will Clark said, and flapped his arms. "That stuff spreads like wildfire. You have to get rid of it now. Now, right away, do you hear?"

"I know," I said, "I know. What should I do?"

Emma Hodges pointed a bony finger at me. "You get someone to spray," she said. "You get someone who knows what he's doing." She nodded toward the street. "You could have brought the bug in on your truck. You could have it on your shoes. Then we could all take it home. Then it gets in our vines. It eats the roots. It destroys vineyards in a summer," she said. And then, in a cold whisper: "You'll kill every plant in the valley, and no one will ever plant another. This is it. This is the end."

I went back home and phoned the oenology department at Davis. They told me that I might be lucky because phylloxera, as Emma Hodges had said, was a root louse, and I might have caught it in its early aerial stage. If it spread throughout Oak Valley, I was told, it could also travel elsewhere in the state. The man I spoke with volunteered to dispatch a team of experts the next day.

So the next morning a half a dozen men and women wearing phosphorescent jumpsuits and helmets with masks descended upon my modest slope of vines, each one of them wrangling an octopuslike hose that ran from a truck filled with chemicals. They sprayed the field in less than an hour. I watched from my bedroom. Tim came out of his and watched, too. I appreciated the consoling hand he placed briefly on my shoulder, but before I knew it, he was gone, back in his room.

The masked team hacked out the diseased plants, one quarter of my vines, and they dumped all of that vegetative matter into another truck, which sped out of the vineyard right away. The ruined vines would be incinerated. The experts inspected the cordons and the roots, and they told me that, to be on the cautious side, I needed to rip out some of them. They urged me to pull out the roots of one hundred and fifty vines. They told me that I was fortunate that it was not the entire plot that they wanted to destroy. They kept telling me I was lucky.

My luck, I wanted to respond, was spent. The love of my life, my old friend, had left me. My son would barely speak to me. I had no friends in town, almost no means of supporting myself. In no way was I lucky. And now this. These were my grandfather's vines they were talking about. Did these scientists realize that? These vines had survived some eighty leaves. I couldn't watch the team rip them out, and so after I agreed to the exorcism, I left a note for Tim, telling him that I would be out wandering the valley for the rest of the day, and I got in my truck and I drove off. I couldn't watch them bring in the tiller. I couldn't watch them gouge at my slope.

When I came home that night, I saw the dark black swath of overturned soil, my field now divided into two distinct plots, and I stopped in the middle of the vineyard road, got out of my truck, and I stood there for a long while just staring at the shallow trench.

* * *

It turned out to be one of the loneliest summers I had known. I took Tim up to the city every other weekend to see his mother and picked him up at the end of the weekend, all without even glimpsing Julia, and when Tim was at the vineyard, he avoided the sun as if it would poison him. He kept his shades drawn in his room. I worked in the bisected field during the day and took a sleeping pill at night. The days were hot and oppressively dry and long. I decided not to make any big decisions about the future right now. I needed time to think, and I couldn't think in that heat. Sometimes I took my sleeping pill as soon as the sun went down. All I really wanted to do was sleep.

In late August, the surviving grapes began to color up, early that season, and in September I began to measure the sugar content with my hydrometer. At this point every year, I expected to lose some of my crop to the birds. I could have tied silver streamers to the vines to scare them off, which was what most vintners had started to do. I wasn't sure whether that really worked. I remember when I was young, I would hear rifle shots in the valley, the vineyard hands actually shooting at the grape-hungry birds or trying to scare off the deer that would wander into the fields. In any case, I hadn't lost all that much fruit in the past to the local wildlife; I figured there was enough to share, even with my much-reduced crop. And the grackles and the big crows came in on schedule, whining from the high limbs of the oaks, diving down to the field and then swinging back up to the trees like big black boomerangs.

One afternoon, I found a crow lying on the brown grass between two rows of vines. It was a huge bird, more frightening in death than in life, its talons open as if it were trying to grab hold of a branch, at the sky, at anything with its dying caw. Its beak was open, too. I got rid of it.

The next day I found two more dead crows. I told Tim about the dead birds, and his reaction troubled me. He asked, "Why are you so surprised?"

The chemicals that were sprayed on the vines to get rid of the phylloxera were not supposed to be toxic to anything other than the louse and its kind. I didn't think that my grapes were killing the birds, but I didn't find the dead crows anywhere else on my property except near my crop.

"I'm not surprised," my son said. "I'm not surprised at all."

He was mad at me, I knew, and probably mad at his mother because we—or I should say she—had decided that Tim should stay on at the vineyard and continue school down here, at least until Julia could find a place for them in the city.

I dreaded walking around my vines, because every time I did, I found another bird on its back, with the startled, frozen gaze of a taxidermed specimen. This went on for a week. I had to wonder what poison was in my fruit, and, of course, I had to wonder what kind of wine these grapes would make.

Eventually I suspected that the fittest birds figured out that the plump berries were no good for them, and they not only stopped dropping down from the oaks to the vines, they left my land completely. The crows vanished from my vineyard that fall. Birds of every kind disappeared, and without birds, the vineyard became eerily quiet.

The skies were overcast every day the month before the harvest, which many vintners deemed fortunate as long as it didn't rain before the fruit was picked. I never quite understood the meteorological connection, but somehow the clouds—or perhaps I should say the diminished sunlight—allegedly raised the level of desirable acidity against the rising sugar content. I had lived in the valley long enough to expect the gray fall mornings and the hour of brightness at around two in the afternoon and then the dark, sultry dusks. I thought that I could read the leaves on the trees and know that if they became limp or if they curled, there was a chance of drizzle.

One day in late September, Tim went off to school, and around noon, someone from the school called to ask me if he was sick. He was playing hooky. I remember this because I never got around to scolding him, for suddenly the oaks lost their rustle and the sky exploded with a spontaneous downpour. It rained and rained, and it didn't stop.

I don't think that anyone could have forecast the two-day drenching that soaked the valley. The gutters of my house overflowed. The ground became muddy everywhere, and when I measured the grapes after the rain, the sugar had risen to 26.5° Brix, which was way too high, much too sweet for cabernet. But there was no reversing the ripening on the vine, and the only thing to do was harvest the crop, which I did as quickly as I could.

"You can either go to school, and I mean really go to school, or you can help me with the harvest," I told Tim.

"Why bother," he said.

"Why bother harvesting?" I asked.

"Why bother anything," he said, and rode his bike down the vineyard road to catch the bus.

I dumped the grapes into the steel vat, and I was unsure how much sulfate to add to kill the native yeast, how much Montrachet to mix in to get the fermentation going if there was more sugar than usual but fewer grapes, given how much of my crop had been destroyed. Whatever I did stir in was not enough, because on the third day after dumping the last of the fruit into the vat, nothing had happened—the fermentation had not begun. I added more yeast—still nothing. Early on the fifth day, I saw some bubbling finally, a slow and uneven fizz. I stood at the top of the ladder and watched the must, and soon enough the juice began to foam with more gusto.

Later that same day the fermentation stuck, it stalled. And it smelled odd. Not like fruit turning, not the sour smell that I was used to, the one all vintners welcomed, but disturbingly sweet, like honey. And the must was thick to the touch, almost syrupy. I added more yeast to jump-start the chemistry, and the must foamed again; a cap formed eventually, and I had to punch down. But the saccharine smell never went away; the rotten-apple odor never returned.

A process that in the past had taken two weeks now took three and a half. The must became stuck several times. This wine was a disaster, and I knew it, but I released the valves at the base of the tank for the free run anyway, and I pressed the pomace. Tim didn't offer to help and I didn't ask him to. For a reduced vintage, there was much more in the way of solid matter that I had to scrape from the filter screens than I had in the past. The skins, the stems, and more dead yeast cells perhaps. I mixed in the bacteria for the secondary fermentation, and I had no clue, none whatsoever, how to adjust the formula. The wine remained sweet-smelling and, if anything, it became thicker each day.

And so finally I ran a hose from the holding tank to an opening on the side of the winery opposite the stairs; I turned the valve at the base of the tank. I heard a single loud gurgle, and then the wine began to pour out through the hose and outside to the slope. I went outside myself and sat on the damp ground up by the top level of the winery and watched the strange wine of my third vintage run down the hill in a trickle at first, then a stream.

The stream soon became a river, swallowing the sagebrush in its way, the sumac, making an island out of a bottlebrush tree, pushing aside stones and branches and leaves, and collecting finally in a puddle, a pond at the base of the hill, a lake that by the end of the day had soaked into the clay—such was the fate of all rivers and lakes in these parts; they flowed for a time, then they dried up—leaving behind only the indelible stain of the wine on the soil.

That night I went inside the old stone house and left a note for Tim, telling him that he was on his own for dinner. I went up to my bedroom and took two of my prescribed pills, and when I woke up, it was still dark out, but judging from the itch and length of my beard, I realized that I had slept for an entire day.

* * *

my days became shorter. I would sleep late into the morning and pop a pill in the early evening. I was aware of Tim coming and going, but our exchanges were brief and infrequent. I had to assume that he was going to school, because no one called me to ask about his absence. At night, I heard him in his room, tapping away at his computer. I rarely left the house. When I needed food, I called a grocer in New Idria who delivered. I didn't bother to collect my mail from the box at the bottom of the vineyard road. I didn't answer the phone, and soon it stopped ringing.

Meanwhile my house fell apart around me. For some reason I never figured out, the heat stopped rising to the second floor, although the first floor remained warm. So my bedroom became something of an arctic refuge, and I ended up sleeping downstairs in the study. I didn't know what Tim was doing to keep warm. He claimed that he was fine. And the rain that had overripened my harvest had continued more or less unabated. At least we were not going through another drought. No one realized it at the time, but we were heading into one of the most damaging and wettest rainy seasons in valley history, in California history. We were heading into a long rain, a single unbroken storm that would last for months; sometimes it would sprinkle and sometimes it would squall, but the rain would never let up.

All of the rain was too much for the gutters to take, and on two sides of the house, they broke free from the eaves and dangled for a while and then fell off and landed on the lawn. I heard what I suspected were shingles sliding off the roof, and shutters falling aslant, scraping against the stone. The roof leaked, too, and I had to set up buckets in several of the bedrooms, although there was nothing that I could do about the rain that ran down into the walls and made the plaster pucker and crack. Outside, the overgrown lawn looked like a marsh, what with all of the puddles and the tall grass and the ungroomed hedges. I was sure that the vineyard had become a bog, as well, but I avoided looking out any window that faced the plot. I couldn't face my vines.

I thought that this was what it must feel like to drown slowly. Every hour, it became a little more difficult to breathe.

I knew that I had to pull myself together, and each day I promised myself that the next would be the one when I would throw out the junk that I was taking and put on a clean shirt and cook a decent supper for my son. The next day, I would take a hard look at my bank statement and figure out if we could afford to live on the vineyard. The next day, I would ask whether the time had come to move back to the city. But the next day came and I slept late, and eventually I moved from the couch to my desk, but all I did was stare out at the rain, the depthless gray of it, the rain closing in, surrounding me, imprisoning me, and before long, I was back on the couch.

This went on for a month.

Late one night my sixth autumn in the valley, I woke up from my deep drugged sleep and heard someone pounding on my front door. At the same time, the phone was ringing. I picked up the phone first. It was Harry Padillo.

"Open your door," he said.

I found him standing on my stoop, holding a cellular phone.

"I've been knocking and calling for fifteen minutes," he said.

So this was it, I thought. It had taken over a year, but finally someone had caught me in my lie. I waved the sheriff into the kitchen. I had to sit down. I wondered if he had told his deputies to wait in the squad car. I guess he knew that I was not the type to resist arrest.

"Jason, are you sober?" Harry Padillo asked.

"It's these pills I take," I tried to explain. My words sounded warbled to me.

"I'm here about Tim," the sheriff said.

I sat up straight. Tim should have heard the pounding at the door.

"We tried calling. We sent over a man an hour ago—"

"Tim's upstairs," I said.

"Tim's not upstairs," Harry Padillo said. "He's been in an accident. He's in Hollister, in intensive care. They've been trying to call you from the hospital, too."

I squinted at him. What was he telling me?

"He drove your truck into a tree on the Oak Leaf Highway."

My entire body shivered. "That's impossible. He's upstairs," I said, and I ran up to his room. The door was open, his computer off. I sat down on his never-made bed. Oh no, I thought. Oh no. No, no.

I looked up and saw Harry Padillo standing at the door.

"Near where the Montoya boy was hit," he said. "He ran straight into a pine. Destroyed your truck. He's just damn lucky a ranger found him when he did. And I should tell you the reason I'm involved, Jason. Tim was drinking. He's old enough that we didn't need to ask your permission to check him out. Anyway, he was skunked. And he went into that tree pretty fast," the sheriff said.

Tim was connected to so many tubes and monitors that he looked like a stunned fly caught in a web, helplessly waiting for the spider to descend. Mostly he had broken bones. Cuts that required stitching. Bruised organs maybe. The doctors were worried about internal bleeding, but so far he seemed okay. His face was a mess, half-bandaged, but he could have suffered serious head injuries, and the attending neurologist was fairly certain that he hadn't. At worst, he had a concussion. He was out of it, on morphine or whatever they'd pumped into him, but I think that he felt me squeeze his one unbandaged hand. I hoped he heard me speak to him.

An emergency room doctor asked me to talk to the psychiatrist on call. The psychiatrist suggested that Tim had intended to kill himself.

"No," I said, "I don't think so. Not Tim."

Julia appeared out of nowhere, running toward the emergency room. An attendant grabbed her and stopped her from barging through the double doors of the intensive care unit. The painter appeared a few paces behind her and took her arm.

After she saw Tim, she found me in a waiting area. Here we all were back at the hospital. I didn't know what to say to her.

"I know it's partly my fault," she said. "I shouldn't have left him with you."

"He's going to be okay," I said.

"They think he wanted to kill himself," Julia said.

She had put on some weight and her hair was longer, not so severely cropped, yet she was so pale with fright that she looked to me much the way she had after her ordeal the previous winter.

"I don't think that," I said. "Do you?"

Julia sighed. "I don't know what I think," she said.

We spent what was left of the night and the entire next day after Tim's accident sitting in chairs on either side of his bed, speaking quietly with the nurses and the doctors who came and went and whose various tests did not yield any results to worry about. We were told that Tim was lucky. The truck was a big enough vehicle to take a hard hit. So everyone was lucky. I was lucky not to have lost my entire crop to the deadly louse, and Tim, well, he was lucky when he drove a truck into a tree but only broke his arm and some ribs, when he only needed two hundred stitches.

I placed my hand against my son's cheek. I expected him to be fevered, but he was cool. His swollen eyelids twitched.

Julia spent the next night at the hospital, too, but I went home and wandered my house. I paced in and out of every room except Tim's room. If I went in there, I would snoop.

I needed to know what he had meant to do. Did he mean to drive drunk? Did he mean to crash on the mountain road?

The next day I held Tim's hand. Some of the tubes and wires had been disconnected. I left him only once to deal with someone from the district attorney's office. The DUI would be diverted if we had Tim see a therapist, which Julia had decided to do anyway. He wouldn't be able to get his driver's license until he was eighteen. He would need to complete certain programs, maybe do some community service and so forth. When I returned to Tim's room, he was sitting up a little higher in his bed, although his swollen eyes were still shut. He was speaking to his mother.

She wasn't listening to whatever he was saying. Julia kept muttering, "I'm the one who should be sorry, sweetie, not you."

I sat down next to him, and although he didn't open his eyes, he turned toward me, and he whispered, he mouthed, "I'm sorry, Dad."

"Don't be sorry," I said. "Just get better."

"I'm sorry," he whispered again, and that was all he tried to say.

And I knew then that he was apologizing for more than merely taking my truck out alone or for driving drunk.

That night I did go into his bedroom. I broke the most basic rule a parent could violate. I found nothing in his night table or his dresser or desk drawers. My son didn't appear to keep a journal. Nothing buried behind the ski boots or old board games in his closet. So I turned on his computer. I didn't know what I expected to find among the documents listed on the screen. A diary? I didn't know if he had any friends for me to call. Would anyone be able to explain my son to me? Would anyone be able to fill me in? And it occurred to me then that if my son knew anyone, it would be an electronic friend.

I toggled the on-line program. I had only gone cybersurfing with Tim, and that was a while ago, so I didn't really know my way around. Right away, I needed a password. Tim's screen name appeared in a box—this was the code name by which he was known to his on-line friends—and then in the blank space below the screen name, I needed to type in the password to go on-line. I didn't know the password—

And then I looked at the screen name again. It wasn't what I would have expected. It wasn't TimothyDark or TDark or TimD or any combination of the first and last name his mother and I had given him. My son's chosen screen name was CMontoya.

My son, my son—I had almost lost him. He had become obsessed with the boy I killed, there was no denying it. My son wanted to be dead, too. And I should have seen the signs, I should have taken care of him. I wanted to go back to the beginning of the summer and talk to Tim about what made him sad. I wanted to go back to the spring and I wanted to stand in front of the door to keep Julia from leaving. I wanted to go back to the previous autumn—

Tim was moved to a private room. He shifted from his back to his side, and, sleeping on his side, he looked more like his old self. Until he woke up. When he woke up, he looked like a ghost of himself. His face was bloated and gashed, his hair had been shaved to a fuzz. His eyes were hollow, and he looked gaunt, as if he had tried to starve himself. He didn't try to talk to me. He would stare at me and then he would fall asleep again.

Julia had conferred with a range of doctors who recommended a program of intensive therapy; he would spend most of the holidays in a clinic and then go and live with her in the city.

Before I left the hospital, I had some time alone with Tim and I asked him, "Is this what you want? Because I only want you to do what you want."

He shrugged.

"Okay," I said. "You know that I love you."

Tim blinked and then he frowned, as if I was lying, as if he didn't trust me. He looked away. And why should he trust me? I had lied about so much.

december. A new year. January. I don't have a clear memory of the weeks that followed. I was all alone again, and I had forgotten how to be alone. It wasn't like swimming or riding a bike. My body didn't remember what to do. I ate poorly. I would open a can of corn and have it cold; that was dinner. I did nothing to make myself feel better. I didn't play music. I stopped reading. I threw out my pills and couldn't sleep. I didn't find any new clients; I was living off dwindling savings. I looked into selling my vineyard.

It rained every day, and some days, when the rains abated, I headed down to my plot of vines with my shears and began to prune in the drizzle. I swung my elbows far apart and then flapped the shears together with all my muscle. I hacked away the summer growth, pulling the shoots and the leaves from the trellis and chucking the greenery behind me onto the aisle of mud between the vines. I selected the shoots to save for the next season, for the next fool who came along and tried to grow grapes in this cruel tundra. I pruned until it started pouring, and then I waited until the rain let up again and I could prune some more. Gradually, I cut vines down to the cordons, but the more progress I made, the slower I pruned. I didn't want this chore to end. I didn't know what I would do with myself when I was done.

One day while I was pruning in the cold mist, I stopped and held the Y-shaped shears in front of me like an impotent divining rod, pointing at nothing but the obvious soaked soil at my feet. It wasn't difficult for me to know what I did and did not want. I didn't want to go to jail; prisons are inhuman places. In my heart, I didn't want to leave the valley, nor did I want to live here alone. I wanted to nurture my vines and make wine. I wanted to lure Julia back to the vineyard and start over again, yes, one more time. I wanted to be a better father to my son, if he would let me, if it wasn't too late. All I wanted now was the life that I had made for myself before.

I began pruning again. I pruned my way down an aisle of vines.

I could imagine myself kneeling on these clay beds in the middle of an arid summer, pulling out weeds, reaching my hand deep into the soil, lifting up a fistful of the dirt, dirt that smelled like coffee, like violets. I could picture Tim lying on the grass, staring at the sun, talking to me, confiding his greatest yearning. I could see Julia wandering down the slope with a pitcher of lemonade and tall glasses. I wanted to make it to that dry day. I wanted to get there without destroying myself on the way.

But how? How could I get there from here?

It was pouring, but I didn't want to head into the house. I was soaked and cold, but I kept working.

I had heard it said that we made our own luck in this world, but I was never entirely sure what that meant. If we made our own luck, did that also mean that we made our own misfortune? There was no god, of that I was certain, and I didn't really know what people were talking about when they spoke of fate. How could any event be preordained when there was obviously so much chance evident, say, in the tides of weather that could ruin a farmer? Chance if you happened to be driving fast down a mountain road when a boy was walking down that road. Chance that this boy's death might in some way destroy your own son. I believed in pure physics, in evolution, in the inevitable draw of all systems toward entropy. And yet.

Without any science to back me up, I had come to believe this: Somehow there was a connection between how you lived, how you behaved, and what happened to you, the turns your life took. I mean that if you were a moral person, a good person, generous and just, and if you helped the people around you in your universe, you would reap certain fortunes. Likewise, if you let a man go to jail for a crime that you yourself had committed, then your entire life would fall apart. I am not so sure that I believe this now, but I did believe it back then. It seemed like the simplest truth: There was a connection between how you lived your life and what happened to you.

The next day I drove down to the state prison in Corcoran, two hours south of Oak Valley—I went to the newly opened annex to the prison, a long steel and cement building that resembled a power station—and I told the guard behind the desk in a building just inside the steep fence that I wanted to speak with Troy Frantz.

The guard looked at a clipboard and didn't find my name. Had the inmate asked to see me? I had to say no, and the guard told me that all visits had to be prearranged and preapproved; I couldn't just show up and demand to see a prisoner. I said that I had traveled far and I begged for a bend in the rules, but the guard shook his head no. He pointed to his clipboard and said that I could call my client and tell him that if he wanted to meet with his lawyer, he should clear it through the proper channels, and I interrupted and said that I wasn't actually Troy Frantz's lawyer.

I had read in a newspaper that the Montoya family had filed a wrongful-death action against Troy Frantz for damages in probable excess of what he could ever earn in his life after incarceration, and I had also read that Troy Frantz had chosen not to fight the civil suit; soon, after certain pro forma hearings, the court would award the Montoya family what they requested. So I improvised; I told the guard that I had been dispatched by Troy Frantz's mother to try to persuade her son to contest the civil suit, for what it was worth to him.

The guard grumbled and tapped his pen against his clipboard. Calls were made. An hour later, I was ushered across a flat unplanted field and through another fence, into the prison proper, to a room much like rooms in the other prisons and jails that I had visited, a bright and low-ceilinged room divided in half by a partition of thick glass.

Troy Frantz wore a bright orange short-sleeved jumpsuit; it was baggy on him, and its one shirt pocket ended up somewhere around his stomach. The cuffs of the trousers were rolled up above his black slippers. His glasses, the oval-framed glasses, were held together with white adhesive tape. The bridge of his nose looked swollen. So did his jaw. What I thought at first might be botched tattoos on both of his arms, an archipelago of black and green and red shapes, were in fact bruises. He had lost his goatee but still had a day's growth of a beard, and his hair, buzzed short, made him appear smaller to me now, as if he were shrinking and shrinking and one day would disappear, probably without anyone missing him.

We sat at the tables on either side of the glass wall, both of us with prison guards behind us. Troy Frantz picked up the phone on his desk, and I picked up mine, and he said nothing. I don't know why I expected him to speak first.

I told him my name and that I was an attorney.

"And my mother sent you," he said.

"That's right," I said. "She believes, as I do, that you should fight the civil suit. Someday you'll get out of here and . . ."

Troy was frowning at me. He removed his glasses and rubbed his brow.

"Are you okay?" I asked.

"You're my first visitor," he said, and looked at me again. "Why hasn't my mother come to see me?"

"Well," I said, and I tried to imagine why a mother would not visit her son in jail. "She's still very upset, I guess, and—"

"Why are you here?" Troy asked.

Because I had to meet you, I had to talk to you. Because you are the man I wronged.

"As I was saying, your mother hired me because—"

"I'm an orphan," Troy Frantz said.

"Oh," I said.

I thought that he would hang up on me and go back to his cell, but he pressed the phone closer to his chin.

"My parents died when I was five," he said.

"I see," I said. "I'm sorry."

"I grew up in foster homes," he said.

Troy Frantz stared at me.

"I know that you didn't kill that boy in the woods," I said.

His eyes looked like small black buttons.

"I've seen your confession," I said. "You thought you hit a deer. And you did hit a deer. I know you hit a deer."

Troy leaned forward.

"You didn't kill that boy," I said. "I know it, and I think that you know it."

Troy swallowed.

"And what I don't understand," I said, "is why you . . ."

And then it hit me. Then I realized what I had to do.

I said, "You don't have to be here."

"But," Troy Frantz said. "But I—"

"I can help you," I said.

"How?" he asked. "Help me how?"

I said, "I'm a lawyer." I said, "I can help you get out."

the only window in the room at the prison where I next met with Troy Frantz was a small square porthole in the steel door. The walls were concrete, whitewashed and blank, and an arctic breeze pouring out from a clerestory of vents made everything in the room cold to touch. The metal table, bolted to the floor, the two metal chairs. In a matter of minutes, my silver pen had numbed my fingers. I had come to the prison a few days after my first visit and was immediately ushered to a room on the left, at the end of a tunnellike corridor, where Troy was already seated, his right hand busy working a pencil across a broad sketch pad. As soon as I came in and sat down across from him, he flipped the pad over.

He set his pencil down, laced his fingers, and stared at me solemnly, arching an inquisitive brow. I asked him how he was faring, and he released a long sigh, his shoulders sank, and he nodded an okay. Then our talk ran something like this:

I said, "As I told you the other day, Troy, I've seen your videotaped confession."

His eyes narrowed to a squint.

"And I know that you initially thought that you killed a deer," I said.

"I killed a boy," Troy said. He closed his eyes all the way.

"No," I said. "You didn't. That's what I'm here to tell you.

Maybe you hit a deer, but you definitely did not hit that boy, and you have to know that deep down. You didn't kill the boy."

Troy opened his eyes and stared at me for a while.

"I can't pay you anything," he said. "I have no money, not a cent."

"I'm not expecting you to pay me anything," I said.

"But you don't know me."

"No, I don't."

"So why are you helping me?" he asked.

"Why am I helping you?" I asked back.

"You don't know me," he said.

How could I earn his trust?

"Well, as I was saying," I said, "I saw your confession. And I looked over the waivers you signed." Here was what I had to tell him: "See, I was there that night at the sheriff's station when you confessed. I was there that night."

"So," Troy said. He looked unimpressed.

"So I was there and heard you say that you thought you hit a deer, and then I was in the woods and I saw a wounded deer."

"Maybe I hit a deer and a boy," Troy said.

"Maybe you did," I said. "Maybe you didn't."

Troy removed his glasses and wiped the lenses on the lap of his jumpsuit.

I waited until he had put his glasses back on. I took a deep breath. I said, "I tried not to get involved. I figured it really wasn't any of my business. What did it matter to me? But I'm a lawyer. Doubt troubles me. And when I heard about how you weren't contesting the civil suit—"

"That's why you came now?" Troy asked.

"That and . . ."

He needed more from me.

I said, "Lately I've done some things in my life that I'm not so proud of."

Troy nodded slowly. "And now you'll do some things you can be proud of," he said.

I shrugged a yes.

"Like helping me," he said.

"Like helping you," I said.

Then Troy smiled, briefly, just a flash before his face melted back into a frown. He stared at me again, his nostrils flaring. "But you don't know me," he said.

To which I had to respond once again, "No, I don't."

"Thanks for coming to see me," he said. "I appreciate it. But I have to tell you, Mr. Dark, I think you're wasting your time."

"Troy," I said, "the last time I came here, I asked you if I could come again and you said sure. So here I am, and I want—"

"I'm sorry," he said. "But you don't know me, and you really don't know . . . I think that . . . I think," he stuttered. "I did kill that boy. I ran him over with his own car. And I should pay the family whatever they want."

"Troy," I said, and reached across the table and gripped his arm. He was as cold as the metal surface. "Listen to me. I don't think you hit the boy."

He swallowed. He looked close to tears.

"Remember when you gave your confession? You decided that you hit the boy, but you weren't entirely sure, were you?"

"I was pretty fucked up," Troy said.

"You were confused that night," I said.

Again he was willing to give me a tentative nod.

"I need to think," he said.

"You know deep down," I said. "You know."

"Now and then, in the back of my mind," he said, "I've wondered. . . . Oh, man," he said, gulping. "Oh, man."

"It's still confusing," I said.

"But how can you be sure?" he asked. "I'm not."

"See, that's what I'm trying to say," I said. "I don't need to be sure. I mean, I think I am sure, but that's not the point. The point is that doubt is enough for me. I doubt you killed the boy."

"This is a lot to take in," he said.

"I'm sure it is," I said.

"It's hitting me now," he said. "If I had any doubt, I got rid of it. I had to."

I patted his forearm again. "Do you remember being confused that night you confessed? That's what we need to go back to. Not what you decided, but the—"

"Doubt," he said.

"Right," I said. "All the doubt you had."

"Okay, let's say I have my doubts," he said. "Then what?"

"Then you shouldn't be in here," I said.

"And you can get me out? You can prove I didn't hit the boy?"

"I think I can," I said.

"How? How can you prove it?" he asked.

How indeed? I hadn't thought that far ahead.

"That's my job," I said. "You'll help me, but that's what I'm here for, and you can leave it up to me."

"All this time," Troy Frantz said, "I've been telling myself I killed the boy and I have to pay. Now I don't know what to think."

"Can I come back tomorrow?" I asked.

He didn't answer me. "I don't know what to think," he said.

I did return to the prison the next day; a guard accompanied me to the white room, where Troy was waiting for me again. He turned over his drawing pad when I came in.

I started talking about the wrongful-death suit that the Montoya family had brought against him.

"But I should pay the family something," Troy said. "It's the right thing to do."

"Why?" I asked.

"They've suffered," Troy said.

"But what if you're not to blame?" I asked.

"Maybe I am," he said.

I knew that I had to work him slowly; the idea of his innocence seemed curiously new to him. I played his game and

said that I didn't think that defending himself in civil court
was tantamount to entering a plea of innocence. I added that
there were different ways to atone for a crime, different ways
to make reparations, which didn't necessarily have to involve
paying out ten percent of his meager earnings for the rest of
his life. All I asked from him was that at the very least he let
me be his advocate for a short while, a few weeks, and then
let me lay out his options for him.

"The Montoyas suing me isn't really the biggest thing on
my mind," Troy said.

"Getting out of here is," I said. "And we'll come to that—"

"No," Troy said. "I mean, yes. But there's something
else."

I waited for him to tell me what this other concern was.

"I'd rather not talk about it," he said.

"Okay," I said. "But can I proceed on the civil matter?
Look, you can change your mind and give the Montoyas
everything you own at a later date, if that's what you want."

And Troy looked at me awhile, and he said, "Thank you,"
as if I had already accomplished what I proposed to do.

Days later I filed a new motion of Troy's intent to go to
trial in the civil matter and then a motion for postponement
until, as his new counsel, I had sufficient time to study the
case before depositions began. I knew that this public
demonstration of whose side I was on would have ramifications for me back at the hardware store—I could no longer
claim a passing coincidental relationship with a man who
was so despised in the valley—but I didn't think about what
these ramifications would be, or I should say that I didn't
contemplate them for very long. A mean stare, some words
behind my back—frankly, nothing new for me. I had taken
a job and I had to do it, simple as that.

Because it was a civil case, I felt that I could proceed with
competence. When the time came, I was at ease in the
judge's chambers, facing off with the Montoya family's
lawyer, who used words like ambushed and manipulated. I
knew how to pretend that I was listening to the judge's ser-

mons about ambulance-chasing and docket clogging and dirtying the good name of due process; I knew how to defer, how to be polite without seeming obsequious. My client's motion to seek a jury trial was accepted; a date was set to make another date to assign the case a place in the long line of cases inching their way toward the court. A civil trial would be at least a year off, probably more like two or three.

I could have phoned Troy, but I wanted to tell him the good news in person, so I drove from the courthouse in Hollister directly to the Corcoran prison annex.

"Thank you," Troy said. "Thank you very much."

"What you need to understand is that these matters can move very slowly," I said.

Troy nodded.

"But I'll be dealing with the plaintiff's lawyer and I'll be looking at the case."

Troy blinked.

"Sometimes these cases never even make it to court," I said. "We might agree to go to an arbitrator. And I'm hoping that in the meantime you'll let me also roll up my sleeves and dig in on the criminal side."

Troy cocked his head.

"I want to talk to you about an appeal," I said.

"An appeal," Troy said.

"To get you out. I want— What's wrong?" I asked.

"I can't pay you anything," he said.

And so we had to dance that jig again. Me: No problem. Him: Why isn't it a problem?

The way Troy put it this time was, "What did you do, Mr. Dark, that was so bad that you have to repent by saving a lowlife like me?"

If I am making Troy out to sound defensive or hostile or overly suspicious to the point of seeming ungrateful, then I am not portraying him accurately. There was something courtly about his gestures—the way he folded his hands in front of him on the table—and a sweetness—he always spoke slowly and softly and after considered pauses—and a certain self-deprecation—a lowlife like me, he'd said, and with that came a single, barely audible chuckle. What did you do? he'd asked, and it seemed more out of concern for my well-being that he posed the question, my sanity, my ability to climb out of my own private dungeon, than out of a need on his part to know my motives.

"I don't think you're a lowlife," I said.

"How do you know?" he asked. "I may have done terrible things."

"Maybe you have," I said.

"I may belong in here," he said.

"Maybe you do," I said. "But you're not a typical criminal, not like any I've ever met." I pointed at the pad in front of him. "Can I see what you've been drawing?"

"No," he said. "Not yet."

Not yet. I accepted that modest offering for what it was. Not yet, implying that perhaps eventually, in time, he would say, Why yes, here, take a look.

"I still want to know," Troy said. "What did you do that was so bad?" His weary bass had a way of echoing in the concrete room.

I wonder now what would have happened if I had said to him, I hit and I ran and I let you go to jail for it. I wonder what would have happened if I had said, I'm trying to get you out of prison without putting myself inside. Would he have understood? I think that it was possible that he might have seen my point of view, but even if he had understood, I doubt that he would have played along with my scheme. I wanted to be honest and forthright, and I needed to feed him something, more than I had given him before, so I began to speak the partial truth.

"Last fall my son tried to kill himself," I said.

I shivered. I had never admitted it before, not aloud, even though I had accepted that Tim had wanted to die on the mountain road.

"My truck," I said. "He ran it into a tree. My only son, my only child."

When I looked at Troy again, he had unfolded his hands and reached halfway across the table toward me.

"I blame myself, like all fathers would, for not seeing the signs," I said. "But worse than that, I think I knew deep down that he was in trouble, and I hid from him when he needed me most."

I described some of what my life had been like the previous autumn at the vineyard.

"And that was really just the last bad thing," I said. "I'm not telling you about the summer before that or the spring or the winter. I'm not telling you about how my wife—well, my ex-wife—I'm not telling you about her miscarriage or about how she left and . . . Now I want her back again," I said. "I always let her go too easily," I added, and although I made it sound like this was an often-thought notion, it was the first time I had stated it so flatly, the fact that I never really fought hard to hold on to Julia when she drifted away from me. "I don't know why that is," I said, "but I always let her get away."

My head ached, my eyes were tired. I could have set my head down on the table and taken a nap.

"Sorry," I said. "I don't mean to babble."

Troy refolded his hands. He frowned. After a while, he said, "A son."

"Tim," I said.

"My own son," he started, and stopped.

"You have a son?"

"My only child also. He . . . Well, he's . . ."

Troy rubbed his temple. He blinked several times. He looked beyond me, behind me, at the door, as if he needed to make sure that a guard wouldn't barge in and tell us that our time was up, as if he needed to make sure he would not be overheard.

Then he said, "I don't know where he is."

"What's his name?" I asked.

"Jared," Troy said.

"How old is he?"

"How old is your son?" he asked.

I told him.

"Oh, that's how old Jared is, too," he said. "It's been two years since I've seen him. Longer. I have no idea where he is."

"I'm sorry," I said. "And his mother? Is she with him?"

Troy sat up very straight and then he slumped again. He took such a deep breath and his mouth curved into such a hard frown—he took so long to answer me—that I thought I had lost ground. I thought Troy would tell me that the mother of his son would not now nor ever be discussed. Too much bitterness, too much anger. And none of my business.

But what Troy said was, "It kills me a little every day I'm not with her. I want them back, too. It's all I'm living for," he said. "I have to find them so we can start over."

my drive home from the prison took close to two hours because the route was indirect and because the persistent rain that winter made the rural roads across the mountain range very slow going. The interstate through Fresno moved, but one mile of a flooded right lane could create an extra half hour of traffic. Before long I was going to the prison so often that I lost track of the number of trips I was making in any given week, and all of that time that I was on the road is lost to me now. Hours and hours, which, all totaled, probably add up to days, to weeks. I don't know if I thought about anything other than my talks with Troy. Early on I had started taping my sessions with him, and sometimes I would insert the cassette into the car stereo and listen to Troy wind his way through the story of his life in brief enigmatic chapters, Troy's gentle drawl somehow warming the used car that I had bought for myself to replace my wrecked truck, his voice, his ongoing confession both caffeinating me for the long drive and lulling me into a pleasing dream.

The prison. The road home. The old stone house.

I rarely went anywhere else that winter. And when I arrived home, I would trudge through the marsh that my land had become and pull off my boots in the mudroom and make a sandwich for dinner and wander back to the study, where I played the taped conversations again, where I did what little work I could, where I fell asleep. I went upstairs only to take a shower in the morning or to empty and reposition a bucket beneath a leak. The house was cold. The house was hollow. Loud echoes in the night, the usual creaks and banging and then a kind of murmuring in the pipes that I would hear only in the early morning. I never slept well.

As I mentioned, the entire state was enduring one of the wettest rainy seasons on record. At the very least it drizzled every day, and usually the rain came down hard, straight down in a gray percussive drench, and I know that from the New Year until one afternoon late in April—it was April twenty-second; there's a reason why I remember the date—I never saw the sun. Even after that day in April, it continued to rain, and as a result there were mud slides throughout California, and countless families fell into a regimen of evacuation and return. You gathered your most precious belongings and ordered your children into the car and rounded up the pets, and then you drove off to a school gymnasium for the night. After the storm, you went home and left the boxes of valuables by the door. Sometimes you went home and found that all you could see was the weather vane on your house; the rest of your world was lost beneath a brown river, the Sacramento, the Klamath, the Eel and the San Joaquin and the Russian all breaking free from tired banks. Even the waterless riverbed running through Oak Valley filled up for a month in the spring, although the high heat of the summer would dry out the basin again.

Eroded roads fell away and farmland became bogs. Grove after grove, avocado and orange and olive, was destroyed, and all of the native vines suffered, too, the strawberries, the grapes. There was talk of entire vintages that would be lost, although some vines, the ones on slopes like my own, did not succumb to root rot or any of the other maladies that too much rain can bring. And the sad truth was that the most ruinous rain, the rain that would cause the most heartache and damage, the most severe mud slides and flooding and loss of life, would not come until the following autumn when the rainy season began again, when the rain had nowhere to go, what with the water table so high and the reservoirs filled to the brim and levees already weakened and the lost flora not having come back because the soil was too wet and the summer sun too severe. The worst was yet to come.

But I'm getting ahead of myself. What I remember about that winter were all of the sandbags everywhere, along the roads, against the levees, in front of the shops along empty main drags, and around any house that I passed, all of the makeshift walls running up and down the swells of the flooded farms. Miles and miles of sandbag walls. It looked to me as if a war had been fought here sometime in the recent past, as if the soldiers were long gone but that the trenches, the lines the armies drew, had been left behind, along with the dead, who would emerge, the bloated corpses, when all of this water evaporated.

This long rain blinded me. I never caught a vista of my valley. I never could see a road beyond the short stretch my headlights illuminated. The rain trapped me, so that I felt like someone or something was closing in on me and there was no escape and little I could do to help myself before I, too, would be carried down the swollen river and out to sea. There were times when all I wanted to do was sleep away the lightless afternoons. There were times when I didn't know why I didn't just pack up a single bag and make my way to the desert, where there had to be some sun. The prison, the road home, the old stone house. That was all I knew during these months, and what sustained me, what kept me going, was my dialogue with Troy Frantz.

Picture me eating a tuna sandwich and sipping some tea and sitting at my desk with only my desk light on. I pushed the play button on my tape recorder.

It's all I'm living for, Troy said. I have to find them so we can start over.

I thought about how it could be or should be me sitting on his side of the table, me who returned to a stark fluorescent cell after these sessions were over, and I wondered what had brought this man to Oak Valley, what had happened to him, what terrible things, as he put it, he may have done. But mostly I sat there and listened to these tapes and thought about the stranger I was getting to know, and what I wanted to do was rush back to the prison to see him and talk some more. How can I explain it? I can only say that I was hungry to talk to him. Sometimes I forgot that I was supposed to be his attorney. My client turned out to be a very good listener.

In a certain sense," I told Troy, "Julia and I were always keeping secrets from each other. I know, I know. Secrecy is a kind of lying. Well, the truth is that our initial courtship was founded on a misunderstanding."

Troy's question was about why my marriage had fallen apart a second time. From a discussion of appellate matters, this was where our conversation had strayed. And I had to think for a minute how to answer him, but then I had started to ramble.

"We were in college together but didn't know each other until our senior year," I said. "I went with my roommate to see his girlfriend in a dance concert. And there was another woman in the dance who immediately caught my eye, a long-legged blonde, who, according to my program, had choreographed the main piece that night."

I described the dance to Troy, and when I did, he closed his eyes, as if that way he could picture it. It was titled something like "In Memory of My Brother," and it involved a lot of very lyrical movement, much swaying, much spinning. The central image of the dance was of the entire ensemble moving in an occasional circle with fewer and fewer dancers with each repetition. The music behind the dance was all cellos, I remembered, cellos and guitars, and at the end, someone switched on a fog machine so that the dancers' lithe twirls began to disappear in the white cloud consuming the stage. Julia was one of the last dancers remaining, and I remembered being completely swept up by her performance, by that somber expression she wore, the grief she portrayed. I made my roommate introduce us after the show, and I was a little thrown when I found Julia giggling with some friends, when she wasn't displaying the same sobriety that she did when she was performing. Nevertheless I said hello and told her how moved I was; I asked her out for coffee.

"This was so many years ago," I told Troy. "I almost feel like I'm making it up."

"Go on," he said.

I told him about my date with Julia and about how I went on and on, telling her that I respected her ability to transform her deep sadness into something so expressive—it was this that I envied about artists, I said—and then when I asked if she wanted to tell me about losing her brother, she said something like: Losing my brother? Oh, well, um, I'd rather let the dance stand for itself. I told her that I wanted to see more of her, and we planned more dates, and soon enough we were seeing each other every day and we became intimate and eventually inseparable.

It was only after some time had passed, a good two months of intense passion, that Julia informed me that I had misread my program, that she had not choreographed the piece that I had been so taken with, that she had not lost a brother, that she was in fact, like me, an only child. She said that she hadn't wanted to set me straight because she thought that was what drew me to her, her loss and her dance about her loss, and she thought I was cute and fun to be with, but she couldn't lie any longer, that it was too mean. Did I hate her? she asked.

"Did you?" Troy asked.

"Not at all," I said. "I was too in love with her by then to care. I had become attracted to her for other reasons, although . . ."

All these years later, in an anonymous prison room, I was filled with belated disappointment.

"Although?" Troy asked.

"In a small way," I said, "I feel—I mean, I felt cheated out of something."

Troy smiled.

"You find it funny," I said.

"No, I understand completely," he said. "You were looking forward to be the one guy who could really help her get over her brother's death."

"Was that it?" I asked.

"Or maybe you just wanted to go where she had been," he said.

"It's true," I agreed. "I'd never lost anyone. I was twenty-one. I wondered what it was like."

"It would be like going someplace where you don't speak the language," Troy said.

"Yes," I said. That was it exactly. There was travel in loss.

"That's what you thought anyway," he said.

"I did think that at the time," I said.

"But it's not such a great place to go to," Troy said.

"No," I said. "It isn't."

He wasn't wearing his glasses and one eye around his brow was a bit puffed up and pink. The side of his right hand was black with graphite. It was his turn.

"Tell me about Lauren," I said.

Lauren was his missing wife.

"Well, she wasn't a dancer," he said. Troy exhaled slowly, as if he were blowing out a plume of cigarette smoke. "Actually she was a singer. She wrote her own songs."

"What kind of songs?" I asked.

Troy didn't say anything for a while. Then: "If you picture, say, a house on a cliff looking over the ocean—"

"Wait," I said. "I asked what kind of songs she wrote, not what the video would look like."

"I'm telling you," Troy said.

"Sorry," I said.

"And there's nothing else for miles and miles around the house—can you picture that? Well, go in the house," he said, "and walk around. All the rooms are empty, there's no furniture. Go outside again, and on the other side of the house, out on the cliff, there's one chair there, and picture her sitting in it."

"Lauren?" I asked.

Troy closed his eyes and inhaled. "She has straight auburn hair, and she is humming something to herself, and soon she'll have to get up and leave the house—it isn't hers, she's just, you know, trespassing—but she doesn't know where she'll go."

Troy looked at me.

"I'd like to hear her songs," I said. "I have a feeling I'd like them."

Troy's face grayed.

"How long ago did you say she left?" I asked.

"Over two years—no, over three years," he said, "counting the year I've been in here."

"Do you want to tell me about what happened?"

"Not really," Troy said. But then, again after a long pause, he said, "We were living in Portland, doing odd jobs. Jared was young. Lauren and I were young, too, for that matter. We had dreams."

He leaned in closer.

"I wanted to make movies," he said. He laughed. "It seems pretty absurd now, but, you know, I thought I could, and Lauren, she wanted to sing the songs she wrote. So we went down to Los Angeles because that's where you go if you want to make movies and write songs, right? And we did okay there for a while, we really did. I mean we got by. We waited tables, did temp work, that sort of gig, but at least we were closer to the scene. Lauren was able to sing a couple of sets at small dingy clubs here and there, and I went to a film school for a year."

Troy licked his upper lip.

"Sometimes Lauren and I would take these long drives through the hills at night. The city looked so great at night. All the lights. But."

"But?"

"The film school was too expensive," he said. "I couldn't afford the second year. I'd spent all the money we had, and for what? Then."

"Then?" I asked.

"I don't know how it happened," Troy said. "The kid got older. Lauren had to work all the time, she stopped writing songs. I lost my job. There was the rent on our small apartment. There were bills. A kid to feed and clothe. I borrowed money from a storefront loan shark. Lauren and I fought all the time. All the time. I hated to be in our apartment with her. I would wander the city at night, by myself now. There were some nights I didn't come home. I was drinking."

Troy stopped. He sat very still.

"And then you borrowed more money," I said.

"And more money after that," Troy said. "I knew there was no way I could pay it back. Ever. Not all of it."

"How much are we talking about?" I asked.

Troy didn't give me a figure. All he said was, "Not a huge amount, but too much for me. I kept the loans a secret from Lauren."

"She didn't ask where the money was coming from?"

"No, and I didn't tell her because I didn't want her to worry," Troy said. "She never asked where I got the cash. So you talk about secrets—that was my secret."

"What were you going to do about the money?" I asked.

"Run away. Pack up the car and just run very far away," Troy said.

"Why didn't you?"

Troy shook his head.

"What?"

"I was getting my car repaired," he said, "and didn't have enough to pay for it and get it out of the shop, and so I was trying to find someone I could borrow the money from. As soon as I got the money and got the car, we would have been out of there. A few days, a week."

Troy stopped.

"Why do I feel like I'm not getting the whole story?" I asked.

"What story do you think you're not getting?"

"Couldn't you have bought some used car for next to nothing?"

"Actually," Troy said, "Lauren took some cash she'd scraped together and when I was out one afternoon, she went and got the car out of the garage. Then she took Jared out of school. Then they drove up the Coast Highway. Then they disappeared."

"Just like that?" I said.

"Lauren called in a few days from her parents' place. They lived back in Oregon. And then she didn't call again. Her parents wouldn't tell me where she went. Then I lost touch with them, too."

I didn't know what to say.

"Oh fuck," Troy said. He rubbed his brow. He looked at me. "I want to find them."

"You will find them," I said.

"How? I'm in here," Troy said.

"You'll find them when you get out of here," I said.

"That's it for today," Troy said, and he picked up his pencil and drawing pad, stepped across the room, and pounded hard on the metal door. Maybe I had pushed him too far. When the guard came and unlocked the door, Troy left without saying good-bye.

"**d**on't we have something more interesting to talk about?" Troy asked.

When I had come to the prison the next day and sat down across the table from him, my instinct was to call in the warden and demand an explanation. Troy's arms were bruised and one cheek was gashed. His nose was swollen, and he was having trouble talking. I never understood why guards looked the other way when an inmate got beaten up.

"What happened?" I asked for about the third time.

"What do you think happened?"

"You get picked on because you're small," I said.

"I get picked on because I don't fight back," Troy said.

"We have to get you out of here," I said. "We have to get going on the appeal."

Troy nodded. "I want out," he whispered.

"In the meantime, I'll see about getting you isolated," I said. I had a suspicion that Troy was being harassed because that was what happened to anyone in the prison world who was linked in some way to the death of a child. That was the argument that I would make to the warden for why Troy needed to be kept in a special ward for a while.

"I'm glad you come and visit me," Troy said. "You're my only visitor."

"I know," I said. Sometimes he seemed so helpless. He didn't belong here. And then my thought was that I would fare far worse in prison. I could never trade places with this man, not for a day.

"I hope you won't give up on me," Troy said in a weak voice.

"Never," I said.

"Even when you discover what a horrible person I am," he said.

"We're going to get you out," I said.

The next time I saw him, Troy looked better. His bruises had faded to grape stains, and the gash on his face had darkened into a thin scab.

"Are you okay by yourself?" I asked.

"Oh, it's much better, thanks," he said. "Not too many

other guys are in the ward right now." He was being kept in
the part of the prison where criminals who were too notori-
ous to be mixed into the general prison population were
held.

We talked for a few minutes, and then before I knew it, as
usual, we were not talking about legal matters at all.

"One night I came home from work," I said. "This was
when we were living in San Francisco. And I found all of
this pottery assembled on the dining room table."

"Pottery," Troy said.

"Tall cylindrical vases and squat round bowls. Plates and
urns. Cups, more vases. Twenty or thirty pieces, all lined up,
all in a series of shiny green and blue glazes."

"The wife went shopping," Troy said.

"The wife had been taking a class," I said. "She'd gone
out and taken a pottery class without telling me about it until
it was over."

"Why do I feel like I'm not getting the whole story?" Troy
asked.

"I thought that she was hard at work on her dissertation,
but she was learning how to throw clay."

"So?"

"Listen, I thought it was great that she was taking the
class," I said. "The pottery was beautiful. She wanted me to
be impressed, and I was."

"So?" Troy asked again.

"I felt left out. Why did she have to keep the class a secret
from me?"

"She did tell you," Troy said.

"Yeah, she told me," I said, "and do you know what happened after that?"

"She stopped making pottery," Troy said.

"She stopped— Right," I said. "As if I had made her
stop."

"And you never kept anything secret from her?" Troy
said.

I was silent.

"What secrets did you keep from her?" he asked.

Plenty, but in our chess game of disclosures, I felt like he was gaining an edge, and it was my turn to lean back in my chair and fold my arms across my chest.

"You never had an affair?" he asked.

I never did, but I didn't answer him.

"What did you keep from her?" he asked.

I said nothing.

Troy leaned forward. He slid one hand up the orange jumpsuit sleeve of his other arm. He looked like he was wearing a straitjacket.

"You want to know how I ended up here in this part of the world?"

"I've been wondering," I said.

"There's not much to say," he said.

He tapped his pencil on the back of his drawing pad.

I stared at him.

"You want to know why I didn't try harder to find Lauren after she left," he said. "I don't know. Half the time I was mad. Half the time I was drunk. I'm telling you there isn't much to say really."

"Tell me what there is to say," I said.

"I managed to pay off some money, but not much," Troy said. "I pawned whatever I could. But I lost my apartment, I was homeless. I'd get some work doing light construction, and I'd sleep in my car or on the beach. Clean myself up in a men's room in a mall, go to work. Eventually I'd start spending my money on tequila and dope."

Then Troy told me about how he woke up one day, and he stank, and he was half-covered in sand. He had fallen asleep on the beach. He had lost a shoe somewhere. He had no memory of the week that had gone by.

"I knew I had to find my family. I'd die without my family," he said.

So he cleaned himself up and he got the money together for a very used and dilapidated car. He began to work his way north. He didn't know where he would find his son, but he suspected that they would not stray far from the coast. It was just a matter of traveling north.

"I figured they were in Northern California or Oregon or Washington," Troy said.

"That narrowed it," I said.

Troy made it as far as Oxnard and then Ventura, and outside of Ventura, he was able to get a job working in an olive grove for a time.

"My thinking was that if I could get Jared and Lauren back, I'd take them back down there. Get Jared in school. Take care of Lauren for a change. And I'd work in the groves. I liked that work, although it was really exhausting. I liked working in the trees," he said.

Then Troy decided it was time to continue north, and he made it as far as Oak Valley. Near Oak Valley, his car broke down. It was a miracle that it had lasted as long as it did.

"I thought it was kind of a bad omen," he said.

"Cars break down all the time," I said.

"It was a sign," Troy insisted. His car needed a lot of work. He found a liquor store. He drank while he waited for his car. He ended up spending what money he had on gin and a cheap seaside hotel. He decided to ditch his car and started hitching rides, and that was how he ended up in Oak Valley.

"I lived in the old wineries," he said. "I was drinking again. I'd go into town and get something to drink, and then I'd hitch or wander by foot to another winery to hang out in for a week or so."

I wondered why I hadn't heard about Troy from anyone in town or seen him myself, for that matter. A stranger had a way of becoming very conspicuous in the valley.

"But all the while, I wanted to keep heading north. I knew that I'd eventually find a small town where I'd find my family," he said. "I was bombed out of my mind, but I knew if I just kept going north, I'd find them."

Troy stopped.

"And then?"

"You know the rest," Troy said.

"I don't," I said.

"I can't talk about it right now," he said. After a pause: "I don't believe that you didn't keep any secrets from Julia."

So we were back to me. And I didn't know what to say. Of course I had kept secrets from Julia, a whole catalog of secrets, but the only one that came to mind was the one that loomed over us now—I mean the nimbus hanging heavily even in the bright room where I sat with my imprisoned confessor—I mean the accident on the mountain road and everything that had happened since then.

My secrets? I started to tell Troy about how for a time I had fallen into the habit of going to the movies by myself when Julia thought that I was working late, and how when she wanted to see a film I had already covertly seen, I would go with her anyway, no matter how little I had enjoyed the movie, and I would pretend that I was seeing that movie for the first time.

I started to tell Troy about that, but the darker cloud shadowed me, and I said, "Sometimes I just felt like she knew me too well. I wanted something all my own."

"Like pottery," Troy said.

"All the vases and the bowls that I couldn't have," I said.

"A kid doesn't help sometimes," Troy said.

I didn't know what he meant exactly.

"With the kid there," he said, "you can feel like you and she have a lot in common when maybe you don't."

I understood. "Did you ever . . ."

"Did I ever what?" Troy asked.

"When you owed all of that money," I said, "did you ever think about just running away by yourself?"

"Oh," Troy said. A sigh. "Yeah, I have to say I thought about it."

"But Lauren ran away from you. You didn't run," I said.

"This is true," he said, and he grinned. It was then, for some reason, that he slid his spiral-bound sketch pad across the table and I got a look at his drawings.

I don't know what I had expected. Sketches of the prison

yard, the guard towers, the electrified fences. Maybe a picture of Lauren drawn from memory or one of his son. But somehow I did know that Troy would be deft with a pencil, and he was. On each page in the pad, he had drawn a landscape, and each landscape was intricately rendered. He aimed for a certain moody photo-realism. He had a fondness for dark clouds and for dusk, which appealed to me; I had the feeling that were I visually inclined, I would have tried to draw what he had drawn. With just a pencil, he had created an entire palette from black and gray and the absence of black or gray. I told him that I was impressed with his technique, and I asked him if he'd ever traveled to some ancient land, because each landscape, a barren hill, the edge of a forest, a knoll in the foothills, contained a loving portrait of ruins.

"I've never been anywhere except the West Coast," Troy said.

And then I looked at each page again, and I looked at Troy, and I had to laugh, because these were drawings of ruins, yes, but they weren't temples or the seats of oracles or shrines. They were much more local. It would seem that Troy Frantz had been busy all this time drawing the abandoned and weather-knocked wineries of Oak Valley.

The pages of the pad had begun to curl from the weight of the graphite, and since they weren't fixed, the corners were smudged. I flipped through the entire pad several times, lingering over each winery. There was the one with the turrets. There was the one with all of the symmetrical windows, the glass gone, the frames smashed. I looked for and found the winery with the cypress trees; Troy had perfectly captured the jagged stucco walls with all of their cracks and ivy, the piles of tiles, and trees reaching higher than the shell of the old winery. Also in the pad, I recognized some other places around the valley without wineries, certain fields of dead vines, the fruitless canes, certain white-faced quarries, and the view from the high rock on a summer day.

"Are you working from memory?" I asked.

"Yeah, memory," Troy said. He took the pad back from me and closed it.

"Then you were in Oak Valley for a while?"

"A couple months last summer," he said.

"Something about the place intrigued you," I said.

Troy didn't answer me.

"You got around the valley, but you haven't drawn any of the places that have been brought back to life. Some of us are growing grapes again, making wine," I said.

"That didn't interest me," he said. He sank a little in his chair. He looked very tired.

everything about Troy Frantz was dark. His complexion, his hair, his often-unshaven face. His black button eyes, his drawings. His past was all shadows, too. You wouldn't think that anyone would want to spend much time with him, and I wondered what he used to be like before—before his money troubles, before he lost touch with his family; I suspected that he had always been something of a gloomy fellow. I wondered about Lauren and whether her temperament had been as dark as Troy's. He had mentioned her lonely songs; were they as bleak as his drawings? Did all of this darkness draw him to her in some way? I never asked him that.

He was dark and he was grim, yet that January and then that February I craved his company, which scared me somewhat when I questioned why. Possibly I liked being with him in that prison room because his darkness matched the rain that I myself was drifting through, I don't know. Driving home and at home, I would play and replay the tapes of my conversations with him, none of which, by the way, I have saved. I kept them awhile, but eventually I got rid of them. I don't have his drawings, either. I never retrieved them from the prison, which I regret, because now and then I am unsure whether Troy really drew the ruined

wineries the way I remember he did, and for all I know, he
was more interested in the mountain range in the distance
and the roofless structure happened to fall within his frame.

I started visiting him almost every day, and our sessions
left me fatigued but high. Almost two months went by, yet I
had the feeling that I had known Troy for much longer. It was
always my intent to turn to the appeal, and we did talk about
his case, I did work on it, but mostly I remember Troy, weary
Troy, often sketching while we talked, grim Troy, gaunt and
stubbled, somehow speaking aloud what I was thinking at
that moment or what I had been thinking for some time. His
dark thoughts were my dark thoughts. My drift seemed
cousin to his drift. And to have stumbled into this friendship
was, well, it was energizing. That is the only word for it.

But I need to say that not all of our conversation was dark
and deep.

"Please don't laugh," Troy said, "but I've always kind of
gotten off on having them be like an inch or two taller than
me."

"Me, too," I said, "me, too."

I admit it. We were talking about what we liked in a
woman.

"And I don't want to put down, you know, women who
aren't like this," he said, "but . . ."

"You like them lean," I said.

"A little skinny," he said.

"I hear you. I'm the same way," I said. And then, as if
someone who might take offense was listening, I added,
"But the smile is the most important thing."

"Definitely," Troy said.

"An amazing smile is key," I said. "It means she's smart."

What else did we talk about?

Me: "I never learned how to cook before I came to the
valley and was on my own."

Troy: "I've always admired people who could make a
meal out of thin air."

Me: "A pasta sauce from whatever is lying around."

Troy: "Or an omelette. Lauren could make something from nothing, and fast."

Me: "Julia, too."

But our conversation did have a way of swerving unexpectedly toward the dark.

"Nothing lasts," Troy said.

Even if I agreed with him or agreed in part, I wanted to challenge him. "That's too grim for me," I said.

"What lasts? Tell me," he said.

"My old stone house," I said. "My grandfather built it over eighty years ago."

"It will fall apart eventually. The roof will go," Troy said, "then the walls. Hey, one good quake, and there goes the chimney."

"The trees around here," I said. "The oak, the pine."

"Oh please," Troy said. "Even the redwoods don't last forever. Eventually they collapse, and when they do, they take out a lot of other trees with them."

"My vines," I said. "For the most part, my vines seem to endure."

"Not forever they won't," he said.

"Okay, nothing lasts," I said. "What's your point?"

"I have no point," Troy said. "There is no point."

Once, I remember, I asked him about his onetime ambition to make films.

"What kind of movie did you want to make?" I asked.

Troy rubbed his nose.

"Come on. Tell me. What would your film look like?" I asked.

"It would be brown and black and gray," he said.

Surprise. I nodded. "And?"

"Okay. I wanted to make a film about a man whose life falls apart. He loses track of his wife after she leaves him. His son, too. He ends up wandering around a valley where there are all of these empty buildings." Troy stopped.

"And then what? That's just a beginning and maybe a middle."

"Where does it go," Troy said, a statement, not a question.

"Does that man end up in prison? Does he confess to something he didn't do because he gets confused and life is bleak and nothing lasts?"

"I don't know," Troy said.

"How does it end?"

Troy looked at me awhile and then he shrugged.

I think we had that conversation ten different times, ten different ways. We always ended up in the same place.

"Tell me how you want your story to end," I would say.

And Troy never responded.

These meetings with him, as I said, always took place in that white box, that cold room, until one day—it was the first week in March—I came to the prison and discovered that the routine for the special-ward inmates had been rearranged. Troy was out in the yard, by himself, walking around the gravel perimeter track. It was drizzling. I got an okay from a guard to go out and walk with him. It was the first time that I had met up with him outside the white room. I didn't take out my tape recorder.

"Hey," I said.

"Hey, Jason," he said. Droplets were forming on the lenses of his glasses, so he put them in his pocket.

"All of this rain," I said. "It's too much."

"I kind of like it," Troy said.

"You would," I said.

We walked around the track. It wasn't much of a turn, a quarter mile, if that, but there was something sort of exciting about the far side of the field away from the prison wall. There was a fence, but you could see through the wire of the fence to the empty field and the second fence beyond that, and then farther off, a glimpse of the interstate and all the freedom that an open road represented if you were inside. We walked around the track again. And one more time without talking about anything.

Then we stopped by the far edge of the track, and Troy asked me, "How's your son?"

We had talked often about the women in our lives, but little about our boys.

"He's doing better," I said. "He's out of the clinic he was at. He's living with his mother in San Francisco and he's back in school. He's seeing a shrink, and Julia says she thinks that's helping a lot."

"But you haven't seen him," Troy said.

"No."

"You haven't talked to him, either?"

"No," I said. I told him what had been going on: "When I call him, he doesn't want to talk to me. When I ask if I can come see him, he tells his mother to tell me no."

"You should try harder," Troy said.

"I know what you're thinking," I said. "At least I know where he is."

The rain was coming down harder suddenly, a light rain, and Troy's face was moist, as if he had been crying.

"I'm sorry," I said. "That wasn't kind of me."

"No," Troy said. "That was what I was thinking. But Jared . . . He probably wouldn't want to see me."

"Why?" I asked.

"Right before Lauren left—this is what finally made her leave—I was drunk. Really drunk," Troy said. "I came home. Jared happened to cross my path. I hit him. Hard. Once. Oh, man."

"The terrible things you may have done," I said.

Now the rain was coming down hard in the prison yard. Both Troy and I were soaked; at least I had a coat on, but Troy was wearing only a thin jacket over his uniform. The jacket and the uniform clung to his wiry body. His face was completely wet and he dug his hands into the pockets of his jacket.

"One night after I'd been hanging out in Oak Valley awhile, one night when it was pouring, I found a car parked on the side of that mountain road," Troy said.

"An old station wagon," I said.

"It was only drizzling when I started walking up the road, but then it really started to rain."

"I remember," I said. "It was the first hard rain of the season."

"I was skunked and just wanted a place to lie down, and whoever it was, probably peeing in the woods or something, had left the keys in the car. I looked around. I didn't see anyone. The fool, I thought."

"You wanted to start heading north again," I said.

"So I drove away, and like I said, I was drunk, and I knew it was a major crime, but I thought what the hell, I'll go a ways and dump the car before I get caught with it. And then I hadn't driven very far at all, and this small deer ran out right in front of me. I hit it. It ran off," Troy said. "I kept driving."

"You were caught shoplifting on the security video in a convenience store," I said.

"I was hungry," Troy said.

"But did you know about the boy"—say his name—"about Craig Montoya?"

"The next thing I knew," Troy said, "I was in this bar, watching television, and I saw my face on the screen. Luckily no one in the bar was paying attention. I looked like shit. I felt like shit. And then I listened to the report, and I thought, Oh no, oh no. I hit him. I ran him over. I thought I'd hit a deer."

Troy was almost whispering, and it was hard to hear him, what with the rain pounding the pavement all around us.

"You did hit a deer," I said.

"But I convinced myself that I had hit the boy," Troy said.

He dumped the car. He took his chances hitching other rides north. He needed another car and started looking around grocery store parking lots for keys left in the ignition.

"The second carjacking," I said. "With the baby in the backseat."

"I swear I didn't see the baby until it started to cry, and I looked in the rearview and saw some woman running after me," Troy said. "I gave the baby to the woman, and then I floored the gas."

He was on the run, fleeing a crime he hadn't committed—his only offense was stealing a car—and then he committed another crime, which wouldn't have happened if he hadn't had reason to believe that he had killed a boy. And he wouldn't have had reason to believe he killed Craig if I had come forward. Everything came back to me.

"I thought I'd hit that boy, and I was a mess when they caught me," Troy said. "And so when they started telling me that they were going to charge me with murder, I thought, Well, yeah, I am a murderer. I'm shit. I deserve what they give me. So I confessed. I would have signed whatever they wanted me to sign."

"You did hit a deer," I said.

"And I guess someone else hit the kid," Troy said.

I combed back my wet hair with my hand. I was shivering. Troy looked cold, too; his lips were turning blue.

"You say that now," I said, "but when did you realize it?"

"Not really until you came along," Troy said. "You confused me. I didn't know what to think for a while. And I have to tell you, sometimes I'm still not sure."

"You've done enough time for the car thefts," I said.

Now Troy was definitely crying. Through the rain, I could see that he was sobbing. "I want to tell my son that I'm sorry I hurt him," he said.

"We have to get you back to him. And to your wife."

"And you," he said.

"Me," I said.

"We have to get you back to your son and your wife, too," Troy said.

I didn't know whether I was crying with him, but my whole body shuddered as if I was weeping. I drew Troy to me and I hugged him.

When he pulled away, he said, "The appeal. I need it now. I need it right now."

I got home that evening and went upstairs to my shower and stood under the stream for a long while. Then I sat on the floor of the tub and let the warm rain pound my shoulders.

* * *

here were my choices: I could draft an appeal based on an error of law, but that probably would not get us anywhere. The various laws on the books that had put Troy in jail could not really be questioned for their constitutionality. Maybe someone more academically inclined, like a true appellate lawyer, might have been able to discern some area of dispute, but I didn't see any avenues to pursue. I could draft an appeal based on an error in due process, but the problem here was that my client had made a full confession and then signed all of the Tahl waivers, giving up his various rights to a trial. Plus, I wasn't sure and would have to skim my procedure handbook to check it out, but I was fairly certain that we had missed deadlines that needed to be met for filing habeas writs, if I wanted to claim, say, that there had been an illegal search and seizure or a sloppy Miranda and so forth. The fact of the matter was that it was virtually impossible for a man who has tendered a plea of guilty to change his mind later. There had been very little due process for me to call into question. All I really had was a transcript of the sheriff's interrogation—a transcript made from the questioning that was videotaped—and I wouldn't find anything useful there. Troy had been arrested and interrogated; a deal was inked; and he had gone before a judge who made sure that Troy understood the consequences of his admission.

That left me with an appeal based on new evidence. Since there hadn't been a trial, there had never been discovery, and, practically speaking, that meant that going through the evidence that existed was at first a matter of organization. I had already made several trips up to Hollister to negotiate my way through various basement files to collect crime-scene photos and forensics reports and then the boxes of physical evidence, all of the plastic bags and vials of detritus that had been collected. I had signed it all out and taken it back to the vineyard, but I couldn't look through the material; I couldn't face it. The folders had remained stacked on my desk and went unperused for weeks, and I found myself avoiding my desk altogether rather than revisiting the accident. My dread only escalated; anytime I thought about digging into the files, I developed a mean headache. I didn't want to go back to that night.

Finally one evening, I sat down at the desk and tried to breathe slowly and I opened the top folder. I examined the photographs of Craig Montoya lying dead in the woods. The pictures were in color and graphic. There were shots taken from every angle, from a distance and then closer and then a blowup of his bloated face, unrecognizable, waxen, mutilated. Streams of dried blood ran from the corners of his mouth.

I didn't know if I could go on. I was nauseous. At the same time, I admit that I was transfixed. I kept looking for myself in these pictures, for my shoe or my arm at the edge of the photo. I had to be there somewhere, but just out of the shot or cropped out because no one thought I was relevant, me, a horrified citizen, Joe bystander, not a criminal. Or I was a ghost who couldn't be captured with silver nitrate. I was a phantom who hovered over the poor dead boy, watching, worrying, but knowing that I could live my life unseen, that I could get away with murder.

There were other photographs, too, which were a little easier to look at—shots of my boot prints and the skid marks of my truck, the snapped birch, a random view into the dense of pine, photos of Craig's station wagon from the field where Troy ditched it, shots of that car's tire tracks—and even without the corpse, these pictures were eerie and left me with the same hangover that I'd had the morning after the accident. My fingertips became so cold that I could barely feel the stiff photos in my hands.

Then there was a box that contained some pieces of fabric and, for reasons I never understood, the shoes that Craig had been wearing, rain and mud and blood-soaked hiking boots, dry now. And finally, a clear plastic bag with the cashmere scarf that Julia had given me. You could see the scarf in the photos, and here it was. Once upon a time my favorite scarf. I felt like I was sorting through a lost-and-found box to claim what was mine and return what wasn't. The evidence was logged, but I thought I could remove the scarf and no one would know. I could destroy this evidence, and no one would probably figure it out. But what if a clerk doing his job made sure that all of the items that I had signed out came back. I was an officer of the court—finally I would be caught committing a felony—and if I hadn't announced my guilt before, I would be broadcasting it now loud and clear. I put the scarf back in the box.

I looked over the various lab reports. Analyses of the mud in the forest, of human hair and other fibers removed from Craig's body, of all of my scatological litter, of blood, so much blood, and of all the evidence gathered from Craig's car. I had seen this kind of chemical notation before, but I had always relied on the summary statements that the lab technicians attached. I was able to see, however, that some of the hair found in Craig's car didn't match the hair found on the mountain road; that much was obvious. And I noticed that the blood test results from the front fender of Craig's station wagon did not appear to be conclusively related to the victim.

The autopsy included photos, too, and the photos were of a boy who looked so swollen and blue, so much paler than the way Craig looked in the crime-scene shots, that I had to wonder whether the coroner had performed his autopsy on the correct victim. Maybe this was an unfortunate child who had overdosed that same night. But it was Craig. Look at what the coroner had to say. A young man thrown a great distance. A boy whose bones were broken in a thousand different ways. Who hemorrhaged all the blood he had in him. Who was hit by a car traveling at a dangerous speed. It was Craig.

I had to rush to my bathroom. That was all my weak stomach could take.

I returned to my desk and buried my head in my hands. I had no new evidence, and under our absurd law, new evidence was what I needed. All of the physical evidence in front of me on my desk didn't help me, not right now anyway; the fact that it wouldn't add up and wouldn't point to Troy was neither here nor there, because by pleading guilty, he had given up his right to have this evidence examined in court. If I could get Troy back to a trial where this evidence could indeed be presented, then I was certain I could make a swift dash to the end zone of reasonable doubt. It would be easy. And at a trial, I could call in a psychiatrist as an expert witness, and he could testify to Troy's state of mind and explain how a man like that could come to believe he was guilty. But how did I get back to a trial? First I had to navigate us back to the plea phase and plead not guilty, and in order to get to the plea phase, I needed brand-new evidence, not the old evidence, which I knew would win me an acquittal—this was the maddening circuit I was going around and around. I wondered if I could claim a new reading of the old evidence as new evidence. It seemed like a tenuous proposal, but I looked for precedents. It didn't take me long to see that I was in trouble.

Here was my problem: New evidence had to pass a difficult acid test. *People* v. *Huskins* said that I would have to prove that the new evidence would have affected the outcome of a trial, that it would have raised enough reasonable doubt in the minds of the jury to lead to a different conclusion than the one already reached. Okay, let's say that I could get that far, that the old evidence as new evidence did fall apart. Then I still faced *People* v. *Henry,* which said that my appeal would have to explain why my new evidence had not been available after a diligent search at the time when we could have gone to trial. And my evidence had been available.

I made my way to my kitchen and found a bottle of whatever I had been drinking the night before, a sweet syrrah, and I proceeded to gulp down three glasses. There was some new evidence that I could introduce, evidence that a diligent search probably wouldn't have uncovered, and oh boy, it would most definitely have affected the outcome of a trial. This new evidence would be quite easy to get ahold of. It would take the form of an affidavit, which I wouldn't have to go very far to secure. I could take out a pad and scribble down my confession.

"How's it coming?" Troy asked the next time I saw him at the prison.

We were back to meeting in the white room, and when I came in, he continued drawing on his sketch pad. He showed me what he was working on. It was another landscape, a view of a mountain range, with no abandoned wineries in sight. I didn't recognize it as anywhere in Oak Valley, but then, that might have been because, unlike all of Troy's other drawings, there was sun in this one. Great columns of sunlight pushing open a mass of clouds.

"The appeal is coming along," I reported.

"Excellent," Troy said.

"You've got some sun in there, I see," I said.

"I don't want Jared to think that all I can draw is rain," Troy said.

I didn't say anything.

"I'm going to use up every page of the pad and give all of the drawings to him," he said.

"What a great gift," I said.

Troy winked at me and rubbed a jag of a mountain with the side of his pinkie.

There was a time in my life when I loved puzzles. I was the child who took apart telephones. I became the man who solved the newspaper crossword each morning before paying attention to the headlines. There was a time when I craved board games. The trivia contests of long drives. I owned a racket for every racket sport known to man. I could play computer solitaire for

hours. But now the puzzle before me left me cranky and
bewildered. This impossible appeal. Now I loathed the
game that was the law.

I needed a new perspective on my dilemma, and I found
myself wandering around my empty house and sitting in all
of the rooms that I never used. There I was at the long table
in the dining room. There I was up on the cold bunk in Tim's
bedroom. I guess I thought that I would suddenly see the
solution merely by changing the angle from which I looked
outside at the rain. The rain pounded the roof. The rain
poured down the windows. It was the same rain everywhere.

There were chores around the vineyard that I had been
ignoring. I had cut back my vines, but I should have bottled
the second vintage weeks earlier, in February, and one day I
did make it down to the winery—I nearly twisted my ankle
on a broken step; the wooden stairs were rotting—and I
began blending the barrels. I finally dumped the ones that
had turned to vinegar, but I still had a fair amount of wine.
Soon I was mixing egg whites into the fining tank.

I think it was while I was letting the wine sit on the finings that my cordless phone rang. My phone rang so rarely
that my heart always fluttered these days when it did.

"Hey," Julia said.

"Oh, hey," I said.

I should explain that we had started talking again more reg-
ularly that winter. Back in January, I called her once a week;
I always phoned her, she never phoned me. I wanted to check
on Tim's progress after he came home from the clinic. I
wanted to hear her voice. And our conversations were so brief
that I often wondered whether they had actually happened.

"So how is Tim looking to you?" I would ask.

"He's looking better," Julia would answer.

"Better? What, like his hair's growing back?"

"Like his hair is growing back," Julia replied. "I've got to
run," she said, and that was that.

Another time I called, I said, "You know, I really want to
see him."

"Well, I do bring it up and, oh, he's just not ready," she said.

"He blames me for what happened," I said.

"He has said he's angry, but— I'm sorry," she said. "I know it's not fair."

"He needs time," I said.

"He needs time," Julia said, "right."

"He's still seeing his psychiatrist?" I asked.

"Twice a week."

"I guess we can't watch him every minute," I said.

"Every other minute, I think about checking up on him," Julia said.

All of a sudden there was a lot of static on the line.

"Got to run," she said, and was gone.

Eventually our conversations became longer, and we began to talk about the rain and what Julia was up to, rounding a corner in her research, working in a bookstore, but we didn't talk about me. We didn't talk about the vineyard, and as I said, I always phoned her.

"Oh, hey," I said when she called me instead. I wanted to disguise my surprise.

"You sound like you're at the bottom of an aquarium," Julia said.

"I'm out in the winery," I said.

"Yeah?"

"Bottling the second vintage," I said. "I'm just getting to it. I've been kind of busy. I've . . ." Then I remembered that she was calling me and that I wasn't the one who needed to fill the empty lapses in our conversation.

"I just wanted to let you know that I might be moving," Julia said.

Moving? Moving where? To another city, out of the state? How far away?

"Oh, really," I said.

"Just across the Bay probably. We could get a much bigger place and pay so much less rent. Tim could still go to the school I've got him in."

"Great," I said.

"I just wanted to let you know," she said. "I mean, so if I called and I said, Look, I'm moving across the Bay, you wouldn't be surprised."

"Right," I said.

"If we do move. I don't know. We may not move," she said. "I do like it here in the Mission."

I didn't know what to say.

"I broke up with that guy you never liked," she said.

"The painter," I said, and I suspect that I probably responded a little too quickly and with too much evident pleasure.

"That doesn't mean—"

"I know," I said. It didn't mean that she would be mooring her skiff in my harbor anytime soon.

"I just wanted to tell you," she said.

"I appreciate it," I said. "I hope you're not too upset," I added.

"You and I are such old friends," Julia said.

I leaned against the vat. I could hear the rain thrumming the slope outside.

"I wish I could see Tim," I said. "It's been months."

"I know," Julia said. "I tell him he should talk to you, but—"

"You do?"

"Then he gets mad at me, and I don't know, maybe I don't push him hard enough because I'm afraid he'll shut me out, too."

"Our son adores you," I said.

"Thanks," she said. "Thanks for saying that."

"You know about his computer name," I said. We had talked about it. "How he was going around pretending to be the dead boy."

"Craig Montoya," Julia said. "Yeah, why?"

"Oh, Julia," I said, sighing. "It's all my fault. It really is my fault."

"Why? Because you made Tim live in the valley and a

boy was killed and he became obsessed with him? That's not your fault, Jason."

But it was, it was, and I longed to tell her why. I longed to tell someone.

"You started to tell me that you were busy," Julia said.

"Oh, with the appeal. Have I mentioned the appeal I'm filing?" I knew damn well that I hadn't. I told Julia now about how I had taken Troy on.

"I didn't realize you were doing any more work for Legal Aid," Julia said.

"It's not for Legal Aid," I said. "But I am doing it pro bono."

Julia didn't respond.

"The guy doesn't belong in jail, and I can't let him sit there," I said.

"So you're on a crusade," Julia said. Her tone was somewhat snide.

"He has no one," I said. "And I can help him."

"This must not be too popular with the folks in the hardware store," Julia said.

"I wouldn't know," I said. "I never go into town."

Julia was silent. Then she said, "Be careful. Just be careful, okay?"

I can't say that I was warmed by the caution in her voice. She sounded suddenly far away to me. Be careful, as if also to say, Don't tell me I didn't warn you. As if to say, You don't know what you're getting into. As if to say, Don't come to me for help. You're on your own.

I got back to the bottling. I wanted to let the wine sit on the finings a while longer, and so I prepared the racks for the new bottles. The first vintage was all stacked and getting dusty on the racks on the right side of the room, and the left side was still empty. The rack on the left was the one that, if it was empty, you could swing aside to get to my grandfather's secret vault. I looked at the empty grid of racks and I gasped.

The vault. I had forgotten about what I had stashed there.

I made a pathetic criminal. It was only a matter of pure luck that I had not been caught. I had intended to get rid of the bags of clothes and my jacket and my boots, all the evidence that would most definitely link me to the accident, but I had forgotten about it. I had lost my mind. I had to get rid of it. Right away. I had to burn the clothes.

I pulled back the rack. I pried open the vault with a crowbar. A waft of musty air surrounded me. And I became very dizzy. The vault was empty.

how much did Julia know and how much did she not know? Back up: When did she find out about the vault? When did she find the clothes? What had she done with them? Did she get rid of them? Did she think that I knew that she had gotten rid of them?

I decided that she must have seen and possibly heard me when I came home late that October night, that morning after Troy Frantz confessed. Yes, because after I came home and moved the bags from the upstairs closet down to the winery, I remembered coming back into the house and discovering her in the kitchen, hacking away at a chocolate cake—

She knew. I was sure of it. She had known all along. She had cleaned up after me. And I began to resent her for not telling me that she knew. Or maybe I resented being exposed, found out, naked all this time. She had known all along and let me destroy myself with my secrecy.

Why didn't she tell me that she knew? Why didn't she try to help me?

I was confused. I didn't want to talk to Julia anytime soon. If I heard her voice, I was likely to snap. She could have helped me and she chose not to, or she thought she was helping me when she got rid of the incriminating evidence, but she hadn't helped me at all. She could have counseled me. She could have held me and lied and said everything

would turn out okay. I could have rested my head in her lap,
and she could have stroked my hair. Everything would turn
out okay.

Now I didn't think that I could ever turn to her. Now I was
all alone.

$f$or months, I had avoided going into town. I
drove to New Idria when I needed food and gas, but every
now and then I needed something that I could find only in
the hardware store. As I was beginning to siphon the second-
vintage wine from the fining tank into the bottles, I noticed
a tear in a stretch of hosing; I ended up having to replace the
entire tube. I had run out of hosing, however, and that meant
running into town; that meant trying to enter the hardware
store without being noticed and sneaking over to the aisle
where I would find my supplies. Then I would approach the
register and pay for my purchase as quickly as possible, staring at my feet all the while.

I zoomed down the main drag and skidded up to the hardware store. My shoulders tensed at the jingle of bells that
announced my arrival, and then, to my dismay, I couldn't
find the food-grade hosing that I wanted in its usual spot.

"Jason," Will Clark said from his stool by the key-copying
machine.

Alex Marquez and Emma Hodges stood on either side of
him, all three of them in a row. For some reason, they were
all behind the counter, forming an inscrutable tribunal.

"I'm looking for some hosing," I said.

"That so," Will Clark said.

"I'm bottling," I said.

"You don't say," he said.

Alex Marquez snorted. He was packing a cardboard box
with cans of food and dried goods. He slid the box across the
counter to Will Clark, who looked in the box and then at me.

"Know what this is?" Will Clark asked.

"Looks like a care package," I said.

He nodded. "And would you care to add anything?"

Emma Hodges looked down her nose at me. She was holding a pair of large scissors. Alex Marquez handed Will Clark a ball of twine.

Will Clark said, "It's for Mrs. Montoya and her daughter." I swallowed.

"See, they've got it kind of rough right now," he said.

"I just need some hosing," I said.

Alex Marquez puffed. "You come in here and have the nerve to flaunt—"

"Flaunt? Flaunt what? That I have wine to bottle?" I asked.

"I guess that means you don't have anything to put in the box," Will Clark said, and closed the flaps of the box and began to tie the twine around it.

Emma Hodges took the box from him and tied a knot and cut the twine with her scissors. She added the box to a stack next to the rack of blank keys.

"So do you sleep well at night knowing the Montoyas are suffering while you defend an evil man?" she asked.

"Troy Frantz did not kill Craig Montoya," I said.

"You know this for a fact," she said. "Even though he says he did it."

"He's innocent," I said. "The wrong man was put away."

Will Clark stared at me. "Aisle three," he grunted.

I returned moments later with a spool of hosing. I paid for it in cash. I left before Will Clark handed me my change.

Outside a light rain had thinned somewhat, and as I was getting in my car, I saw a round black figure waddle toward me. I recognized the mother of the boy I had killed. She was wearing a black plastic rain scarf. Her ankles were swollen, her lope difficult. Mrs. Montoya was dragging some kind of shopping cart behind her, and I wondered if she had walked all the way from her house. That was too far, but I didn't see her car or truck anywhere on the street. I didn't know if she saw me when she entered the hardware store. I wanted to wait until she came out. I wanted to talk to her. I wanted to tell her that she had focused her wrath on the wrong man, but I drove away before she emerged.

•

I replaced the torn hose and spent the rest of the evening and the next day and the day after that siphoning my wine into bottles and racking the bottles in my cellar. It took a long time without any help, but I enjoyed the mindless repetition of the chore.

When I was done bottling my second vintage, I decided to open a bottle of my first. It would take another year before it was finished, but I wanted to sample it now anyway, and so I took a bottle inside and removed the cork—the cork slid free from the bottle without a pop, as if it had been greased—and I poured a glass.

I had made it. We had made it, Julia and Tim and I, and it looked so beautiful, the clear ruby mass of the cabernet in the crystal, that I almost didn't want to drink it. But I held it up to the light and then I rolled the stem of the glass in my fingers and I sniffed the bouquet, and what I smelled was a certain spring field, a meadow somewhere far away. A dry place, a sunny place, a familiar place—but where?

I smelled violets and I smelled tall rye, a hint of sage.

I took a sip. I took another.

I closed my eyes and I could see the field now, the meadow.

Julia and I had just come to California. She was pregnant with Tim, though we didn't know it yet. We had decided to get out of the city for a day and had driven nowhere in particular up the coast road until we found a forest. We got out of our car and hiked through the trees to a meadow—the meadow ran up to a cliff—and we found a clearing in the meadow where we could spread a blanket. There was no one in sight. We had the Pacific to ourselves. We could hear but not see the waves crashing against the rocks a hundred feet below us.

We were all alone, and I took off my shirt. Julia ran her hands up and down my arms and across my chest. She took off her shirt, too, and she lay on top of me, and our bare chests pressed against each other. She told me that her back would burn, and so, without letting her slide off of me, I reached into my backpack and found the suntan lotion and managed to get the cap off and squirt some of it on Julia's back. And then I massaged it in. Julia sat up and I rubbed the lotion across her breasts. She took the tube from me and began working my chest with the cool balm. She rolled me over and rubbed my back.

How had so many years slipped by? I drank another glass of our first cabernet and lingered there, in that meadow, rubbing a lemon lotion all over the body of the woman with whom I thought I would spend the rest of my life.

I sat at my kitchen table and drank the whole bottle, but I didn't get drunk at all, not at all.

The next morning I woke up when the phone rang. I woke up in Tim's room, although I didn't remember wandering up there.

"I haven't seen you in a while," Troy said.

That would be because I've been avoiding you.

"Sorry," I said.

"I was getting worried you had second thoughts or something about my case."

"Never, Troy," I said.

"So how's my appeal?" he asked.

"I've made a lot of progress," I said, nearly gagging on my lie.

"That's great. When will you be done with it?" he asked.

"Soon," I said.

"When will you come see me?" he asked.

"Soon," I said.

"Soon," he echoed.

"I'm close," I said. "Don't give up hope," I said.

I had made no progress. I was not close at all. No appeal seemed reasonable, but I needed to come up with something. I had phoned various lawyers I knew for advice, including my friend back in Legal Aid, and all of them concurred that there was little I could do. One of these attorneys, however, a law-school acquaintance who had a criminal appellate practice, had encouraged me to go back and look for errors in due process. He had also recommended that I limit the remedy I was seeking. Trying to file a habeas writ to get my client out of jail completely would make the judges hostile; trying to renegotiate the sentence might get me further. What I really wanted for Troy was for him to be able to enter a new plea, and then in my wildest dreams I would secure a demurrer and the charges would be dismissed and Troy would go free. He would get in a car the same day and continue on his journey north to find his family.

But I couldn't see it. I couldn't solve the puzzle.

When I went downstairs, I noticed the empty wine bottle on a lower step. I sat on the step and held the bottle up to my lips. I blew air across the bottle and issued a deep note.

And then I saw it. A way out. Maybe.

I needed to drive up to Del Norte County. I needed to contact a psychologist. And a zoologist. And I had to hope that I would find some precedents to bolster my scheme.

"a good contract is lean and mean," I told Troy two days later. I hadn't slept at all and realized that I was probably a little manic. "An appeal should be the same way."

Troy sat at the table with his hands folded as usual, although he didn't have his drawing pad with him. He watched me while I circled him, pacing the edge of the small room, around and around him like a dizzying electron.

"I don't want the appeal to look like we're groping around

in the dark," I said. "I don't want to load it with extraneous points."

Troy nodded and followed me around another lap. He was sitting on the edge of his chair.

"The fact is that I've always taken your confession, your plea, to be our biggest liability, and it is a hurdle. But after trying to see a way around it, over it, beyond it, I realized that I could just dive right into it."

Troy stroked his chin.

"When someone confesses, it can be for either of two reasons," I said. "As a tactical move, a concession made during a negotiation. Or as a genuine expression of sorrow and remorse, as an acceptance of responsibility for something you've done. The court doesn't really differentiate between the two, although it should."

"I thought I hit that boy," Troy said. "I convinced myself I hit that boy."

"You thought you should pay," I said.

"I did, yeah."

"Excellent," I said. "And you'll be telling all of that to the therapist I've arranged for you to meet. I can't present evidence with this appeal, but I'm going to try to attach a psychological review and see what happens. Regardless, I think I'll be able to show that while you were being questioned, when you made your confession, when you waived your rights to a trial, you were acting in good conscience. You wanted to do the right thing."

"I did, yeah," Troy said.

"And the district attorney did not."

Troy grinned, but he looked confused.

"There you were, a moral man," I said, "acting in good faith, telling the truth simply because you believed the truth should be told. And there was the sheriff and the district attorney, trying to nail you at any cost, playing a game with you, angling, strategizing, acting in bad faith."

"Oh," Troy said.

"You were being honest and forthright and they were taking advantage of you to close the case fast."

"I see," Troy said.

"This appeal is not about evidence," I said, "even though the evidence would prove your innocence."

"It's not?" he asked.

"No, because I'd have to offer some explanation for why you didn't present the evidence at a trial. The appeal is not even about your innocence."

"It's not," Troy said.

"No, although I think that your innocence will become obvious. I know, it doesn't make a lot of sense. Welcome to the criminal-justice system. See, the appeal has to be about how your rights were violated. And then if we go back to a trial, we'll look at the evidence and talk about your innocence, and then back at a trial, you won't carry the burden of proof the way you do in an appeal. The people would have to make the case, and all they have is a case based on dubious physical evidence, a case they can't win."

Troy frowned.

"Let me walk you through the actual appeal," I said. "First of all, you were drunk when they picked you up."

"But I sobered up," Troy said. "I'm sorry. I don't mean to be difficult."

"No, please," I said. "Be difficult. You were drunk, and then you say you sobered up, but how did the sheriff and the district attorney know that? How did they know when you sobered up?"

I reached into my briefcase and pulled out a report that I'd retrieved from the DMV up in Del Norte County. It was the Breathalyzer test that Troy had been given when he was arrested. The officer didn't need to prove that Troy was driving under the influence in order to arrest him—he had a warrant—but he was a rookie and he must have thought he was helping the cause by piling on another charge. He had tested Troy and begun filing the report, although he never finished it. He was probably told to drop it, but he had transmitted the report to the DMV and never asked to have it erased, so it was in limbo in the DMV computer. It was my proof of Troy's insobriety.

"Jason, by the time I confessed, I felt like shit, but I was sober," Troy said.

"I know. But when the charges were explained to you," I said, "the sheriff didn't necessarily know that you were sober enough to understand them. It's not like they gave you another Breathalyzer."

I removed a folder from my briefcase, the transcript made from the videotaped interrogation. All day long the police had gone in and out of the room where Troy sat, talking to him for fifteen minutes here, an hour there, leaving him alone for long stretches, then coming at him with questions. The transcript was over one hundred pages long, but nowhere in it did I find any explanation of the charges, which to me meant that they had probably told him what they were holding him for early on, before he sobered up.

"The Sixth Amendment," I said, "guarantees that you have to be informed of the charges against you, but there's no record that you were informed, and certainly not at a time when you could have reasonably understood what you were being accused of."

"I see," Troy said.

"I think that borders on coercion," I said, "which is a legitimate basis for an appeal. And then, my second point . . ."

I flipped through the interrogation transcript until I found a threat, or something akin to a threat, made late in the day. I showed Troy the highlighted page.

"They told you that they could make a deal then, that night, but that as the evidence was processed, that deal might evaporate," I said. "That pressure is unfair. That's in part why you agreed to the plea, isn't it?"

"I thought I was acting out of good faith," Troy said, "trying to do the right thing."

"You were, you were, but that's not the point here," I said.

"The point is that they can't offer you a deal and put a time limit on it."

"Isn't that done all the time?" Troy asked.

"You were not necessarily sober when they informed you of the charges," I said. "They questioned you over a long day and into the night, and then when they offered you a deal, you had to take it right away, without getting to sleep on it, without getting to think it over."

Troy swallowed. "They did talk a lot about the death penalty."

"Oh, that's because they were ready to file for felony murder," I said, and slapped the table. "Which brings me to my third point. Back to improperly informing you as to the nature of the charge."

From the transcript again, I knew that the sheriff and the district attorney had never offered Troy any evidence of a carjacking. Grand theft auto, yes, but there was no evidence, at least none offered during the interrogation, that Craig Montoya was present when Troy took the car, and then the whole upstate car theft was not necessarily a carjacking because the woman had appeared as Troy was driving away, not when he initially stole the vehicle. At least no one had suggested an attempted kidnapping of the baby in the backseat. All they had were two grand theft autos, yet they bargained with Troy from the point of view of having two carjackings, with one being bumped up to a murder charge. They started out from a higher position on the ladder of offenses than they should have, necessarily making Troy climb higher himself than he had to.

I explained all of this to Troy, and I said, "And since the deal you accepted was ultimately founded on that false representation of the charges, the deal itself should be called into question."

"They didn't play fair," Troy said.

Understatement of the decade. I pounded the table again. "It was particularly not fair since you repeatedly turned down the opportunity for counsel. You were accepting your culpability, anxious to put this horrible episode behind you, taking responsibility for your actions, speaking openly and honestly, but they were screwing you every which way they could to make sure they didn't have to go to a grand jury with evidence they didn't have and knew they probably never would have. It makes me angry."

I genuinely believed that the district attorney had violated Troy's rights. I was the last person who should be pointing this out, but Troy had been denied his due process.

"I should have had a lawyer," Troy said.

"Yes," I said. "Even to plead guilty, you should have a lawyer. The DA was thrilled you didn't ask for one, and you know what else? If you had agreed to their original accusation—I mean, if they had insisted on trying you for murder one and you pleaded guilty, they would have had to get you a lawyer, because you can't plead guilty to a capital offense without one."

"Normally I don't trust lawyers," Troy said.

I raised a brow.

"I've had some bad experiences in the past with lawyers," he said. "But I trust you."

I trust you, he said, and his words bounced around the room. And I wanted this man to trust me; after all, I was a double agent, wasn't I? I needed his trust so I could believe that what I was doing was right. I needed his faith to liberate us both, and so in retrospect I think that was why I didn't really hear what he was telling me, what I should have questioned right away. What bad experience in the past with lawyers was he referring to exactly? I heard only, I trust you, and I moved on.

"Here's another point," I said. I realized that I was shouting, and so I lowered my voice. "The district attorney and the sheriff unfairly placed the burden of proof on you."

"How?" Troy asked.

"They never checked out your story."

"I had the boy's car," Troy said.

"But you had no contact with the boy," I said. "There's no

proof of it. Your fingerprints and fibers will be in the car, sure, but not on the corpse. There's hair on the corpse, but you had no contact with the boy, so it won't be your hair. Not that anyone fully analyzed the lab results. And you said you thought you hit a deer."

"I did, yeah," Troy said. "The sheriff told me I was full of crap and that there was no deer."

"You did hit a deer," I said. I pulled another two sheets from my briefcase. One was the blood test from the sample taken from the bumper of Craig's car. The results were inconclusive. The second sheet was an examination of the same results by a biologist in San Diego, who confirmed my suspicion that the blood on the front bumper could indeed be deer blood.

"The people have an obligation to check out your story," I said. "Checking out your story would have meant waiting for the forensics, but they somehow knew not to wait. They knew they could flip you before the blood tests came back. Look, if you'd given them an alibi, they'd have had to check the alibi before they went any further."

"The burden of proof," Troy said.

"You thought you were guilty, but you weren't sure. So you were holding out, and then finally, you decided you must have hit a boy and not a deer, and so you didn't fight them anymore," I said. "Isn't that what happened? It's like they were waiting for you to make a case for yourself, for you to come up with the evidence that would save you, rather than them presenting you with the evidence that proved your guilt. Do you see how I'm saying they changed the rules on you?"

Troy's shoulders sank. He leaned back in his chair. "Will this be enough? Will this do it?"

I sat down. I honestly didn't know. Maybe not.

But I looked squarely at Troy and I said, "They didn't play fair, they deceived you, they made you do their work for them. And I think that they knew exactly what they were doing. I have one more point." I paused, and then in one breath: "Just because you didn't have a lawyer present doesn't mean that you shouldn't have been afforded the information your lawyer would have asked for and been given. You see, they denied you—deliberately denied you— potentially exculpatory information."

Had there been a trial, I explained, there would have been reciprocal discovery. The people and the defense would have traded their evidence.

"During the trial, each side can edit. But in a sense, you get to read the unedited story first," I said.

So Troy didn't have a trial, and therefore no discovery. And my point was that the people had to present him with all of the evidence that they had when they had it.

"I'm saying that the discovery should extend to the plea negotiation, if the defendant is going to waive his right to a trial. The procedural code needs to protect defendants who waive the right to counsel, too."

Troy cocked his head.

"I'm saying that before you plead guilty, you should see all of the evidence, no matter whether it helps the prosecution or it helps you. I've got Supreme Court cases all the way back to *Brady* v. *Maryland* and up to *Kyles* v. *Whitley* that affirm reciprocal discovery."

Troy was squinting at me. Did he know that I was probably applying my precedents too broadly?

"What?" I asked.

"What did they have that would have helped me?" he asked.

I tapped the folder containing the interrogation transcript. "Remember this is all on video, too," I said.

Then I pulled out the photographs from the crime scene. I showed Troy the pictures of Craig dead in the woods; looking at them, we both flinched. I showed him the photos of the forest and then of the road with the skid marks of my truck. My truck.

"When they were questioning you, they showed you these photos," I said.

"They made me sick," Troy said.

"Me, too," I said, which may have sounded strange. "But they didn't show you these photos," I said, and I pulled out the pictures of the stretch of road and the field where Craig Montoya's car was found. "We're not talking about lab reports that hadn't come in yet. These are photos they had at the time of the interrogation, photos that they could have and should have but did not, I repeat, did not show you."

Troy looked at the photographs and shook his head.

I found the photo of my truck's skid marks on the mountain road. I placed it next to a photo of Craig's station wagon's tracks in the mud by the field.

"They don't match," Troy said.

"They don't look anything alike," I said.

The marks my truck's tires made were broad and jagged, and, by contrast, the station wagon's worn treads left delicate and narrow impressions.

"If you'd seen all of the photos, and then if you'd been given a chance to have your story checked out, you might not have pleaded guilty," I said.

"I don't know if I would have been able to see the difference between the tracks," Troy said. He looked at the photos again. "But that doesn't really matter, does it?"

I grinned.

"Another car hit that poor kid," Troy said.

"I know," I said, and stopped smiling.

"That poor kid," he said.

"It's very sad," I said. "But it wasn't you."

"So I'm in here and the real killer is out there somewhere," Troy said.

The back of my neck tensed. I could feel myself blush. I stood and paced again.

"It's like they lied and told you they had recovered the murder weapon, when in fact they hadn't," I said.

"I feel foolish," Troy said.

"Don't," I said. "You were ripe to be picked. All you wanted was to be reunited with your wife. With your son."

Now it was Troy's turn to blush.

"That's why I want you to talk to the therapist," I said. "You were so tired that you were almost looking for a way out, a way to sleep. And when you woke up, you were in jail."

I explained the remedy we would seek with the appeal. There was no verdict to set aside. We just wanted to go back to the arraignment.

"Then a trial," Troy said.

"Or not," I said. "We might actually plead guilty, if it's two counts of grand theft auto they come back with and we can get you out right away with time served. Or it's possible that the DA won't even file new charges at all."

As I got up to leave, Troy stood to shake my hand.

"Thank you, Jason," he said.

"Look," I said, "it may not work."

"Thank you anyway," he said.

The next day, Troy met with the psychologist, and he saw her several times over the next week. I filed a notice of appeal. Days after that, I brought Troy the statement of appeal for him to sign, and I filed it later that afternoon. And so we had climbed aboard the great train of the law, its wheels turning in a slow chug, pushing forward toward the next station.

I went down to see Troy again after the appeal was certified. I didn't have any news for him. The date was April 22, and I remember that during my drive down to the prison, the clouds broke and the first wash of sun in months splashed across the interstate. The next day, it would rain again, but that afternoon it was sunny and the night was clear.

Troy looked different. I had only known him a short while, but I thought that he had changed. He greeted me at the door of the white room as if he were welcoming me into his modest home. He asked if I wanted anything to drink. Soon a guard brought me a can of soda.

I haven't mentioned it, but once Troy was moved to the ward for isolated prisoners, the only people he spoke to were the guards, and they regarded him with as much fondness—

read: bending the rules—as they could. It turned out that one
guard in particular, the tall and balding man with small eyes
and a wide derelict smile whom I usually saw leading Troy
around, was something of an amateur artist. He had won
some local prizes for his desert watercolors and he brought
in slides of them for Troy to see. This guard thought that
Troy should enter his drawings in a statewide penitentiary
contest, and Troy told the guard that they were for Jared and
only Jared, once Jared was found. The guard said, I think
your son would like them even more if they were framed and
had a nice blue first-prize ribbon attached.

Troy and I sat there in our white room and clinked soda
cans, and we didn't say anything. It was his eyes, I realized;
that was what was different about him. He had stopped
wearing his glasses. I didn't know how badly he had needed
them, and I doubted anyone wore contacts in prison, so I
wondered whether his eyesight had somehow improved over
the last months. In any case, his dark eyes were not quite as
black or dull as they once were. His eyes looked browner to
me, as if some hard dark surface had worn away.

"So what about you?" Troy asked.

"Me?"

"You're helping me get out of here so I can get back to my
son," he said. "But what about your son?"

"My son," I said. "Oh, he still won't talk to me. I'm waiting for him to—"

"You know where he is," Troy said.

"I do," I said.

"If I could talk to my son," Troy said, "I would tell him
that it would be okay if he was mad at me for years. But I
would also tell him that no matter what, he would always be
my son." Troy drew in a deep breath and exhaled fast. "I
would tell him that's just the way it is."

"You will get to say all that someday," I said.

"But you know where your son is," he said.

I wondered if the world looked different to Troy through
his new eyes.

"If you wait too long," he said, "he'll be gone."

"I know," I said.

"Don't wait too long," Troy said. "Don't wait."

When I left the prison, I drove north and eventually crossed over the Diablo Range, but instead of finding the mountain road and making my way home, I continued west and north and drove the additional hours to Berkeley. It was almost disconcerting to be driving without the windshield wipers going at full swipe; I kept checking to make sure my lights were on, that I had enough gas, because I was sure that I was forgetting to do something. The night was dry, that was all, and once I got used to it, I was able to drive faster.

Julia was living on the top two floors of an emaciated but generously turreted Victorian. She buzzed me in and I climbed the steep flights up to her apartment, fully expecting to be reamed out for showing up unannounced at nine-thirty on a school night.

But Julia, dressed in an old sweatshirt and jeans, gave me a friendly hug and said, "I didn't tell him it was you. He's in his room." She pointed toward the back of the house.

"I couldn't stand it anymore," I said.

"This has gone on long enough," Julia agreed.

Her hair was pulled back into a loose ponytail.

"I'm sorry I didn't call," I said.

"Talk to him," she said. "He can handle it. Just talk to him."

I knocked on Tim's door. The music he was playing was loud and I had to knock again.

Tim didn't turn around from his computer. He said, "I hope you're bringing me coffee, because I am going to be up all night with these guys."

"Hey," I said.

Tim spun around on his swivel chair.

He looked good. He had gained some weight and his cheeks were tanned. Even from across the room, I could see a faint scar that traced the arc of his left eyebrow, but other than that, I saw no outward evidence of his injuries.

I wanted to hug him. I wanted to hold him.

I didn't say anything at first. I crossed my arms and leaned against the door frame. I thought that I would be nervous, but I wasn't at all. I was so glad just to see him and have him see me that I could have gone away for a while and come back another time.

"What guys are these?" I finally asked. "You said you were going to be up all night with these guys."

"The Beats," Tim said. His voice cracked. "I'm writing a paper on the Beat poets. Hey, Dad," he said.

To hear that word again, Dad. It was like a doctor shaking my hand for the first time. Congratulations, Mr. Dark, you're the father of a healthy baby boy.

"I know I should have called first," I said.

"I wouldn't have taken the call," Tim said, and swiveled around toward his computer again. He tapped a key.

I decided to take a chance and I crossed the room and sat on the bed.

Tim reached over to his stereo and turned down the volume.

"I've missed you so much," I said.

Tim swallowed.

"You don't know how much," I said.

"How's the vineyard?" Tim asked.

"Wet," I said. "Very wet."

"The vines are okay?" Tim asked.

"So far, but with all this rain, I don't know what kind of fruit we'll get."

I wasn't choosing my words with any great care, but I realized that each one carried a measured weight for my son. I don't know what kind of fruit we'll get, not what kind of fruit I'll get.

"If you're mad at me for years, that's fine," I said. "If you don't want to talk to me or see me for a long time, that's fine. But I have to tell you—I came here to tell you—that no matter who you are, no matter what you do, where you go in the world, you're my son and always will be and I love you. That's just the way it is. There's nothing you can do to change that."

Tim stared at the computer screen.

I had said what I wanted to say, or as much as I thought I could, and I stood up to leave my son alone.

Then, in a weak voice, Tim said, "I have been pretty pissed, I guess." He looked at me. He looked back at the computer screen.

"Okay," I said. "That's okay."

Tim glanced at me again.

"Because of how your mother and I hurt each other all over again," I said.

Tim shrugged.

"Because you hated living out at the vineyard, especially after your mother left."

Tim closed his eyes.

"Because I didn't take care of you last fall at all. I was lost in my own world. I'm sorry, Tim. I'm so sorry. Can I . . ."

I stepped over to him. I reached down to hug him. I did hug him. His shoulders were broader. He was stronger. I hugged him and he hugged me back. Then I sat back down on his bed.

"I haven't told anyone," he said. "Except my shrink, but he says as long as no one is in danger and no one is going to harm himself or someone else, the secret stays with him. So you don't have to worry."

The secret? What secret?

"I haven't even told Mom," he whispered. "She has no idea."

"You lost me," I said.

"I'm not really mad at you, okay? I was, but I'm not anymore."

"Okay," I said.

"It's just that . . . We can pretend to be really tight, you know? You and Mom and me. But then we don't seem to talk about anything real."

Now Tim was facing me and he'd pulled his chair a foot closer to the bed, and while I wasn't sure what he was talking about, I didn't want to stop him.

"The thing is, I really liked the valley and living there, and you and Mom were, like, so cool about everything, but then shit would happen, and it was like, ooh, nobody is supposed to know. Suddenly there are rules about what we can talk about."

"We can talk about anything you want now," I said.

"And Mom was so unhappy after she lost the baby, and you were like oblivious or something. And it was just so sad. I couldn't stand it. Everything got so sad, Dad."

I nodded.

"Sometimes I wished I had told Mom. Sometimes I wished I'd called the cops myself, just to get it over with."

My heart thudded. I was beginning to make sense of what my son was telling me.

"I kept thinking you were going to get arrested," Tim said. "Then I was going to get arrested."

He knew. My son knew.

"And I actually worried that if I told Mom, then she'd have to turn us both in, and you know, like she'd be all alone, and then she lost the kid, and then it just got worse and worse and worse." Tim stopped. He was breathing fast, trying not to cry.

"Tim?" I swallowed. "Why were you worried about getting arrested?"

He wrinkled his brow. "You know," he said.

"I know why I might have been, but why you?" I asked.

"I destroyed the evidence," he said. "You can go to jail for that, can't you?"

"Yes," I said, "but I don't . . ."

The clothes in the vault.

"Oh," I said. "Oh, Tim."

"I never told Mom," he said. "I promise. I never told anyone."

"When did you find them?" I asked.

Tim paused. Then, softly: "Well, it was that day I came home from school early. I saw that the closet door in the empty bedroom was open a little. And I found the bags with your boots and jacket and stuff. And then—I don't remember when it was—a few days later maybe, I saw that the closet was empty. After that? I don't know, it wasn't like I went looking for them, but I was messing around down in the wine cellar and I checked out the hiding place, and I kind of put it all together. What had happened."

It turned out that he had found the secret vault on his own the year before.

"What did you do with the bags?" I asked.

"I took them into the woods and burned them," he said in a flat voice.

Tim was staring at his unlaced hiking boots. He was shivering.

"I didn't want you to get caught," he said. "But I hated you at the same time. Then when Mom went away, it was like we were doing hard time together."

I couldn't fathom what it must have been like, knowing both that your father harbored a dark secret and that this secret could do him harm. I couldn't imagine how alone Tim must have felt, what with no one he could tell. Why hadn't he come to me? Why didn't he ask me what was going on?

"How did you figure out that I was in an accident? Just from the hidden clothes?" I asked.

"It wasn't hard," Tim said.

"But I don't think Julia—I don't think your mother figured it out," I said.

"That's Mom for you," he said.

I sighed so loudly and with such force that for a moment I thought that I would pass out. This was the first time I had talked about the accident. This was the first time I had talked with anyone about my crimes, and the relief I felt, the liberty and then the fear, was too much for me. I had to clutch the bed board to keep from keeling over.

"It was an accident," I said. "I hope you know that it was an accident."

"I know," Tim said.

"But he was just a boy like you," I said.

"A little older," he said.

"Things were going well for us," I said. "I thought I could do my own penance in my own way."

"So you let some guy take the rap," Tim said.

I nodded. And how did I explain that? I could see the judgment in his squint. What was right, what was wrong—there was no way I could spin it.

"Mom says you're the guy's lawyer now," Tim said.

"I am," I said. "I just filed an appeal for him."

"Why?"

"I think that if I can get this guy out of jail, well, then maybe things will get better for us again. I don't know," I said.

"Things are fine for me now," Tim said. "They're fine for Mom, too."

He was telling me not to mess with their life. I heard what my son was telling me.

"I still love your mother very much," I said. And I want her and you to come back with me to the vineyard. Now, tonight. Pack your bags. Pack up your computer. Please come home.

"I was sort of obsessed with him," Tim said.

"Craig," I said.

"I thought his poems said it all," Tim said.

"What poems?"

"Didn't I show them to you? The poems that were in the school literary magazine?"

"No," I said. "I didn't know that Craig wrote poems."

"After he died, his sister gave all of his poems from his journals to the lit and they ran all of them," Tim explained. "They were awesome. I'm writing poetry now, and it's kind of because of Craig, although I'm not writing about what he wrote about."

I wasn't sure I wanted to know, but I had to ask, "What did Craig write about?"

"Death," Tim said. "Killing himself."

"What do you write about?" I asked.

Tim shrugged. "Whatever. The old women doing tai chi in the park across the street."

"That's sweet," I said, and I knew immediately that it was the wrong thing to say.

"I write about driving into trees, too," Tim said defensively.

I nodded. "I'm glad you can write about that. I'd like to read your poems. If you'll show them to me."

"Okay," he said. "Some other time. So."

"So," I said.

"I've got to work on this paper," he said.

I stepped across the room and reached around my son to hug him again. He hugged me back but let go long before I wanted to let go.

"Thanks for helping me," I whispered. "I mean, after the accident."

"I shouldn't have," Tim said.

"Maybe not," I said.

"I don't know what I'd do now," he said. "Look, Dad, this was cool and all, your driving up, but . . ."

"But?"

"I like it here," he said. "In the city."

My son had taken a long, hard fall, and part of it was triggered by the death of a local boy, but a significant part of it had to do with me, his father, about whom he had fretted and panicked, whom he had wanted to defend from peril, whom he had come to resent. I was to blame for a major quotient of his anger and his despair——me, his father, the one who should have looked out for him——I was responsible, and my penalty had been his silence, his retreat. There was little I could do to repair what had been torn between us and noth-

ing I could say except, "I hope I'll see you soon, Tim man."
But when I saw him next, I knew, would be up to him.

I left him at his computer and I shut his door and made my
way toward the kitchen, where Julia was sitting at the table,
doing nothing, her eyes closed as if she was meditating.

"So I talked to him," I said. I didn't sit down.

"You were protecting us," she said. "That's why you
didn't come forward about the accident."

I gripped the back of a chair. "You were listening?"

Julia glared at me. "Or were you protecting yourself?"

"You shouldn't have listened, Julia. That was between
Tim and me—"

"Of course I listened," she said. "Wouldn't you? He
refuses to talk to you for months, and he won't tell me why,
but he says it's something related to why he tried to kill himself on that goddamned road. Wouldn't you listen?" She was
yelling at me now.

"Please don't shout," I said.

"I'll fucking shout if I fucking feel like it," she yelled.

"You shouldn't have eavesdropped," I said. "Tim didn't
tell you because it was between him and me."

"You were protecting us, and he was protecting you,"
Julia said.

"Yeah, it's ironic," I said.

"It's fucked is what it is," she said.

I stared at her.

"You should have told me what happened," she said.
"Why do I feel like you betrayed me?"

Because I had betrayed her with my secrecy.

"And you let someone go to jail for you." Julia grimaced.
"No, it's worse. You helped put him there—you had a hand
in it—and I have no idea what the hell you think you're
doing now."

"Trying to turn everything around," I whispered.

"I should call the police," she said.

Would she really do that to me?

"I really should," she said.

She looked like she might cry, but she didn't.

"I remember when I met you," she said, "and you were clumsy and you were shy and you were sweet, and now . . ."

I held my breath.

"I guess that was a long time ago," she said.

I needed her faith in me. I needed her respect.

"Julia," I said.

"I don't have anything to say to you," she said.

Tim burst into the kitchen. He stared hard at his mother and then at me. His face was red.

"Tim," I said.

"Just get out of here, Dad," he said.

"Son."

"Please," he said, and shot back to his room.

Julia was up on her feet and chasing after him. She glanced back at me. With a single blink, she echoed my son: Get out. She ran down the long hall, and when I heard her talking to Tim, I knew that my son would be okay.

I went down to the street. The pavement was wet, my car was wet. It had started to rain again.

"Look at it this way," Troy said. "He could have told you to get out before you had a chance to talk to him."

"I suppose," I said.

He wiggled his pencil across the bottom of his sketch pad.

"Seriously, Jason. Think about how long it had been since you'd seen him."

The drawing Troy was working on was of a small square house high on a bluff overlooking the ocean. It reminded me of the empty house he had evoked to describe Lauren's music.

"You'll see him again sooner than you think," Troy said.

I wanted to believe what he was telling me, but I wasn't so sure. I had told him about being chased from Julia's

house, but I hadn't told him specifically what disclosures led
to my ejection.

Troy darkened the oceanic horizon. He rubbed the waves
with the side of his hand.

"A house with a view," I said. "I wouldn't mind hiding out
there awhile."

I was tempted to tell Troy the whole truth. Talking about
it with Tim had provided only passing relief, and Julia's dis-
dain had left me cold. I had spent so much of my life standing halfway in shadows, offering fragments of the truth to
give the impression that I was revealing the whole. I rarely,
if ever, stood all the way in the light.

Troy brushed his pencil along the slope beneath the cliff
house, articulating the dense of brush and flowers. He
squinted at the drawing. He shaded more of the hill.

"I've been thinking about what I'm going to do after the
appeal goes through," he said.

Ten days had gone by since the appeal had been certified,
and it was too soon for any word from the higher court just
yet—it could be another month before we knew where we
stood—but anytime I saw Troy, he expressed his confidence
in the matter.

"After you find your family," I said.

"I want to go somewhere very far away from here," he said.

"So that's the Atlantic, not the Pacific," I said.

"I want to live in a big city."

"You can get lost in a city," I said. "What would you do
there?"

Troy smiled.

"What?"

"You'll laugh," he said.

"I won't," I said.

He slid the drawing pad across the table. His scenes were
always potent in mood. The roof of the house, the ocean,
everything reflected a hopeful sun.

"I want to go to law school," he said. "I want to help people the way you've helped me."

"Listen, I'm not really a very good lawyer," I said.

"I want to be just like you when I grow up," Troy said. He winked.

Now I had to laugh.

"If only you knew," I said.

"I do know," he said. "After the appeal goes through—"

"Troy," I said. "Let's wait and see what the court says."

"They're going to say, Let him out," he said. "Put that man back on the street."

I looked at the source of light in his drawing; his sun cracked fissures through the darkest clouds. It was contagious. I found myself nodding slowly and then nodding fast in agreement. This man would walk free.

"Maybe everything will turn out fine," I said.

"Everything will," he said.

I left the prison in a profoundly better mood.

A few days later, however, some news came in that, while not terrible, was not good. The appellate court announced that they would not hear oral arguments in the matter of *People* v. *Frantz*. I thought about keeping the news from Troy, but I decided that I had to tell him. When I went to the prison, he was jogging by himself around the perimeter track of the paved yard. He wasn't wearing his usual uniform; he had on a pair of baggy shorts and a T-shirt, and I could see that, while he wasn't a big man, he was in good shape. He told me that he'd been taking good care of himself in the last months, doing a lot of push-ups and sit-ups and various other stretches and crunches. He waved and jogged over to me.

"You have news," he said, catching his breath.

I told him.

"But it doesn't really mean anything," he said.

I told him that we could read what we wanted to read into this development.

"Maybe the judges are just realizing that the other guys are wrong," he said, "and they have no interest in hearing them say anything they don't already know."

For some reason I hadn't thought of it that way.

"Maybe they're already on our side," Troy said. "Maybe they'll give us the verdict we want faster than we thought they would."

I corrected him and told him that the court would not exactly be issuing a verdict.

"Whatever," he said. He poked me in the gut. "I haven't gone to law school yet."

I looked off at the fields beyond the prison fence.

"Come on," he said. "Buck up."

So much had gone wrong in his life. How could he be so sanguine?

He must have read my mind. He said, "I look at it this way. I've done some rotten things in my life. But that's all over with. Now everything will go my way."

I took a deep breath. Maybe he was right.

"You and me both. Here's our second chance," he said.

I shrugged.

"Or third or fourth," he said.

I laughed.

He began bouncing on his feet. He began to jog again. When he was on the opposite side of the field from me, he clapped his hands, and when I looked at him, he turned in a cartwheel and then kept jogging.

I suppose that to some degree I was afraid that everything might be turning out well after all. If my fortunes were indeed improving again, then I could blow it again, too. And yet I was beginning to believe that I had done the right thing. The risk had been worth it. I had known that this man should not be in jail and I had come to his aid, and while my advocacy was unorthodox and my prolonged deceit born from admittedly deep self-interest, I was close to securing him his freedom. I began to believe that the appeal would work. I had followed the right path, I told myself, I would save us both. On the way home from the prison that afternoon, I played the radio and sang along to all of the pop songs, humming when I didn't know the words.

Progress on all fronts in my life was slow but undeniable. One night Tim called. We didn't talk about his mother or the screaming or anything that we had discussed. We spoke about his impending calculus final and we talked at length about the latest software developments, or I should say that I let Tim talk and I just listened. And as for Julia, well, at least she hadn't called the police and I didn't think that she would. In my mind, I composed and refined the careful apology I would offer her when she was willing to see me again.

Another good development involved money. Just when I needed the cash, my friend in the public defender's office called me up. She had followed the progress of my appeal for Troy, and while she said she thought that there were more worthy candidates currently in the system who might benefit from my pro bono representation, she did appreciate my ardent effort. Everyone deserves to be heard, she said. And she offered me a range of freelance assignments, all of which I accepted. In a blink, I was very busy. I had legal work again, and I needed to nurse my long-neglected vines.

All of the rain had eroded some of the slope, and the beds of vines needed to be shored up with fresh soil. I found the soil elsewhere on my land and packed my pickup with dirt and then slowly went about packing in the new loam. All of the rain also meant that my vines were more likely to fall prey to mildew, and so I sprayed more than I usually sprayed to combat every imaginable mold interloper. But in truth my vines had survived the long rain just fine on their own. These sturdy ancient vines. The spring shoots had formed buds. The plants were flowering on schedule. There seemed to be fewer flowers than usual, but the vines were sprinkled with white petals just the same.

The band of missing vines in the middle of my plot disturbed me. A gully had formed where the roots had been ripped out, and the soil had blackened as it dried in the early June sun. It looked fecund to me. It looked like grapes could grow there again.

New vines might not make it. It would be difficult for the

roots to establish themselves in the beaten earth, but then again, the ground was much more moist than usual. I knew, however, that if I had wanted to replace my lost vines, I should have ordered the rootstock the previous fall and probably sunk the plants in the ground in February or March at the latest. I knew this, yet I could picture the field the way it used to be. I could imagine the vines in their fullest plumage, and I wanted to see it again.

It took some calling around, but eventually I found a place that would ship me bare rootstock this late in the season. I could buy cabernet vines grafted onto a reliable louse-safe, disease-free rootstock. My order for one hundred and fifty vines could be met. Apparently these plants had been ordered by a northern vintner who had watched his fields turn into swampland and there was no way he was going to put new plants in such wet ground. I was warned about how these vines had been heeled in for longer than plants should live above ground, and I was given no guarantees about how long they would last once I did plant them. At least I got a good rate.

And so one day early that summer, I began to dig a deeper trench into the gully between my two plots of surviving vines. I mixed an ample amount of fertilizer into the dark earth. I sank new posts for the new trellises. And then the vines arrived on the back of a truck, exposed to the white summer sun but wrapped in damp muslin. I soaked the roots in buckets and troughs of water overnight, and the next morning I got up before dawn and cut back the tops of the canes, leaving only eight inches or so above the node of the graft, saving two or three choice buds. Then I trimmed the one-year-old roots, too.

I made small mounds of dirt in the trenches, spacing them generously apart, and then I placed each plant on its own dome of soil, spreading the roots out all around, making sure that none of them overlapped. Once upon a time, I had destroyed some thriving bougainvillea when I repotted it and broke its fragile root ball, so I may have been more tender at first than I needed to be with the young vines, but eventually I realized that these were much heartier plants. I pressed the roots against the mounds of dirt and then began covering them with more soil so that they were completely covered, and I pressed that dirt down and added more, and I stepped on it, I packed it in. I tried to shape a berm around each plant.

When I was done, the grafts of the vines stood at about three inches above ground, and the stubby canes didn't look like much, nothing more than a series of metered markers all lined up in neat rows. It would be another year before they flowered, and years beyond that before they produced viable fruit. That hardly mattered to me. I was intensely proud. My hands, arms, and knees were covered with dirt and my shoulders and back ached from more work in the field than I was used to, but I felt woozy with the power and promise that anyone who has ever planted anything knows. I could look at the rows of vines on either side of me and believe that with luck, someday these markers, these stakes would look like them, too. Meanwhile these old vines would shelter the new ones as if they were raising them, watching over them, teaching them how to endure the most inclement climate.

This was in June, when the days were long and the sun still benign and the nights cool. This was when I believed that one more time my life was turning around. I had an old rocker that I liked to drag outside and set on the grass and sit in while I watched the slow yawn of the dusk.

Then, sometime in the late morning on a day early in July, I received a fax from a clerk in Hollister. I read it twice and then hopped in my car and sped down the vineyard road.

troy stared at me without blinking. I wanted to lay out the ruling carefully. I wanted him to understand point by point what the appellate court had decided.

The three judges had all rejected the notion that Troy had

been denied due process because he had been denied reciprocal discovery during the plea negotiation. The court said that discovery was part of the procedure connected to a trial and that Troy had therefore waived his right to discovery when he waived his right to a trial. Also, the court maintained that I had not offered reasonable proof that the withholding of potentially exculpatory evidence was willful on the part of the prosecution.

"However," I said.

Troy gripped the sides of the table between us.

However, the court said that it could not pretend that the information contained in my appeal did not exist and that, were it known, say, by a jury of Troy's peers, it could affect the outcome of a trial. The judges had looked over the interrogation transcript that I had submitted with my brief and—in a two-to-one opinion—agreed that the charges against the accused were not fairly laid out and that the basis of the deal offered was not fairly put forward to the defendant and that no one should be told to take it now or leave it; that was not playing fair. The defendant put himself in the position of acting as his own counsel—that was his right and his doing—but that meant, in the opinion of this court, that the people had an obligation to determine whether he was in effect fit to act in that capacity, just as a court would determine whether a defendant was fit to stand trial.

"Furthermore," I said.

Troy bounced in his chair.

Furthermore, the court came to the conclusion that the prosecution's inadequate investigation into the accused's version of events amounted to what the author of the opinion called "sloppy, sloppy work." And the court felt that there was enough reference to new evidence—although the new evidence itself was not submitted—to suggest that there could have been reasonable doubt in the mind of a jury to acquit the defendant had there been a trial. The court went beyond the scope of my appeal to say that it could see an ending to this story other than the one already written. It did, however, limit the relief granted to the relief that I had requested.

Troy jumped up and hugged me.

"You did it," he said.

"I got lucky," I said, and in fact, I know that luck might have been paramount to my legal maneuvering, because after I left the prison, I talked to my friend in Legal Aid, and she told me about how I had tapped into an ongoing political debate among the appellate jurists that I had not been aware of. It had to do with some of the judges on the higher bench wanting to make a statement about how too many cases were being rushed through the system at the expense of due process and that the courts of appeal were having to do far too much cleanup work, rather than, say, the kind of loftier review of laws to which they would have preferred to devote their energy. Frankly, the debate was over my head, but I understood the idea that I had reached the judges at just the right time. Another month, another week, and they might have been in a less charitable mood.

"So now what?" Troy asked.

The case would be remanded to the lower court, where the plea agreement would be reviewed. But Troy would have to remain in jail, because the ruling made it clear that he could be held over without the prosecution having to go to the grand jury for an indictment.

"Now I have some work to do," I said.

there was no time to rest. The next day the superior court judge set aside the plea agreement and ordered a new arraignment. Days after that, I got a call from Eric Dreyfus—he had decided to handle the case himself—saying that he was ready to go back to court with clarified charges. And days after that, Troy was put on a bus and driven up to Hollister.

The air-conditioning system wasn't working in the court-

house, and so the air in the fake-paneled courtroom itself
was as still and hot as the air outside. Eric Dreyfus looked
like he would melt in his gray suit. His assistants took off
their jackets. Mrs. Montoya, dressed in black, seemed about
to faint, and her daughter fanned her with a legal pad. I had
expected many people to show up in court, some of the Oak
Valley crowd, and there were a few familiar faces sitting
next to and behind Mrs. Montoya—Alex Marquez made an
appearance—but perhaps because of the heat, the crowd was
much sparser than I had anticipated.

Our side was empty. Troy was brought in wearing his
prison best, and he was seated next to me at the table. A
courthouse guard stood next to the prison guard, Troy's fellow artist, and then the judge came in. The judge was a short
man with no hair and a red face, and he was talking before
he sat down. He spoke in a whining tenor. He asked the district attorney to present the new charges, and maybe if I
hadn't heard them before we had gone into the court, I
would have been surprised, but Eric Dreyfus had warned me
what he intended to do and I, in turn, off in a basement conference room before the session, had warned Troy.

One charge of carjacking and one charge of murder in the
second degree.

Frankly, I was dumbfounded that the district attorney
wanted to go to trial at all, what with the evidence so clearly
favoring the defense. Did he really think he could win this
case?

And then it hit me. I stood up to make a motion, but I had
to sit down.

"Counselor?" the judge asked.

Troy was headed for a trial, and if I failed to defend him
well, if I somehow faltered along what should be an easy trot
to acquittal, then he might face a harsher and longer punishment than the one he was currently serving out. A trial was
inevitable, a trial with higher stakes, and what if, what if I
had made Troy more vulnerable than he was before? After
all, that was what I had done with my vintner clients whom

I had tried to usher out of bankruptcy. I got involved; I made their lives worse.

Troy nudged my arm.

"It's this heat," I said, and I thought, There is no turning back now. I rifled off a series of motions, starting with my demurrer, where I declared that there was no real corpus for these charges, and that motion was immediately denied. I argued, then, that the charges against Troy required a grand jury indictment, even though I knew how the judge would and did rule; the appellate court had removed that step.

It was time for Troy to enter a plea. Both of us stood.

He cleared his throat. "Not guilty," he said.

Bail was denied. I asked for a speedy trial. Preliminary hearing dates were set for the end of September, early October. Then Troy shook my hand, and he was led away.

There was no turning back.

On the way out of the court, Eric Dreyfus pulled me aside. His eyes narrowed. He said, "No deals this time." A sinister grin broke across his face, which, even in that stifling heat, made me shiver.

I threw myself into Troy's defense. I broke the case down into several parts and attacked each part separately. I would begin with the inconclusiveness of the evidence against Troy, focusing particularly on the deer blood on the bumper of Craig's car. That alone would be enough to raise reasonable doubt, I thought, but I wouldn't stop there. I would use the fact that the sheriff hadn't adequately checked out Troy's story in order to segue into a discussion about the interrogation, with all of its abuses and misrepresentations. And from there, I would try to explain how it was that an innocent man would admit to doing something he hadn't done. Troy would have to take the stand—that was key. I had ordered another review by a neutral psychologist whom the DA had approved of, but I felt certain that if Troy remained honest and if he expressed his sadness about letting Lauren and his son get away and his ensuing funk and his deepest desire to find his family now, he would have the jury rooting for him, cheering him on. He could do that for the therapist, but I wanted him to speak to the jury directly, and I didn't think that the prosecution would look good trying to break him down on cross.

Discovery began, and soon I was looking at the various analyses of the evidence as they came in from an independent lab. The reports were not as favorable to our side as I would have liked. The lab said that the sample of blood taken from the bumper of Craig's car was too small to supply a definitive reading. Another report claimed that the skid marks that were photographed were open to interpretation; possibly they came from the same vehicle, possibly they did not. All of this information didn't necessarily help the prosecution, but then again, I would have rather had concrete exculpatory results to support my argument than data that merely raised doubt.

I was particularly disturbed when I learned that the hair fibers taken from Craig's body in fact pointed to Troy. Craig had ended up with hair on him that was similar to Troy's hair, and now I would to have to find a witness who could dispute the finding. However, the forensics experts whom I was likely to call to the stand might prove no match for the experts that the district attorney would be able to rally.

I began to understand why Eric Dreyfus was willing to go to trial. He probably believed he could win. We were both looking at the same physical evidence, and it would be his spin against my spin. But beyond the physical evidence, I was pretty sure that the prosecution didn't have a case; if I couldn't raise enough reasonable doubt with the lab work, then I would have to rely on what the people did not have, namely, Troy himself. The further we went into discovery, the more I realized that Troy would definitely need to testify to tip the scales of justice in our favor.

He surprised me, then, when I outlined our defense and he

said he wasn't so sure that he wanted to take the stand. He paced back and forth in our prison meeting room.

"I just don't know what it will be like when I start talking about my life in Los Angeles," he said.

"It's okay if you cry," I said. "The jury will cry with you, that's what we want."

"I'm just not sure," Troy said.

"I can see how you'd be worried that the DA might somehow turn your words against you, but if you just tell the jury the truth, I promise you, Troy, we'll come out ahead."

"You have all the evidence," Troy said. "You have the interrogation—that worked for the appeal. You yourself said that would be enough."

"It probably will, but why risk it? We have you, and you are a defense attorney's dream client," I said. I stood and faced Troy. I told him, "You're a good man, and the jury will want to put you back on the road north. I won't win this case—you will."

Troy bit his lower lip and nodded once, quickly, giving me his reluctant assent to go forward with my strategy.

July flew by. August. The heat that summer was as dry and severe as the rainy winter had been wet. The sun seemed to hang lower in the sky, pressing down on the valley with greater weight, casting no shadows until the very edge of the day. Fortunately, there was enough water in the ground so that my new vines endured and, with my additional conscientious watering, my older vines survived the long fever. The fruit began to darken.

Tim was involved in a summer math and computer program at his school, and I didn't expect him to come down and see me yet, but our conversations remained frequent. We spoke briefly and often and never about anything of consequence, but I preferred that in a way, at least for the moment. Julia remained silent. I would ask Tim how she was doing and he would always answer me the same way, he'd say, Mom's cool. Now and then she answered the phone when I called, but she never spoke to me at length. I would replay what she had said to me in her kitchen, and one day soon I hoped that she would give me the chance to begin at the beginning and explain as much as I could explain. But I couldn't afford to dwell on her right now, not when I had to move forward with a confident stride.

In September my grapes began to color up. I measured the sugar with my hydrometer every morning. The harvest was near, and so was the trial. I was so busy and so tired at the end of the day that I slept with greater ease than I had in years.

Discovery dragged on; the DA's office and I traded witness lists. The psychological review was complete and looked good for us, although the doctor who met with Troy did tell me, off the record, that she thought he was a charmer—her word—and I was not entirely sure what she was implying. And then before I knew it, I was back in court for the preliminary hearings and the voir dire. The judge who ran the arraignment presided over the trial.

It only took an afternoon to empanel the jury. I would have preferred more women—there were only four—but given the fiscal distress that had plagued the county, I was satisfied with the economic background of the panel. I thought that the jurors would understand the hardship that Troy had endured; his troubles would hardly seem alien; change a few variables and they might see his life as what their own lives could have become.

The jury was sworn in, jeopardy attached. The trial began the next day. It would not last long, a week, two weeks tops.

I drank a lot of coffee before I delivered my opening statement. I thought I did well, considering that I've never been much of a performer and considering that I had to avoid looking into the audience. I was afraid that if I noticed Emma Hodges or Will Clark or any of the other scowling valley citizens, I would have lost my place. I didn't even want to look at Troy, who was wearing a suit that was two sizes too big and who kept nervously tapping a pencil. So I only looked at the jury, and I took my time and talked about how the first obligation of our justice system was to protect the innocent. I couldn't help but compare myself to Eric Dreyfus, and his oratory, I thought, had been dry.

He began to mount his case. By now I was prepared for how he would go about presenting the physical evidence; he placed particular weight on the hair found on the corpse. I was ready to ask sharp questions of the people's experts on cross. I couldn't really challenge their credentials, however, because the prosecution had found impeccably established forensics authorities who were practiced at courtroom delivery. I would bring in my experts in time, and while I knew the jury was being persuaded by the people's case right now, I would eventually get my chance to debunk every reading presented so far. But I also began to realize that in the end, based on the physical evidence alone, the score would probably be tied. Based on the evidence alone, the jury could go either way with its verdict. And if it came down to a contest of experts, the people might even have a slight edge. When I became nervous, I steadied myself, knowing that Troy's testimony would shoot us into the lead for the home stretch.

A few days into the trial, the district attorney called Mrs. Montoya to the stand. She started crying the moment she was sworn in. I probably should have waited a few minutes, rather than moving for a recess right away; I should have waited until those tears became so obviously prejudicial that the judge would have to order Mrs. Montoya to take a breather and compose herself. But I asked for a break before Mrs. Montoya had a chance to say anything, and the judge overruled my objection.

"I miss him, I miss him," Mrs. Montoya said. "Oh, how I miss him," and she sobbed. The question put to her by Eric Dreyfus had been, Do you miss your son?

"Your Honor," I said.

"The defense objection is noted, Counselor," the judge said.

"I miss him," Mrs. Montoya said.

People in the audience were crying.

"Describe for us what your life has been like after your son was killed," Eric Dreyfus said.

Mrs. Montoya wept some more, and finally the judge cautioned her. She took a deep breath and talked about how her family had fallen apart. She said that she couldn't clean up her son's room; it remained exactly as he had left it when he last slept in his bed. She couldn't throw away his clothes. Sometimes she sat in his closet, clutching his soccer silks.

Now members of the jury had become teary, too.

"Your Honor," I said.

"You'll have your chance," the judge said to me.

Mrs. Montoya did not testify for very long, and then I did have my chance to question her, but what could I possibly ask? I wanted her off the stand as quickly as possible, and I didn't say anything other than to express my sympathy for her loss, which may have sounded over the top to some people because I spoke softly and my voice cracked.

"All of us are very sad," I said.

After Mrs. Montoya stepped down, the people rested. It was only ten in the morning on a Friday, I remember, and the judge decided to break for the weekend. I would begin calling witnesses first thing Monday morning.

I went home. It was the last week in September and I wondered if I would be able to harvest my grapes that weekend; they were just about perfect for picking. I was about to head down to the vines when the phone rang at twelve-thirty.

It was Eric Dreyfus. He said that he had some material he thought I should look at. I asked him to fax it to me, and he said that I might want to come in and talk about it with him that afternoon. He said I might want a continuance. His condescending tone made me angry. This was a tactical ploy. He had dug up something that he had probably known about for weeks but had kept hidden until the last possible moment, and now he was complying with the rules of discovery, but barely. I had to take him seriously, however, because after I called my witnesses, he would have another turn to present whatever he had found out.

An hour or so later, Eric Dreyfus escorted me to a chair in his office and closed the door. "How's the vineyard?" he asked. "You must be almost ready to harvest."

"Cut to the chase," I said.

"Fine," he said, and handed me a piece of paper.

It was a revised witness list. The first name on it was a detective from the Los Angeles Police Department.

"I'm going to make a motion," Eric Dreyfus said, "to introduce a prior—"

"You can't introduce prior bad acts," I said. As far as I knew, Troy had never been arrested before he was apprehended upstate. He had no record. Maybe Eric Dreyfus had indeed realized that the case was coming down to a tie on the physical evidence and maybe having Mrs. Montoya make the jury cry was not enough for him.

"A prior investigation," Eric Dreyfus said. "The police in L.A. were looking into—"

"Wait," I said. I had no idea what he was talking about, but I didn't want to appear blindsided. "A conviction isn't necessarily relevant, so it's unlikely an investigation would be allowable. If my client was a target, that's not—"

"I'll be arguing for a pattern of behavior—"

"What behavior?" I asked.

"What behavior?" Eric Dreyfus asked back.

He was bluffing me.

"You're talking about the money Troy owed," I said. Was that it? "Sure, Troy got into a little trouble, but I don't think that is in any way relevant."

Eric Dreyfus scratched his nose.

Maybe he wasn't bluffing.

"Look," I said, "once the jury hears about how his wife got their car out of the shop and grabbed their kid out of school and then just disappeared, I think they will feel nothing but sadness for Troy. Whatever money he owed—"

"His kid?" Eric Dreyfus asked. "Did you say that Troy's wife got his kid out of school? His wife did that?"

"Her name is Lauren," I said.

"I know her name is Lauren," Eric Dreyfus said. He leaned back in his swivel chair. He tossed his half weights on his desk. "We've been looking for her. We want to put her on the stand, but no one can find her. Jason, surely you must know that Lauren didn't run away with the kid."

"Jared," I said.

"Yes, Jared. Surely you know that Jared was murdered."

Murdered?

"And Troy refused to participate in the investigation," Eric Dreyfus said, "which is in part what I want to introduce."

"Troy's son is dead," I said. "That's what you're trying to tell me?"

Eric Dreyfus tossed a file across his desk. I paged through it slowly. It was material supplied by the Los Angeles police pertaining to the investigation into the in-broad-daylight homicide of Jared Frantz.

"I think you need to talk to your client," Eric Dreyfus said.

I could feel my face redden. "You could have faxed me the file," I said.

"Actually that's not what I wanted to show you," he said.

He handed me a large black book, an unlined blank book filled with blue-inked scribblings. All but the last few pages had been used.

"And I was going to fax this to you, but the copies we made aren't very clear," Eric Dreyfus said. "You're holding the original."

I opened the book. There were three words written on the first page. At the top, in neat capitals: *JOURNAL*. At the bottom: *CRAIG MONTOYA*.

"Mrs. Montoya just came in with it today," Eric Dreyfus explained. "She found it in Craig's closet, under a pile of his clothes."

"I've heard the boy's poems are wonderful," I said, "but how on earth are they relevant?"

Certain pages had been flagged with yellow tabs, and I

turned to one of them. The boy's handsome cursive was easy
to read. I skimmed the page.

"Never mind," I said.

"You can sign that out with the clerk. If you're interested,
that is," Eric Dreyfus said. "And since this came in so late, I
could see how you might need to make some adjustments in
your strategy. I know I would." He couldn't help himself. He
chuckled. "Your guy was okay with the deal he had. He was
getting off easy. Then you came along. Now we can go all
the way with this."

I crossed the prison field at a clip. The inner gate
closed behind me. Down the familiar bright corridors. Down
a long hall of private rooms and offices. I didn't nod hello to
the guards. I went right in the white room, where Troy was
waiting for me. I didn't sit down.

"I've been thinking. The way you talk about your vines,"
Troy said, "has really made me want to do something like
that. I mean garden. I mean grow something. I just want to
sink my hands into some dirt and . . ." He looked at me.
"What?"

I stared at him. I locked him in a gaze. I said, "Did Lauren
really run off with your son?"

Troy frowned.

"Did she?"

"You know she did," he said.

"And your son is alive," I said.

"Jason," Troy whispered.

"Did you know Craig Montoya?" I asked.

"What's going on here?"

I repeated my question.

"You know I never met him," Troy said.

"Funny," I said. "He met you."

I placed Craig Montoya's journal on the table and opened
it to one of the flagged passages toward the end of the book.

Troy read the page. He looked at me. The pupils of his eyes dilated.

"You knew him," I said.

Troy breathed in. He nodded. His brown eyes went black.

"You saw him the day he died," I said.

Troy nodded again.

"You've been lying to me," I said.

Troy was silent.

"And Lauren?" I asked. "Please. The truth. Tell me the truth."

"She didn't take my son, no," he said. "I wanted to find her, I wanted to—"

"But your son?" I asked.

Then tears streamed down his face.

And so there it was. We were so very much alike, Troy and I. We both lived with secrets that would ruin us.

Late in his journal, Craig Montoya wrote:

All I want is to be nobody nowhere with nothing to do. Used to be I could be nobody on the field. Nobody passing the ball to somebody else who was nobody. It used to be a game we played. It used to be fun. Now they say, The way you play, son, you could go all the way with that ball. The way you play, anything you want is yours. You can be rich. You can be famous. Yeah, great, but everything dies anyway. The flowers and the trees and even you, you idiots, everything dies. All the vines in the valley, they'll die all over again. Grapes are dead fruit. Wine is spoiled juice from dead fruit. Think about it. So like what's the big deal? Soccer, it's just a game. It's now. It only lasts as long as you play it. Fuck off, leave me alone.

I'm tired. I'm really tired. I wish I could sleep.

And what's going to happen when next fall is over anyway? Then the winter and the spring, and I go away, I study hard, I get good grades. After college, I make lots of money so Mom can fix the roof and maybe take it easy. So she can tell Dad to fuck off for good.

But what if I can't do it? What if I don't want to do it? It's not fair. I didn't ask for this. It's like my whole existence is all about getting everyone to say, Oh, yeah, his father was a total drunk but he did one thing okay, he raised that boy. Ever see that boy kick a ball? I'm so sick of hearing people say that.

Sometimes I think the best times are way over with. Way, way over with.

I don't want Mom to cry. I don't want her to cry anymore. I don't want to let her down. But I'm so fucking tired. I just want to go away.

Nobody knows me anyway. Nobody on the team. Nobody at school. Not even Mom, no one. I smoke dope, I drink. I do all kinds of things, and nobody knows about it. Nobody cares as long as I score. Nobody knows what I can do. I could disappear. Then they'd get it. Maybe. Probably not. I should blow my head off. I should jump off the rock, I should dive off that rock. Will they get it then? Or will they say I slipped?

This passage and most of the ones preceding it displayed the same gloominess. But then, pages later in the journal, in an entry labeled with a day late in the last July of his life, Craig wrote:

Troy is hip. Troy is cool. Troy has been around. He gets the big picture. The vista grande, he calls it.

I thought he was going to kill me when he popped out from behind the vat in the old winery. I thought he found my stash and was going to kill me for it. I've heard about that, people getting knifed for a few lousy dime-bags. But he was like, Go ahead and smoke out, I don't care. He was a little drunk, but not like Dad gets drunk. He was friendly. He said he was sort of lonesome. He said he was glad I found him because he needed someone to talk to.

He told me the story of his life.

I can't imagine it. Watching your son get blown away. Watching your son die. That must have been so fucking dismal. I'd go live in empty wineries, too, man. I don't get why his wife bolted. I mean I get why she was freaked, but she shouldn't have run out on old Troy like that. Not telling him where she went. Making him so miserable.

So Troy is trying to find her now, but I don't know why. It sounds like he's better off without her. Anyway, Troy's car broke down and he hitched to the valley and now is like regrouping or something. Getting his bearings, he says. No, restoring himself, that was how he put it. He asked me to bring him some wine. He'd just about polished off whatever he'd found in the old winery, which couldn't have been very much. I would know, I've looked. I told him there was a better place for him to hang and I drove him to another winery where there's a roof at least. And I got him some food. He tried not to gobble it down, but I knew he was hungry and I said go for it. I got some of Dad's booze, which I somehow don't think the old man will notice missing. We fired up a little reefer. And then Troy and I partied all night.

It was an amazing night. Troy knows the stars, he can point them out. When he gets a little wasted, he makes up stories about the constellations. He says he could teach me things, and I believe him. Mostly, though, he told me about a film he's going to make one day. It's about a man who watches from an upstairs window while his son goes to the mailbox and some freaks pull up in a car and shoot the kid dead for no reason. Then the wife runs away, and the man spends the rest of his life trying to find her.

I said to Troy, Sounds a little autobiographical. Troy said, Like is there any other story worth telling?

So I ask him, How does it end? Does the man find her? And Troy looks all wistful. And I say, The man meets this bummed-out kid in an empty winery and they go and find the woman.

I said, C'mon, man, let's head out tonight, Troy, and Troy said, Don't you have school tomorrow? And I told him, It's summer, man, c'mon, and he said, What about a summer job? And I said, Fuck that, and he said, I can't go, I'm restoring myself. Or something like that.

Tomorrow after work I'm going to bring Troy some dinner and we're going to hang. Troy is cool. Troy sees the big vista.

The next passage in the journal included a short poem, and it was dark—it was about wanting to disappear, and the final stanza mentioned suicide—yet the entry that followed the poem seemed buoyant to me, full of life:

Troy is totally into my poetry. He wasn't freaked by it at all. He says I have talent. He says I should say fuck off to anyone who tells me what I should or shouldn't do and that I should just write poetry if that's what I want to do. I told him I do like playing soccer, I mean I used to, and he said, Play soccer, write your poems. He said, This is your time. I like the way he said that. This is my time. He's right. He's totally fucking right. This is my time. This is my time.

And even though the poetry scribbled out and revised on the pages that followed was often bleak—there was a poem about a man getting so drunk that he hit his wife; there was one about a house burning down, probably an arson, probably set by an angry child—I thought that the journal entries themselves fountained with exuberance.

I had to work late and showed up late and Troy looked kind of relieved I came at all, but I brought a lot of food with me, leftover chicken and then a couple bags of chips and some beer, of course, and we ate it all and drank a lot and smoked a couple of cigarettes, and then Troy had me read him my latest poems, which he dug, and he read them back to me so I could hear what they sounded like, and yeah, you know, they weren't bad, if I don't say so myself. They weren't bad. Troy said they could be put to music, and I don't know about that. He said they reminded him of the songs his wife used to write and sing. I said we should find her. You and me, we could drive off and find her. But Troy is like still restoring himself. He was tired of that winery, so we drove and found another for him to crash in, and I said, Tomorrow we should go find her, we really should drive north and find her. And then what? he asks.

And I said, It's simple, we drive across the country. Which Troy is totally into. We get the hell away from here, all three of us. I said, Tomorrow, and he said, Okay, maybe. Okay, maybe, which like means soon, but I'm thinking by August, he'll want to go. We're going to find his Lauren, and then we're going to drive across the country. See some of the world. Who knows where we'll end up?

I read Craig Montoya's entire journal in one sitting after I came home from the prison. And then I began reading it a second time, slowly and carefully, imagining the voice of the boy I killed, a sincere baritone reading each entry and poem to me. I could read only as far as the passage above, however, before I sank into a deep haze and had to close the black book and put my head down on my desk. Partly I was angry at Troy for his deceit and for toying with Craig's mind, but mostly I couldn't bear the weight of this boy's loss. I could see him now as I always did on the mountain road, walking up the highway in the storm, glancing over his shoulder at my truck—

It took so long to make a life, for a baby to be born and then for that baby to become a boy, a man. So much went into the nurturing of that child, raising him, the making of a poet—maybe a poet of teenage funk, but who knew whether he would have gone on to write greater poems or novels or who knew what else this boy would have someday been capable of? No one would ever know. There it was, the icy truth slapping the shore over and over and over. There it was, I had to face it. It took so much to make a life, and so little to end it. A car skidding on a wet road, that was all. I had to face it: What was lost was a life, what was lost was a voice.

I fell asleep with my head on my desk and didn't know when or how I made it to my couch on the other side of the room. I woke with the sunrise and went down to my vines and sliced off a bunch of grapes. In my kitchen, I squeezed the bunch into a beaker and floated the tube of my hydrometer. The fruit was ready to pick.

That day I was grateful for the straightforward and consuming labor of the harvest. All I had to do was work my way down the aisles between my vines and cut the bunches free with my scythe and toss the bunches into a bucket. All I had to do was dump my bucket into the bay of my pickup and then fill the bucket again. Down another row. Down another. The sun was high and hot while I stripped each vine of its berries. A series of menacing clouds loomed over the Diablo Range but didn't deliver any rain just yet, and the afternoon was gray and cool enough so that I was able to work steadily until dusk. At dusk, I drove the pickup to the upper level of the winery and dumped the grapes down the chute to the vat below. I would have liked to pick the grapes into the night, but I was spent and regrettably had to go inside. I say regrettably because the moment I stopped working in the field, I began to mull over everything that the day's chore had eclipsed.

I had trusted Troy Frantz, and for the most part, I had been completely honest with him in turn—more honest than with anyone in my life, even Julia, I think—and I wasn't sure I wanted to know his true story now. His lies were disheartening, but then again, who was I to claim the high road? I had bluffed, I had played both sides, I had conned him, just as he had conned me. So I shouldn't have been so hurt or bothered, but I was.

When I left the prison, I never wanted to see that man again. There was one problem in that I was his attorney, and technically I couldn't quit; he would have to fire me, and the court would have to approve the dismissal, which it might not be willing to do in the middle of a trial. But I couldn't put Troy on the stand, because he would be destroyed on cross. Under pressure, he might perjure himself, which I couldn't knowingly let him do. Even without his testimony, the people could use the dead boy's journal to demonize my client and the jury would convict him and probably ask if they could levy penalties more severe than the ones on the books.

I thought I knew Troy Frantz, but I didn't know him at all. I had thought of him as a friend, but he was a stranger.

That night, I never went to sleep. I drank some wine. I read Craig's entire journal again. The last entries looked as if they had been scribbled in a hurried hand; the handwriting was difficult to read. In early September, Craig wrote:

> *Tomorrow we hit the road. I told Troy, It's now or never. I told him, I'm going crazy waiting. And he*

*freaked out on me again. He got all mean and said I
don't understand what's involved. He told me I was
too young. He asked me to bring him more money, but
I've given him all I've got and as much as I could take
from the register at work without getting caught. I'm
not taking money from Mom's secret jam jar. No way.
I'm not going that far.*

*So he's all mean, but he still wants to party, and we've
been getting really stoned and really plastered lately.
Practice started and I'm like so slow. The coach is
pissed. It's like I never played this game before.*

A few days later, another entry:

*I told Troy we've got to tell the rest of the story. Boy
gets girl back. And he tells me there are no happy end-
ings out there beyond Oak Valley.*

*He told me this and then I went home and today he
wasn't at the same winery. I had to drive around and
I finally found him hanging at one of the places I took
him to before. And I said to him, Hey, man, are you
trying to ditch me or something? And Troy says, Smart
kid, you figured it out.*

*I wanted to cry but I wasn't about to cry in front of
him. I don't know why he's so mad at me all the time.
I don't get it. Aren't we going to drive across the country?*

The school year began. With soccer practice after school,
Craig had less and less time to hang out with Troy, and Troy
didn't want him around. Craig was ruined.

What did I say? What did I do?

*Troy said he's leaving the valley without me. I said,
Right, in whose car? I said, You need me to drive you,*

*and he said, I don't need you and I don't need anyone.
Troy said he doesn't know if he'll ever find Lauren. He
said he's not sure he wants to. Troy told me to stop
coming to see him. He said I am not in his big vista.*

*But I think if we just could get on the road going north,
he'd change his mind.*

*I don't know, I don't know anymore. I mean I'm begin-
ning to think what's the point. I wish I were nobody.
Nobody nowhere.*

*Nobody knows me, not even Troy. Nobody knows what
I can do. I could jump off the rock. I really should. I
wish I could sleep.*

*Maybe Troy will change his mind. If we could just get
on the road going north. I'll pick him up, and I'll say,
Let's just drive, man, and maybe he'll say, Okay.
Maybe he'll say, Let's go.*

And this was the last passage Craig wrote. It was dated
one day before the accident. Troy had led him on. Troy had
given this boy hope, so why did Troy let him down? Why
did he push him away? I read the journal, and I came to the
conclusion that Troy and I were accomplices in Craig's
undoing. First Troy wrecked his mind, and then he somehow
stranded him on the mountain road. That was what I
assumed. Then I hit the kid, I delivered the coup de grâce.

I had stayed up all night reading Craig's journal and
brooding, and when the sun began to lighten the sky, I went
out to my garage and got in my car and headed down the
vineyard road. Soon I was winding along the mountain highway. I drove beyond the spot where I had wiped out on the
way to the hospital with Julia, and I drove past the tree that
Tim plowed into. I came to the scene of the accident. I
slowed the way I always slowed when I came to this stretch.

Craig had looked over his shoulder at me, and I think that
at that moment he had wanted to die. The world had let him

down. He was hiking up to the high rock and he had wanted to dive into the ravine below, but then I had come skidding along instead.

I drove into the turnout a quarter of a mile up the road and got out of my car and began to make my way up through the trees to the cliff. By the time I reached the clearing, the sun had illuminated enough of the valley so that I could see its entire reach, the jagged fan of notches, the shape of a leaf, the passes, the folds of hills, the layering of woods and the open fields, the bald slopes of the quarries, the acres destroyed by too much rain and the acres where vines still managed to grow.

I stepped to the edge of the granite shelf. My ankle turned on a patch of moss. There was something clean about the morning air. The sage, the mint, the pine. I let myself sigh until I felt as though I had no more air in me. I held my breath.

That October dusk when I killed the boy would never end. I would forever ask, What if I hadn't hit him? What if he had made it here, to this cliff, and taken a long look down into the deep canyon below? Even though it was dark and raining and even though he would not have been able to see very far, it was possible that he would have considered jumping but then, in the end, crept back from the cliff. It was possible that he would have stepped back the way I stepped back now, and it was possible that Craig Montoya would have run back through the woods and seen a car drive by and hitched a ride down to the main drag and another ride home.

Maybe the boy would have ended his life, but maybe the boy would have changed his mind, and that was what I had stolen from him, the chance, the moment when he would have stepped back from the high cliff and run home.

Somber clouds hung over the valley, and so I needed to harvest the grapes faster. The forecast was that it would pour the next day. I was working my knife as fast as I could, tossing the bunches into my bucket, and I somehow didn't notice a car drive up the vineyard road. I didn't hear any footsteps, and when I stood up to stretch my back, I gasped at the sight of Julia standing at the end of the row, Julia wearing jeans and a sweatshirt and holding her own scythe and bucket.

"I figured you'd be in the middle of the harvest," she said.

"It's not supposed to rain until tomorrow," I said, "but I don't trust these skies."

"Never trust these skies," Julia said, and then, without further conversation, she began to slice off bunches of grapes and to fill her bucket with fruit. When she saw me staring at her, she said, "There will be plenty of time to talk later."

And so we worked on either side of a row of vines and we worked our way down the slope, and after an hour of silent labor, I finally asked after Tim.

"He's really doing well. He likes his new teachers so far. He's going to try out for a play again. He's playing the guitar."

"The guitar," I said. "That's great."

"Right now he's hanging out at a friend's house across the Bay and asked if he could stay over. And like I said, I figured you'd be in a middle of a harvest. . . ."

"This was always your favorite time of the year out here," I said.

"My favorite time of the year anywhere," Julia said.

"It's great to see you," I said.

She looked at me through the vines and winked, and then she continued lopping off the grapes. We worked for most of the afternoon, and needless to say, the harvest went considerably faster. There was some drizzle, some mist, but no hard rain just yet. We would need another day to finish. The next day was Monday, however, and I was supposed to return to court.

After we dumped the grapes into the vat, we went inside and foraged around the kitchen until we found the ingredients for a simple dinner. We still were not speaking much, but somehow our work in the field and now our dinner preparation, the sautéeing of vegetables for a pasta sauce, the tossing of a salad, sufficed. When we sat down to eat, I opened a bottle of cabernet from our first vintage.

Julia took a sip and closed her eyes, and when I asked her to describe the taste, she said, "I see Tim when he was about five, playing with some kids, rolling down a hill."

"You see Tim," I said.

"His hair is covered with grass. He's like a cat rolling in the dirt on a hot day."

"It's a good wine," I said.

"We made a great wine," Julia said. She clinked my glass.

We ate the pasta and the salad and drank much of the wine, again mostly in silence. And then I revealed what the wine tasted like to me. I reminded Julia about our picnic on the edge of the meadow once upon a time.

She reached across the table and gripped my hand. Then she let go of it.

She said, "I was mad at you. I was so mad."

"I know," I said. "I'm sorry."

"I mean, I'm still mad," Julia said. "The way you deceived me. And Tim——what all of this did to Tim. I can't talk about that yet."

"Thank you for not calling the police," I said.

"I did seriously consider it," she said.

"But you didn't."

"I couldn't."

"There's so much I wish I could undo," I said. "That boy, I held him——"

"Jason," Julia interrupted.

I was silent.

"I honestly couldn't see how you lived with yourself," she said, "letting someone go to jail like that. But then again, I see that you weren't able to live with yourself—you knew you were wrong—and I do see how you're trying to fix everything now."

"You're still mad," I said.

"Oh, I don't know what I am. I'm not sure that what you're doing now is right, either, but I'll try to support you. No matter what. Jason, we're great friends. I've missed talking to you."

"And I've missed talking to you," I said. "I was hoping you'd come back."

Julia straightened her back. She rubbed her neck. "I'm not back, Jason. I'm just visiting."

"Just visiting?" I asked.

"Just visiting," she said.

I drank more wine. I refilled my glass.

"I want your friendship," she said. "But we're not going to be together again. You know that."

A bird fluttered in my chest. What Julia was telling me was not a surprise, yet I became cool with the shock of bad news.

"You've been holding out hope," she said.

I shrugged.

She reached across the table again and held my hand, but this time she didn't let go. "You do know that I will love you always," she said.

"I know that, yes," I said.

"This is what I want," she said. "This dinner, this wine, this time with you. Our friendship back, that's why I came down. I don't want to make you miserable. But that's what I want and I have to be clear about it for a change."

"Okay," I said.

"You can tell me to leave," she said.

But I didn't want her to leave. When I spoke, what I said was, "You've always been stronger than me."

"I don't know if that's true—"

"It is. You've always been stronger," I said.

It was chilly in the house. I went into the living room and made a fire. Julia brought the wine in and we sat on the couch, I with my arm around her, she with her hand on my knee, and we watched the blaze.

"What's going on with you?" she asked. "I have to tell you, sweetie, you look like shit. When I saw you out in the vineyard, I thought, Something's going on."

"I'm fine," I said.

"I'm the one person you can talk to," Julia said. "That's what I've been trying to tell you. What's going on?"

"Nothing. Really, I would tell you. Nothing," I said.

We listened to the wood crack and hiss.

"Well," I said, "actually I'm sort of torn up."

And then I told her everything. I told Julia about Troy and all the lies he had told me and what I knew to be the truth about him. I showed her Craig Montoya's journal. I let her read some of the passages.

"That poor boy," she said. "What does this do to your case?"

"There's a chance I might get him off," I said. "A chance, but not a great one, and I'm not so sure I want him walking the streets anyway."

"Obviously Craig became the son he'd lost," she said.

"So then why did Troy ditch him? Why did he let him down?" This was what I wanted to know.

"Well, only Troy can tell you that," she said.

I rubbed my eyes.

"What will you do?" she asked.

"What should I do?" I asked back.

"I don't know," she said.

I leaned forward and rested my elbows on my knees and Julia massaged my shoulders. For a moment I relaxed.

We had reached a point in our lives that we had come to before and—I would be naïve to think otherwise—would arrive at again. We were like the neighbors who lived on either side of a house that one day was abruptly and inexplicably abandoned. First we both studied the emptied house between us from the distance of our respective porches, but eventually, we each stepped a little closer for a better look around, and that was when we noticed each other, watching through bare windows and across empty rooms. Empty rooms where in time we would meet up, where we would search the closets together and the cellars, the upstairs, the attic, collecting artifacts from the former tenants, a single cuff link or a bottle of homemade preserves, where we might dance, where we would convene day after day until, inevitably, the house would be let or sold again, and Julia and I would return to our own houses with a certain mixture of reluctance and relief, to our separate rooms, which were cold with our longing but which we decorated with our salvaged loot. A photograph behind cracked glass, a broken chair. The next time we descended upon the house, we would be older, and we would be both friendlier to each other and more distant, but we would meet up again and again, such was our union, a marriage that had run its course but a marriage that somehow lasted, too, surviving all others and the test of time.

I don't want to pretend that I necessarily arrived at this understanding then, that night during the harvest when we sat on the couch in front of the fire, or that I came to this conclusion soon after that evening. This understanding, if I can call it that, came later, and I have to confess that when Julia stopped massaging my shoulders, I wanted to say, Don't stop yet, don't stop. I wanted to kiss her. I wanted her back. I always would.

Julia slept on the couch. The next morning, I went up early to Hollister and met with the judge. The district attorney supported my motion for a delay; he wanted more time, too. The judge gave us four days and ordered us back to court that Friday.

I returned to the vineyard by late morning and joined Julia down in the field. We clipped the grape bunches with great speed. The wind had picked up and it was drizzling. By three that afternoon, it was raining, but we had finished harvesting the fruit and dumped it into the fermentation tank. We added the sulfates, mixing them in with the long pole, and a short while later, we added the cultured yeast. Now we had to wait for the grapes to turn.

We were out in the winery when Julia said, "I don't exactly want to tell you to go driving in this weather, but . . ."

The rain began to come down hard, straight down; it was a fierce pounding.

"But what?" I asked.

"I'll call Tim," Julia said. "He loves having the house to himself, and I can stay here and help you with the crush."

"But what?" I asked again.

"You need to go and talk with this guy," she said. "One way or another, you've got to deal with him."

"I thought you'd given up on me," Troy said.

I placed both of my hands, palms down, on the table in our prison meeting room.

"I would understand it if you did," he said.

The cool air spilling out from the high vents seemed particularly chilly that evening.

"The truth?" Troy asked. He held his breath. "I lose it sometimes. I don't even remember what it is."

I got up to leave. I reached for my briefcase.

"Wait," Troy said. "Please. Wait."

I sat down again and folded my arms across my chest.

"I lied about my year in film school," he said. "I never went to film school. The closest I came to it was working in a video store on Sunset for a few months."

Troy hadn't shaved for days. It looked like he hadn't slept; his eyes looked as though they had receded into their sockets. Even his prison uniform was wrinkled and worn-out.

"Lauren did write songs. That part was true," he said. "But she never performed them anywhere. She should have, I really wanted her to. They're beautiful songs. I would give anything to hear her sing again. Just one song. I think that's why I've hung on as long as I have, to find her, to hear her sing one more song."

I wanted to believe him, but why should I?

"Sometimes I'd come home at three in the morning," he said, "all skunked out of my mind, or sometimes after I'd been gone for days, or sometimes after I'd lost another pathetic job or I'd spent the day wandering the city—and she'd sit on the edge of the bed and just sing to me. She would soothe me to sleep. Her voice alone could do it."

A single tear ran straight down Troy's cheek.

"Jared was a good kid," he said. "He was smart. He was strong. He was an athlete. He didn't play on any teams, but he was always running around, playing out in the street with his friends, picking up a game of basketball. I wasn't around. I wasn't there for him. He was fifteen. He was really on his own. He had a close bond with his mother, I know that. But he and I . . . I mean, he never fought with me, but I could see the anger in his eyes, the way he glared at me."

Troy tried to imitate his son's glare.

It occurred to me that I had no reason to believe that what he offered me now was the absolute truth. I had no way of knowing whether he was conning me again. But something about the way he spoke to me now was different from all of our conversations in the past.

"What I told you about borrowing money," Troy said, "that part was true. I owed so much money. So much fucking money. And I knew I couldn't pay it back, and I knew I had to leave town, and I was going to run. I was going to run away by myself. Without Lauren or Jared."

I believed him. I believed it all.

"Lauren was so sad," he said. "She'd gotten to the point where she was sad all the time. She didn't need me around—I made matters worse. And finally when I was told by one of the guys I owed money to that I had to pay up, I made a date to hand over some cash, but I planned on skipping town before that day came."

The week wound down and Troy didn't leave, and finally the day, the hour of the arranged meeting arrived. It was a hot summer morning in Los Angeles, Troy said.

"There wasn't any breeze that day. Lauren had gone out, I don't know where—but she took the car. We just had the one car. Jared was home. I saw the car of the guy I was supposed to pay pull up to the mailbox at the corner. I was trapped. I had to get out. I told Jared to go down to the car and tell these people that I'd be down in a minute."

I tried to speak, to ask a question, but my throat was dry and I couldn't get the words out. I wasn't sure that I needed to hear the rest.

Troy continued slowly: "Jared was carrying his basketball, and I saw him bounce it a few times as he approached the car. I was watching from the window of our apartment on the second floor, looking out over the street. Then I don't know what happened. I don't know whether one of the guys in the car looked up and saw me watching. I don't know whether they figured out that I was going to slip out the back. I don't know. There was a shot. A single loud shot from the car. Jared flew back ten feet. He landed on his back. And the car sped off with a screech. And I ran down the stairs, and he was dead. He was dead. They shot him, but it was all my fault. That beautiful boy. He was gone."

Troy exploded with tears and buried his head in his arms on the table.

I cleared my throat. "The terrible things you did," I said.

After a while, Troy calmed down and he told me about how Lauren came home around the time that the ambulance showed up. She had to be sedated. She knew that Troy was in some way to blame for what had happened, although she never knew the entire story. She left town the same day that she was released from the hospital, and Troy never saw her or heard from her again. Meanwhile, the police were all over him. He was a suspect in their investigation into the murder, and Troy hired what sounded like a rather inept lawyer, who told him not to cooperate with the police, which naturally made them dig even deeper into his life. And what followed this incident, Troy's years of drift and wandering, the way he made his way up to an olive grove near Ventura, the way he worked his way north up the coast—all of this was more or less the same story that he had told me before; the only difference was that it was only Lauren whom he wanted to find.

"She always liked my drawings," he said. "Even the doodles I'd make in the margins of the classifieds. The drawings I've been doing are for her."

"You have no idea where she is," I said.

"None," Troy said. "And the thing of it is, I know she would never want to see me again. Why would she? But I want to make up to her for all of the rotten things I did. I took her child and I can't give him back, but—"

"You think you can start over," I said.

Troy shrugged. "I have to make this up to Lauren somehow. If it's the only thing I do with the rest of my life, I have to make up for what I did to her."

"Why did you lie to me?" I asked.

Troy looked at me and swallowed.

"Did you tell me your son was alive because I told you that I had a son I wanted to get back to?" I asked. "Did you think you'd hook me that way? Did you think that would make us bond?"

Troy grinned. "It did."

"Did you think that if I knew the truth, I wouldn't want to help you?" I asked. My voice was getting louder.

"Yes. That was what I thought, and to be honest," Troy said, "I still don't know why you helped me."

"Or was it that you couldn't face the real truth?" I asked. "So you made up an easier story to tell. You were to blame for your son's death and you couldn't face it."

"How about all of the above," Troy said. "All of the fucking above."

"You didn't have to lie to me," I said. "An attorney defends his client, no matter what the client did."

"Your lawyer works harder for you when he thinks you're innocent," Troy said.

I didn't want to argue with him.

"So you ended up in Oak Valley, living in some empty winery," I said, "getting drunk and stoned, and then this kid came along. I read Craig's journal. He thought you were cool. You were kind to him."

Troy nodded. "He was like Jared in so many ways."

"Smart," I said, "strong." Tall and lanky, an athlete, beloved.

"It was . . . it was like getting a bit of Jared back," Troy said.

Julia had been right.

"So you hung out for a summer," I said.

Troy nodded.

"Your chance to be a dad again," I said. I'm not sure whether you need to be a father who has fathered badly to understand what Troy saw in this stranger boy who meandered into his life, but I got it, I understood all too well. Here was his second chance.

"So why did you turn on him?" I asked. "Why did you tell him to go away?"

"I let it go too far," Troy said. "I'm no good. I'm shit. Jared was gone and that was my fault. I would have screwed Craig up."

"Don't you get it? You did screw him up," I said. "Couldn't you have just disappeared?"

"No car," he said.

"So you stole Craig's?"

"One afternoon he comes to me where I'm hanging out," Troy said. "And he says, Okay, this is it, Troy. We're heading out to find Lauren. And it starts to rain. And I'm thinking, He just won't go away. So we drive awhile along that mountain road. And then I think, Fuck this, I can't lead this kid astray. Not to mention his parents are going to freak and I'll probably get picked up for kidnapping. So when the kid pulls over to the side of the road to get out and go pee in the woods, I chuck his backpack and I steal the car."

I knew the rest. Craig despairs. He hikes toward the rock. I come along.

"When I heard the boy was dead," Troy said, "it didn't really matter whether I'd actually killed him or not. I stranded him. I left him out there. I might as well have—"

"But you didn't," I said.

"When they questioned me," Troy said, "I truly thought I deserved to go away to jail forever. And see, one way or another, I knew I was going to go away. They had enough on me, I was pretty sure. One way or another, they'd connect me to the boy."

And they could connect Troy to Craig. It was Troy's hair on Craig's corpse after all.

"They were going to connect me," Troy said, "and I knew that I had to take a deal, and I waited all day and took the best they offered me."

He traced an imaginary circle with his finger on the table.

"My life is one big circle," he said. "I try to spin out of it, to break free from it, I try to do something right, but I just keep going around and around."

We sat across the table in the white room for a long while, staring at each other.

Finally I said, "I don't want to put you on the stand."

"I could tell the truth," Troy said.

"The truth won't help you much. Plus you lied to the psychologist," I said. "You gave her the same lies you gave me. You have no credibility. Nothing you say has any value, not a word."

Troy sank in his chair.

"I'm fucked," he said, "aren't I?"

I didn't answer him. I said, "I have to figure out where to go from here. I'm supposed to start calling witnesses on Friday."

Troy pounded the table with his fist. He startled me.

"I'm never getting out of here," he said. "Why don't you just tell me that and get it over with? I'm never getting out of here, right? I'm never getting out of here."

Again I didn't answer him. I told him that I would see him Friday.

"I just want to hear her sing one song," Troy said. "One more song."

When I turned back toward him as I left the white room, he looked to me much the way he had looked when I had seen him the first time that night at the sheriff's station. Fragile, small in the world. If he disappeared, no one would know. No one would care.

I tried to convince myself that I didn't know this man. I tried to convince myself that I had never known him. Troy Frantz was an enigma when he confessed to my crime and he had remained an enigma when I visited him in prison. At long last, he had told me the barest truth, but he was still a stranger. And I thought that if I could feel no compassion for him, if he could have me think that he was getting what he deserved, forever spinning and spinning in his hopeless circle, then it would be easier for me to let him face a certain conviction and longer prison term. To walk away. But driving home in the rain, I knew that he was neither a stranger nor an enigma, and the fact was that I did know him.

He had been a loquacious boy who learned to read late. He was fast and spry but never found a sport he liked. He was the child whose shirts and jeans were always a little too big, too baggy. The boy who hung out with the older kids on the street but could never quite keep up with them when they tore off on their bikes; the kids his age picked on him. A boy who had moved around a lot, which meant that he had to learn how to lose himself by himself in his own improvised games; give him a golf ball and a stick and some trees as targets, and he was all set. He was a boy who could spend hours in the low nest of an olive tree, whittling a branch into a blade. He took summer art classes in a suburban park, and when he was instructed to draw a sycamore or a toy sailboat in a pond, he looked elsewhere, until he landed on an old man sitting on a bench, leaning on his cane, and Troy drew him instead.

He grew up believing that he would always be alone in the world, never understood, never held. When he was a teenager, he fell in love a hundred times a day, hoping against hope that someone would smile back. Then one day when he was twenty, a woman did smile back. It seemed impossible, but it was true. She seemed like a piece of the sun, radiant, yet cool to the touch. He was certain that he would chase her away—after all, he had his dark moods, the days when he still wanted to climb a tree and whittle a weapon—but she stayed. She stayed and she soothed him with her breeze and her balm, her song. They liked to take long drives up and down the coast, going nowhere in particular. They liked to drive into the desert and sleep outside. They liked to make complicated omelettes together, to read books aloud together—anything together. This woman was his salvation, and he adored her, and when she told him that they were going to have a child, he thought, I don't deserve this much luck, nobody does.

The big city came next, the move south, with all of their child's toys crammed into the trunk. Exploring that new city was exhilarating for a time. There was nothing quite like arriving in a place and believing that these wide boulevards, these bony hills, these dry basins were yours to conquer. The days slipped away fast, and the nights were even shorter. Were they happy? Yes, very happy.

And yet, deep down something bothered Troy. Deep down he suspected and he feared and, face it, he knew that too much that was too new was happening too soon and too fast. The boy needs a new jacket. The wife looks tired all the time. Our apartment is our home, but wouldn't it be nice to live on a quieter street? Before long he felt as if he were running a race with his old self, his younger self, and he couldn't keep up. I mean that when he was younger, it was easy to dream. Now that dream, the grand plan, seemed too ambitious. So the question became what to give up. Should he stop thinking that he could become someone who was known in the world for making something other people would look at and admire? Should he figure out instead how he was going to buy a new car or a house? Which mattered more?

Then there was a cold snap, a rainy winter that would never end. How had it happened? Once upon a time, there were not enough hours in the evening to spend with the love of his life, sprawled out on a mattress on the floor and talking in the dark. Suddenly they had nothing to talk about when they were together. Once upon a time, the boy seemed so content; he ran to the door when Troy came home. Suddenly the boy couldn't be bothered to say hello. How had it happened? Troy had no idea. He wandered the city every dusk. He thought, It would be so easy to disappear.

This was who Troy Frantz was. The child and the boy and the man I am describing. He wasn't a stranger, I knew him. Change a few facts and I was Troy. Our lives were not all that different, although somewhere in the late summer of our respective youths, our stories diverged. Would I be wrong to say that Troy's life was merely a darker rendering of my own? Was his cold snap colder? Had he drifted along a faster current? Was my time dusk and his midnight—was that it?

These were the facts of our lives: Both of us had squandered our luck. We had hurt the people who loved us most. Our negligence had tragic consequences. I suppose that I could look at myself and say that my son was still alive; he had survived, yet in the end, that had little to do with me. I was not the one who had given a lonely boy hope and then literally stranded him in the middle of nowhere during a storm, but I had killed that same boy and let him lie on the road all night, and the truth was that I had tried to move on with my life as if the accident had never happened. Troy and I were not so different. We were men who lied, simple as that, men who ran, and at least Troy had started to tell the truth, which was more than I could say for myself. I could have contrasted our felonies and decided that his crimes were graver than mine or that he deserved the harsher punishment, the more arduous penance. I could have decided that he deserved to be in jail and I did not; let me remain free. But who was I to make such claims? I couldn't make them any longer. I couldn't pretend.

Here we are at the end of the century, drifting through a heroless age. We have no leaders we can trust, no visions to invest in, no faith to ride. All we have are our own protean moralities, our countless private codes, which we each shape and reshape according to our own selfish needs. We don't dare think too far ahead. We can't see too far ahead. Here we are, trapped by whatever season we find ourselves enduring, waiting out the weather, staring at a drought sun, stupefied, helpless—or scrambling like fools to make it home before the rain really comes down and the dry river floods and the hills crash into the valley. Where do we find the courage to do what we know is right?

I was tired, I was spent. Where would I find the courage? Show me, tell me: Where?

The rain pounded the lawn around my house and ran down the slopes of my land in a steady flood, and even inside, I was constantly aware of the torrents drumming my roof and draping every view with a gray hallucinatory gauze. There was no escape. I don't remember ever feeling dry during the bleak sunless days of the storm that autumn—my feet were always wet, my face damp—and partly that was because I had to deal with the possibility that the house and especially the winery would flood, which meant building a sandbag wall at the top of the hill. Julia stayed another day—she went home to check on Tim and then made it back—and then she stayed yet another day, and together she and I constructed a snaking barricade of sandbags, a running pyramid of plastic bundles of dirt and gravel and sand, which diverted the flood stream around the threatened stone structures. It was hard work and we needed to do it quickly, filling the bags and wheeling them over to our makeshift wall and flinging them atop the bags already laid down. It was a tedious chore. I lost track of when the day began and ended, when it was night. Sometimes we took refuge in the kitchen and shared some soup. Most of the time, it seemed, I was outside piling sandbags.

Meanwhile, the grapes began to turn. The must foamed, and Julia took charge of monitoring it and eventually punching down the cap. She had stayed on at the vineyard and claimed that it was because she had abandoned her dissertation again—which was news to me—and had nothing better to do; later she told me that she was worried about me and thought I might float away in the middle of the night and never be seen again. She also said that rain or no rain, she missed this life, making wine and working the land, even if that meant coping with the rain.

Like I said, Julia went to check up on Tim, but we also talked to him twice a day. He was apparently quite content to have the house to himself. Don't hurry back on my account, he told his mother.

He had grown up, Julia said. "He doesn't really need us anymore."

"I guess not," I said. "Is that a good thing?"

"I don't know," Julia said, "is it?"

When we ran out of plastic for the sandbags, I had to drive into town. This was on Thursday. The vineyard road had become a treacherously narrow track because the sides of the road had eroded and either fallen away or turned into pure mud. The main highway had narrowed to a single lane, as well, and when you needed to pass a car coming in the opposite direction, it was like a game of chicken: Who would give up first and pull over to the side of the road and risk floating off into the meadow?

I made it to the hardware store, climbed over the sandbag wall, and went inside, where the shelves looked emptied. I suspected that there had been a run on supplies, but the low level of stock could also have been evidence of a larger migration that had occurred during the last months. People were leaving the valley. People were giving up and running away, although I didn't know where they were going or what they would do when they got there. I was surprised and lucky that Will Clark still had the supplies on hand that I needed, the bags and the sheets of plastic that I wanted so that I could seal off all but one door into my house and garage, and I was glad that only he and Emma Hodges were in the store.

Emma Hodges looked at me but didn't say anything, and I didn't speak to her, and the only words Will Clark uttered were prices and the total amount I owed him. I had decided to gather whatever other supplies I thought I might need, flashlights and flares and that sort of thing, and Will Clark took what seemed like an unnecessary amount of time to punch the buttons of his register. When I went back outside, I knew why he had taken so long.

Who it was, I would never know. All I know for certain was that it could not have been Emma Hodges or Will Clark who had pulled this mean trick, although that hardly mattered, because they did play a part, delaying me while someone else came along and opened my car doors and rolled down all of the windows. Whoever it was also propped open my hood and trunk. The rain was so hard that during the twenty minutes that I was in the store, the trunk had filled with a half a foot of water and the seats of my car were soaked. Then the engine wouldn't turn over.

I could have gone back inside, but that would have given everyone too much satisfaction. I sat in my drenched car and waited awhile, then tried the ignition again, and it wheezed, it moaned, and yet it still didn't start; but that wheezing and moaning was heartier than it had been during my previous attempt, so I decided to wait.

An hour later I was able to start my car and head home.

I didn't want to alarm Julia and so I planned not to tell her about the prank, but as soon as I peeled off my rain poncho and the coat beneath it, my boots, my layers of socks, I plunked down in a chair and spilled out what had happened.

"That town," Julia muttered, and that was her only response.

She stood behind my chair and worked her fingers along my neck and upper spine until I began to relax. She set down a bowl of a thick bean soup that we had made a large pot of and were working our way through, a bowl and a slab of bread and some wine.

"I don't know what I would have done without you these past couple of days," I said.

The rain slapped the windows next to the table.

"I'd rather be here making a stand," Julia said, "than anywhere else worrying about you."

We ate in silence, and then I asked her if she could stay on at the vineyard for the rest of the crush.

"I'd like to, sure," she said, "but why are you asking me this?"

"And do you think that you could come down to the vineyard from time to time and take care of the vines and the barrels—"

"Jason? What's going on?" she asked.

I told her my plan, as much as I had a plan. There, at that moment, at the table in my kitchen, I had come to a decision about the motion that I would file the next day in court.

"I can't let you do that," she said.

"It's what I should have done a long time ago," I said.

Julia frowned.

"There is no other way," I said.

"Look, it's late," she said. "You've had a miserable day. Why don't you wait until the morning before making any decisions. Why don't you wait and we can talk about it after we've had a chance to sleep," she said.

"Okay," I said.

"Do you promise? Do you promise me that you won't make up your mind until the morning?" Julia asked.

"I promise," I said, I lied.

After Julia went to sleep on the couch, I retreated to my desk and began working on my motion. It took me several hours to draft it and revise it and check my precedents and the procedural code—I had never filed a motion like this before—and before long it was morning, although, again, I couldn't really tell because the rain obliterated the daybreak.

I showered and dressed. I was too anxious to eat anything. Julia was still asleep when I was ready to leave, enviously lost in a dream that made her smile. I kissed her forehead and whispered good-bye.

I waited for Troy in a small gray basement room at the courthouse in Hollister. He looked terrible when the friendly guard from the prison ushered him in. Troy had shaved that morning, but he'd missed a few patches, and his hair looked barely combed. He had already changed out of his usual orange jumpsuit into the blazer and rumpled trousers that he wore for the trial. I suspected that he hadn't slept since the last time I had met with him; his eyes were raccooned and bloodshot. He met my glance and then looked away as if I were a one-man jury and he didn't like the verdict that he read in my stare. The guard hesitated but then broke the rules and removed Troy's wrist and ankle cuffs. The guard nodded at me and then left us alone.

Troy rubbed his wrists and forearms.

I sat across from him and removed a folder from my briefcase. I handed him the motion and said, "I need your signature on this so I can file it. Technically you're the one filing it, not me, even though I prepared it."

Troy skimmed only the top of the first page of the long document. He shook his head. "I don't get it," he said.

"It's a petition to get a new lawyer," I said. "Read the whole motion." I straightened my tie. "It's a motion for a new counsel based on defense counsel misconduct."

Troy looked at me. "I'm the one who lied to you," he said.

"No, Troy," I said. "I lied, too."

He continued reading the motion. His ears reddened. His entire face turned red.

The document was what I said it was, a motion for a new counsel, but it was also my signed confession. I began with the accident on the mountain road. I talked about my panic and how I drove away. I confessed everything, I left nothing out.

Troy didn't look up at me when he had finished reading the motion.

"I'm sorry," I said. "I'm very sorry. And I know that doesn't begin to—"

"Fuck off," Troy said. His breathing quickened.

"This will get you a new lawyer," I said. "The new lawyer will use my confession and the people will probably not even pursue the grand theft charges, which is all they have on you. You've already done the time."

"The time," Troy said. He shook his head slowly. "You have no idea."

"I know," I said. "I'm sorry."

"How long will all of this take?" he asked.

And here was where I made a crucial mistake. I should have been vague and said that it would take no time at all, but I answered him truthfully, and I calculated roughly how long it would take to get a new attorney and then how long after that before a mistrial might be declared, if that was the way the judge went, and then how long it might be before there was another trial or perhaps a rearraignment and so on.

"Months?" Troy asked. "I can't wait that long. I can't wait anymore."

"Troy, try to—"

"Fuck off," he shouted. "What am I going to do?"

"Like I said, this will get you out eventually—"

"I trusted you, you asshole," Troy yelled. "I trusted you. And then I finally told you the truth, and all along . . ."

There was nothing I could say. I had no defense and I

knew that my repeated apologies would only make him angrier.

"You're my friend," I said. "I deceived you. I'm sorry."

Troy stood up. His face on fire, his fists clenched.

"You are not my friend," he said.

He was breathing very fast now.

"I want you to pay," he whispered, and that made me shiver, not the words so much as the chill in his voice.

I stood and faced him. I had nothing to say for myself. I would no longer practice law, I thought. I would probably face fraud charges. Not to mention the civil suit that would now be redirected at me. Was that enough? Possibly not.

"What's going to happen to me now?" Troy asked.

"I'm trying to tell you—"

"Shut up," Troy said. "Just shut up. I need to think."

"Troy," I said.

"Will you shut the fuck up?" he screamed.

And then he swung his fist at me. His right hand flew into my chin. He hit me hard. I fell back into my chair and knocked it over. I may have blacked out for a few seconds.

"Guard," Troy yelled.

I realized that I had knocked the folder with my motion off the table when I fell, and I managed to gather together the papers and slip them into the folder, and then, standing, I slid the folder back into my briefcase.

All of this was happening very fast, and Troy's punch had made my vision blurry. I don't know exactly at what moment the guard appeared.

But I did see the guard step into the room, his hand on his gun.

And I did see Troy stand behind the door, shut the door after the guard, and in a blink punch him squarely in the jaw the way he had punched me.

The guard fell back against the wall.

Troy had his hands on the collar of the guard's shirt. The basement room was partially unfinished; there were exposed pipes running along one wall. Troy slammed the guard back into the pipes.

The guard was reaching for his gun.

Troy had grapsed the guard's neck and chin and he pounded the guard's head once, twice, hard against a pipe running along the wall, which was enough to knock the man out. He slumped over in a heap.

I jumped over to the guard and noticed that the back of his head was bloody. I pressed my ear to his chest and could tell that he was breathing; Troy hadn't killed him.

And when I looked up at Troy, I saw that he had grabbed the guard's gun. He was pointing it at me.

"I can't wait any longer," he said. "I can't wait."

"Troy," I whispered.

"I'm fucked now. I'm so fucked," he said. "I'm fucked forever."

Assaulting a peace officer would not help him walk free, no.

"Let's go," Troy said.

"Go where?" I asked.

"Don't say anything or I will kill you," Troy said. He pulled me up to my feet and pushed me in front of him. He stood close behind me. He had the gun at my back.

"We can't just walk out of here," I said. I nodded at his gun.

Troy took off his blazer, all the while managing to aim the gun at me, and he folded the jacket over his wrist and hand so that his weapon was concealed.

"Don't say a word," he said.

"We can't just walk out of here," I said again.

But that was exactly what we did do. The basement of the courthouse was empty that morning; we didn't pass anyone. At the end of a narrow hall, the exit was guarded by a man reading a paper and eating a doughnut. Beyond the exit was a loading dock, and beyond the loading dock, the prison van that had brought Troy here. Beyond the van, a large and mostly vacant parking lot.

We headed down the hall toward the exit, Troy close behind me, the gun pressed against the small of my back. A phone rang and the guard took the call.

As we approached his desk, I thought about saying something, but then I knew that Troy would use the gun and that after a few seconds, one or more of us would be slain.

The guard looked up briefly and nodded once. Whoever had called him was making him laugh.

"Wave and say good-bye," Troy whispered.

We passed the guard. I did what I was told. On the way out, we didn't have to go through a metal detector.

"Bye," Troy said.

The guard waved back without looking up again.

We were outside in the rain. The rain pounding the prison van. The asphalt. The few cars parked around the lot.

"Your car," Troy said. He jabbed me with the gun.

We walked over to my car at the far end of the lot.

"You drive," Troy said.

I got behind the wheel. He sat in the passenger seat, with the gun aimed at me.

I started the car. "Drive where?" I asked.

The rain came down that day. Californians would remember the storm because flash flooding closed all of the schools and colleges and long stretches of the freeways. The main streets of small towns were washed away, drowned in a murky tide. Stores were ruined, businesses lost, and huge swathes of farmland were rendered unarable. The damage ran into the billions. Thousands of homes had to be evacuated, hundreds were destroyed, and mostly because of the mud slides. It was the mud that fell free from the cliffs and that poured down every drenched hillside, the mud along the riverbanks that couldn't hold, the mud running everywhere that inspired the most panic and caused the most harm. Most of the deaths that day involved mud. Mud trapping a trucker in his cab. Mud carrying away an ambulance while rescue workers were trying to revive a woman who went into cardiac arrest. Mud bringing down the roof of a grocery store. Mud everywhere.

As I drove away from the courthouse with Troy, I had to worry more about the uncertain road than the gun pointed at me. I had both hands on the wheel. I stared straight ahead. I could see only a few feet, if that, beyond my car, my headlights illuminating nothing and my wipers providing no relief. The wind had kicked in, and so the rain came at my car from every direction, sometimes horizontally. And the constant shifts in gusts disoriented me, so I had no idea where we were headed, except to say that we were generally driving south. Troy seemed to know where we were in the world, and he would snap directions at me and tell me where to turn. Eventually we were on a fast road, a highway, with only occasionally another car in sight, and then after a while, we stopped passing anyone.

I tried to apologize several times, although each time I said, "You don't know how sorry I am," it seemed to mean less and less to him, as if each apology cheapened the previous one, as if the more I begged for his forgiveness, the less likely he was to grant me his absolution.

We followed a road that carried us into a forest and then hills, and I said, "I know this is a mess we're in, but I think we can fix this."

Finally Troy spoke. He said, "You can't fix anything."

And he was right. Assault, escape, armed kidnapping—these crimes would not be forgiven.

I kept driving.

Minutes later Troy said, "All I wanted was to find Lauren."

This, too, seemed impossible, especially since the road had narrowed and the wend had become more difficult to negotiate and my tires were slipping with each turn. I thought we would either drive right into an oncoming truck or we would skid off the road.

"I just wanted to find her," Troy said.

"I'm sure you will someday—"

"I won't," Troy said.

"You don't know that," I said.

"I do know," he said.

I didn't know how much time had passed or how far we had driven. We could have been driving for an hour, or we could have been driving for days. I had to assume that someone had figured out what had happened back at the courthouse. I had to assume that someone had noticed that Troy and I didn't make it to court on time or that someone had walked into the basement conference room and found the guard. But if we were pursued, if there was an all points bulletin out for a fugitive and his captive, I saw no sign of it. No other car in my rearview mirror. Nothing but flood warnings and traffic reports on the radio, which Troy turned off after a while.

So we headed deeper into the storm along an unfamiliar winding road, which after a while I realized was the mountain road. Were we headed back to the scene where our lives had first collided, Troy's and mine, back to the scene of the accident? I didn't know, I didn't ask. I didn't think that Troy wanted to kill me, but I thought he could. Look at him: He was so drained, so lost, leaning against the door, glancing at me, checking the road, me again. Sometimes he appeared to forget he was aiming a weapon at me, and he would let the square nozzle droop or point it away from me, at the dash; then he would remember his role, and he'd aim the gun at my neck again. Soon we would come to the rock with the view, and then we would follow the haunted trail of the road, and then where?

All I could do was drive. I gave myself up to the road.

And then, before we came to the rock, we approached one of the curves along the cliff where the road hung over a sheer drop, a deep ravine, where the roadway itself was bolstered by a grid of steel supports. We came closer and closer to that curve, and from a distance of about twenty yards, we could see that the road had collapsed and that the steel framework had given out. I couldn't tell if it was a mud slide from the slope above the road or if the earth beneath the arc of girders had fallen away, but it didn't much matter, because the road was out and we would have to turn around.

"Oh, man," Troy said.

I thought that he was upset about our interrupted escape route, but then I noticed what he was looking at: Right at the edge where the trestle had collapsed into the canyon, there was a car poised on the rough tear of the broken road, a car that was teetering, its hood angled down into the fatal drop and its rear wheels off the ground, spinning. I couldn't tell whether the car had been crossing the span when the road gave out or whether the driver had not seen the missing link and had started to drive across or braked too late.

Closer, I could see that there were passengers in the car, behind the wheel and in the backseat. It was a large and square-rumped blue sedan.

Closer still, I saw that whoever was behind the wheel had slumped forward and that the passengers in the backseat were children, trapped, waving frantically at us.

We came to a stop and Troy and I hopped out of the car. The rain soaked us instantly, and it was a cold rain, cold enough to make my fingers immediately numb.

Troy was standing next to me, but I noticed that he wasn't holding the gun anymore. He had tucked it into his belt, beneath his untucked shirt. He tugged at my elbow and started jogging over to the car. He shouted something at me, but the rain pounding the road and cliff was so loud, like we were standing beneath a waterfall, that I couldn't make out his words.

But I knew what he was telling me. The car was about to go. It was teetering back and forth on the jagged precipice, and with each wobble, it pointed a little farther down toward the ravine.

The driver was a woman. Her head was against the steering wheel; she was out, unconscious, maybe dead. The children were both boys and they were bobbing up and down and making the car teeter even more. One good shift in the wind and that car would sail a hundred feet straight down into the granite glen.

Troy motioned to the children to relax. Calm down, he was trying to say, and I think that they saw that we had come to their rescue. He crept close enough to the car for him to mime that he wanted them to roll down the windows. Troy was on one side of the car, on the ravine side, and I was on the other. I could see now that none of the wheels were touching a surface and that the car was balanced on the break in the pavement, balanced on its driveshaft.

When the kids had the windows down, Troy told the boys to stay right where they were, not to move an inch. The boys responded with a simultaneous timid nod.

He looked at the car. He waved me over to his side. I shouted that I was going back to my car to get some rope that I had in my trunk—I thought that maybe we could tow the sedan off of the edge—but Troy grabbed my arm when I moved away and he pointed to his wrist and shook his head: We didn't have time.

I shrugged: What should we do? This much was obvious: If we got the kids in back out first, the car would slide into the canyon. And if we tried to free the driver first, we would lose the kids.

The hood of the blue sedan dropped a few inches lower and the car creaked.

The car tilted forward again, and the children shrieked. The woman at the wheel—the mother of the boys, I assumed—moved her head slightly. She wasn't dead. If she had been dead, Troy and I could have each grabbed a child and let the car go down.

The rain blew in gusts and slapped us in the face and then came at us from behind, pushing us toward the cliff. A piece of the road on the opposite side of the break fell away and crashed into the canyon. In about a minute, the car would slide off the jag and everyone would die.

I didn't know what we could do except watch. I was
bouncing on my toes. My arms were outstretched, as if I
could somehow telekinetically hold the car up.

While I was standing there picturing the worst, Troy shuffled around the sedan, studying its exact relationship to the
slope. And then before I knew it, without saying a word, he
scrambled around to the front fender of the car and carefully
lowered himself down the mud and rock and broken pavement beneath the spinning left-front wheel—the mud coated
his shirt and his jeans and his arms, soon his face—and his
foot slipped at one point, but his boots gripped a notch of
granite—and he managed to slide along the slope beneath
the car, beneath the front fender, and somehow he managed
to stand on a ridge and stand to his full height, and somehow
he was able to push up with all of his strength so that he
lifted the car up the few inches that it had dipped down since
we had arrived on the scene.

Troy had lodged himself beneath the left-front fender and
the slope—he became a human wedge—the car looked as if
it were resting on his left shoulder and that he were holding
it up with his extended right arm—and I couldn't really tell
how much force he was actually applying against the balanced car, but what I could see was that he had steadied the
sedan from slipping any farther, at least for a few moments
longer. Gravity was against us, but he had bought us more
time.

Troy grunted. I could see that he was straining. And it was
obvious to me then what I should do. We had to take this one
step at a time.

Very cautiously, very slowly, I opened the left back door
of the car, on the ravine side, and at the same time that I
opened it, I instructed the boy on the other side of the car to
open his door carefully and to climb out onto the road.

The boy did what I said. He was the older of the two and
seemed to understand the equilibrium we needed to maintain. As he climbed out, he pulled his brother across the
backseat after him.

I got in the car. The sedan tilted forward and creaked.

I heard Troy grunt.

The car shifted back to where it had been moments ago.

The woman in the front seat stirred and mumbled something.

The boy standing out by the break in the road slowly pulled his brother out after him, and then when I could see that the boys were out of the car and in the rain, I nodded at them to move away from the car toward safer ground.

I inched toward the middle of the backseat. The car didn't move. It had worked. I started laughing because I couldn't believe that the car had held, and I think my laughter might have roused the woman behind the wheel. She leaned back and her head rolled and she moaned. Her face was a bloody mess.

My heart thudded now that I was in the car—I mean it really beat hard, because I knew that the car could go at any second and that if it did, the woman and I would go with it.

We had to move faster now. I pushed the front passenger seat forward and leaned over it and slipped one hand, then the other beneath the shoulders of the injured woman. At that point her eyes were open and she seemed to understand what I wanted her to do. I tugged her torso and she pushed with her feet, with what strength she had, and I was able to get her arms and stomach into the back and then reach for one leg, the other, and pull her back onto me.

The car creaked again and wobbled more than it had before, and the older boy appeared on the ravine side, and he pulled at his mother's feet, pulled her enough so that her feet were on the ground and she was able to lift herself up. I pushed at her back, and then the woman was out, standing, then on her knees, crawling away from the edge, and it was just me in the backseat, ready to ride the car into the fold of the mountain.

I heard Troy grunt again.

I slid across the backseat and I put both feet down on the

pavement and I stood carefully and I was back in the rain, the cold gusting rain.

The injured woman was lying on the road, her children huddled over her. They were safe.

The car remained miraculously poised, its wheels still spinning.

I crawled around to the front of the car to Troy, who held his position. He was drenched with rain and mud. He looked up at me.

I could see the stone strength of his arms beneath his wet shirt.

I smiled at him. I gave him a thumbs-up to say that the family was safe.

I got down on my knees next to the car and as far as I could go on the pavement without sliding down the slope. I held out my hand.

Troy tried to reach toward me, but when he moved his right arm, the car began to shift down again. He couldn't grab my hand without the car coming down on him.

I tried to extend my arm farther, and he tried to grab hold again, but the car slipped and shifted.

He looked at me and he smiled a strange, puzzled grin.

His right foot began to slip. Mud was streaming down the ledge where he was standing. His foot slipped some more.

I yelled his name.

He looked at me again, his left foot slipping now, and his brown eyes went completely black.

Then both feet slipped at the same time. The car tilted forward. First it came down right on him, pinning him beneath it, crushing his chest, knocking out his last breath. Then the car slid forward and the tumble of rock and road and mud beneath it fell away—I had to crawl back quickly so I wouldn't fall in, too—and the car plunged down, down, straight down, flipping once, flipping again, and finally diving headfirst into the ravine, taking Troy with it.

If there was any noise when the car crashed, if there was an explosion, I didn't hear it. If Troy cried out one last time,

I didn't hear it. All I could hear was the rain beating the ground around me.

A man was dead, a family saved. And the rain kept coming, without pause, without memorial. It rained and it rained and it rained.

Some mornings my last autumn in the valley, I would hike through the woods that bordered my vineyard and get lost. I would head out for no reason in particular, to clear my head, and I would make a few capricious turns; in a matter of minutes, I would have no idea where I was. The trees should have been familiar to me, each ancient oak distinct from its neighbor, but for some reason they all looked the same. All of the trunks flaked the same gray bark. All leaned at the same cant. All of the slopes and dry streams became indistinguishable, all of the dark alleys through the trees. The rain would begin to come down in a befuddling mist, and I would slump against a trunk and sit there on the wet ground, waiting for the drizzle to subside long enough for the sun to break through the clouds and offer me some sense of direction, some clue that east was over there where a blackened branch had fallen and west behind me. I would pick myself up and head for the branch and eventually begin to recognize certain trees, like the one with its roots exposed and splayed every which way like an old man's arthritic fingers grasping for anything to hold on to, the powdery soil, the world slipping away from him. Eventually I would reach a familiar clearing, a bald cove of reedy grass, and then another familiar landmark, a lone pepper tree or the run of a rail fence or the remnants of a shed, and this was how I made my way home. I had been wandering through these woods for the better part of my life, but they became foreign to me that fall, a desert of nomad sand, unmappable, ever shifting.

"There you are," Julia would say when I made it back and found her in the winery. She had taken charge of finishing the crush. She was busy siphoning the young wine into the barrels, managing the hosing and heavy casks by herself.

"Here I am," I would answer. I watched her work. I had no desire to help.

"Did you get lost in the woods again?" she would ask.

I hummed a vague reply. "No one called," I said.

"No one called," Julia said.

"No one came by with a warrant," I said.

"Sorry to disappoint you," she said.

She rubbed her nose with the back of her wrist. She sealed off a barrel and then looked up at me.

"What?" she asked.

"I hear a siren," I said. I was forever hearing an approaching siren that season.

"No, you don't," she said. "Hey, could you hold this?"

I took the siphon from her and held it until she was ready to fill a new barrel with wine from the vat.

"Could you steady the barrel for me?" she asked.

I grabbed hold of the barrel as if it were a calf we were about to brand.

"Okay, here I go," Julia said, and she opened a valve at the base of the tank and the thin blood of the grapes poured into the barrel.

In this way, Julia enlisted me in the winery work, and in this way, she coaxed me into the routine of the day—the vineyard chores, making our meals ("Will you cut up some tomatoes for the salad? Would you sautée a zucchini for the couscous?")—drawing me into a life in which I was a reluctant participant. She took care of me that autumn, staying on at the vineyard after the crush was over. Every other day she drove all the way to Berkeley to check on Tim and then back to the vineyard. Tim certainly appreciated this arrangement; it was all any high school senior wanted, a house to himself, no parents around. And when it came time to head up to Hollister for the formal hearing into what had happened in the courthouse basement a month earlier, Julia went with me.

"You don't trust me," I said.

"Got that right," she said.

She knew that I wanted to clear Troy's name.

"The story is written," she said. "Don't muck it up."

"It's written wrong," I said.

"You don't need to do this to yourself. You'll be disbarred, you know that. You could be prosecuted for fraud. The Montoyas will definitely sue you, and they'd have grounds for psychological damage—"

"I know," I said.

"The story is told," Julia said. "Let go. Move on."

"I can't let go," I said. "I can't move on."

We arrived at the courthouse and worked our way down a series of anonymous corridors. I had thought we would listen to the entire proceedings, but in this matter, I was a witness and not an attorney, and so my presence in the hearing room was limited. Julia and I ended up sitting on a bench outside the chamber where a panel was looking into the security breach at the courthouse. We were reading a newspaper when Mrs. Montoya and her lawyer appeared at the end of the hall.

I watched Mrs. Montoya lope toward us. When she noticed me, she pulled her black shawl up higher around her neck. Her lawyer attempted to screen me from her view, but I offered her my seat on the bench, which she took. The lines in her face ran deeper than the last time I'd seen her. She had dyed her gray hair black, which, given her sickly pallor, made her look even more frail.

We must have faced each other for a minute before she

spoke, and I could read the same concerned expression in both Mrs. Montoya's attorney's and Julia's faces. They both were saying, Let go.

"I'm happy he's dead," Mrs. Montoya said.

I didn't say anything.

"The man who killed my boy is dead," she said. "He's dead. It's finished. It's done."

But the man who killed your boy is not dead.

Julia inched toward the edge of the bench.

"Now I have peace," Mrs. Montoya said, and coughed. "I have peace," she said. "I can rest," and then she looked away.

She had peace, she could rest, and who was I to take that away from her? Just when you thought you understood how your son died, let me tell you what really happened. Let me take away your belief that ultimate justice has been delivered. Let me take that away and leave you wondering and worrying whether you will ever prevail on the playing field of a courtroom. Let me take away your peace, and let me tell you this, that your ordeal will never end.

I couldn't. One more time I said nothing.

And so perhaps it was out of cowardice again or maybe because I understood what my ex-wife, my old friend, was advising me, or perhaps it was because I believed that this was what was best for a mother who had lost her son—or all of the above—that when I was called into the paneled room where the committee of four men and two women sat at a long table, when they solicited my account of the relevant events, I gave them what they wanted, the story as they already knew it, unembellished, a truth so partial that it was perjured.

At the end of my testimony, I was asked if there was anything that I wanted to add to the official record, and I leaned forward in my chair, and even though I knew that my comments would probably be dismissed as the obliged good word put in by Troy's erstwhile advocate and nothing more,

I made sure that everyone in the room knew that on the same day that Troy Frantz had badly beaten a guard and taken a hostage at gunpoint, he had also saved three people from certain death and in the process lost his own complicated life. I will not pretend that anyone cared, but at least I said that much.

Julia waited until we were back in our car and driving home before she asked me what I had told the panel.

"It still seems impossible to me," I said, "that no one found my motion in my briefcase. I left my briefcase on the table that morning." It had been returned to me with my confessional brief tucked neatly inside. "Anyone could have gone through my things."

"Jason," Julia said.

"It just doesn't seem possible that someone out there doesn't know the real truth."

"Jason, what did you tell them?"

"I did what you wanted me to do," I said. "I let go."

Now we were supposed to get on with our lives. Julia had asked me if she could move back to the vineyard for a while; she said that through and through, she had been happy here. I liked the idea of her taking over the day-to-day work in the winery, and so she transformed the bedroom where she had been sleeping into more of a permanent nest, buying a dresser and writing table for it, a used armoire, a bed frame for a futon. She seemed content for a while, at least as long as I remained in Oak Valley.

Julia stayed on the following winter after I was gone and she became briefly but intensely involved in the larger world of winemakers, entering our first vintage, now ready to drink, into all manner of contests, in which our cabernet was always praised. Judges labeled the wine with words like eucalyptus and vanilla and violet. We needed money and so she sold that vintage to a distributor for a good price; she did the same the following year. Meanwhile she tended the vines and reaped another harvest and bottled another vintage. She stayed on at the vineyard much longer than I expected her to, but inevitably she longed for the rhythm of the city again, and inevitably she needed a more regular income. She hatched a plan that I knew wouldn't work—she would raise money for an art museum for part of the year and work at the vineyard on weekends and some months during the summer and fall, and indeed, as it turned out, she couldn't divide up her year that way. In time she stopped going down to the vineyard, and since I was no longer living there, the place was once again abandoned.

Julia and I speak often—recently she moved to the Southwest when she changed jobs—although we haven't talked much about the people we've seen, our occasional romantic ventures; that history, we keep to ourselves. But she remains my confidante and the mother of my son. I don't see her or Tim nearly as often as I would like, but somehow all three of us remain in touch, a family in diaspora, and Tim now attends a college in the East—he chose our alma mater—and he and I maintain a fairly fluid written correspondence, a weekly back-and-forth on-line. I am hoping that later in life we can take a trip somewhere, just my son and me, a rafting expedition, or maybe we can find a cabin somewhere serene and hang out for a week, because I want to talk to him for days and days. I want to do nothing in particular with him. Make a feast, watch an old movie. I suppose I am asking for his friendship—and as a friend, his trust—but I don't take for granted that I will have it. I long for there to be a laziness between us, but years may go by before that exists.

Back to my last autumn in the valley: The crush was over and Julia had moved into the old stone house, and I still went on long walks in the woods and kept getting lost, and what I came to believe was that I didn't belong in the valley.

Finally one day I said to Julia, "I can't stay here."

"Where will you go?" she asked.

I didn't know.

"What will you do?"

I didn't know that, either. I would finish up my pending legal work and I wouldn't take any new cases. Early into the new year, I would leave; I would head north.

"I'll be here when you get back," Julia said, which was a pleasant notion, even though I knew—and I was right—that she would leave the vineyard before I returned.

Before I left Oak Valley, I went for a drive, one more tour of the ruins, what ruins were left, and I ended up at the winery where the stand of cypress had grown up around the fermentation vat. The trees were tall now, sturdy, amply plumed and very green, and all of the walls of the old winery had crashed down; all traces of the structure were obliterated by weeds and grass and a thick swell of brush. Maybe you could tell that there had been a winery here once upon a time, but not necessarily. A stray roof tile, a lump of stucco—that was all that was left. And I thought that a stranger who happened on this glade would probably see a curve of handsome trees, a fountain of green in a dry brown scape, and nothing more.

Little made sense to me. Nothing added up.

Why was it Troy Frantz who had fallen into the ravine that morning and not me? Were his crimes graver than mine—was that why he died and I survived?

I envied him for dying a hero. I envied the way he had known what to do and done it without hesitation or deliberation. He had saved the family, and yet he had died. Nothing added up.

I suppose that in one sense, he broke free from the circle he had talked about, his desperate coil. His last act afforded him that, a chance to live his life differently, selflessly, if only for a few minutes. He had managed to jump off a train that kept traveling the same circuit, while I, while the rest of us keep going around and around the same loop of track. We go through droughts, then floods, then droughts again. There is a growing season and then a harvest, then another growing season. We make wine, we age it, we drink it, we make more. Here we are applying the law: A criminal is punished and then the criminal is ushered back into the world; elsewhere, another crime goes down. Here we are ambling through our various romances: We fall in love, we fall out of love; if we are lucky, we fall in love again, often with the same person for whom we misplaced our passion. Around and around, until one fine day, something happens and we are released and we fall free from our tedious orbits. But death shouldn't have been the price of Troy's freedom. He should have had another chance. We all deserve it, and what will never make sense to me, what will never add up, is why I keep getting these chances to begin my life over, and why this man, even with all of his truancies, never did.

After I left the valley, I would think about Troy often, and I thought about Craig Montoya, too, although I thought about them differently. The only way to describe it would be to say that when I remembered Troy, there would be storm clouds looming offshore and blowing in toward the coast, that there was darkness when the day should have been bright—that I thought about him the way you think about people close to you who have died: You can't see them or speak with them and so you cannot apologize for all of your wrongs against them the way you could have, should have were they alive. All peace made after they are gone seems contrived. It will probably sound strange, then, if I admit that when I thought about Craig, I saw sun and I saw light. It was as if he lived on in the strangers I would meet. What I mean is that instead of an absence, I sensed his presence.

About six months after I had left the valley, for example, I made my way to the northern border of the state, a vacation town on the coast, and I was working in a bookstore that was only open during the summer. One afternoon, I decided to go to the beach, and I found a deserted stretch and fell asleep on a blanket on the sand. I woke up when two boys standing next to me eclipsed the sun. They must have been about sixteen or seventeen; one was blond, one dark. They were wearing rubber surfing skins and they each carried a long white board. The blond one politely asked me if I would mind watching their stuff while they surfed—by stuff, he meant a mound of keys and wallets and towels and tubes of sunblock—and while it didn't seem necessary, since we three were the only people on the beach, I was delighted to perform this easy role.

The boys headed out into the tide—they were amateurs, unsteady on their boards, and the waves were not all that rough—and they spent about an hour riding toward the shore and tumbling into the Pacific foam and then paddling back out to sea. I kept my eye on their belongings. When they were done, they came back to the beach and we talked for a few minutes about their surfing, and then they were gone. I knew that it was silly, but I was so grateful for that evanescent hour, so elated, and then so alone after the boys left—

But I was not completely alone, you see. For the remaining hour that I stayed on the beach, I thought that someone was watching me from the bluff. Someone I couldn't see. Another boy was with me, perched at a distance, keeping an eye on me, maybe smiling. And I don't mean to imply that I saw a ghost or anything of the kind. I mean that I knew that Craig was present somehow, basking in the stupid simple joy that I had felt in being trusted by these stranger boys while they surfed. Craig was there, absolving me perhaps—I don't know or want to make too much of it. He was there.

But then again, Craig was gone, he didn't really exist— and the feeling that I was being forgiven was passing and at best abstract. How could I possibly expect to be forgiven? By whom?

I drifted north up the coast. I ended up in a quiet town. I found a job there. As I said, I worked in a bookstore. But a season went by, and I began to feel too settled. I stopped sleeping. Long walks didn't relax me. Wine at night didn't relax me. I became restless, and so I gave my notice at the bookstore and eventually headed farther north up the coast, until I found a new quiet town, where I took another bookstore job and where I lived above a store that sold boating supplies. Then a few months passed, and once again I became uneasy with the routine of my life. Once again I moved on.

In another town, I became a carpenter's assistant; I learned how to build cabinets and tables. In the next town after that, I worked at a travel agency. Or was my next job the one running the pro shop at an indoor tennis club? The towns, the jobs began to blur. A clothing store, a flower shop. I never earned much money, but I anonymously mailed roughly ten percent of whatever I did earn, in cash, to Mrs. Montoya. I remained a stranger wherever I lived.

This went on for over two years.

Finally I was lingering in a onetime fishing village on the coast in Washington State, working in a nearby library, and getting ready to move one more time when I realized that my town-to-town drift itself had become a kind of routine. My drift itself had become too familiar and too easy. And I knew that I couldn't wander any longer.

I had to make some decisions, and the simplest one was to return to Oak Valley and sell the vineyard, since Julia wasn't living there. Two weeks after making this decision, I started working my way south. I drove all day—winter storms meant that I couldn't drive too fast—and I slept in the first motel that I found at dusk.

Then one afternoon when I was making my final push toward Oak Valley, somewhere along the road between San Jose and Hollister, I switched my car radio to a station that played new music. I heard a voice that I liked, a gray and mournful alto, so I stayed with the song to find out the name of the woman singing. Her low notes were like the deep sighs of a cello and her higher range reminded me of the way laughter can echo through a canyon and change shape and end up sounding rather eerie, almost dissonant. The song was about heartbreak, and yet the singer's voice had a certain float to it; I mean that despite her despairing lyrics, there was something hopeful about the way her voice would slide one line into the next.

The song ended and the deejay announced that this woman would be performing that night in a program spotlighting local artists at a club in Salinas. She didn't have an album out yet, but the deejay was certain that it would be only a matter of time before she did. And then he said her name, and I became dizzy, my ears buzzed. I had to slow down and signal my way over to the shoulder of the highway.

The name of the singer was Lauren Frantz.

I didn't continue on to Oak Valley. I drove to Salinas instead. I found a motel and tried to sleep until it was time to find the club, which turned out to be a smoky barnlike dive on a narrow rural road outside of town.

I found a stool at the bar and ordered a burger, some beer. There was a modest crowd huddled around an array of small tables facing a platform with a microphone. Two men were singing a soulful duet. They finished; the crowd clapped. An emcee introduced another folk duet, who came up to the stage and performed a three-song set. A woman followed them. Another woman after her. I could tell who the singers' friends were by which tables issued the loudest applause.

And then the emcee announced Lauren Frantz. The applause was welcoming but scattered. I couldn't clap at all. My hands were numb, heavy on my lap, my heart agallop.

She was a small woman and when she sat on a stool behind the microphone, her guitar blocked most of her body. She sang the song that I'd heard on the radio. Her bangs fell in her face and she kept having to comb her hair behind her ears. She stared straight ahead while she sang, at no one in particular.

I closed my eyes. I could picture myself making my way through an empty house. I could see myself wandering through the rooms but never quite finding the woman singing.

Lauren finished the song and the crowd clapped longer than it had for the previous performers. She sang a second ballad, which was a little more buoyant than the first one, but still pensive. She delivered her third song a cappella, and while she sang it, I held my breath.

Then she was done and she grinned and bowed to grateful applause, and then she slipped offstage and a trio, a woman and two men, took her place.

I followed her as she moved through the club. She spoke briefly to a man who told her something that made her smile. She came over to the bar, accepting the compliments of the people who noticed her brush by, and she sat down and had a beer.

I was three seats away. I tried not to stare too conspicuously.

Then she pulled on a thrift-shop overcoat, which she wore with the cuffs folded back. She picked up her guitar case and headed for the door.

I followed her out.

"Lauren," I called after her.

She turned around. She set her guitar case down.

She didn't look anything like what I expected her to. I think that I had expected her to be fair and fragile, anemic, easily frightened, but she was dark-haired like Troy, although not nearly as pale as he was. I thought that her hair must have been auburn once upon a time—hadn't Troy told me that it was?—because in the light, I noticed traces of red here and there. She wore a wide bracelet of fishing tackle, and, on both hands, a collection of silver rings. She wore a pair of dusty cowboy boots.

She waited for me to say whatever I wanted to say.

"I really enjoyed your music," I said.

"Oh, thank you," she said. "Thanks a lot."

Her speaking voice was deeper than her singing voice, maybe half an octave lower.

"The last song was the best," I said. "Well, actually I liked them all."

I took a step back. I didn't know what to say. Or there was too much that I could say and I didn't know where or how to begin.

Lauren leaned against the doorway. Someone came in the club and she stepped aside and picked up her guitar again.

"I'm glad," she said. "I'm singing here tomorrow night again," she added, "so tell your friends."

"I'll be sure to do that," I said.

Then she nodded good night and left the club.

•

I stayed in my motel another day. A storm swept in from the west. It was still raining hard when I went back to the club that night.

The program was exactly the same, the lineup of performers, what they sang. This time, however, I knew who

Lauren was, and from my perch at the bar, I watched her arrive and shed her coat and tune her guitar.

She sang the same songs. The crowd was warm, but not as loud as the night before. She ended up at the bar again, and this time, I moved over and sat next to her.

"Hello again," I said.

She didn't appear to recognize me.

"I was here last night," I said.

"Oh, right," she said. "Did you bring your friends?"

"No, sorry," I said. "I'm not from around here, so I didn't have any friends to call. But look, I came back. I wanted to hear your songs again."

Lauren smiled. She combed her hair out of her face the way she did when she was performing. She swiveled on her stool so that she was facing me.

"Since I didn't bring anyone, can I make it up to you by buying you a drink?" I asked.

She bit her lower lip. "Oh, why not," she said.

I waved over the bartender and had her order what she wanted.

"So where are you from, then?" she asked.

"Nowhere really," I said. "I've been moving around a lot for the last couple of years."

"Me, too," she said.

"I guess I'm headed home now," I said.

"Home?"

I told her about the vineyard. I also told her that I was planning on selling it.

"Do you want to sell it?" Lauren asked.

I nodded. I shrugged. I shook my head no.

"What about you?" I asked. "You say you've been moving around a lot?"

"Mostly in the Bay Area," she said. "I was in Monterey for a while. I worked at the aquarium there."

"Wait," I said. I gripped my beer bottle. "Are you telling me that you've been in the Bay Area all this time?"

"All this time?" Lauren asked.

"These last few years?"

She nodded. "You know at one point, I wasn't staying all that far from your vineyard," she said. "I was in Hollister. But that was maybe four and half years ago."

I had to rub my eyes. This news was too cruel.

"Are you okay?" she asked.

Too cruel. Troy had been working his way north and looking for her, and if only he had kept going, he might have ended up in the same city where she lived.

"Thanks for the drink," Lauren said.

And the chances might not have been all that great that, even in the same city, he would have found her, but he wasn't that far from her. He wasn't that far.

"I should be going," she said, and stood.

"No, wait," I said. "Let me buy you another—"

"I should go," she said.

I waved over the bartender and ordered her another beer.

She sat down. "Then I should eat something, too," she said.

I ordered us a plate of fries. I apologized if I had suddenly seemed aloof. "It's just that . . ."

She blinked.

Tell her, I thought. Tell her everything.

"You have such a pretty voice," I said.

Lauren laughed.

"No, honestly. I was driving and I heard your voice, and I had to come hear you sing live. Tell me about your music," I said.

"About my music?"

"How you come up with a song, what inspires you, that sort of thing."

"That sort of thing," she said, and looked surprised. "No one ever asks me that."

She glanced back at the stage and then she began to answer my question. The plate of fries came and soon we were dipping them into a pool of catsup while Lauren told me about how she kept two notebooks, one for her lyrics and one for her melodies. She told me about songwriters whom she admired. She told me that ironically she didn't think of her music as being especially downbeat. She wrote sad songs, she said, but composing them gave her great joy.

"Enough about me," she said. She shifted her stool and inched closer to me. "What sort of work do you do?"

I flattened my hands on the bar. I started to speak, but I was out of breath.

"Jason?" she asked. "Do you need help? Is something wrong?"

I looked at her, and I could see that she was searching my face for what it was that I wanted to disclose.

"What's wrong?" she asked. "What?"

Then I told her that I had known Troy.

She sat up very straight. She eased herself back on her stool, away from me.

I told her that he was dead. "I'm sorry to tell you this," I said.

Lauren tried to speak and couldn't. She cleared her throat. "I knew," she said. "I heard the news."

Then I told her about how Troy had died a hero. I described the car on the cliff and told her about how he was strong when he needed to be strong.

Lauren stared at me without blinking.

I told her how I had come to know Troy; I explained that I had been his lawyer. I described our fast friendship, and then I talked about Troy's lies, although I decided to spare Lauren the exact content of these lies and merely say that they endangered our case. But I said that Troy's lies were ultimately beside the point. Because he was innocent. Because he had been falsely accused. I told her about how he had confessed to a crime that he didn't commit. I told her about the accident on the mountain road.

And I looked at Lauren and I explained how it was that I could be so certain that Troy was innocent.

I said, "You see, I know because I am the one who hit the boy and drove away. I kept it a secret from everyone. I am the one who killed him."

All around us, there were people moving about the club and the music was loud, but we were alone at one end of the bar, and I wasn't really aware of anyone except Lauren. Her face had paled. She glared at me without saying a word. I thought I would die in the heat of her gaze.

Finally she said, "I don't know why you had to tell me all that. I didn't need to hear any of that."

"I'm sorry," I said.

"Rot in hell," she said.

"Lauren," I said.

"Fuck off," she said. She covered her eyes with her hand. "Go away."

"I have to tell you something else," I said.

"Leave. Go away," she said, although she was the one who stood. She was crying.

A couple of people at the opposite end of the bar were watching us. We probably looked like arguing lovers.

"Listen. Listen, please," I said. I stood, too. I knew that I didn't have much time left, so I spilled out the rest fast: "Troy was on his way north. He wanted to find you. He got waylaid. He desperately wanted to find you and in some way make up for what he did."

"That," Lauren said, "is just too mean. How dare you come here and tell me that. How dare you. As if he, as if that—as if you could possibly make a difference."

"He loved you," I said.

"Go away," she said. She was sobbing.

"I had to tell you," I said.

"Now," she said. She pushed at my chest.

I fell back onto my stool. People at the bar and in the back of the club noticed. The bartender flagged the bouncer.

Lauren shoved me again, hard, and I nearly fell.

"I'm going," I said, and I stepped away from her. I left the club.

Outside it was still raining hard, and the rain was so cold that I couldn't feel my keys. I fumbled with the lock on my car and by the time I got in it, I was soaked. I was shaking. I couldn't drive. The rain came down harder.

I don't know how long I sat there, leaning back in my seat, but it was a long time.

Someone knocking on the passenger-side window startled me. I opened the door.

Lauren slipped into the car and shut the door and didn't say anything.

"I'm sorry," I said. "I shouldn't have—"

"So you're headed back to your vineyard now," she said.

"Yes," I said.

"To sell it," she said.

"To sell it or . . ."

"Or what?" she asked.

"I don't know," I said. Which was the truth, I didn't know.

"I have to tell you something," she said.

She paused, and I let her take her time.

"I knew without knowing that you had something to do with Troy," she said.

"You did?"

"In the back of my mind, I think I knew. I try not to think about him, but of course I do," she said. "In a strange way, I am glad to know that he was strong, like you say. I am glad to know that he thought about me."

More silence.

"I can't forgive you," she said.

"I know," I said. "I should have told you who I was right away. It was cruel of me to toy with you like that—"

"No," she said. "I don't mean forgive you for that. I mean that I'm not the one to forgive you, that I can't forgive you for everything you did."

"In my life," I said.

"In your life," she said. She reached out for my right hand. She took it and squeezed it once. And then she got out of the car and was gone.

The vineyard road needed work. I nearly drove into a ditch. But I made it up to the twin eucalyptuses and left my car there. I went down to the winery first and retrieved one of the bottles that hadn't been sold off, one from a precious reserve.

The old stone house was damp. There was no power, so I had to rummage around for some candles. There was no heat, and I had to go up to my bedroom and wrap myself in a blanket. I sat in the rocking chair and poured myself some of the cabernet, and I listened to the house creak in the storm. A high branch scraped the eave.

I thought about my grandfather. I pictured him lying on a cot in a French vineyard house turned army hospital and wondering what he would do when he finally could go home. Slowly he had recovered and hobbled around on crutches, and he had watched the vineyard hands returning to the fields that they had neglected during the war. Maybe it was autumn and he watched them salvage a harvest. My grandfather was inspired. It was a simple vision, to grow grapes, to make wine.

I thought about my father. He had tried to make an empire out of his father's acre and for a while he had succeeded, before the climate got the better of him. I thought about how he had ended up, all alone in this cold house, vacantly staring at the browning valley. But what I never fully appreciated was how he had managed to hold on to the original plot of vines, if for no other reason than to will them to me. Now they were all I had.

I couldn't know whether Tim would ever have any interest in becoming a vintner, but I realized that I had to keep that option open for him. It was all I could do really, maintain the vineyard for my son, probably without him recognizing my purpose until after I was gone. I had to go away and return in order to understand that this was my obligation.

Tending a modest crop, reaping its fruit—these are the quiet chores to which we can retreat and devote ourselves when we have betrayed our better instincts and become the agents of tragedy and despair. Working our land, we might find renewed mission—and not in an attempt to remake a squandered fortune, but in the day-to-day, the year-after-year pursuit of protecting an inheritance for our children. Maybe I am only fooling myself, but this is how I think I can transform my regret into something worthwhile. This is how I can begin to atone. I don't think that we can say that we make our own luck, but I do think that we can say that we make our own redemption, or so I want, so I need to believe.

I blew out the candles and went to bed. The rain stopped while I was asleep. I slept well—not long, but deeper than I had in years.

That was last night. This morning, I woke up early and headed down to the vines. They are a mess, an impossible overgrown tangle, and the job of pruning them frankly overwhelms me. But then again, it is winter; it is the right time of the year to cut them back, down to the cordons, save a few sprigs. And today the sun is everywhere. And I know what I need to do. And I have done it all before.